ALSO BY MARY BLAYNEY

Traitor's Kiss / Lover's Kiss
Stranger's Kiss

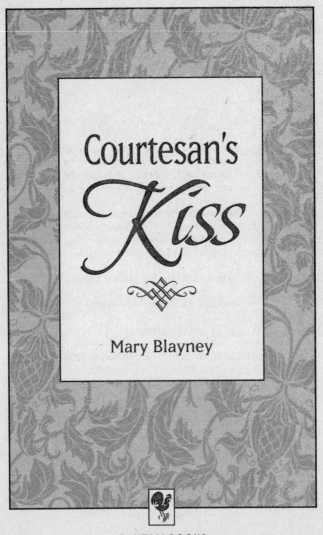

Courtesan's *Kiss*

Mary Blayney

BANTAM BOOKS

NEW YORK

2010 Bantam Books Mass Market Original

Copyright © 2010 by Mary Blayney

Published in the United States by Bantam Books, an imprint of The Random House Publishing Group, a division of Random House, Inc., New York.

BANTAM BOOKS is a registered trademark of Random House, Inc., and the colophon is a trademark of Random House, Inc.

ISBN 978-0-553-59313-6

Cover art: © Aleta Raton
Lettering: © Ron Zinn

Printed in the United States of America

www.bantamdell.com

2 4 6 8 9 7 5 3 1

Mary Jean Murray Walker
and
Barbara Zurawel Wallner:

*All through high school we
plotted stories together with
no idea where that would lead.*

Chapter One

A Travelers' Inn
The Cotswolds
July 1819

"NO IS THE most valuable word in the English language." Mia Castellano raised two fingers to her mouth and tried to think of someplace, anyplace on earth, where women were as powerful as men. "Indeed, *no* is the most valuable word in *any* language."

"You cannot mean that," Miss Cole protested, her sweet face losing much of its charm when she frowned. "Shouldn't a young lady always be obliging?"

Mia knew she would say that. She just knew it. Mia stood up and walked to the sideboard, drawing in the scent of the rose-filled arrangement. When everything else went awry, the scent of roses always refreshed her heart. She poured herself some tea and offered some to Miss Cole. After serving her, Mia began to put some of the sweet and savory treats on a plate.

She paused, turned back to this chance acquaintance,

and looked her straight in the eye. "Of course, one likes to be obliging as often as possible, but think how often we are compelled by good manners to do something we do not truly wish to do." She could sum up most of her life with that thought, at least until she herself had realized the power of "No."

"Oh, yes." Miss Cole's words echoed with long suffering.

"It is the curse of being a lady, is it not?" Mia continued.

"Even this trip to London," Miss Cole went on with growing enthusiasm for the subject. "I want nothing more than to start my first Season. I thought we should leave next week after Aunt Marjorie's birthday, but Warren *insisted* that he had to be in Town this week."

"If you had said 'No' quite firmly, what would have happened?"

"Why, I do not know." Miss Cole thought through the conundrum for a moment. "My brother would have gone without me, I expect."

"Precisely." Mia set the plate on the table between them.

"You know, I do believe you are right. Mama would have allowed me to stay to help her with her packing and I could have come with her. We would have been very crowded, but I could have sent most of my trunks and even my maid ahead with Warren."

"That is proof, is it not? *No* is the most important word in the world." Despite her initial annoyance at not having privacy, Mia found it rather enlivening to share the inn's sitting room with a girl as young and unformed as Miss Cole. Someone she could actually help, if not tutor, in ways to make the most of her Season.

"Excuse me," Mia began as she took her seat again. "But why are you going to London in July? The Season has ended and the new one will not begin until next winter."

"Yes, I know, but my older sister lives in London and has just given birth. Mama insists that we need six months to prepare for the Season. The truth is she cannot wait to see her first grandchild."

Miss Cole did not seem to mind that a baby would upstage her Season. What a generous soul.

The two young women sat in companionable silence. Mia considered what to suggest next. It was so much more worthwhile than dwelling on her wounded heart.

The door burst open with a rudeness that matched the manners of the man who entered. Lord David Pennistan came into the parlor with his usual ill humor. He was nothing if not belligerent. Add to that unfriendly, closemouthed, and secretive.

How perfectly awful that Elena's husband had chosen him to act as her escort. But if she were ever to say "No!" to the Duke of Meryon, it would be over something much more important than the company of a man who regarded her with disgust. She hoped he could feel her disdain. His opinion meant less than nothing to her.

"We will leave now, Miss Castellano."

Lord David did not bow or in any way acknowledge Miss Cole, manners being completely foreign to him.

"The horses are ready and we have another seventeen

miles to cover before we stop for the night." The clamor of the hectic posting house added to the sense of urgency.

If he had asked politely, Mia might have agreed, but his idea of conversation consisted of a series of commands that would annoy the most amiable of women.

"No, Lord David." Mia flicked a glance at Miss Cole. "I am not quite ready."

Lord David gave a curt nod. "Five minutes and we leave."

He closed the door without waiting for her agreement. That would cost him. "You see how well 'no' can work."

"Yes, but if you will excuse me, how can you say no to such a handsome man?"

"Quite easily." Oh my, this girl had so much to learn, Mia thought. What a shame that she would not be in London to show her the way. "Yes, his expression is compelling and the broad shoulders impressive." Blond and handsome could be said of all the Pennistan men, Lord David included. "But he never smiles, has no conversation, and when he does speak it is to tell me to do something that I would rather not, *and* he is traveling without his valet."

"Without a valet!"

Mia knew that would shock the proper Miss, and it was so much more polite than the truth.

"Yes, indeed he is. He says that since this trip is so short, it is more efficient to send his valet ahead with his trunks. But, I ask you, how can a man manage alone? He must shave himself and tie his own cravat, not to mention polish his own boots."

Miss Cole nodded. In truth, Mia agreed that a man could manage for himself for a few days, but the list of what the ton considered essential would convince Miss Cole of Mia's most important point. "The word *no* was invented for men like him."

Mia picked one rose from a small vase on the table, held it to her nose, and then tucked it into the buttonhole of her traveling gown. "I promise you that halfway through your first Season, you will realize that making a match is about more than how a man looks at you and how many flowers and sweets he sends."

"Yes, I am sure you are right." Miss Cole spoke as though the conversation made her uncomfortable. That was unfortunate. This subject was too important to ignore.

"Miss Cole, your Season is about finding the right match. And to that end it is in your best interest to collect as many admirers as possible. To make it clear that you have high expectations and more to give than they can even imagine. And I assure you, Miss Cole, men have very good imaginations when it comes to women."

"You mean I should be a flirt?" Shock echoed in her voice.

"No, I do not. I mean you should charm every man you meet and not stop until all of the ton is at your feet. Then you shall have choices."

Miss Cole laughed. "I do not see how using the word *no* will have all of society bowing before me."

"It will make it clear that you are more woman than girl and that you know your own mind. Men find that very attractive. It implies that you are not constrained by society." Mia leaned across the table and touched Miss Cole's hand. "Promise me you will use the word *no* at least four times today."

"I shall try."

Miss Cole agreed easily enough, though Mia would have liked to hear a more determined tone.

"I shall try after we reach London."

That meant never. "Are you afraid that if you say 'No' your brother will abandon you?"

"Not precisely, but if he is irritated he will not give a thought to my comfort and it will be a miserable trip. He is prone to bursts of temper that leave me in tears."

"But once you see the power in the word, you will not need to cry because he will be doing as you wish."

Miss Cole bit her lower lip.

Mia wished she could think of a way to convince this girl that future success merited the initial discomfort. She was proof of that. What could be worse than ending an engagement? And yet, after just two months, she was beginning to see that it had all been for the best.

Finally, Miss Cole nodded cautiously. "It seems to me, Miss Castellano, that the tone is as important as the word."

"Oh, very good." Hope lived! "Sometimes imperious works best. I pretend I am a queen. Other times my 'No!' is a command and I pretend I am Wellington and the word carries all the authority of his rank and success. And there is the 'No' that is a contest of wills. I think of a courtesan whose lover is begging for her favors."

"Oh my. I have never even seen a courtesan, much less heard one speak."

"Well, you will when you reach London. You will not socialize with them, of course, but you'll see them in shops and at the theater. Indeed, from my observations I think courtesans have a very advantageous way of life."

"That cannot be!"

"Think on it." Mia ticked off the reasons, raising a finger for each one. "They decide with whom they will sleep. They have their own houses. They make the rules. They have control of all their own money, and they can dismiss a lover far more easily than a woman can rid herself of a husband."

Miss Cole giggled.

The girl showed more embarrassment than intrigue at the frank discussion. Mia reached out and patted her hand again.

"I am sorry if that offends you. There are times when I speak too bluntly and this is one of them. Please, forget I made the comparison. If marriage is what you want, then I encourage you to take your time and consider all your choices. All the possibilities. The Season is ideal for that. I myself am headed in a different direction."

"You're not going to London?"

The girl had a brain, Mia could tell that, but she did seem to take everything quite literally. "No, I am going to Derbyshire to see the Duke and Duchess of Meryon." She picked a small bit of the lemon bar and nibbled, enjoying the sweet tart flavor she loved as she decided how best to explain the visit. "You see, the duke's wife is my guardian. Indeed, she has been my guardian since long before she married the duke last year. The duke's brother is escorting me as he has just finished business in the Cotswolds near where I was visiting."

"A house party. You are going to a house party at the Duke of Meryon's estate?"

"Yes, yes. It will be grand," Mia lied. She picked at the rest of the lemon bar on her plate and Miss Cole did the same.

Mia would not call a gathering of family a house party. Especially one where she would have to explain why her engagement had ended. Please, she prayed, not in front of Lord David. But no matter how private the discussion, the facts would dampen everyone's good spirits. *Mia is back and we have no idea what to do with her.*

Well, she now had an answer for that. If she did not, never had, fit in anywhere, she would create her own life and live it on her own terms.

No tears, she commanded herself as she felt them threaten. *If you cry people will think William broke your heart.*

The door burst open, again, and an even more impatient Lord David leaned into the room. "Miss Castellano, the horses grow restless."

"No, my lord, I am not yet ready."

"Yes, you are, Miss Castellano. Now."

He aggravated her so much that she did not even deign to answer the boor.

Lord David came fully into the room and she could feel his anger. She stood up to face him.

"No, Lord David. We can leave after I have finished this conversation."

"Miss Castellano, this conversation *is* finished." Lord David grabbed her cloak from the hook on the wall, swirled it around her, and then swooped her up in his arms and headed for the door.

Oh my. The sensation of power overwhelmed her even in the arms of a man she detested. A thrill flashed through her and she wanted to struggle against him with the secret hope that he would know her rebuff was really a longing for more. How romantic it would be to be mastered by someone who could read her mind and not take no for an answer when she did not mean it, someone she actually found attractive. Not a man who had witnessed the most hideous moment of her life.

Not Lord David Pennistan.

Mia looked over his shoulder at the shocked Miss Cole and made herself smile. She might have lost the battle but the war had just begun.

The rose crushed between them did little to mask Lord David's scent. Not cologne. Only a gentleman would use something that refined. His coat smelled of tobacco as well as leather and pine as though he spent a lot of time out-of-doors, in a saddle.

Thinking of herself as an actress on an informal stage, she buried her face in Lord David's shoulder and trusted that other travelers would think her overcome with fatigue or grief.

Mia decided that, under the right circumstances—that is, with a different man—this could have led to a very interesting adventure.

The way he dumped her into the carriage and slammed the door made it clear that Lord David Pennistan did not share her excellent imagination.

Chapter Two

DAVID SLAMMED THE DOOR and threw the rose she had been wearing to the ground. Crushed between them, its sweet smell had blended with her perfume. The scent lingered, tangy, steeped in spices that reminded him of incense and flowers like carnations and jasmine. A heady mix that aroused him almost as much as her beauty.

Damnation, I have work to do. Work that did not include accompanying a stubborn woman to Pennford.

The cotton mill, he reminded himself. *Forget her and think about the mill.* He was so close to securing what he needed, so close to success.

Tonight he would complete his presentation for Thomas Sebold. The man's financial support was as essential as the plans he was going to share for the mill.

David set a pace to match that of the much-too-slowly-moving coach. The letter that made this trip mandatory lay burnt to a cinder in Gabriel's fireplace in Sussex. David did not need it in front of him to remember the wording.

Since you are coming north, the duchess would appreciate it if you would escort her ward. Since she and Viscount Bendasbrook have ended their engagement, we both feel it would be wise for Miss Castellano to retire from society, for as long as a year, and spend the time at Pennford with us.

David wondered how much the duke and duchess knew about the scandal. The ton lived for details behind the obviously unhappy end of the engagement between Miss Castellano and Lord William Bendasbrook. No doubt someone would have sent the details north to Derbyshire.

Surely Lord Arthur had known she was engaged to the viscount when they kissed. What David had wondered for weeks now was whether Mia Castellano had wanted Lord William to find them in the embrace. Surely she had not expected him to be with William.

God only knew what either Arthur or the girl had been thinking, if they had thought at all. Reasoned thought did not appear to be one of Miss Castellano's strong points.

Escorting her was not a test of his control, merely a chore he could not refuse. Meryon's last line made that clear.

If you write to the trustees, I will have the estate's half of the funds for the support of your first manufacturing effort ready when you arrive.

The duke knew David would balk without the promise of that reward. His brother could have saved ink and paper if he had just written "Bring her and you can have the money."

David reminded himself of the greater goal. The cotton mill would take him one step closer to financial independence on his own terms. He ignored the irony in the fact it would take his brother's money to do it. He refused to even consider the truth that he had failed at a bid for independence once before. Only in his nightmares did he consider the consequences of failing again.

Mia Castellano should be the least of his headaches. Would it be better to ignore her antics or force her to accept that he was the one in charge?

"SIGNORINA!" MIA'S MAID grabbed the strap as the coach lurched forward, even before Mia settled on her seat. Losing her balance, Mia fell to the floor and Janina screamed, which did not help at all. Mia should have been the one screaming and Janina should have been helping her up.

Mia stayed on the floor. It smelled of dirt and brandy, but that did not bother her as much as the fact that she would have bruises tonight.

Once the coach settled into a more comfortable rhythm, Mia found her way from the floor onto the seat. Her skirt had a tear at the seam, easy enough to fix if Janina had brought her sewing kit. Her hair felt all in a tangle and she reached into her reticule for the traveling set that Elena had given her last Christmas. Mia pulled the combs out of her hair. They had taken so long to fix properly. She began to ruthlessly work the knots out.

Without a word, Janina sat beside her and took the comb in hand. "More gently, Mia. Your hair deserves the same kindness you give the rest of your body."

Mia smiled. Sometimes Janina's English made for very interesting mental pictures. The feel of Nina gently combing her hair helped Mia relax. Someday her lover would do this for her, and as relaxing as it might feel, she knew it would be as erotic as a kiss.

Mia drew a deep breath and closed her eyes. Not that she could rest. When Janina held a comb she felt it an invitation to speak.

"Oh, Mia, I told Romero this trip would be horrible, but now I fear it is ill-fated."

"Because Lord David is in as bad a mood as I am or because you had to leave Sussex and Romero?"

"Well, both," Janina admitted honestly. "But once we are settled Romero can come to me and he will find work wherever we live."

"He told you this?"

"Yes, he promised. Since he will travel in his work as a master gardener, he can make his home anywhere that I am, because you know, Mia, that if he works with a great landscape architect there will be much demand for his presence at each site to install what the architect devises."

While Janina chattered on, Mia wondered if she should tell Janina of the risks of having a beau or even a husband who traveled so much of the time. A vow of fidelity came easily when you rested in your lover's arms but proved much harder when miles separated you.

Mia had seen that firsthand the one time she had traveled with her father and the other musicians. She had spent her days with the courtesans who flocked around them. The women were like a gathering of peacocks after the time Mia had spent with the mother hens of her home, her aunt and her governess.

The lively group of cyprians had laughed and played with her as though she were a treasure they had discovered. Her "unseemly fascination," as her aunt called it, had begun then. She watched for courtesans in the theater and when they were out shopping, and knew by the way they smiled which one her father was the patron of.

Courtesans were only one way a man could be tempted. Janina herself was proof of that.

Ah, well, Mia knew better than to give advice to someone as lovesick as Nina. Besides, she and Romero were nowhere near married yet, despite the fact that by the time Janina had refreshed her hair the girl had already named their first child.

They sat back and Mia did her best to find a spot that would induce sleep or at least a light doze. She tried to let herself be soothed by the sway of the carriage and the warmth of the noontime sun. But the road had so many ruts and bumps that the carriage could not settle into a rhythm.

And how could she forget that as soon as Janina did not have a distraction the travel sickness would start? Her maid's dislike of travel counted as another reason why this trip could prove less than pleasant. "Janina, you must let me know if you are going to be unwell."

"Oh, I will be fine." The young woman waved her hand as though carriage travel was not, for her, a preview of hell.

"I wonder why you do not travel well. Papa and I never had a problem with it, except on very rough seas. And you have as much of his blood as I do."

"Oh, please, Mia, do not remind me of that crossing when I finally came to England. It is so much better that you were not with me."

"And I am so happy you finally agreed to brave the crossing. I missed you so much last year."

"And I you. Do you know how I sneeze around cats?"

"Yes."

"I think that and travel sickness come from my mother." She rummaged through her bag.

"More than that. Your beautiful smile and delicate hands." Mia looked at Janina's hands. "What is that? Are you sure you should eat it?"

"Oh yes." She took a bite and then another of the sweet that she took from the box in her bag. "Romero gave me these. His mother made them and he says they are made especially to soothe a nervous traveler, but they taste like ordinary lemon bars. Sprinkled with some nut crumbs, I think." She closed the lid on the box, then used a cloth and some water from the bottle strapped to the carriage wall to clean her fingers.

"They smell like lemon with lots and lots of honey."

"Oh, would you like one?" Janina said as an after-thought.

"No, no, thank you. I ate quite enough lemon bars at the posting house."

Janina pressed the box to her heart before putting it back into the traveling bag next to her.

"Would you like to lie down and rest?"

"You are too kind, Mia. But no, thank you, if we talk I will not even think about vomiting. So tell me if Lord William will follow you. It would be so romantic."

"No, he will not. I am the one who broke the engagement."

"Oh, that is what must be said when an engagement ends."

"Yes, but his lack of trust insulted me so that I insisted that we part."

"Mia, we both know that he thought your flirtation with the Duke of Hale's son too intimate. And, cara, we both know it was."

"In light of what happened I suppose you are right." Mia closed her eyes. "I will never forget how William looked when he found us together. Honestly, Nina, we were only kissing. Nothing more."

"He could not believe you would kiss someone else when you were engaged to him. It was not unreasonable for him to be hurt."

"But all I wanted was to make him a little jealous. Who knows what would have happened if Lord David had not been with William."

"You think it was Lord David who convinced him to cast you off."

"No, no, not at all. But if you could have seen the way Lord David looked at Lord Arthur—as though he was on the verge of a challenge, and then suddenly remembered that I was not *his* fiancée."

He had ignored her but it was clear that her stock could not be much lower in his eyes. Being around him made her feel the worst slut in the world, when all she had wanted that evening was proof William loved her with a passion that would last forever.

"I only wanted to make him a little jealous," she said again. "Just a little. So he would stop treating me like one of his madcap friends and more like his future wife."

"But the viscount would dance with you and escort you to dinner and to any shop you wished to visit. He would play cards with you and he took you to Astley's and insisted that your skill on horseback exceeded the talent of anyone there." Janina might as well have said, "Only you could want more than that."

"I wanted him to kiss me with something that felt like more than two lips pressed to mine." Janina was in love. Surely she should understand. "I wanted him to show me the passion that is as much a part of him as being Italian is a part of me. That was all it would have taken to convince me that I had found a place in life where I truly belonged."

She stopped and bit her lip. William did not love her. Not enough. Which was exactly what he had accused her of. Not accused so much as gently suggested. So gently that she picked up a book and threw it at him so that he would do something besides smile at her as though his heart could not stand any more pain.

She wanted William to sweep her into his arms and show her passion. Instead he had suggested that they end their ill-advised engagement. What else could she do but pretend she wanted that more than he did?

"Romero thinks he will come after you and beg you to take him back."

"And you told him to stop spouting nonsense. You are so practical, Janina."

"Yes." Janina nodded with conviction. "I think Lord William is too short to be your husband."

"That is unkind. William Bendasbrook is a gentleman in every way, and manly in all the ways one could want from a husband. His height is nothing more than a distraction."

"Then you did love him!"

That question lay at the heart of the matter. In truth, Mia feared she was the one who had not loved enough. And if she did not love someone as ideally suited to her as William, was she even capable of love, fidelity, or finding someone to share her life with?

While she considered what to tell Janina, Mia heard the sound of hooves pounding along the dry road and nearly swooned at the idea that Romero understood the situation better than she did and that Lord William was almost upon them.

Chapter Three

THE RIDER PASSED and called a halt to the carriage. Even through the dust his thoughtless gallop had raised, Mia could tell that it was not Lord William. This man did not have nearly the command of his horse that William did.

"A highwayman!" Janina yelped. "Help us!"

"It is not a highwayman. Will you stop shouting, Nina."

The gentleman stayed at the head of the team and waited for Lord David to ride back from some little way ahead. Not a thief, but he definitely wanted them to stop.

Dear God, she hoped nothing had happened to the duke or duchess.

Mia opened the door and jumped down, not waiting for the grooms to lower the steps. She almost fell, the drop steeper than she expected, but she found her footing and hurried to where Lord David and the rider were talking.

They stood in the shade at the side of the road, beyond the hearing of the coachman and servants.

Lord David did not appear particularly interested in the stranger's words. He was scowling. That and exasperated summed up his usual expression.

"Is it Elena or the duke?" Mia stopped a moment to control her breathing. "Has the baby come early?" *Please, please let Elena be safe.* It would be more than she could bear to lose someone else she loved.

"Miss Castellano, rest easy. I am sure everything is as it should be at Pennford." Lord David settled his horse as he spoke.

Rest easy might be another command, but he spoke in such a matter-of-fact manner that she felt relief instantaneously. Mia relaxed her hands, not sure whether she had been praying or despairing. She stepped into the shade, and while she waited for an explanation she stared at the ever-changing patterns in the shadows as the tree branches swayed in the lightest of breezes. If fairies lived in these woods, this would be where they came to dance at twilight.

"Miss Castellano."

She started. Mia hated the way Lord David began every sentence with her name as though he had to remind himself who she was.

"This is Mr. Warren Cole." He made the introduction with the most perfunctory of good manners.

"Mr. Cole." The name had a familiar ring, but she could not place him. She closed her eyes for a moment and recalled her friend from the posting house. "Ah yes,

Miss Cole's brother, who is escorting his sister to London. How do you do, sir." She curtsied and waited.

"Miss," Mr. Cole responded. He did not dismount and gave her no more than an insincere bow from his neck. "My sister insisted that I bring you your hat and your fan. She said that you were compelled to leave quickly and would not want to be without them."

Mr. Cole handed her the items, the hat crushed and without its feathers.

The young man gave his full attention to Lord David. "I am using the return of these fripperies as an excuse to speak with you about the behavior of this young woman in your charge."

Miss Cole had not mentioned that her brother was a pompous fool.

"I am Miss Castellano's escort, not her brother or husband. Speak to her directly."

Mr. Cole looked surprised, but did as he was told, looking down on Mia from atop his horse. "What in the world possessed you to fill my sister's head with such vulgar ideas?"

"Vulgar ideas—I did no such thing!" Mia looked at Lord David for support, hoping he would dismiss the man for his rudeness, but the dolt sat his horse, staring off into the trees as if he had more important things to think about than protecting her.

"You told her that she should say 'No!' more often, that the Season exists to buy and sell young women for a bride price, that a woman would have more control over her life if she went into trade."

What a shame, Mia thought, that she had *not* told Miss Cole to hold their conversation in confidence. It was such a basic idea that she had not thought it necessary.

"I never said that last, Mr. Cole. But the rest is true and you know it. I would call my conversation with your sister frank, not vulgar." She had to crane her neck to look him directly in the eye. The sun near blinded her and made it impossible to see his expression. "I did not suggest that she go into trade. Not at all. But I did discuss with her that courtesans have more control over their lives than married women do."

"Your words are offensive, even to me, a gentleman and, I assure you, a man of the world. To use such a term in my sister's hearing, much less discuss the advantages of a whore's life, is beyond vulgar and makes me question whether you are indeed a lady yourself."

Mia took a step back, his use of the word *whore* making her feel as though he had punched her in the heart. She raised a hand to her chest to ease the pain.

"That is more than enough, sir." Lord David edged his horse close to Mr. Cole's, making both the man and his mount nervous.

Lord David dismounted and stood beside her. "I will not tolerate insults to the lady."

Thank the saints Lord David had been listening. Mia turned her back on both men and pretended to be overcome with tears. She fumbled in her reticule for a handkerchief, but apparently Janina had not thought to put one in. A hand appeared over her shoulder with a handkerchief and she nodded thanks as she took it and dabbed at her eyes.

"You had best keep an eye on your relation, Lord David, or she will ruin you and your house."

Only a nodcock would threaten a Pennistan. Their tempers were as well known as the family's rank.

"That's true—if fools like you must announce wild stories. Listen to me, Cole. Keep this to yourself or you will regret it."

"Are you threatening me?"

"Oh, no," Lord David said with a laugh. "If I threatened you there would be no need to ask."

Lord David had his back to her and she could not see his expression. Mia could imagine it easily enough. A stare that would have unmanned a pirate. A mouth no more than a thin line of disgust. She was relieved that for now it was aimed at someone else.

"When I see you in London, my lord, I will give you the cut direct."

Mia pressed her lips together to keep from laughing out loud at the pathetic threat, even as she wondered if this confrontation would come to blows.

"Cole, you had best research my connections before you think to do that or you will be the one on the outs with the ton."

She turned around in time to see Lord David slap the rump of Mr. Cole's horse. The next thing she saw was Mr. Cole on his way back from whence he had come on a horse not entirely in his control.

"Thank you, Lord David." Mia tried for meekness and kept her eyes down.

"Look at me."

With a grimace she raised her eyes to his and he shook his head.

"Your eyes are twinkling. You enjoyed every moment of that." He made it sound like a grievous sin—and besides, it was not true.

"No, I did not *enjoy* it. No one likes to be insulted. But I did admire your rescue."

"Miss Castellano, climb back into the carriage, like the little piece of baggage you are. I have no doubt Mr. Cole told the truth, with the exception of his last crude comment. Our last meeting showed just how wild you can be. I can see that you have learned very little from the experience and are still a hellion."

"And you are a pedantic bore." She hated his patronizing tone, his implication that she was too wild when all she wanted was a little bit of adventure. "You know as much about having fun as I know about boxing. Which is to say nothing at all." She folded her arms to keep from throwing his handkerchief at him.

"Do not provoke me," he said in a threatening tone. "I assure you that Lord William is ten times the gentleman I am." He leaned closer to her. "I do not treat women gently."

Mia could not look away from him. His eyes held hers. Dark blue eyes that sent a tingle from her heart to her toes.

"Signorina."

Janina's voice sounded unusually timid and Mia turned around, welcoming the chance to end the competition without actually losing, no matter that she was not sure what a loss would mean.

She didn't look at Lord David again, but allowed him to lower the carriage steps so she could climb inside more easily.

"I am not feeling well. If we move there will be a breeze and I am sure that will help."

"Yes, Janina." Mia settled herself on the seat and handed her maid Lord David's unused handkerchief. "Wet this. If you press it against your forehead it will help, I am sure."

"It is not my forehead that hurts."

As the carriage moved forward Janina moaned and Mia reached for her hat.

"Here. Please, please use this if you are going to be ill and we cannot stop the carriage quickly enough."

"Oh, but it would ruin your beautiful hat. This is the one that you were wearing when Lord William proposed."

"Yes, well, it's already ruined and it is no longer one of my favorites." Mia reached for the bottle strapped to the wall as Janina rapped for the carriage to stop, practically leaped from the steps, and was sick before she reached the side of the road.

DAVID PENNISTAN PUSHED HIS HORSE into a canter and then a gallop. The horse needed the freedom as much as he did. Run as he might, David's mind could not lose the image of Mia's expression in that moment before her maid had called to her.

He'd meant to discourage her; instead, he'd seen awareness and challenge in her eyes. It fired the lust he'd done his best to ignore.

Bending low, David took off into the woods, following an old deer track he knew would lead to the same ford as the road. He had to concentrate to keep his seat. Just what he needed to dispel thought of trouble in a lilac dress.

The trees rushed by him, the occasional branch snagging his coat, bruising his hat. The horse knew what David wanted and gave it to him. They were both on the edge of losing control, close to catastrophe but so aware of life in them, around them, they were at one with it.

This was the way it felt to be in the top mast, watching the play of the sea all around him, no land in sight, just miles and miles of rolling blue waves, the deck a thousand miles below. When one misstep would mean death. His short career in the navy had been headed for failure even before the shipwreck, but when he thought about those months, the highlight would be his time on top of the world when he felt the same elation he felt now.

David slowed Cruces about a quarter mile from the ford that crossed some nameless tributary of the Severn and waited for the carriage to catch up with him. Finally he saw it coming around the last bend, moving so slowly that he would have to revise their travel time.

The carriage passed him and the coachman raised a hand to his forelock. David gave a jerk of his head in response. He nodded to Miss Castellano, who raised her hand to knock on the roof of the carriage. It slowed to a stop, which only took a moment since they were hardly moving anyway.

She did not lean out the window so he came closer to hear her latest demand.

"My lord, the coachman must be allowed to drive more slowly. My maid is unwell."

"He will drive at the usual pace or we will arrive in the dark."

"No! There is a full moon and two grooms besides you to protect us."

David heard the maid moaning. He could see that the servant rested her head in Miss Castellano's lap while her mistress waved a fan to cool her. These two behaved more like sisters than maid and mistress.

"My lord, if we move as fast as you would like then the inside of the carriage will not be fit for travel."

"We will stop a moment after we ford the stream."

With a nod to John Coachman, who had heard the conversation, David rode ahead to test the ford.

Miss Castellano must have learned her peculiar attitude toward servants from her guardian.

It had taken them all a while to realize that the new duchess truly cared about the servants' wives and children, and whether the basket weighed too much to carry easily or the schedule for beating the rugs rushed them too much. Even the duke called it unconventional.

David put Mia Castellano out of his mind, or at least banished her to a quiet corner, and gave the ford and his horse his complete attention.

Cruces made his way across the natural ford without hesitation. The horse stepped onto the bank and responded instantly when David urged him back into the water.

David stopped to speak to the coachman, well aware that Miss Castellano was leaning out the window so she would not miss a word.

"The only spot that is less than calm is about five yards before the opposite bank," he called out.

"Aye, my lord," John Coachman said. "I remember it from the crossing coming south. A right bit higher the water was and still the horses had no complaint."

"The bigger problem is the underwater moss—algae, my brother Gabriel would call it. Whatever the word, it will be slippery and I do not think you can avoid it. It's in the shade right where the ford ends."

"Aye." The coachman climbed down from his seat and went back to talk to the grooms.

Lord David rode up to the coach door.

"Will it be dangerous?" Miss Castellano asked, as though it were her fondest wish.

"Not really, but in the interests of safety I will take you across with me on my horse. I do not expect any mishap, but you are too valuable to risk."

"Nonsense." She pushed open the door and stood on the edge. "If you truly were concerned for items of value, you would take my trunks with you. I would be desolate if they were lost."

He had no time for her version of flirting. He would

not beg her to let him carry her across. Touching her at all was unwise.

She waited for one of the grooms to lower the steps and announced, "I want to ride on top while we cross the river. It will be much more fun that way."

"You cannot. There is no way for you to climb up to the seat. And I will not lift you." He should never have phrased it that way. David knew it the minute the words left his mouth.

"Of course I can do it." She laughed at his concern. Pulling her skirts up to a most unladylike height above her ankles, Miss Castellano climbed, with casual grace, up into the driver's seat, then straightened her skirts and sat with the demeanor of a grand dame.

"Cor, look at that," one of the grooms said to the other. "I never even seen circus women who could move like that."

Lord David turned his head and stared at the boy who had spoken. He did not have to say a word for the two grooms to be reminded of their positions. The young men hurried to their spots at the back of the carriage where they would see nothing of the crossing, only the trunks stored between them and the riding compartment.

The boy was right, David thought, as he rode around the carriage, inspecting the wheels and the frame of the conveyance. Not about the show of ankle so much as her amazing agility. That made the mind wander.

As he came up to the driver's box he noticed that she had put her hat on, ruined as it was. Still, the light breeze caught her curls, their color between brown and gold. She did not seem to mind the disarray of either her hair or her hat. He watched as she pressed her lips together, barely able to contain her excitement.

"My lord, you must smile more. You look so much friendlier when you do."

David bit back his smile. He didn't want her to see him as anything more than an irritated protector. "Sit still. Do not distract the driver. Listen to me. The river is higher than usual but it should be an uneventful crossing."

She nodded, pretending to be as serious as he was. But he could see the devilment in her eyes.

"If you do anything to upset the crossing you will have to fend for yourself."

She nodded, her eyes growing more severe. "I am not a fool, Lord David. I think you prefer to take the fun out of everything. This may not be dangerous but it will be an adventure. Stop trying to spoil it."

"If it were dangerous or if I trusted John Coachman less I would drag you from that seat no matter what you wished."

I'd like to see you try. She did not have to say the words; her expression spoke volumes.

"Now you look like a petulant schoolgirl."

She gave him that look from beneath her lashes that made him think she might welcome a masterful hand. But only on her terms. If he tried to total the number of times she had said "No" on this trip, David expected he would lose count somewhere in the hundreds.

He gave her a discouraging scowl, aimed as much at his thoughts as at her. Falling in behind the conveyance, he stayed on the right side where he could see if she caused any trouble or panicked. Though he did not think her flaws included panic, not when she so valued "adventure."

The coachman set out slowly. Mia turned her head this way and that, looking down into the water as if trying to find fish, stretching out a little, apparently to watch the horses' footing.

All went well and David breathed a sigh of relief—a moment too soon. The back right wheel caught the moss just as the horses pulled up onto dry land. He watched, powerless, as the wheel slid into the water, coming to rest at an awkward angle.

At his nudge, Cruces stepped into the deeper water, so David could circle the carriage and take a good look at their predicament. He stared at it, ignoring the cries and commotion from the others. It would require brute strength to right the carriage without upset, but on the list of possible disasters it ranked fairly low.

First he faced a bigger challenge, figuring out how to calm a hysterical woman.

Chapter Four

"*Io vado a morire,*" a woman's voice wailed. David recognized it as the maid's and then heard her mistress's irritation as she called down to her, "You will not die, Janina. Be quiet."

None of them needed the maid's cry as a call to action. When the carriage jerked as the wheel slipped off the moss, the grooms knew exactly what had happened.

David dismounted as well, after checking on Miss Castellano, whose only sign of distress was the way she gripped the side rail of the box. He gave a moment's thought to taking her to safety but decided against it for at least three reasons, only one of them truly practical: The more strength they had pushing the conveyance the less likely any sort of rescue would be necessary.

David joined the grooms along the right side of the carriage and pushed up as John Coachman urged the horses. The water felt numbingly cold but strength brought on by need helped him ignore the discomfort.

They struggled with the back of the coach and for a moment David feared the wheel would not set back on the ford shelf.

"I don't think—" one of the grooms began, huffing the words out with short breaths.

"Push," David spat, refusing to allow the groom's doubt. The carriage hit dry land a moment later, the two grooms and David none the worse despite trousers wet to the knees.

"What an excellent piece of teamwork," Miss Castellano called out, applauding as she spoke. "You are a fine driver, sir," she added to the coachman with one of her brilliant smiles. "I felt as safe as if I were in a chair in my own home."

"Thankee, miss." He blushed hard and Lord David wondered what Miss Castellano would do with this latest conquest.

No wonder Lord William had grown tired of her behavior. She flirted with every man she met, no matter his age or state in life. Praise and smiles won them over every time.

"Lift me down, Lord David," she called out to him, even though he had begun to move ahead.

"No," he called over his shoulder and rode on, out of sight of her amused pout and out of hearing range of her laughter.

*   *   *

IF HE THOUGHT his use of her favorite word would upset her, then Lord David Pennistan was much mistaken. Mia wanted to keep her place on top of the coach, but thought she should see how Janina had weathered the crossing.

"Do not climb down, signorina." Janina leaned out the window, her face rather more pale than before. "Stay up there, if you please. I would prefer to be alone."

"All right. It is not much farther and then you can go to bed."

"*Grazie,*" the maid said as she disappeared back inside.

Mia felt selfish but her seat in the driver's box was too entertaining to abandon when she really could not help Janina. She decided she would make sure that her sister had a bed of her own at the inn.

Mia loved the fresh air and the expanded view from the coachman's seat. Why did anyone sit inside when they could be up here and watch the world of nature parade by? The trees and shrubbery, the birdsong and the small animals were far better company than the velvet squabs and ticking carriage clock.

She supposed it would cause some raised eyebrows when they reached the inn. She would pretend that she would have been sick if she rode inside. Or she could say that the inside of the conveyance felt wet after they crossed the ford. Everyone would understand that she wanted to avoid a chill.

Or she could convince John Coachman to make it look as if she had cajoled him into allowing her to handle the reins. No, that would not do at all. To be driving such a team would show a shocking lack of feminine grace.

By the time they reached the inn just outside of Worcester hours later, fatigue made her bones ache. Mia felt so road weary that she did not care what people thought. The sun had set, and the last light faded as they came into the empty stable yard.

Most likely they were the last to arrive this evening. Light poured from every window, and Mia assumed any number of travelers had arrived ahead of them, headed home from the London Season.

Lord David had arranged for a private parlor and told her that a cold dinner awaited them as soon as she found her room and freshened up. At her request, he asked for another room for her maid, but reported back that the inn had no extra beds available.

Mia was surprised but appreciative when Lord David gave Janina his arm. She did need help with the stairs; her knees barely supported her. Mia hurried ahead, her energy renewed by the obvious comfort of the inn.

At the top of the steps she all but ran into Lord Belfort and his wife. Newly married, the two were bickering; Mia could tell by the tone of their voices.

"Good evening, my lady." Mia curtsied in greeting. The Belforts, Lady Belfort especially, looked startled, and Lady Belfort drew next to her husband, their squabble apparently forgotten at the sight of a friend from last Season. Though Mia would not call Lorraine Belfort's brief curtsy welcoming.

Mia gave them her most gracious smile, determined

to test the depth of their lack of sympathy. "Lord David Pennistan is escorting me to his brother and my guardian, the Duke and Duchess of Meryon."

Mia added the titles, in case they had forgotten that she had friends in high places. "Lord David has secured a large parlor for my use. I would love it if you would join me for dinner."

Lord Belfort nodded but his wife put a hand on his arm. "Thank you, Miss Castellano, but we have our own room and would prefer to dine alone." Lady Belfort swept by her, down the stairs, leaving her husband looking slightly apologetic as he followed.

Well, the Belforts were no different from the rest of the ton in their opinion of her broken engagement. Mia prayed that Lord David had not heard the exchange, but as he and the slowly moving Janina reached the top of the stairs he commented, "Belfort looked disappointed."

"Well, they are newly married," Mia said, pretending that she was not hurt. Lord David did not comment any further, out of kindness or, more likely, because he was preoccupied with his own thoughts.

He left the two women at their room and Janina all but collapsed onto the pallet near the bed. Mia untied her own dress, and unlaced her corset. Then she stretched out on the bed. It felt wonderful not to be moving.

With a sigh she thought about Lady Belfort's snub. With her engagement over, Mia would know who counted as friend.

Janina would never fail her. Her baseborn sister was

the one constant in her life; they were loyal and loving, each to the other.

Mia wished she knew how Elena would react to the news. William was Elena's nephew, and they were very close. If Elena felt a need to take sides, Mia was sure family would win out over a ward. After all, there was no blood between her and Elena, and over the last year, Mia knew, she had been more trouble than anything else.

As for William, well, she had been a fool to think that they could still be friends. Did he miss their adventures together as much as she did? Mia sighed.

"I hear the sigh that is as good as tears. Stop thinking about Lord William. It is over."

Janina sounded better. Her voice was stronger. Mia turned to check her color. Still too pale.

"I was wondering what will happen the next time I see him. The first time he was very cordial but last time, at that country ball in the Cotswolds, he ignored me. Completely."

"Then you will ignore him." Janina lay on her back, her eyes closed, arms folded across her stomach, and her face toward the ceiling. Except for the rise and fall of her chest she looked as if she was ready for her coffin. Mia looked away.

"But he sent me that letter apologizing and saying he would stop to see me at Pennford on his way north for hunting."

"You will not go hunting with him?" Nina asked, sounding shocked. "That would stir up all sorts of gossip."

"Hunt with him. Well, I suppose it would be an adventure, but I would definitely not fit in, now that we are no longer engaged." Mia sat on the edge of the bed and met her sister's eyes. "Besides, I do not think I like hunting. It reminds me too much of my life. Always trying to avoid a trap of someone else's making. Rules are the trap the ton makes. And I had no choice but to try to follow them. That ended in disaster. Now I just want to be left to make my own choices."

"Only widows can do that. Which is too bad since you must marry first and one cannot count on a husband dying."

Mia laughed. "There is another way to make my own choices. Courtesans make their own choices. The salons they manage and the music they encourage appeals to me."

"That is truly one of your more outrageous ideas."

"Perhaps." Mia stretched out again, well aware that Janina had not rejected the suggestion out of hand. "When I come of age the Duke and Elena will have no choice, just as I have had no choice for too long." No choice but to leave Naples and settle in Rome with Elena and her first husband after her father died. No choice but to move to England when Elena decided to do so after Eduardo died. No choice but to go through a Season on the fringe of society with no vouchers to Almacks. No choice but to live with the false sincerity of people, once Elena had married the duke. No choice but to tell William she did not want to marry him. No choice but to travel to Pennford with a man who saw her as nothing but trouble.

"Soon you and I will have our own home. I will play

the pianoforte and entertain other musicians and I do not care if they are part of society or not. Then I will not care if they whisper, 'Mia Castellano does not belong in London society.'"

"Please wait and see what happens after this Season. If you are away awhile I am sure people will forget. Perhaps the mad king will die, or the Regent's wife will take a lover and have another child. Now that would be a serious problem, would it not? No one would think about Mia Castellano. Your adventures would seem tame by comparison."

Janina started to stand up and Mia jumped to her feet to help her.

"I am better," she said with surprise. "I want nothing to eat yet, but I do feel well enough to help you into a fresh gown." As Janina spoke she put one of her hands on the wall to steady herself.

"No new gown. There is not a soul here I want to impress." Mia led her maid to a chair and made her sit. "I can manage."

"But, Mia, Lord David is so handsome."

"You and Miss Cole have read from the same book." How many times a day would she have to hear this?

"But the serious look, the sadness around his eyes makes him so much more of a mystery. It makes a woman curious, does it not?" Janina's own woeful expression lightened as she spoke.

"And what would Romero say about that?" Mia teased as she ran a brush through her hair.

"We have talked about it and he knows I am as true as he is."

The two were very close. If Romero did join them, wherever they settled, Mia might start to believe in love again.

"If you could entertain Lord David with some of your outrageous adventures," Janina continued, "then I am sure his sadness would disappear."

"Yes, I could do that," Mia said thoughtfully. She stopped brushing her hair as the glimmer of an idea presented itself. She tapped her mouth with two fingers but could not keep the words back. "You know, Janina, I could try to seduce him."

"Mia!" There was no doubting the shock in Janina's voice. "That is a foolish idea. He is Elena's brother-in-law."

Mia's outlandish suggestion had the desired effect. She was sure that Janina was no longer thinking about her upset stomach. "Well, I only mean to tease him into a kiss. Besides, he already thinks I am a woman with no loyalty and loose morals and he would never tell the duke."

"Has he said that to you?"

"Not exactly." With a deft hand, Mia pulled her hair back to her crown and waited while Janina found her simplest combs. "I have hardly seen him since that awful night. But today he has treated me as though I were a pariah who could taint him if he said more than five words to me."

"By the end of this trip I am sure he will see you differently."

"Yes, I think you are right. Especially if I do my best to have him kiss me." She fixed the two combs so that her hair was swept back and cascaded down her back. "I think I will leave my hair down tonight."

"It's a look better suited to the bedroom than the dining room." Janina made a move to take the brush, but Mia raised a hand and backed away.

"I have but three days." She added, "I need all the advantages I can find."

"It is very daring."

Mia could not tell if Janina meant challenge or caution. "He cannot like me any less than he does already."

"What if the duchess finds out?"

"How could she? I will not tell her and I can't imagine that Lord David would."

"If Elena does find out, the duke will insist that Lord David marry you."

"And I will say no. What will they do? Keep me in my room until I come of age? Fine, between the two of us we can arrange for where we will go and what we will do after my birthday."

"No is an amazing word," Janina agreed. "If you are serious about kissing him, then you must wear a new dress."

"A new gown would be too obvious."

"As if leaving your hair like that is not."

Mia shrugged. "I will wait to wear the new ones when we arrive at Pennford. They will distract Elena from my ruined engagement."

"I am sure she will understand about Lord William. I

am sure she will." Janina spoke with more worry than conviction.

"Then you are more certain than I am. She and William are very close and he has never irritated her half as much as I have."

"Elena is a new duchess and close to her lying-in. She does not think of Lord William at all these days."

"Well, I can only hope that she is not thinking about me, either. In the meantime I will not worry about it." Except at night, just before sleep.

Janina nodded and sank into the chair, as if she had used all her quota of energy for the day. Mia told her that she would have some dinner sent up and made her way down the stairs with a book, in case she needed an excuse to stay in the parlor with Lord David after dinner. It would be a fine opportunity to practice being a silent distraction with her book as a prop.

Mia nodded to the servant who opened the parlor door for her, and then she stopped on the threshold. Lord David sat at the table. He ignored the plate of food and mug of ale, preferring the stack of papers at hand, others spilling out from a leather satchel leaning against the side of his chair.

The line between his brows hinted at an internal argument. As she waited for him to notice her, Mia saw that the candlelight made his hair darker than it appeared in the daylight.

His brows were full and his eyes more deeply set than the duke's. Lord David's air of aloofness, if not mystery, made him so much more fascinating than his brothers.

His brother the duke was a tyrant, but one expected that from a duke, though he did smile more since his marriage. "Open" and "friendly" perfectly described Lord Gabriel, as well as his sister, Olivia. Mia had never met Lord Jessup, which was odd considering how many times she had been with the family since Elena's official engagement ball. According to William, David's brother loved games and was a stranger to serious thoughts.

She waited a full minute but Lord David did not look up, did not stand up, did not offer to fill her plate.

She would have to find a more direct way to draw his attention.

Chapter Five

MIA DECIDED THAT she would not garner Lord David's attention with outlandish behavior. That would only add to his ill opinion of her. She decided on behavior that was subtle and genteel.

Putting some cold ham on her plate, Mia rattled the dishes and made a loud clink of serving fork against platter. She took very little of the fish, unable to actually name it, and some haricots verts served cold and dressed in the Italian way. She chose a roll, realizing that she was rather hungry, and a slice of cheese—a hearty British cheddar, she thought. A white wine, nicely chilled, completed her meal and she sat, knocking the table so hard that it wobbled and everything on it moved. How could she have forgotten her perfume?

Lord David still had not acknowledged her presence or touched a morsel of his very full plate. He must be hungry.

"Put those papers away, Lord David, and make some conversation while we dine."

He looked up at her, pushed the papers aside, and reached for his fork as he did so. He cut into the well-cured ham, took a bite, and chewed.

"Tell me what you are studying so thoroughly."

He raised his eyebrows, his mouth too full for any other comment.

"If you please," she added, and took a very small forkful of the beans.

He swallowed, wiping his mouth with the serviette. "I am studying the design of the Long Bank Mill near Styal."

"Where is Styal?" The English had such strange names for towns.

"Near Manchester."

"Why are you studying the design of a mill?" she prompted, feeling like a mother encouraging a child just learning to speak.

"I want to build one like it."

"Build" sounded like it had to do with trade. That could not be. "What does this mill do?"

"It makes thread out of cotton roving."

"I have no idea what cotton roving is but I do know you are speaking of trade." When he did not deny it, Mia could not suppress her shock. "You are going to involve yourself in trade! You must be teasing me."

"No, I am not teasing." He sat back in his chair. "And cotton roving are the fibers twisted by the slubber to give it the strength to be spun into yarn."

"Thank you." She pretended she believed him. "Slubber" could not possibly be a word. "But that does not make your story any more believable."

"The duke is providing half of the money, and I am going to oversee the construction and establishment of the business."

"But that's," she hesitated, "that's shocking. I would never have expected you to do something so unusual." Mia tasted the fish, which had been cooked in an herb-flavored wine sauce. To disguise its age, she suspected.

"Manufacturing is the future," Lord David said. Then, after a moment of silence, he continued. "Once I secure the other half of the funding I will be ready to move forward. I will supervise the construction and find someone to run the factory for me."

"That's not as bad as it sounded at first. It does still hint of trade and you are the second son and the brother of a duke."

"I am well aware of that and I do not care. Neither will the people who will have work and those who will be able to afford the items made from the cotton." He picked up his mug but went on before tasting it. "Once I am confident that the mill manager is reliable in all ways and is as interested in an honest profit as we are, I will move on to the next project."

He addressed himself to his food, and she thought about his plan as she buttered her roll. "The ton will be shocked."

"I do not plan to go to London for anything but business. I have no use for the Season or the ton."

"You are joking." She waited, and when he did not respond she wondered. Could it be he felt the same way she did? "You must care. Everyone cares."

He leaned close to her over his papers. "I spent seven years in Mexico. My experiences there forever changed how I see the world. I have no use for mindless diversions."

"Yes, I understand travel will do that. But there must have been a social world there. One you could enjoy. Or were you deep in the country with only wild men for company?"

They had both stopped eating and she waited for him to speak. Who would have thought conversation with him would be so intriguing?

"Miss Castellano, where I landed they had never heard of England. No one even thought to ask about my station in life."

"Where was it? How could they have never heard of England?" She did not mean to sound so skeptical but she found it hard to believe.

A muscle in his cheek moved and then he spoke very quietly. "I was on my first voyage as a naval midshipman and the sole survivor of a shipwreck. It took me seven years to find my way back to England."

MIA CASTELLANO stood abruptly.

Now what had he done? David knew he would find out, because she would not hesitate to tell him. Miss Castellano was not inclined to silence.

"I thought to have a civil conversation with you, my lord." Moving behind her chair, she pushed it in with unnecessary force. "But pleasant conversation is too much to ask. You've tried to find a way to shock me, to make me wonder if you are serious, until you come up with something that leaves no doubt in my mind that you are toying with me."

David said nothing. Elena had warned him about Miss Castellano's hotheadedness, and he understood her passion. Not that Pennistans were always diplomatic and deliberate.

"Shipwrecked in Mexico, my lord! How ridiculous." She looked up to the ceiling as if praying, then at him with her eyes narrowed. "If that's true, then explain how it is that I have never heard the story before. It would be the first thing anyone in society would say about you."

She had raised her voice only a little, but her anger was obvious from her theatrical tone, her flashing eyes, her expressive posture. Miss Castellano waited no more than a second for him to answer.

"Lord David, no one, I tell you, no one anywhere in society, no one in the Pennistan family, no one has ever mentioned that you were missing for so many years."

She drew a deep breath to fuel her tirade and David made a Herculean effort not to even glance at her décolletage.

"If I had swallowed that, no doubt you would have told me something even more preposterous. That you have a wife and five children waiting for you in Manchester, or that you prefer the company of men, or that you kill people who take God's name in vain, or that you resorted to cannibalism while you were supposedly shipwrecked."

She did have a vivid imagination, but so far she had not named a truth. He opened his mouth, not to speak, but just to see what she would do if he did try to have his say. She shook her head sharply.

"Do not try to justify your behavior. Unless you mean to apologize. I will leave you to your cold dinner, your papers, and your wild tales of trade, abandoning society, and, oh yes, your shipwreck in Mexico. I will leave, which is, I am sure, what you wanted all along."

Miss Castellano left the room, without slamming the door, which surprised him.

Quiet descended at last, but the air still sizzled with the last sparks of her temper. David laughed. Out loud.

He had told her the absolute truth.

He had set aside his papers and did as she asked, had a conversation with her. She had been a good traveler, never once complaining about her maid's illness even though it must have made the trip very uncomfortable. He'd seen how Lady Belfort's cut had hurt her feelings and even noticed that she left her hair down this evening so as not to trouble her maid further.

With all that in mind he had done his best to be a pleasant dinner companion. And failed miserably.

The result only illustrated his complete lack of social grace. "Let that be a lesson," he announced to the empty room. Instead of telling her that he was hoping to build a cotton mill, that he had been in the navy, and that yes, he had been the only survivor of a shipwreck off the coast of

Mexico, he obviously should have made an effort to find a subject more conformable, like the colors favored in this year's fashions, or even suggested renting a horse so she could ride tomorrow if her maid was still unwell.

Refilling his mug, David abandoned the meal, and moved to the desk so he could return to work, clearly the only thing he was fit for. First he'd write the letter to the trustees of the Meryon entail.

As he opened his writing box and organized quill, paper, and ink, he recalled the lively hour he and Lyn had spent discussing how to approach the trustees with something so unconventional as investing in a cotton mill. That was after hours of far more tense debate convincing the duke first. God, but his brother took his role seriously.

"I'm determined to leave the estate in even better condition than I found it," Lyn had said. "Father worked hard so that the finances had a sound footing. I am not going to undermine that even to support you, David."

That was not the vote of confidence that David hoped for, and it left him feeling like the beggar he was.

If he was not so convinced that manufacturing would create even more wealth than the thousands of acres of land the dukedom owned, David would have walked out then and there. Land, land, land had been the measure of Meryon wealth for more than five hundred years, but times were about to change, so David had pressed on.

The winning argument had come from his heart, and he knew that if it failed there was no point in hoping to convince the duke. "Brother, I learned firsthand in Mexico how hideous it is to be without resources, what a nightmare it is to be under someone else's control with no idea of what the next day will bring, to have almost no hope.

"Providing work for as many men, and even women and children, as possible will help to put an end to the unrest and will give everyone faith in the future. If there is any good that came from the shipwreck, it is my understanding of how the poor live and what might help them most." He did not need to add that it was something that the Duke of Meryon could not begin to grasp.

The duke, his brother, nodded, and David did not have to listen to what he said to know that the duke was convinced. He could see it in his eyes, in the sympathy in his voice.

Ever cautious, the duke insisted that the trustees agree.

"You don't need their approval, Lyn, and I'm not saying that to save me writing a letter."

"I have found it best to keep them informed."

The duke pushed his chair back and raised his feet to the desktop, a sure sign that they were now both on the same side.

"Never think I mean to include them in the process, David. The point is that one never knows when their support will be needed for something over which they do have control."

"So let me outline what I will tell you and them." David remembered pacing the room as he ordered his thoughts. "The plan to work with Thomas Sebold to develop a second mill like Long Bank is sound on several levels. His mill is profitable."

"That's key. The trustees' interest in profit is only exceeded by their lack of imagination."

"Yes, but I will try to be more tactful in my wording."

"I trust you will. You may be blunt in speech but your letters are always reasoned and thoughtful." Lyn did not expect any explanation for that fact, any more than David could give him one. The duke laughed as he put his feet down and sat with more authority. "Even with a profit I do not think the trustees will be impressed by the housing Sebold provides for his employees."

"But I will make it clear that we are adamant on that. There is a precedent for it in our family, so they will not be surprised. We all learned from Father and his experience in France during the Revolution. He would never let us forget. Neglect of servants or mill workers is a sure prescription for unrest and revolt."

"You know, David, that explains *our* inclinations, but Sebold had none of those experiences. When you meet him next, do ask what motivated him."

"My biggest concern is whether Sebold will be amenable to moving the site to a different city. Once he agrees to that it will truly be our project."

"But not in competition with him. It will increase his profits as he is an equal investor. He would be a fool to argue over where the mill is placed unless the site is inadequate in some way."

"It is, in fact, superior. Closer to the canal, with a large group of veterans eager for employment."

"Yes, yes, but I want you to understand one important fact."

David straightened.

"I support you, I will make that clear to the trustees, but if you fail to find the rest of the money, if Sebold should refuse, you will have to move on to another project."

David had agreed, and now in the quiet of the parlor his brother's choice of words haunted him. Failure. The most noteworthy event of his life had been the total failure of his naval career. The shipwreck was only the final devastating stroke. And he'd saved his own life by doing precisely what had led to the ruination of a possible career. He'd disobeyed orders and been the only one to survive.

He would not fail again. He would prove that he could contribute something to his family name. He would rather be compared with his brother Gabriel and his interest in scientific study than with his brother Jess, who had gambled away his inheritance and had been too busy trying to win it back to attend the duke's wedding.

With Gabriel as inspiration and Jess as warning, David wrote the letter to the trustees quickly, pleased that despite the speed it appeared legible and blot-free. He stopped midsentence, rereading to see if it sounded too subservient. As he considered how to finish, he raised his head and caught sight of the shawl Miss Castellano had left behind, draped on her empty chair.

Damnation. Mia Castellano thought he had been teasing her. Did she think "civil conversation" nothing more than a discussion of who courted whom and what she would wear to the next party? Try as he might he could not see serious discussion centering around whether the Regent would outlive his father and be called King George IV.

His attempt to treat her as though she had as much intelligence as beauty proved the opposite. Odds were that even when she matured, Mia Castellano would be no more than a empty mind encased in a lovely face and a tempting body.

The sooner they reached Pennford the better. Then Lyn could decide how to deal with her.

Chapter Six

"HE IS IMPOSSIBLE." Mia walked smartly across the room, loving the way the silk of her dress whirled around her. What a shame there was no one else to enjoy it but Janina. "I would have been happy to talk about his plans but he has to tease me with the unlikeliest stories."

"So you are not going to tempt him into kissing you?"

"It's hopeless. He made me angry from the moment I walked in the room. I did not realize how much he can annoy me. It's as though he thinks of me as his sister." That was a lie but it was easier to say than to try to explain the sudden roil of feelings that both excited and confused her.

How could she be attracted to a man who held her in such disregard, who did not know how to flirt or do anything but work?

"I will tell you this, Janina: As soon as we arrive at

Pennford, I am writing to the agent who handled the rental of Elena's house in Bloomsbury, the house we lived in when I first came to London, before you arrived." Janina's absence had been part of the reason her first year had been less than perfect.

"I will write and ask him to help me find a place to rent. I can use my correspondence with the agent as proof I am serious about my independence."

Janina nodded and closed her eyes. "I am listening, but I feel easier with my eyes closed."

"Oh, dear. I hope you tried to eat something." Mia dropped to her knees beside Janina's pallet and felt her head, feeling like a selfish witch for not asking after Nina as soon as she came into the room.

"They brought a very nice beef broth and then I ate some bread and one of Romero's sweets, but too much food made me sick and now I have such a headache that I cannot stand up without the dizziness, and ooh, my body aches as though I have been traveling in a donkey cart and not the duke's fine carriage."

"Your head is warm. You may have a fever. You use the bed tonight, Janina. I will sleep on the pallet."

Her maid opened one eye and did not move. "No, I cannot."

"Do not argue. I am the one in charge and you will do as I say."

"I am afraid if I try to move I will be unwell."

"Then we will wait until you have convinced yourself that you can stand up so that you can lie down in comfort."

It took the better part of an hour before Nina felt well enough to move. Not five minutes after that, Mia could hear the deep breathing that meant sound sleep. Janina might think her too generous, but Mia needed her maid healthy and whole.

For a dozen reasons, but most importantly because she did not want to face Elena without Janina nearby.

Mia reached around and undid her own dress. Her singular dexterity did come in useful sometimes, like today when she had climbed up onto the driver's box after Lord David had refused to help her.

"Che diavolo!" Mia whispered. Janina had the ties all tangled and she would need two mirrors to see how to undo them. The room did not boast even one.

She went down to the common room, hoping to find a daughter of the house who would come up and help her.

The room smelled of hops and smoke. And men. She made no move to enter or even swish her skirts to attract attention but her one glance stilled all conversation.

That did not bother her as much as the sight of Lord David seated at a table, his newspaper announcing he did not want company. He had a private parlor, but here he sat in the common room. One would think he'd prefer solitude, rather than face the possibility of conversation when he so obviously had no skill at it.

"Is there something I can do for you, my dear?"

The gentleman who had spoken to her looked rather nice, well-dressed and well-groomed, but Mia knew better than to respond to that sort of invitation.

"No," she said, using the imperious, queenly version of the word.

Quiet prevailed and when Lord David did look up, his bored expression conveyed his disinterest. She knew it for a sham but she also could tell that, like this morning, he would wait until the last moment to step in. Mia did not know whether to be annoyed by his lack of gallantry or pleased he thought she could handle this herself.

"Good evening, gentlemen." She gave a vague curtsy to the room, not eyeing anyone particularly. Speaking loud enough for all to hear she went on, "I am looking for the mistress of the house. My maid has taken ill."

Some bowed, a few only nodded, but not one of them cared about a woman with a sick maid. The gentleman who had approached her chuckled. "I'm so sorry." His tone made a joke of it. "Why not let me escort you back to your room."

Mia shook her head and stepped back, but the man, not a gentleman despite his dress, came out into the hallway with her.

"Perhaps we could go somewhere else."

His tone of voice suggested something so improper that Mia did not have to pretend outrage. "No," she said even more brusquely. "My maid is ill and if you cannot solve that problem then leave me alone."

"Your protests charm me but they can be overdone."

Admitting defeat and now profoundly relieved that Lord David sat nearby, she marched into the common room, over to the table where he waited, and sat down. "I need your help."

"Hmmm" was all he said, though he did glance at her for a moment.

"Janina is sick and I need someone to help me undress."

"But that man offered to do just that."

She banged her fist on the table, which hurt more than she thought it would and also stopped conversation once again. She did not want the attention of anyone but Lord David. Though she whispered the words it did not diminish her rage. "Stop insulting me. Stop right now. Help me find a maid and please beat that man to a pulp."

"Beat him to a pulp." Lord David seemed to consider the suggestion as he eyed the room full of men, most of whom were nodding. "With pleasure, Miss Castellano." Lord David put the paper down and took her arm, escorting her from the room.

Murmurs followed them.

"Her husband?"

"No, she would have come to him right away."

"Her brother?"

"They don't look alike."

Lord David turned to the man who had been so importunate. With a speed that took everyone by surprise Lord David shot his fist into the man's nose and then grabbed him by the cravat. "Let's finish this outside."

David pulled him out the door, followed by the entire population of the common room, both local and traveler alike.

"Her lover," one of the men muttered to the others.

"May well beat her next," another suggested.

"Neither. He's a gent that loves a good fight and that's all there is to it. Hurry or it'll be over before we're out there."

Mia watched them leave, all their interest in her forgotten. It could be he had punched the man quite deliberately to distract the travelers from her embarrassment.

A woman came from the kitchen just as Mia remembered what had started this. She still needed someone to help her.

"Miss." The woman introduced herself as the innkeeper's wife.

"I do so beg your pardon, Mrs. Wills," Mia began, but the woman seemed unperturbed by the incident.

"It happens all the time, miss. It's good for business. Lord David will pay us for the inconvenience when, in fact, the crowd will be thirstier than ever."

"You know Lord David?"

"That we do. He's been traveling through here for years now. He and my son often put on amateur boxing fights. They are well matched, they are."

Boxing! And he took offense at her behavior.

"Come along, now, miss, before they return. You say your maid is ill."

The innkeeper's wife entertained her with a delightful mix of caring and coarse. For the next few minutes, as Mrs. Wills untied her dress and unlaced her stays, she treated Mia to stories that made her laugh and gasp.

Mrs. Wills told her about the time that a family left one of their children behind, quite by mistake, and did not return for three days, and about the newlywed couple who was with them now, who had broken the bed with their before-dinner use of it.

"The Belforts!" Mia exclaimed. She hoped so, though she could never, ever refer to it. Still, it would make her feel so much better. How unbelievably embarrassing.

"Discretion is an innkeeper's most important virtue. Stories, but no names."

Mia thought for a moment. "How many newlywed couples are guests this evening?"

"Only one," Mrs. Wills answered with a smile that showed her crooked teeth. "I wish I could have offered you a bed for your maid," the older woman began, deftly changing the subject, "but we are full up tonight."

"Oh, that's quite all right. I lived in Italy during the war with Napoleon and I am used to inconvenience." Who would ever have thought that she could so casually talk about those years of deprivation and worry? "So, Mrs. Wills, now I suppose I am one of the stories."

"Oh no, miss. The crowd in the common room came tonight because they heard that Lord David would be here and more than ready to fight. If that man had not been so rude to you, I'm sure someone else would have picked a fight with him."

Mrs. Wills bid her good night and left Mia marveling at what men were allowed.

Mia tossed and turned, and not because of the pallet. When she had traveled with her father she had grown used to them.

Tonight had reminded her of that descent into the debacle that had been her engagement. One ill-timed kiss had ended her engagement and jeopardized her place in society, but Lord David could start a brawl in a public place and not suffer any consequences. It was maddening and wrong.

She counted the beams in the ceiling, measured how often Janina snored, and heard when the men retired for the night—quietly enough, but the sound of their drunken steps was impossible to mask.

Quiet settled with the slam of one door and Mia wished it were as easy to close the door on what had been one of the worst chapters of her life. Bad enough to make her realize that what she had wanted so intensely was forever out of reach.

At first she made excuses for the lack of passion between her and Lord William. It didn't matter. With him everything was so much fun, even the most mundane outing. They were *sympatico* and that would be so much more lasting than passion. It had taken her months to realize that marriage meant more than having adventures together.

The realization came one day at the Pennistan house in Richmond.

They had all been at dinner for hours and clearly had spent too much time with the children earlier in the day. When the duke's brother Gabriel had suggested charades, everyone agreed instantly, except for the duke and Lord David. As a result, both of them felt the brunt of merciless teasing for their lack of good humor.

The duke stood and waited for them to quiet down. Mia expected him to insist they observe more decorum.

"Before the evening descends to a level suitable for the nursery, I have an announcement," he began.

They all sobered. The duke was not smiling.

"God willing, the duchess and I will welcome a new addition to the family within five months."

No one said a word. The duke's first wife had died in childbirth. Though he tried to smile as he spoke, Mia could see that the all-powerful Duke of Meryon was afraid.

The duchess herself had smoothed over the awkward moment. Elena hurried from her spot at the other end of the table, pulled her husband close, and kissed him soundly.

His brothers cheered. His sister, Olivia, called out, "It's wonderful news, Lyn!" Everyone rose to their feet, toasting the couple with the last of their wine. William bolted from his spot, shook hands with the duke, and kissed the duchess on the cheek.

That gesture reminded Mia of the blood relationship Elena and William shared: aunt to nephew, despite their closeness in age. They, too, were family.

Not a one of them shared their excitement with her. Yes, it was Elena's moment, but William showered all his attention on her aunt and never once looked at Mia or gave any sign that this was a future they would share, too.

Mia had never felt so much an outsider, so unnecessary. She had no place in this family, any more than she had ever been part of any family. Not since her mother had died.

Mia pushed the thought to the back of her mind that

evening. Elena looked positively radiant and Mia gave her own best wishes to her guardian with sincerity.

The rest of the evening was vastly entertaining. Lord Gabriel's crazy gyrations called for laughable guesses from all of them. Mia was inordinately pleased that she guessed which line from Shakespeare he pulled from the box: "What light through yonder window breaks?"

Her natural inclination to theatrics made her own "Out, damned spot" much easier.

When they were drinking tea, Elena had asked her to play the pianoforte for them. But it had been so long since she had been near one that she had declined. Elena had chastised William for not giving Mia time to practice. William had shrugged off the comment, insisting that listening to someone play an instrument was boring, and the subject was forgotten. By everyone but Mia.

As she brushed her hair that night, the truth about her engagement came to her with a clarity she had never before recognized. A lifetime of tribulations, disappointments, trials, and even death marked a marriage. An unselfish love made it worth the effort; passion made it a worthy adventure.

She did not know if William loved her that way, or if she truly loved him with the kind of passion that existed between the duke and Elena. Having fun and being in love were two different things.

She had tried to talk to Elena about it, but her guardian knew such deep love that she insisted the connection grew stronger with marriage and every day, and night, thereafter. That assumed the right sort of love existed in the first place.

The fact William found listening to music boring haunted her. He would move restlessly around the room while she did her best to entertain him. Finally she realized, with profound disappointment, that he would never grow to share her love of music.

From then on Mia tested William. Tested his love, wondering where William hid the passion he showed for the adventures that were his idea of a good life, and if his passion was for her or for the adventures they shared.

And she began to practice the pianoforte alone. He had not reacted with anything more than easy amusement, leaving her to play while he spent the time at his club or at Jackson's.

When she danced more than once with the same man, William teased her about her weakness in arithmetic. When she walked on the terrace with an older gentleman, William found them and suggested that she come back inside as the night promised a storm, even though the sky showed the moon and stars. That was the closest he came to acting the jealous fiancé.

He ignored her trifling indiscretions until that evening with the son of the Duke of Hale, when she went one step too far and William and Lord David had found them. Within days her world changed forever. She'd wondered, more than once, if William would have cared at all if Lord David had not been with him.

At night, alone with her thoughts, the past haunted

her. The embarrassment she had caused, the hurt she had suffered.

At first Mia had been shocked at the way the ton had shunned her when she and William were no longer together.

She had tried so hard to belong. Anger soon followed. The last straw came when she was not even invited to a musicale, much less asked to play. Music should transcend rank and, even here, the ton had turned their collective back to her.

That night Mia began to consider a life that was not dependent on anyone else's whim or want. It had only been a way to escape the pain at first, but it was growing more and more real every day.

She fell asleep, awash in self-pity, desperate to find a way to live life on her terms.

Chapter Seven

"NO, LORD DAVID," Mia Castellano insisted, "I have no idea how long my maid will be ill and I will not wait here until she can travel. Travel sickness is a burden to Janina and when she is ill she prefers to be alone. It is one of the reasons I rode with the coachman yesterday."

David could see that this "No" was not halfhearted. They were in the same parlor they had shared last night and had managed a polite if silent breakfast until he had suggested, quite generously he thought, that they delay a day until her maid was well again. He could work anywhere. He finished his coffee and poured more from the pot.

"One day will not be enough. She seems much worse than usual and I would estimate a week before she can travel. You will leave me behind long before that."

"How perceptive."

She stood up as though she had enough of the discussion. "Janina is very important to me. I will find someone to care for her and she will stay here until she recovers and is able to join us later."

David could see that she would not budge. But if he let her have her way this time, he feared there would be no end to the demands she would make.

"Be reasonable, Lord David," she began.

"I am always reasonable," he interrupted, exasperated beyond endurance. "We will wait one day," he said again, this time much more firmly.

"No," she repeated with an irritated edge in the one word. "If the entire party stays behind it will only add more pressure for her to recover. Janina will pretend she is well and will most likely not recover for months. I will not endanger her health that way."

"So you are willing to travel without a maid and risk another scene like last night?" The woman was a confusing mix of spoiled and generous. Impossible to understand or predict how she would react to anything.

"My lord."

The way she said his name made it sound like she doubted his intelligence. He nodded.

"We are stopping at a Pennistan holding this evening, are we not?"

"Sandleton. Yes, we are."

"Sandleton. Thank you." Her nod was as queenly as her "No" had been shrewish. "I am sure there is a girl there or in the village who would be willing to wait on me until Janina is well again." She raised two fingers to her lips then dropped them. "I know, I will ask the lady who is to act as chaperone this evening. She will know someone who would like to travel to Pennford, to have a small adventure. We can take Janina's things with us and then she can travel by the mail when she is better."

"Hmmm," he said to cover his surprise at her good idea. If he did as Miss Castellano suggested it would simplify the situation and allow him to deliver her to Pennford and arrive in Manchester on schedule.

"There must be a pianoforte at Sandleton. I will play very quietly, which will keep me from worrying about Janina and you will not have to distract me from my concern with the dreaded 'conversation.' You can work on your mountain of papers and we will not be in each other's way at all."

"Very well. We leave in an hour." Though the suggestion that they would "not be in each other's way at all" was as likely as snow in Mexico. "I would be impressed with this morning's gesture of loyalty, if I did not know how mercurial it can be."

It was an arrow that found its mark. Miss Castellano took a step back, her eyes betraying how wounded she felt by his reference to her broken engagement. After a long moment she smiled a little. "Congratulations, my lord. Now you have spoiled both my dinner and my breakfast."

She picked up the serviette that had dropped to the floor when she stood, tossed it on the table, and moved toward the door. He watched her progress, debating an apology, but one that would not give her the upper hand, when she stopped and faced him again. He was relieved to see her eyes no longer wounded but bright with feeling.

"Lord David," she said, her words tinged with regret as well as anger. "You know nothing, nothing about me other than that regrettable incident." She raised two fingers to her lips again, but it was not enough to keep her from finishing. "If you have never once made a terrible mistake, then do feel free to mention that incident hourly. But if, despite having 'Lord' before your name, you are as imperfect as the rest of us, I will thank you not to speak of it again."

With that she left the room.

David stared at her still-full plate and noticed that she had forgotten her shawl and her book. He stood and added them to the papers. If he thought to keep her at a distance he had succeeded. Her petulance would make for a miserable day of traveling, though it might keep her quiet. He wondered how long it would be until she smiled again.

To his surprise she was in the stable yard when he came out. They were one of three groups preparing to leave. He stood waiting for her, watching, after he handed her shawl and book to one of the grooms with the direction to put it in the coach.

David saw her turn to the Belforts who were right next to them, waiting for their baggage to be loaded.

"I hope you travel safely to your destination," she said

pleasantly. "Will you have many more nights on the road?"

"Uh, three more days, Miss Castellano." Lord Belfort Wiggins answered, with a try at civility that was not anywhere equal to hers.

"I hope all the beds are as comfortable as the ones here."

Before either one of them could answer, Miss Castellano turned toward her carriage, pressing her lips together as if to keep from laughing out loud. The Belforts were clearly embarrassed. Over what, Lord David had no idea. On the other hand, the Belforts deserved whatever barb she had delivered, after the way they had treated her last night. It would have cost them nothing to be kind to her. Of course, he thought, that was the pot calling the kettle black.

Miss Castellano took Lord David's arm as they crossed the stable yard. "That, my lord, was very small of me, but I wanted to show you that a pinch is so much more genteel than a body blow. As a boxer you should understand the difference."

"Yes, I do. And I know that what I said at breakfast was far closer to a knockout punch."

"But good practice for what is to come," she said, seeming to accept an apology at which he had only hinted. "There is a vast difference between a cut and an insult. Not to mention a snub."

"We do not have the time to discuss the philosophical difference between insults and snubs." The subject seemed like dangerous territory to him. Most likely, they would end up demonstrating insults on each other.

"Lord David, I live for the day when you decide any time or place is suitable for conversation."

She left him feeling the same confusion he thought the Belforts must have felt. Had she snubbed him or simply ended the conversation as she thought he wished?

David watched Miss Castellano speak to the groom and the coachman, offering them something from a box but not offering him any of the treat. Finally, Miss Castellano climbed into the carriage without another glance his way.

If she was in a bad humor, it lasted only three hours. Or at least that was how long quiet reigned. Not that he actually timed it, but they had reached the first sign directing them to Stafford shortly before she called to him. For once they were on time and should arrive at Sandleton before dusk.

"Lord David!" Miss Castellano leaned out the window at a precarious angle. He rode back beside her and she settled safely on her seat. "Do come and ride inside the carriage awhile. It is so very boring with no one to talk to. We can compare insults we have received and given."

"That seems a subject that will invite discomfort, and there is nowhere for you to run off to."

"Then I will thank you for rescuing my shawl and book and then we can discuss some other subject of which we both have knowledge."

"Miss Castellano, I think we would find it difficult to agree on what color the sun is."

"Gold, of course."

"Yellow," he answered.

"You are deliberately being difficult, but I am so desperate for something living to talk to that I will overlook it."

David rode into the woods and pulled a branch of wild roses from a wildly blooming plant. They were almost the color of her costume.

He shoved them through the window of the coach onto the seat opposite her. "Here is something living. Talk to it."

Her long-suffering expression mirrored exactly how he felt, but then she smiled and gave her attention to the flowers.

"Oh, good afternoon, Miss Rose. You and your friends are such refreshing company. It's so lovely of you to call, and the scent you are wearing is delightful. Spending time with you always lifts my spirits."

She waited as though listening.

"How kind of you to say so. And I think that blushing red suits you marvelously as well. The white near the center only emphasizes the depth of the hue."

The conveyance bumped over a root and settled as quickly. "Yes, you see all your friends are nodding in agreement."

She listened again.

"I know. He quite swept you off your feet, or from your branch."

David stared off into the woods so that she would not see him smile.

"He is a fine figure of a man but, I must tell you, my dears, his manners leave much to be desired."

Silence again.

"Oh, I suspect that there is more there than you think, but it will not be anything but the most mundane experience."

She said the last as though it were the worst criticism one could make of a man. David rode ahead, sure that more insults were to follow. She could be charming, but like the roses there were thorns hidden in the most unexpected places.

After a while the sound of her voice faded and he actually looked around for another flower to stir her imagination. He decided against it, afraid she would misinterpret his gesture.

The sun heated the air, hot even for July. And humid. Over the next hours, as they headed steadily for the Great North Road, David had to fight to keep his eyes open. He jerked himself awake and turned back to see how the rest fared.

The coachman was nodding as well, and David turned his horse back to the carriage just as the man fell from his box and hit the ground with a sickening thud. The horses sensed the lack of control instantly and picked up their pace. The grooms, both of them, jumped from the back of the conveyance to see to John Coachman's injury, which left no one but Miss Castellano to take charge of the horses.

He urged Cruces to a spot opposite the window.

"You do not have to rescue me. Go see how the

coachman is; I can climb up and slow the horses." She shouted her suggestions and did not seem at all afraid.

The horses picked up their pace and Miss Castellano fell back into her seat. If he did not act quickly the team would soon be out of control.

"Stay right there!" he shouted to her, and could not think of another woman who would need to be told that.

David thought first to ride to the lead horse and grab the bridle, but they were already moving too fast for that, so he urged his horse parallel to the coachman's box and made a grab for the edge. He missed on the first try and lost ground as the team sensed a race and pulled ahead.

Now the carriage picked up speed, too fast for him to effect a rescue of its passenger. He would have one more chance to jump into the driver's box before the conveyance moved beyond his reach. The consequences of that would be disastrous.

"I can jump safely," Miss Castellano yelled from her seat. "I've done it before."

I've done it before. Of course she had. No matter how many times she had jumped from a moving carriage, her guardian would hardly thank him if he let Miss Castellano demonstrate that skill now.

"But my trunks. Please, I need my clothes. Try just one more time."

Oh yes, he would be delighted to risk his life for her gowns and jewelry. The carriage rocketed over a rough patch of road and even the redoubtable Mia Castellano let out a very small shriek. At least she realized how fast the carriage moved, that she could not jump without some injury. He could banish the thought of holding her unconscious body, bones broken as surely as her hat had been yesterday.

Desperation made an excellent companion, bolstering his energy as it did. This time David waited until the conveyance swayed toward him. He kicked free of his stirrups and pulled himself up into the box though he could feel his shoulders protest the effort. *Thank God a hundred times ten!*

The coach swerved to the right toward an embankment that led to a lake, and he had a horrible picture of his passenger tumbling over and over like dice in a cup as the conveyance slid and spun into the water.

The horses slowed a little, either because his horse no longer raced alongside or because they felt the weight in the box and knew the coachman had returned. Their less panicked gait would make it easier for him to reach for the reins that were trailing in the dirt between the last horse and the box.

He needed something with a hook and searched through the items that littered the driving box. A rain cape, a pistol wrapped in linen, a bottle of water, or maybe gin, and a few coins. Nothing with the appendage he needed.

David considered jumping onto a horse's back, but that was more of a challenge than lowering himself between the vehicle and the horses to reach for the reins.

If anything went wrong it would be deadly, and not

just for him, so he would have to convince the Fates that nothing would.

As he took off his coat he heard Miss Castellano's voice. "Take this!" He turned around to find the curved end of an umbrella stuck from the open window. God bless a woman who could think at such a time, any time. Beauty and brains rarely came in the same package.

He took the umbrella. The handle gave him the extra reach he needed and on the third try, with no more insult than a face full of dirt and some doubly strained muscles, David caught the loop at the end of the reins, drew them up, and took control of the team. He slowed the over-heated horses gradually. They finally stopped in the shade of some trees much too close to a part of the road filled with a lethal run of ruts and rocks.

It felt as though the curtain had dropped on the play before the last act. The air was charged with the same energy he felt racing through him.

He swung himself down from the driver's box and with a quick glance at the horses, which appeared winded but fine, gave his attention to Miss Castellano.

Kicking the door open, she jumped into his out-stretched arms. She wrapped her arms around his neck and he swung her in a circle before setting her down. David did not release her and Mia did not move away.

"What an adventure, my lord! Trapped in a runaway carriage. Rescued by a handsome man. It would make a wonderful scene for a theatrical vignette."

"You are amazing. I cannot imagine any other woman

reacting with enthusiasm to this debacle. Tears and swoons would be more like it."

She smiled at him, flattered if not thrilled by his praise.

William had found his match, David thought, a female who loved adventure. The viscount had been a fool not to give her what she needed and never let her go.

Chapter Eight

DAVID SAW THE MOMENT her jubilation disappeared, the moment she realized the closeness of their embrace or read his thoughts. No wonder Lord Arthur had given in to temptation. One kiss was a poor substitute for what he wanted from her. He wanted this excitement next to him in bed, her sense of adventure explored with her legs wrapped around him and him deep inside her, that look of wonder when she understood what a man and woman could truly share. A kiss was nothing by comparison.

Her expression changed from elation to intrigue, an expression so close to temptation that it sobered him immediately.

Damnation, he was her protector for the next twenty-four hours. Surely he could reach Sandleton and their chaperone without compromising both of them. He set her away from him. She raised a hand to her hair and continued on as if nothing had passed between them.

"What good fortune Janina insisted I take the umbrella. Why didn't John Coachman have one?"

"One can hardly drive a coach while holding an umbrella." He turned away. The horses were winded and in need of some water and rest, and he had to see to the others.

As if she read his mind, Miss Castellano's grin disappeared and she raised a hand to her mouth. "John Coachman! I hope he is not badly injured. I will go back while you tend to the horses." Without waiting for his agreement she ran off. The coachman and the grooms were out of sight but still she began to hurry back toward them.

By the time David turned the carriage and headed back down the road, she, too, had passed from sight. When he reached the group he saw a tableau he had not expected.

One of the grooms sat on a log, his head in his hands. The other groom had the coachman propped up against a tree, but now stood around like a girl with nothing to do but wring her hands.

Blood seeped from a wound on the coachman's forehead. Miss Castellano worked at staunching the flow with a white cloth he suspected she had ripped from her petticoat.

She glanced at the grooms. "What is the matter with you two? Don't just stand there. Bring me the water flask from the coach. Don't sit on that log. Go help Lord David!"

One of the grooms scrambled to obey as David observed her command of the situation. In his experience, when faced with an emergency women fell into two classes, those who wailed and worried and those who took direction well. He could not think of a time when a woman had taken charge.

He left his horse and the team in the shade and walked over to the gathering. Miss Castellano looked up at him and continued her ministrations as she spoke.

"John Coachman has come to his senses, my lord. But he is feverish and complains of headache and has been sick to his stomach." She added the last in a conspiratorial whisper. She stood up, faced him, and spoke quietly. "The same complaint that Janina made."

David nodded, aware of what she suggested. She wondered if some kind of pestilence had settled among them.

"Leave me alone!" the groom who sat on the log shouted to his partner. "My head spins like I drank five nights running."

The healthy groom stood up and stepped back from his compatriot, who leaned over the log he sat on and made a terrible retching sound.

"I think we have added one more to our list of sick and injured." God help them, illness had claimed a third member of their party. Concern replaced his earlier annoyance.

"We are close to Sandleton," Mia said, not taking her eyes from the groom, who kept on complaining about his stomachache, the heat, and his "bleedin' eyes."

"We have about five miles left to travel," Lord David said.

She nodded and continued to attend to the coach-man.

"Let me, Miss Castellano. You will ruin your dress."

"All the excuse I need to buy a new one." She brushed at the dirty fabric as she spoke. "I will check and see if the groom is feverish."

"Listen to me, Miss Castellano; go no closer to him."

She did as he asked despite the rudeness of his com-mand. "If it is some kind of disease then I have already been exposed to it."

"Climb up into the coach box. I will join you shortly."

She wanted to argue; he could tell by the way she opened her mouth and then pressed her lips together. He never would have guessed that Mia Castellano would be so well behaved in an emergency.

Once again she tried to brush the dirt and blood from her already ruined dress, and, with a curt nod, she went over to the coach. He would have had to be a eunuch not to enjoy watching her climb onto the top. She had the makings of a fine acrobat, if all else failed her in this world.

The grooms, both of them, helped the coachman into the traveling chaise. The sick one traveled inside with him, while the healthy one rode Cruces.

David climbed up beside Miss Castellano, taking up the reins. He could practically see her mind working as she conjured up one deadly illness after another. One that would scar her for life, one that would cripple her, one that left her an invalid.

He knew her thoughts because his mind was hell-bent on the same course. They needed a distraction, both of them. It did no good to create disaster before it befell them. "I thought I heard you say that you have jumped from a carriage before."

"What?" Her puzzlement lasted only a moment. "Oh yes, once, when William agreed to a race to Richmond with me as his passenger. The reins snapped and we both had to jump. I had watched the acrobats at Astley's Circus and had a fair idea of how to drop and roll. William twisted his ankle quite badly but I did no more than dirty my fingernails."

"That sounds like a singularly stupid thing to do. You were both very lucky." There, that should irritate her, though David did wonder exactly why she watched those female acrobats so carefully.

"Poor Janina," Mia began, ignoring his comment. "I wish I had been more kind. She really is ill."

They rode in silence until the village came into sight, then Miss Castellano found her voice again. "I will do whatever you want me to do, my lord."

This was exactly the kind of person he wanted as second in command on a ship, he thought. Calm, able to act when necessary, but willing to take orders from a superior. He found it rare and impressive in a man, much more so in a woman. The woman whose favorite word was *no* had disappeared.

"We will not drive up to the house. I will send the healthy groom for the surgeon and have him meet us at the gate to Sandleton. We will wait there so he can give us his medical insight regarding the coachman and the groom. After he has made his observations I will decide what to do."

"Then you think it may be something serious?" She did not wait for him to answer but gave her own suggestion in a whisper. "Smallpox."

He did not answer her.

Chapter Nine

DIO MIO, *SMALLPOX,* Mia thought. Panic flooded through her. She wanted to scream and run away as far and as fast as she could. Instead, she folded her hands together to still their shaking and prayed that when they found the surgeon, he would ease her worst fears. It did not have to be smallpox. It could be something else, anything else that would not scar her for life.

"Please tell me you have had Jenner's vaccination," Lord David said, undermining that small bit of hope.

"Well, during the war in Italy, but my father thought it might be no more than a ruse. The smallpox destroyed whole villages and everyone felt panic. It seemed a miracle that the process should be made available."

"It might have been a placebo."

"Placebo? That is an English word I do not know."

"A placebo is something that is used to soothe while not necessarily effective as medicine."

"Yes, yes, exactly. It could have been a placebo."

"Then there is the word *reconnaissance*."

"It sounds French, but I am not familiar with that word either." All of a sudden Lord David could not stop talking.

"Yes, reconnaissance is another word from my brother Gabriel. It came into use during the war. It means to survey an area before taking action."

"You mean the way one might examine the boxes at the theater before deciding whom to visit?"

"I suppose you could use it that way. What about the word—"

"Stop!" She put a hand on his arm. "I do not want an English lesson right now, and if you are trying to distract me it is not working." She would not apologize for her barely civil tone. Mia raised her hand to her lips. "If I could just scream at the top of my voice then I might stay sane for the next hour."

"Yes." Lord David nodded. "I understand."

They were the kindest words he had ever said to her and calmed her more than his annoying attempt to distract her.

They arrived at Sandleton and Lord David jumped down from the driver's box. He did not offer to help her down and Mia knew why. As much as she liked the feel of being in his arms, the look on his face the last time he'd touched her told her it was a dangerous business. They may have shared a certain physical awareness, but they were mismatched in every other way.

Before she could tread down the wayward path of wondering what it would be like to make love to a man she did not otherwise care for, she saw the groom approaching, accompanied by a very young man. Mia could hardly credit that one so young could be an experienced surgeon.

She would not panic. At least not out loud. It would do no good, would not keep her healthy.

The surgeon did not actually examine the groom or the coachman and maintained a healthy distance from Lord David. Despite that, they spoke so quietly she could not hear what they were saying to each other.

She wanted to hear every word they exchanged but she stayed in the driver's box, knowing that her presence would make them more circumspect, as if the truth would send her into hysterics.

Mia waited with as much patience as God had given her and distracted herself by studying what she could see of Sandleton from the gates. She made mental notes, intending to write to Janina that night. She would describe it to her, let her know that it would be the ideal place to recuperate when she was well enough to travel, and she would reassure her that it was no more than a half day's trip from the inn in Worcester.

Daylight remained strong, the air still as early evening settled around them. The house appeared rather small for a ducal estate, but the elegance of the architecture made up for the scale. The symmetry of the façade reminded

Mia of the Pennistan house in Richmond, which Janina had especially liked.

It was redbrick, with a windowed brick pediment at the crown of the top floor. There were four windows, three large and one small, on either side of the front door, which was reached by five shallow steps. Mia preferred a more dramatic entry but she knew Janina liked as few steps as possible since she carried the bundles.

The floor above the ground floor had windows that echoed the ones below, with two over the door that made for a pleasing line. The two chimneys on either end of the house framed it lovingly and rose to an impressive height above the roof.

Mia preferred the majesty of a grander estate. In a house this size, where did one find privacy? How could one practice on the pianoforte without disturbing the others in residence?

Mia counted the trees that lined the road leading to the house. Janina would want every detail of the garden so she could tell Romero about it. Her beau knew herbs and fruits, loved to work with anything that grew. According to Janina he knew every tree.

Mia could not name them but could count twenty trees, ten on each side of the drive, not in a line, but then neither was the road. It angled to the left so that you could not see the house as you approached the gate, but one did have a view from the verge to the left of the gate where the carriage stood now.

A breeze moved the shrubbery and the leaves on the

trees. The sky and the feel of the air promised rain. Not too soon, she hoped.

When she could stand it no longer, Mia prepared to jump down from the box. She might not be able to hear what the men discussed but she could easily guess the plan.

She would rescue Janina's bag and the sweets Romero had given to her and put them somewhere safe until Janina joined them. As Mia stood, gathering her skirts on one hand, she saw Lord David and the surgeon approach her. Lord David introduced the surgeon as Mr. Novins and suggested that she stay up in the driver's box.

"Can you tell me when your maid first felt ill, Miss Castellano?"

Mia explained that Janina did not travel well, but then last evening she had complained of feeling not only sick to her stomach, but also hot. And her body ached.

"I told the surgeon what the groom said," Lord David explained. "That his partner was suddenly stricken about twenty minutes before the coachman collapsed and fell."

The surgeon turned to Lord David. "I will send a messenger to the house and tell the Cantwells to vacate the premises. Then you, Miss Castellano, and the servants with you, will be quarantined there for seven days. By then we should know if this is a contagion and what kind it is." Mr. Novins gave Mia his attention. "There will be no greater chance of disease with the quarantine. You have already been exposed to whatever it is."

"Smallpox." Mia could not help the edge to her voice. "You fear we will contract smallpox."

"Possibly," he agreed with maddening calm. "But it could be that all three illnesses are unrelated."

"Mr. Novins, that would be entirely too much of a coincidence." She would not be treated like some stupid chit who did not want to know the truth. Mia hoped her tone made that clear.

"It would be a surprising coincidence, but not impossible. Or, miss, it is not necessarily smallpox. It could be some other disease."

"I think that more likely." If not any more reassuring.

Lord David nodded and turned to Mia. "We will not go to Pennford until we know." He folded his arms across his chest.

"Of course not." The thought that he considered her so selfish infuriated her. "I would never take a chance like that. Never. I will do as the surgeon says and count the days."

Lord David nodded but his expression conveyed his own dislike of the situation. He would be counting, too.

"And in the future, my lord, Mr. Novins, do not equivocate because you think I will become hysterical. Anger and hysteria are two different things, which you should know, Lord David, after seeing Janina. She is often hysterical."

"Very well, Miss Castellano. I will assume your English and your temperament are up to hearing the details." The surgeon bowed to her and she nodded back.

"Lord David?" Mia asked, hoping for equal assurance from him.

"Miss Castellano, your English is excellent. Your temper, if not your temperament, is legend."

She understood that he did not mean that as a compliment.

"The question remains," he added, "whether you are up to this challenge. We will know in a week whether you are inclined to hysteria or just temper tantrums."

A woman hurrying down the drive distracted them. Without comment Lord David abandoned her and went to meet the newcomer, who wore the dress of a housekeeper.

It was just as well they had been interrupted. Lord David's lack of faith hurt and she did not want him to see it.

"You have handled this crisis with equanimity, Miss Castellano," Mr. Novins called up from the ground.

"Thank you, Mr. Novins." How lovely that even in this dark moment, someone appreciated her. "It has been a difficult trip."

"I have every confidence that you will arrive at your destination safely, if later than you hoped." Mr. Novins took a step closer, which meant he had to crane his neck even more. "I will look forward to speaking with you when the quarantine ends."

She smiled with all the charm she could muster. "Thank you, Mr. Novins."

He blushed and managed a "You're welcome."

Mr. Novins counted as one of the sweet ones, Mia decided. He deserved better than someone who could turn him to her bidding so easily. Maybe he already had someone special in his life.

"Will Mrs. Novins worry about you or is she used to the unexpected?"

"There is no Mrs. Novins." His expression firmed. "Not anymore."

"Oh, I am so sorry to mention a painful subject. You are widowed." Mortified, she closed her eyes and wished she could disappear.

"No, no, I beg your pardon, Miss Castellano. An engagement. I had hoped to be engaged this summer."

She wondered if his young lady had shared the hope. Before Mia could decide how to find out details, the housekeeper reached the gate. She spoke from the other side of the wrought-iron rails. She listened to Lord David and when she answered him, she spoke in a raised voice so that Mia and the surgeon could hear easily.

"I will not leave the house, my lord. I have had the vaccination for smallpox and will stay to serve you and your guest, and care for the ones who are ill."

"Very good, Mrs. Cantwell, as long as you are aware that we do not yet know what disease this may be. There are any number for which there is no vaccination."

Typhus, plague, influenza. Mia listed them silently.

Mrs. Cantwell looked surprised. "It does not matter, my lord. I understand and will stay. I will never give up my post."

Lord David seemed to expect no less. "And Mr. Cantwell?"

"He will stay, but he has not had the vaccination."

The housekeeper's expression conveyed such disgust that she did not have to add the words "He knew it would hurt."

"Hmm" was Lord David's only response at first, but then he nodded firmly. "Mr. Cantwell will leave the house immediately and stay in the village. Tomorrow he will ride to Pennford with a message from me advising the duke of our delay."

"Lord David," Mia began.

He glanced at her. "I'll talk to you in a minute."

"Oh, really." Mia expected his dismissal, but she still felt mortally embarrassed. "Then I'll climb down and stand over there with the groom until you have time to give us instructions."

"Yes," he said, missing her sarcasm.

Dio mio, she thought. She was joking, but he had every intention of treating her like one of the servants!

Mia climbed down from the conveyance, on the side away from curious eyes. There were more important considerations at the moment, like their possible death. And whether the chaperone would be willing to stay.

Mr. Novins nodded to her but did not approach or offer his arm. She accepted the separation as necessary because of the threat of illness and addressed her greatest concern.

"Mr. Novins, do you not think that someone should return to the inn where we stayed last night to see if my maid improves and if anyone else has taken ill?" She spoke in a rush, afraid that he would interrupt before she made her point. "If it is some contagion, it started there or even at the first posting house." Mia thought of Miss Cole and her odious brother. She prayed they were well away from any infection.

"Yes, you are quite right. Someone should be sent. I will discuss it with Lord David."

"No, Mr. Novins, I will discuss it with Lord David."

The surgeon nodded so readily that Mia suspected he feared the dreaded hysterics from her. Or Lord David's reputation had preceded him.

"I can understand your upset, Miss Castellano, but I suspect that Lord David's concern for you is what makes him less than understanding."

"Thank you," she said with skepticism, turning away from him to go and wait with the other outcasts.

"In addition," he went on, seeming not to have noticed her simmering anger, "men like Lord David are too used to controlling their world to face mortality with equanimity."

"And the same cannot be said for women?" Mia stopped short, and faced him again with her challenge, her irritation now expanding to include all men.

"No, it cannot. Women face death in childbirth. They learn from their first confinement that death is only a breath away."

Mr. Novins's gloomy words reminded her of Elena. Mia wondered if her guardian worried as much as her husband did about the impending birth of their first child. Now there would be one more worry added.

"Here comes Lord David." Mr. Novins raised a hand, acknowledging him. As Mia watched him approach, Lord

David did not take his eyes off her. He looked aggravated, as though he did not approve of something she was doing, had done, or would do. Well, why disappoint him?

"I look forward to more such conversations with you, Mr. Novins. It's a joy to meet such a true gentleman."

"Miss Castellano. Mr. Novins." Lord David nodded to both of them. "I will send a letter advising the duke that the quarantine is only a precaution." He took a moment to look quite pointedly at Mr. Novins. "Novins, wait to be sent for. I do not want you to court illness unnecessarily even for company as tempting as Miss Castellano's."

Novins nodded, but did glance her way at least.

"One more thing, Novins. Mrs. Cantwell suggested that Mary Horner might be asked to come help with the sick."

"Absolutely not." Mr. Novins spoke with surprising force. He certainly thought it his duty to protect women.

"Mrs. Cantwell says she has been vaccinated."

"Yes, but once again, my lord, this is not necessarily smallpox. I will not risk a young woman's health for your convenience. Besides, Miss Horner is busy enough caring for her mother and her three siblings. She is needed at home."

"I will tell Mrs. Cantwell and we will manage, Mr. Novins." If the surgeon's adamant refusal embarrassed Lord David, he didn't show it.

"I could send one of the boys who help me," Mr. Novins added in a conciliatory tone. "They have been vaccinated and are well compensated for the risk to their health."

As if money matters when one is dead. Mia could never understand that logic, but Janina insisted that she would if she had ever been poor. Oh, Mia did miss her maid, and felt like the most selfish person in the world to have left her alone.

Right now it was too easy to imagine what it would be like to face death with no one who cared nearby. Her eyes filled. *No tears. No tears. No tears,* she reminded herself. Not before the worst happened and, please God, it would not.

"Thank you, Mr. Novins. When you come tomorrow I will let you know if more help is needed." With a nod of farewell, Lord David took Mia's arm as if she were a child and had not proved herself an adult.

"Into the carriage, Miss Castellano, and once in the house keep to your room for the rest of the day."

Mia pushed his hand off her arm. "I will walk to the house." She used the freezing tones his arrogance deserved. "Have someone bring my trunks and Janina's bag as soon as possible. I will write to Elena myself. And to Janina."

Without waiting for permission or direction, Mia walked toward the house. She could feel Lord David, the surgeon, everyone, staring at her, but she kept on, her head up, her back straight.

Janina would not die. She herself would not become ill. But there was no chance in the world that Lord David would turn into a charming gentleman, even if he faced death from some dread disease. *A week, seven days in a veritable prison with a bore like Lord David Pennistan her only company.* The prospect was daunting.

Mia had all the clothes she could possibly need but no maid to help her dress. She was to be a guest in a house with no one to entertain her. At least there was a house-keeper. Mia had no idea how to cook.

She had turned the corner on the curving drive so the others did not see when she stumbled. Mia regained her footing easily but when she pushed fear of illness to the back of her mind, the thought that upset her most grew to monstrous proportions.

The chaperone. What had happened to the woman who was to act as her chaperone?

Mia looked back toward the gate where the house-keeper was still in earnest conversation with Mr. Novins. Mia was certain the odds were very good that she would be spending the next week with a man she did not like without a lady to act as chaperone.

There was no chance, no chance in hell—she used the word quite firmly and on purpose—that, when this was over, anyone, up to and including the duke, would convince her that she must marry David Pennistan. She would tell Elena that in this first letter and hope to kill the idea before anyone gave it life. She would rather die first.

It struck her that if the disease was smallpox, then death was entirely possible.

Chapter Ten

THE CARRIAGE PASSED HER as she walked. Lord David drove the team and did not offer her a ride, never mind that she would have declined. She hoped he would hurt himself carrying her trunks upstairs.

"Oh dear, I hope Lord David doesn't hurt himself carrying everything upstairs."

The housekeeper had caught up with her and spoke in an even voice, as if almost running had not winded her at all.

"He will have the groom to help him." Mia heard the edge in her voice and when she spoke again tried for a more ladylike tone. "Do you think we will be able to convince the chaperone to stay through the quarantine?"

Mrs. Cantwell slowed her brisk pace. "I'm sorry, miss, but I could not find anyone willing to come, even for only one night."

"What did you say?" Mia stopped abruptly, her shock not at all theatrical. "No one would stay? Even if they were paid?"

"I apologize, Miss Castellano. I most sincerely do, but I was not surprised."

"But why would anyone refuse?"

Mrs. Cantwell started toward the house again before she answered. "Miss, do you know why the duke keeps this estate?"

"I assume it is part of the entail."

"As to that I do not know, but it came to the duke's grandfather to redeem a gambling debt. My grandmother kept house here then. My family has been here even longer than the Pennistans."

Mia heard both pride and condescension in Mrs. Cantwell's voice.

"The fact is that Sandleton has been used for their pleasure ever since. Their very personal pleasure."

Oh, this must be like the hunting boxes she had heard about, where men brought courtesans. Mia had always wanted to see one. "Let me assure you that this is anything but a clandestine meeting. The duke and duchess both know we are here." How odd that she, the lady, must reassure the housekeeper. "Lord David has some business with Mr. Cantwell, some business that would not wait. So we made this small detour and then it only made sense to stay the night."

Mia waited for the woman's nod of understanding before she went on.

"My maid became ill and stayed behind at the inn

where we were last night." Mia explained the whole mis-adventure in detail. This woman had suspected her of being a courtesan. Mia felt both shock and a little pleas-ure, but was determined to correct that misapprehension. She would make a decision about her future when she chose and not because of a servant's gossip.

Had Lord David come here with a cyprian? The pig. How could he not consider *her* reputation? He must have known what the villagers thought of the gatherings at San-dleton before planning to bring her here. She shook her head. Hardly. He was not the sort to elicit any sort of con-versation from the local gentry or even storekeepers. Meet them in the boxing ring, of course he would, but actually converse with them? Never.

She tried again. "Mrs. Cantwell, Lord David is a self-ish oaf and he finds me as irritating as I find him. I am sure it never occurred to him that there was anything inappro-priate about stopping here."

"That is rather frank of you, miss. But I do appreciate it." The housekeeper paused. "But then where is Lord David's valet? Has he taken ill as well?"

"Oh, no, Mrs. Cantwell. Since Lord David expected this trip would include only two nights he sent his valet ahead to Pennford. I am sure he will regret that now." She tried not to smile.

"I see." Mrs. Cantwell stared off, looking toward the house, as if trying to decide whether to believe what Mia knew was the absolute truth. Finally the housekeeper nodded to herself. "The new duchess is your guardian, Miss Castellano?"

"I am almost twenty-one but, yes, she has been my guardian since her first husband died. He was my guardian after my father died."

"How upsetting for you to lose so many loved ones. But you are so lucky to be able to call England home now."

Mrs. Cantwell sounded as if she thought that Mia had landed in paradise when she set foot on English soil.

"The Pennistans have always been generous employers. Lord David himself never fails to write when he is coming to see Mr. Cantwell."

Mia could hear the change in her attitude. Not fawning, not at all, but eager to undo any damage her initial supposition might have caused.

"Miss, I will do my best to see to your needs this week."

"Oh, Mrs. Cantwell, I know that we will all be doing things that we are not accustomed to and I assure you that I am very capable of caring for myself when it is necessary."

"Thank you, again, miss." Mrs. Cantwell glanced at Mia. "If you can unpack your own things that would be a great help."

"Of course. You have more pressing responsibilities. There is one thing though. I am not at all skilled at cooking."

"And why should you be?"

She gave Mrs. Cantwell a smile of such gratitude that the woman patted her arm and murmured, "There, there."

She and Mrs. Cantwell made their way through the empty house. No servants gathered to greet her, no maids bustled up the stairs with hot water for the travel-weary. Mrs. Cantwell did not offer tea and biscuits but hurried Mia up the stairs to the first floor.

The stairway was elegant, rising from the middle of the entry hall and then splitting to the left and right and ending at a set of double doors on both sides. To the right the doors were closed. To the left the doors were open to show a wide passage with a series of paneled doors on each side.

Mrs. Cantwell gestured to the right as they turned left. "That wing is for the family only. For the duke or whichever of his brothers is hosting the party, and also for their personal guests."

Mia noticed the housekeeper did not say wife. This was most definitely not a family retreat like the Richmond house. "Do the men of the family come often?" Mia asked, too curious to care that she sounded like she was a visitor on a tour of the house.

"The duke has not been here since he married his first duchess."

But what about Lord David? Mia did not ask, would not ask. If she had to know, she would ask the man himself.

Mrs. Cantwell escorted her down the passage to a room as far as possible from the bedchamber Lord David would use. "Your room, miss."

Despite her disappointment over the size of the house, Mia thought her bedchamber lovely. "The gentle pink and pale blue is so feminine. They're colors that make a woman feel pretty."

"Thank you, miss. It's what makes having a lady here a pleasure. You appreciate all that it takes to make a house a home."

"Indeed, I do, and I realize that you have other people to attend to. I can settle myself and even help with the patients if need be."

"Oh, no, Miss Castellano, that would not be at all proper. The other groom will help me. There is a nice library. I am sure you will find entertainment there."

"Is there a pianoforte?"

"Usually, but it sustained some damage during a house party last year. Lord David had it sent out for repair."

"It's been in repair for over a year?" Mia could not hide her dismay. And then wondered if Lord David had hosted the party.

"Lord David is not musical. I think it has not been a concern."

Not musical. Well, that was hardly a surprise. It was one more thing they did *not* have in common.

"I shall manage with the library then, Mrs. Cantwell." But it will be very dull, she thought, and was so very disappointed to have no music to distract her.

Mrs. Cantwell curtsied, explaining, as she moved to the door, that the sick needed her attention.

Left alone, Mia set about making the room her own. It had its small size against it, but very charming was in its favor. Tucked into a corner, the room had three windows and a fireplace, plus a small writing desk. The connecting dressing room had the same dimensions as the bedroom, a grand space for one's clothes with a small daybed for the maid. Her trunks were already in place.

She moved the ornaments around, taking the elegant statue of a woman in pink tulle from the writing desk and placing it on the mantel as a balance to the longcase clock that ticked with quiet comfort. She moved the inkstand to the left of the desk as she preferred it, and dismissed the ugly potpourri bowl onto a shelf in the clothespress.

Opening the trunks, Mia rooted through her frocks until she found the three that she could manage without help, hanging them on the wall hook shaped like a butterfly. She could iron out the creases if necessary but hoped that the wrinkles would hang out. All the while, she considered the next seven days. How exactly would she entertain herself without a pianoforte? Who had ever heard of a boring adventure?

Chapter Eleven

MIA WENT BACK into the bedroom and stood at the window, looking out over the back of the property. A great expanse of well-kept lawn rolled up and down in a gentle slope to a small river or large stream. It looked ideal for trout, and if one could fish it would be a fine distraction. In any case, the prospect alone entertained her. The grounds were much more extensive than the small house deserved.

Mia turned her back on the window and hurried to the desk, remembering that Lord David had told her to write her letter "with dispatch." No doubt he would send Mr. Cantwell off at first light, so her letters had best be written tonight.

Besides, ignoring responsibilities had never been one of her failings, unless it was something she didn't want to do.

The writing desk had paper, quills, and fresh ink and she sat staring at the paper debating what to say. If she died she would want Elena to be sure that her money was used wisely. To support Janina first and foremost. Would Nina want to continue as a maid, or would she prefer a life better suited to her family, if not her birth? She and Romero could start their own business. Mia's capital could give them the independence that she herself had so craved.

It would take Nina years to recover from Mia's death—if she survived this illness herself. If they both died their branch of the Castellano family would end. How discomfiting to think that in a few years no one would remember that they had ever existed.

Mia felt a tear drop on her hand. *No tears, you stupid woman. Stop the maudlin thoughts.*

Mia dashed off a short letter to Elena. *We are safe and I am adequately chaperoned.* Elena would suspect it an outright lie, but she could use it as proof that her ward's reputation remained intact until Mia could decide how to handle the situation.

With assurances that this quarantine meant nothing serious, another lie which Elena would probably see through, Mia signed the letter with her love and sealed it.

She spent longer on her letter to Janina, suggesting that, once she had fully recovered, her maid send notice to Romero in case he should want to come and escort his beloved the rest of the way to Pennford.

Mia debated telling Janina about their quarantine. She decided not. If something deadly had been unleashed, they would know of it at the posting house by now. The Belforts could have taken it home. It could be spreading through most of England.

The panicky feeling came back and Mia folded her hands and prayed for calm, for good health for all, and that she would come through this test with fortitude and good will.

Prayer made her feel better, even though she had long ago given up the Roman Church for the Church of England. It could be that God still listened no matter how the prayers came to him.

Mia almost ran to the stairs but then slowed as she descended, hoping Lord David noticed that she had not tried to ring for a servant.

The entry hall was empty and the door stood open. Mr. Novins waited outside some little way down the front steps, talking with Mr. Cantwell, a man who looked as capable as his wife. Finally Mr. Cantwell made his way down the road to the front gate, leaving Mr. Novins looking quite lonely.

Flirtations began in less intimate settings, but right now Mia wanted to know more about the woman Mr. Novins wished to marry. Mary Horner. Why else would he be so adamant in his refusal to allow Mrs. Cantwell to ask for her help?

If the man had already given his heart and the woman deserved the honor, Mia would do all in her power to bring them together, not pull them apart. She might be considered the worst kind of flirt, but she had never, would never, set her sights on a man whose heart was truly engaged.

She caught his attention and asked him to take her letters as he had Lord David's. The surgeon assured her that he would pass her letter to Janina to the postmaster and her letter to the duchess on to Mr. Cantwell, "who will be on his way first thing in the morning." Mr. Novins went on. "I hope your fears do not overcome you, Miss Castellano."

Concern filled his voice—a concern Mia would have welcomed, if she had been ill.

"Mr. Novins, the only fear I have is that I will be bored into a decline."

"How brave of you, dear lady."

"No, sir, there is no bravery involved on my part. One does what one must. Like Miss Horner, taking care of her mother and her siblings. Now there is a brave woman."

"Yes," he said and, after a dispirited sigh, went on. "Though I would say Miss Horner is noble rather than brave."

"Noble is an even greater virtue."

"Do you think so? I think nobility and an inclination to act the martyr are too closely aligned. There is no denying bravery."

Mia could argue that. But she did not want a philosophical debate. She wanted to know more about his feelings for Miss Horner. Dear God, men spent too much time on nonsense and not nearly enough on the important issues. This called for a more direct approach. "Miss Horner is a friend of yours." She did not make it a question.

"A friend?" When he took time to think about that, Mia did not need his answer.

"Oh, I see, dear sir. She is more than a friend."

He looked around as if someone else might be listening. Mia laughed.

"Mr. Novins, here is one advantage of a quarantine, which is a phrase I never thought I would use. Mrs. Cantwell is with the sick and Lord David is writing to the duke. There is no one else here, no servants, no other guests, not even any pets. We are completely private." Maybe she should not have said it. Mia rushed on before he had a chance to think about that. "Please, tell me about Miss Horner."

For a moment Mia feared she appeared too forward to the very proper Mr. Novins, but after a long pause he nodded, started to move closer to her and then stopped himself.

"Mary—" Mr. Novins reddened. "I mean, Miss Horner does the flowers for Mrs. Cantwell. She helps with the housekeeping whenever Mrs. Cantwell's aches send her to bed. Miss Horner is one of the most generous women I know. Sometimes too generous."

"Too generous?"

"Yes." Now he did take just one step closer to her. "I think that generosity to self is as important as generosity to others."

Dio mio, *he has started another philosophical discourse.* She bit her lip to keep from snapping at him and then considered what he said. "Is there a point where one can give too much?"

Mr. Novins stopped and redirected his thoughts. "If it keeps you from your own wants and needs, then it is more than one should give."

"No," she answered promptly. She had been through this herself. "Not if you are happy. When I nursed my father I had to give up my music lessons, but I wanted nothing more than to be with him for as long as he was alive, for every minute. In an odd way it remains one of the happiest times of my life."

Mr. Novins looked down. Even though she could not see his expression she knew defeat when she saw it.

"The question I would ask you, sir, is if Miss Horner is happy."

"I do not know."

"Then ask her."

He looked shocked at the suggestion.

"Yes, it really is that easy. You risk looking foolish, but if she is not worth that risk then your heart is not truly involved."

He stared at the pot of flowers near the door a little longer, but looked up the moment the hall clock began to chime the hour. "Do you think Lord David will be much longer? It's growing late and I have to make a call on one of my patients."

Oh, Mia wanted to hit him over the head with a book. Just when the conversation moved to an issue dealing with pride the man decided, like all others, that he did not want to discuss it further.

"Miss Castellano." Mr. Novins cleared his throat. "Can we discuss this further? Perhaps I could take a few moments to visit with you when I come to see the patients."

"That would not be wise, Novins," Lord David interrupted without giving a thought to the rudeness of eavesdropping.

Mr. Novins straightened, smoothing his hair with his free hand. "You would prefer I not call? I beg your pardon, my lord, do you disapprove of me?"

Bravo, Mia cheered silently. The surgeon had a backbone.

"You mistake me, Novins. Your help today has proved invaluable. I will put my letters with Miss Castellano's. Pass them on to Mr. Cantwell. I will expect you tomorrow, as early as is convenient."

Novins looked momentarily confused, then bowed to Lord David and took his leave without so much as looking at her again.

"The way you address a question without actually answering it is near brilliant, Lord David."

"Miss Castellano, do not provoke me."

He did not turn to face her, so she circled to see his expression. The grim turn to his mouth made her want to shake him. Arguing would not make this quarantine any more tolerable.

"I am not happy about this enforced exile either, my lord, but we must simply make the best of it."

"That is easy enough to say when you will only miss some shopping and gossip over the tea tray. I have business in Manchester, appointments that I will miss. This is time that I cannot afford if I have any hope of success."

"I am sure the duke will understand." Mia stepped closer to him, close enough that she could see a muscle working in his jaw, as though he ground his teeth trying to control his temper. "The duke, he is your brother after all."

"Yes, yes, he is." Lord David rubbed his chin with his hand. "It's Mr. Sebold who will take any delay as offense and may well rethink his commitment. And I cannot, will not, face Meryon with another failure."

"Oh, yes, I see." This fear she understood completely. "How odd that failure haunts both of us, for I dread the prospect of facing Elena with the further ruin of my reputation."

Lord David did not have an answer for that but she could see by his expression that until now he not considered her worries at all.

"Did it never occur to you that because this quarantine leaves us together without a chaperone, some might suggest it calls for us to marry?" Mia bit her lip. That sounded much too tentative. Stepping back from him, she tried for a more authoritative tone. "I want to make it perfectly clear to you, sir. I will never, under any circumstances, marry you."

Lord David might have been only half listening before, distracted by his own worries, but now she had his complete attention. After searching her face, he shook his head as he answered. "Miss Castellano, I cannot believe you are serious. We will not be compelled to marry because of a quarantine. Stop manufacturing difficulties. We have enough as it is."

"That may be true but the Fates do not always play by

fair rules." She wanted him to swear that he would not be coerced into an alliance that would be a disaster.

"Marriage," he said again, as if it were the most preposterous idea he had heard this year. "No one would expect it of me." .

Mia should have been relieved but was not. Her temper edged up a notch. "What do you mean, no one would expect it? Are you implying that I am not lady enough to be compromised?"

"I am not." The words were filled with such exasperation that she wanted to kick him. "I mean that no one expects me to marry *anyone,* much less a beautiful woman so much younger than I am. I assure you that you will never hear a proposal from me."

Beautiful? He thought her beautiful. Mia smiled, despite her ill humor. "You are saying that just to make me happy."

"Miss Castellano, I have more to worry about right now than how to make you happy."

"Which shows how mistaken you can be, Lord David. We will be living in very close quarters for the next week. Not as close as when you were aboard ship, supposedly on your way to shipwreck in Mexico, but we will be living closer than most married people do.

"Most husbands spend the day at their clubs, and if they do attend the same parties as their wives everyone knows how gauche it is to be seen with your spouse."

He pursed his lips. She reached over and tapped his cheek lightly with one of her hands. "Indeed, sir, keeping me happy is very much in your interest." Mia twirled around, making sure that her skirt brushed up against his leg, and swept through the nearest door. Oh, she loved that sort of exit and so rarely had a chance to use it anymore.

Let him think that she was annoyed. It was better than admitting that touching him, that the barest tap on his cheek, had sent such a surge of awareness through her that running away seemed the wisest option.

Chapter Twelve

THE DOOR SHE PASSED THROUGH, quite mind-lessly, led to the kitchen. With a quick study of the foreign space she found fruit, cheese, and bread and made herself a simple supper that she took up the back stairs to her room.

Settling at the small table near the window, she enjoyed the view while she ate, until she saw Lord David walking slowly across the lawn toward the copse of trees where the stream ran.

If he had not considered her worries, she was honest enough to admit, at least with herself, that she had not given a thought to his, either. He was the brother of a duke. He had the choice to pursue nothing but his boxing and other trivial activities so favored by men, but he had apparently chosen to do something more with his time.

If music, and the much-missed pianoforte, had made

her days more meaningful, what had Lord David found that was worth the risk of failure?

Lord David was out of sight and Mia stared at the trees swaying in the evening breeze. Fatigue made her bones ache, but no one went to bed before the sun had fully set.

Mia counted all the evenings she had longed for the solitude of the country, when the noise of the city kept her awake. Now the extreme quiet of this almost empty house would have the same effect as the noise of the city. She would never be able to sleep, or would awaken in the middle of the night.

Lord David came back in sight, smoking one of his awful cigarillos. As he walked toward the house, he looked neither left nor right, but at the ground before him, obviously lost in thought. Even from a distance he looked strong and rugged, more like a land steward considering plantings than a gentleman.

She had never met anyone like him. He must have slept through the part of his education that included the right way to treat a lady, to show that you were interested in her appearance, what she thought, whether she needed a shawl or a fan.

It should annoy her that he did not seem at all interested in those things. Instead she found it intriguing.

Which was ridiculous, and a sure sign of boredom. She would dispel Lord David, his appeal, and his worries from her mind. She had to find something to do that would make her forget all about him for a few hours at least.

Despite Mrs. Cantwell's insistence that she could not help with the patients, Mia found her way to the servants' quarters in the attic. There were two rooms only, set up as dormitories, one for each sex. They were unoccupied except for the coachman and the sick groom. Despite the large well-aired space Mia could feel sickness in the air, an atmosphere of aching pain overlaid with both fear and determination in both patients and nurses.

Mrs. Cantwell demonstrated to the one healthy groom how to care for the two sick men. He watched her with a reassuring intensity. "Use damp cloths to wipe the fever from their faces and hands. It eases their discomfort. And you must keep them covered even when they complain. . . ." Her voice trailed off when she realized she no longer had the groom's attention.

When Mrs. Cantwell saw who had come to visit the sick, she stood abruptly and tried to shield the two patients from Mia's view.

"Mrs. Cantwell, I know you think this is wrong, but please. I have been caring for the sick since I was twelve when I nursed my father through his last months. There is nothing I do not know about caring for the sick. I could help. Truly." How strange to have to plead to do such work. Why did no one want to see her as anything more than an ornament?

"Absolutely not in my house, miss. We will manage quite well for the few days this will last."

But what if it is more than a few days? Mia did not voice her fear but knew that if any of the rest of them took ill, the rules of a civil house would no longer apply. For now she felt she had no choice and left, disappointed that the woman could not be convinced.

With an apology for intruding in the sickroom, an apology Mrs. Cantwell accepted as brusquely as Mia offered it, she went back to her bedchamber, gathered up her plate and utensils, and headed for the kitchen to wash them.

This time it occurred to her how unique it was to place the kitchen on the main floor, in a wing attached to the back of the house. Who had come up with this idea? Indeed, it would be so much easier to move food to the dining room. No stairs to travel, no dumbwaiter to deal with.

Besides the sink and washing cloth, she knew nothing about kitchens and no magic descended endowing her with knowledge of how to cook anything, even something as simple as baked eggs or chicken broth.

She washed, dried, and shelved the dishes with the rest of the ironstone the servants used and was taking a casual inventory of the pantry, out of nothing more than curiosity, when Lord David came in from the outside, still smoking his cigarillo.

"Miss Castellano!" His pleasure at seeing her was as shocking as it was sincere. "I was just thinking about you."

"You were?" She smiled and thought that a little flirtation might be fun.

"Yes, you surely know more about the kitchen than I do."

"Only enough to know that having one on the main floor is not usual."

"It seemed practical when the old oven caught fire and smoke ruined the old kitchen below-stairs. The house is not used that often and the Cantwells are aging. Putting the kitchen where it would be more convenient for them made sense."

"More convenient for the servants?" How could he complain about the way she treated Janina when he had moved the kitchen to accommodate a butler and house-keeper?

He ignored her. "You must know how to cook. That would help Mrs. Cantwell immensely."

"You can insist all you want, my lord, but the answer is no, I do not know how to cook."

His smile disappeared along with all traces of his short-lived good humor. "Miss Castellano, you use the word *no* the way others use please and thank you. Mrs. Cantwell cannot do everything for the next seven days."

"Nor do I expect her to. I offered to tend the sick, but Mrs. Cantwell will not hear of it."

"I'm not surprised you have more experience comforting men than cooking." His sarcasm wounded her, but before she could explain her father's last months, he went on. "My sister, Olivia, is skilled at all manner—"

"Lady Olivia is an amazing woman with unique skills." Which was a very nice way of saying that dear Lady Olivia's love of cooking was not typical of a gentleman's daughter. "I know enough about food to choose or approve a menu, but this 'knowing enough' does not include cooking a chicken or," she shuddered, "killing one."

Lord David paced the kitchen once, moving from the fireplace to the larder and back.

"There must be other ways I can help."

"I doubt I will need anyone to advise me on the latest fashion."

His tone of derision was the last straw.

"You were delighted at seeing me when you thought I could cook a meal but now that I can't you are an ogre once again." If he was not going to make even the slightest effort to be good company then she would not, either. "Look at me," she demanded and was surprised when he obeyed her. "I hate that foul-smelling tobacco. Take it outside and leave it there, or better yet, stay with it."

He took a deliberate puff and blew the smoke out in a circle.

She grabbed the cigarillo from his hand and dropped it in the sink, still half filled with water, and went to the door where she turned to face him with her arms folded across her chest.

Instead of trying to retrieve the cigarillo, Lord David caught her at the shoulders and held her with more pressure than was necessary.

She refused to let her smile of triumph fade but it felt more forced, and she hoped he did not see that she was just a little afraid of—and excited by—his temper.

He pushed her back against the door and stepped so close that she could feel the heat from his body. "Do not aggravate me, Miss Castellano. I am not a man to be toyed with."

Mia wanted to laugh with the pleasure of it. To have him so close, to feel his power rush through her thrilled her even more than doing riding tricks on a horse.

He dropped his hands from her shoulders. She wanted to rub the spot where she might well have bruises tomorrow, but decided she would rather not betray weakness.

"Very well, my lord." She swooped away from him, down and under where his arm blocked her, while she thought of the best way to couch her challenge. "I will leave you alone until you wish for my company." *Until you beg for it,* she added to herself. He did not answer, but Mia could feel his eyes on her as she left the room.

Dio mio, not a moment ago she had rejected him completely. Even now she knew she could barely tolerate Lord David's rude behavior. But suddenly she wanted very much to seduce him into a kiss to see if she enjoyed it as much as she had the feel of him.

It would answer a question, one that she had never been able to ask of anyone, since she numbered no courtesans among her acquaintances here in England. Was it possible to make love to a man you did not like very much at all?

She shivered at the thought. The idea fascinated her now that the imaginary man had a name.

Mia dashed up the stairs, turned to the left at the top, and continued down the hall to her bedchamber. Once again she was drawn to the window and stared out at the landscape and the darkening sky.

The sun dipped toward the western horizon, no longer casting shadows. Mia watched it fall from view and listened to the sounds that welcomed the night. Crickets and frogs sang to their own tune. Could she write a piece for the pianoforte that would imitate their sound, or create a tune that would remind the listener of a warm summer night surrounded by nature?

Better to dwell on that than on what a downward spiral her life had become from the night that William and Lord David had interrupted her with Lord Arthur. She could date it from that moment. After weeks of uncertainty and finally a demand she come to Pennford, she now faced one of several unwelcome futures. The possibility of illness, the possibility of disfigurement following the illness, and the probability that all of this would be followed by a confrontation with Elena that was bound to make the months until her majority miserable for all.

Only then would this bad patch end. On her twenty-first birthday she would have all in place to set out on her own. That is what she should think about; not everyone must dwell on the possibility of failure like Lord David.

She would start with where to live. Not London. There were too many bad memories and unfriendly faces there.

Abroad would be best. If the life of a single woman of independent means was too limiting and she did become a courtesan, then living abroad would be much less embarrassing for Elena. Her eyes filled, as she was overwhelmed with regret for the way life had pulled them apart.

Denying the upset, she tried to think of a city she would enjoy. Someplace where she spoke the language with a charming accent, where they appreciated music, and where she could afford the cost of establishing herself.

Vienna. The city was growing, recovering from the wars and becoming as international as Paris and Rome. Yes, Vienna should be at the top of the list. She turned her head away from the window and ignored the tears that trickled down her cheeks.

Leaving England should not feel so hard.

With the deep, deep sigh that was as much a relief as tears, she considered living in England. If she wanted to stay, she could choose a place other than London.

Mia lay down on her bed and stared out the window as she considered where. Brighton. The Regent's Pavilion at Brighton attracted all sorts of people, from royal to roué, and would never appeal to the staid Duke of Meryon or his wife. But the Prince Regent was aging with neither wisdom nor grace. His circle of friends did not seem to appreciate music or anything but drink and revelry, something she enjoyed as much as the next person, but in moderation. The Regent himself was proof that nothing ruined one's looks or health faster than excess.

Mia mulled over several other possibilities, but really she had not seen all that much of England north of London. There was plenty of time to decide. It would be more than a year before she reached her majority. She did not have to make a decision tonight about anything more than what time to retire.

Jumping up from her bed, Mia changed the angle of the clock so she could see the time in the morning.

Lighting a candle, she searched through her bag and found a book that Elena had given her when they first came to London.

She lost herself in the adventures of a girl off to Bath, away from home for the first time. Mia considered the similarity of their stories. The likeness ended when the heroine, whom Mia judged as none too bright, met two young men and found it a challenge to make her preference known, constantly falling under the influence of her brother and her best friend, who had fallen in love with each other.

True, she and Catherine both enjoyed adventure. Mia put her head against the high back of the chair and smiled.

Would Bath suit her? What better spot than a place people visited for relaxation and fun? And Elena disliked Bath.

They had visited once and her guardian had insisted they leave within the week. Mia had loved it, had found herself the center of attention whenever someone came to call. It had been before her come-out and was the scene of her first nasty argument with Elena over Mia's flirtatious behavior.

Her visit last spring with Mrs. Giddings and her daughters had been disappointing in some ways, but it did prove she had a talent for charming old men. And Bath was full of older, wealthy gentlemen.

When she turned twenty-one Mia would not have to answer to anyone. Not Mrs. Giddings or Elena. She could flirt outrageously, and there would be a constant stream of visitors so that there would be no danger of forming attachments and, if she wished, many, many opportunities for seduction.

Closing her eyes, Mia pictured a house on the Crescent where her salon would be the one everyone visited, as popular with artists as it was with society. A place where gentlemen could mix with men they would never usually meet. It would be easy to find a lover in such a group. Or not. As she wished. And she would send them away when she grew bored.

Yes, Bath might be the perfect spot, she decided, and dozed off with that thought.

Some sound awoke her. She sat still, trying to determine the source of the noise. It wasn't noise, but the lack of it. The clock had stopped its soothing tick, tick, tick.

Mia jumped up and found the key, winding the mechanism carefully, and then realized that she must find a clock still running to know the correct time. In the next moment it occurred to her that she could wind all the clocks. She could perform that helpful task quite easily without any training at all.

Chapter Thirteen

DAVID CAME IN the kitchen door, tossing the tiny end of the cigarillo into the banked fire. It flared for a moment, and then the room fell into darkness again. Locking the door, he prepared to make the rounds to be sure the house was secured. A silly precaution in a house under quarantine, with a sign on the gates announcing it, but Mrs. Cantwell had asked him to see to it and he would.

As he came down the passage from the back of the house, he heard a low singing as someone, some woman, a woman who could only be Mia Castellano, passed by the passage and went into the main salon. He recognized the tune, "Greensleeves," but the words were not familiar. He moved closer for a better look at what mischief she had found.

"Midnight, the witching hour," she sang in an almost charming alto whisper, "when all our dreams are bad ones.

Midnight, the wishing hour, when all our dreams are glad ones. Dreams, dreams that blend our world with all we wish and all we fear. Dreams, dreams that blend our world with what we want and all held dear."

She stopped singing but kept on humming as she found the key for the tall clock and carefully wound it. She had to stretch to reach the keyhole, her lithe body lit in silhouette by the moonlight from the window nearby.

David did not need to be reminded that dreams could be an insane blend of reality and illusion. Without closing his eyes he knew that. He could still feel the warmth of her shoulders under his hands. He could still feel the longing to pull her to him and show her just how much he wanted her. He stepped back behind the door as she left the salon and passed him to go into the small salon, singing her song again.

"Oh, take me back to days gone by when love was new and hearts did plead. Take me back to nights so sweet when dreams of love were filled with need."

Need. No one so young could understand true need or she would never have used a word so mundane, even if it rhymed. David could hear the turning sound as she wound the clock in there and wondered what possessed her to do this chore at midnight.

He stole into the room she had just left. He could still hear her singing and would know when she had gone to bed.

Seven days of this. Of running into her four or six times a day. As they had proved in the last twelve hours, it was impossible to avoid each other in a house this size.

This was Eros's idea of hell. To put a man in close confines with temptation in the shape of a girl. One who had no idea what she risked when she did something as simple as let her skirt brush against him.

Add to that the irony that he was her only chaperone, and the one person she needed protection from was him.

He did not want to imagine how Elena and Lyn would react if he could not control himself. No doubt his dreams would be filled with possibilities, up to and including a duel with swords where the duke unmanned him with one well-placed thrust.

Mia came out of the small salon and made her way up the stairs. "Dreams, dreams that curse our souls and wound our hearts. Dreams, dreams that make our lives more worthy of our living."

He listened for a while and heard the tune fade as she went into her room. David checked the latch on the front door, the windows in the hall and the two salons, and, sure that enough time had passed, made his own way upstairs. He had his hand on the latch to his room when Mia opened the door from the other side. She jumped back, startled, and then laughed. "You frightened me half to death," she said, stating the obvious.

"I trust you have a very good reason to be visiting the family suite."

"The double door was wide open and I knew that meant you were not abed yet," she explained without guile. "I wound your clock."

He stared at her. She never said exactly what she meant. He had never caught her in a lie, but he knew that she bent the truth to suit her whims. When they talked, he spent half his time trying to decipher the truth and her version of the truth. She was bold, but at the moment looked as insecure as a new midshipman.

She had been winding clocks downstairs. But no matter what the truth, David knew in that moment Mia Castellano was a test he would fail.

He stared at her. Just stared until he spoke his thought without censor. "I can see there is no chance on this sweet earth that you will leave me alone, allow me any peace at all. I am bound for hell. You are like a curse I cannot undo."

If she had stood there one minute more he would have taken her to his bed whether she wanted it or not. But Mia Castellano must have heard the ultimatum implicit in his tone, if not his words, for she curtsied, swooped under his arm as she had at least two times before, and ran down the passage, pausing at the doorway to whisper, "Good night, Lord David."

David went into his room, closed the door, and leaned against it. He felt more than need. This was hunger, aching, longing, craving, and still something that went beyond those words to a desire that blinded one to honor and responsibility. That drove a man to demand what he needed regardless of the consequences.

The first time he had seen Mia Castellano, at his brother's engagement ball, he had no idea who she was. He had thought her looks exotic, and when she had waltzed past him, the sound of her laughter had stayed in his head all night.

She had caught him watching her and given him a smile that held all the allure of a courtesan.

Surely she was no more than an adventurous girl, he had thought. His brother would never invite anyone but the best of families to his engagement ball.

He'd watched her flirt her way through the ballroom leaving a trail of charmed fools. Not every eye was on her but no one would forget her; she was like a bee wrapped in butterfly camouflage.

When they were finally introduced and he realized she was engaged, to Bendasbrook no less, he had been all but rude to her and ignored her at every meeting since. He did not need the temptation or the trouble it would cause.

Avoiding her now, however, would be a challenge.

David needed those dreams of Lyn's vengeance. In vivid detail. He knew he needed something, anything, to quell his libidinous thoughts or he would do something that would define failure in an entirely new way.

CLOSING HER DOOR, Mia turned the lock and leaned against it, patting her chest to calm her racing heart. *Dio mio, I have been like a child in five different ways.*

She went into the dressing room and did no more than toe off her shoes before she sank onto the bench. Covering her face with her hands, Mia tried to decipher what had frightened her so much.

He was like a banked fire. And she behaved like a child who had spent the day adding little bits of kindling, trying to coax the fire to life when it had been simmering underneath and more than ready to flare into flame that would consume anyone fool enough to stand too close.

What she had seen in his eyes so shocked her that she had not even heard what he said.

Disgust and hatred aimed at her, directly at her.

Mia could not pretend that she did not know why, that she had not pressed him, teased him, and played the coquette at a time when he faced a disaster of monumental proportions. Lord David was the one in charge, and no more able to control the situation than she was.

Lowering her hands so that they now only covered her mouth, she stared at the pink and blue patterned carpet. She felt sick, not from some hideous disease but at the thought that he could hate her.

No. She stood and began to undress. He had only needed someone to vent his anger on and she had been standing there. She understood that. She threw things when faced with too much to bear. The hate in his eyes was aimed at the Fates that had put them in this horrible situation.

Leaving him alone would be the best way to make amends. She put her dress on the hook along with her stays and chemise and wriggled into her nightdress, a cool light cotton that was one of her greatest extravagances.

She would spend all day tomorrow reading about the stupid girl at Northanger Abbey. Catherine Morland would be the perfect companion for the stupid girl at Sandleton.

Chapter Fourteen

ON THEIR SECOND MORNING at Sandleton, Lord David Pennistan woke with a headache and swore. He never had headaches. He considered them the province of women, but he could not deny the dull pulse of pain at the back of his head, just above his spine.

He'd seen the surgeon again yesterday and never thought to ask what kind of pain to expect with the illness or where it would start. If he had asked he would have a better idea if this was a very bad sign or merely the result of a poor night's sleep.

Damn him twelve times twelve for not making the effort to dose himself with Jenner's vaccine. David pushed himself out of bed, relieved that a headache was his only symptom. The newly risen sun helped him decide that a walk may be all the treatment his headache needed.

Like the morning before, he found hot coffee with

bread, chicken, and cold eggs on the table in the dining room. Miss Castellano still slept, no doubt. It would be fine with him if she kept to her room for a week.

He had not seen her at all the day before and by evening had wondered if she had run away. Patently impossible, but how else to explain why someone so ubiquitous one day became invisible twenty-four hours later?

Finally, just before dark last night he heard her making the rounds and winding clocks, singing new words to "Barbara Allen." Not only did she avoid his room but she had not come into the family suite, leaving all the clocks there unwound.

Whether deliberate or not, her absence had made it easier for him to come to his senses. They were a man and a woman in close company, unusually close company. Add to that her inclination to tease any man close enough to see her face.

He knew that from their first meeting, and only had it confirmed in the harshest of ways, when he and William had found her with Lord Arthur.

He needed only time and distance to talk himself round, to remind himself that he was a gentleman and she a woman without scruples eager to test her wiles on the only man available.

After a hasty breakfast, David hurried up the steep attic stairs on the first of his thrice-daily visits to the sickroom. Basil, the healthy groom whose name David finally thought to ask, sat with John Coachman and Ralph, the other groom. The coachman looked feverish and seriously ill.

"Ralph's awake, my lord, but he says keeping his eyes closed makes it less likely that he will be sick again."

"It's good news that he is on the mend." Neither one of them mentioned the coachman, who showed no sign of improvement.

"Mrs. Cantwell left to sleep for a few hours. I'm to run for her if either man takes a turn for the worse."

"Very well. I'm going out for a walk and will stop back when I return."

"Very good, my lord."

"Does your head ache, Basil?"

"No, my lord." The boy shrugged. "My back hurts from all this bending over but my head is clear."

"Good, good."

"Yes, sir, my lord."

David made his way down the narrow stairs. Pressing his fingers into the back of his neck relieved some of the tension, if not the pain. Passing through the dining room again, he grabbed some of the bread and a leg of chicken.

The front door was still bolted from the night before. He pulled it open and stepped out into the sunshine of an already warm day. As he ate, he felt summer fully upon them. He hated the heat and, worse, the damp. It reminded him too easily of Isla Mexicado. The constant steaming humidity had been the only thing worse than the blazing sun.

David headed down to the gate from habit before he remembered that he could not walk to town today. Something rested on the ground just outside the gate and he decided to keep on in that direction.

Two baskets.

He picked up both after checking the contents: some meat pies and a loaf of bread with no indication who had sent them.

As he stood there considering the gifts, David recalled the time in Isla Mexicado when the village chief had been poisoned by an anonymous gift of his favorite fish. The man had been arrogant and stupid to eat the food, or else he had no concept of how much his slaves hated him.

The townspeople here had always seemed amiable and none were beholden to Sandleton or the Pennistans for their income. Most of the land had been sold off years ago and the house kept only because the fishing was so good.

Surely this food would be safe to eat; no villager would be inclined to poison them to eliminate the possibility of contagion. England and Mexicado had more in common than any Englishman would believe, but surely that kind of barbarism was not part of it.

"What a generous offering."

Still mired in an internal debate, David had not heard Novins approach. Today he drove a two-wheeled dog cart with a single horse. He slowed and stopped on the other side of the gate. Several packages heaped beside him explained the need for the conveyance.

"Yes, very kind." David opened the gate, but stood back.

"I am coming in." Novins urged the horse through. "It is impossible to know what illness we are fighting without seeing the patients. I've made arrangements for the surgeon in Pegford to call on anyone who has need of care. I will quarantine myself at my own home, which is outside of town anyway. My servants have been sent away for the week."

"Well thought out, Novins."

"Thank you, my lord. Would you care to ride up to the house with me? These packages are for you and Miss Castellano, my lord. Sent from Pennford."

Lord David put the two baskets he had at hand next to the others and hauled himself up into the seat next to Novins. "The packages are for us? I didn't think Cantwell would be back until tomorrow at the earliest."

"And you were right, sir." Novins urged the horse into a trot. "Mr. Cantwell will start back today. The duke sent one of the stable lads with these items. Since the moon is full, the boy offered to travel by night. There are letters as well. They arrived less than an hour ago. Since there seemed to be some urgency I came up immediately."

The ache in David's head ratcheted up a notch. What could be so urgent that the boy had to travel at night? Their arrival at the kitchen door precluded any more conversation. David helped Novins unload the cart. In the kitchen, the surgeon shed his hat and began to organize the packages.

He handed David two letters and a weighty satchel similar to the ones that the mail courier used to transport estate papers from Pennford to London.

David accepted the bundle and dropped them on a

chair nearby. "Novins, take a minute and tell me who sent these baskets." He lifted one and nodded at the other.

Novins's cheeks reddened, though David had no idea why.

"The bread could be from Miss Horner." The surgeon's voice hinted that all bread looked the same. "I do not recognize the other, though they look like meat pies."

"Yes, they do. Surely a thoughtful gesture on someone's part." David left the slightest question in his voice.

"Yes, indeed, the people here are generous."

"Novins, given your work you must know the truth." David rubbed his forehead. "Generosity lasts only as long as people do not fear for their lives or their livelihood."

"Indeed you are wrong, my lord. Some people are selfish through and through, no matter if they are happy or ill." He put his hand on the basket that held the bread. "Some are so generous they give despite their own want to strangers. There are those who would risk their lives to care for others. It is my work and to be expected, but Mrs. Cantwell's loyalty is her only motivation."

"That's a singularly noble assessment." For his part David remained skeptical. "I will ask Mrs. Cantwell if she can identify the senders."

"Very well, my lord," Novins said, though David could tell the surgeon did not understand why.

"I know someone who was poisoned by such a gift. I remain cautious. Would it not be easiest of all to eliminate all of us who might be contaminated?"

"Including me and Mrs. Cantwell? For how are the senders to guarantee that only the visitors eat the pies?"

"Hmm" was all David could think of to say as he mulled over what Gabriel called his "paranoia." His man-of-science brother had pointed out he behaved that way whenever he felt ill or threatened. Both, in this case, if you counted a headache as illness.

"Your silence makes me hope I have convinced you, my lord. I will leave you to your letters and visit the patients. With your permission I'll report to you before I return to my own quarantine and a year's worth of books waiting to be read."

David gave him a nod, understanding why the thought of a week's quarantine made the surgeon smile.

As much as he wanted to keep his headache a secret, David would tell the surgeon about it before he left the house whether Novins asked him or not.

David did not take the letter from Pennford to the study but carefully opened the seal while still in the kitchen. Lyn had not dated the letter and wrote with less than his usual care.

David,

God's blood, brother, you do manage to find every possible predicament. Elena says that the letter from Mia is full of utterly useless assurances of your well-being and that all the proprieties are being observed. I will not tell you what my wife said in response to that bit of fiction.

Elena and I have no doubt of your discretion. Unfortunately Mia is prone to create complications by her very breathing. Be careful of her mischief and come home as soon as you are allowed.

Advise me if you require another medical opinion.

As I recall Sandleton is lacking in any reading material of an intellectual variety. When I explained Sandleton to Elena and the sort of books kept in the study, she begged me to tell you not to allow Mia near the room.

If, by some unlikely chance, you grow bored with erotic drawings and anecdotes, I have included the most recent Edinburgh Review *and a bag filled with all the details on the Stone Bank Mill, water wheels, and steam engines, all from your rooms here. I trust you have everything else with you.*

You may have need of them. I have included a letter from Thomas Sebold. Even before this last delay I see that he has decided to seek a partner from among his cohorts in Manchester.

David picked up the second letter, already opened and refolded. He unfolded it, swore at the indecipherable scrawl, and dropped it back on the table. He would finish Lyn's letter and then find his magnifying glass to help him decipher Thomas Sebold's deplorable handwriting.

I know your willingness to escort Mia is the reason for this most recent delay and Sebold's withdrawal. I had no idea that Sebold's commitment was so tentative and I apologize for the way our request undermined the project. Rest assured that once the trustees' cooperation is firm the Meryon dukedom will support your efforts to find another partner for the mill project.

Hopefully David's letter to the trustees would be well received, as well as the fact that Meryon himself supported the idea. Then he looked at the next sentence and winced.

> *About steam engines. I personally find the invention unproven and would advise against such an investment at the present time. Water wheels have been in use forever and last as long.*

David felt as though he spent most of his time trying to convince his brother to stop looking at how previous dukes had handled their responsibilities and move into the future. The duke might be far-thinking when it came to the well-being of the poor, but if an open mind involved anything mechanical, his brother still lived in the last century.

He began to mull over a reply. *The damn engine was invented before either one of us was born. More than two hundred are already in use. A steam engine will allow us to build a mill closer to the source of coal and save money and time.*

Oh, hell times ten, he would not waste his energy on a letter. They could discuss it, or argue it out, in person.

David shook off the disappointment and read the closing.

> *Elena and I both want you well and whole when we see you next. Olivia and her husband promise cinnamon rolls and prayers respectively. Garrett said to tell you that if his prayers work and you do not take ill he will "beat the hell" out of you in the boxing ring for worrying us all so.*

Sometimes I doubt our brother-in-law's insistence that he is now a man of peace.

Lynford

David understood his brother's skepticism. Olivia had fallen in love with a man as unconventional as she was. For an Episcopal priest Garrett had some very eccentric beliefs.

The baskets sat on the table where the servants met for meals. He put them on a chair, out of sight, until he could ask Mrs. Cantwell who had sent them. He would tell her he wanted to send his thanks.

With only a little curiosity, David placed the note to Mia enclosed with his letter on the odd-shaped package awaiting her attention.

He scooped up Sebold's letter and the satchel. With an "Ooof" at its weight, David lugged it into the study. Setting up his work here seemed the surest way to keep Mia from an examination of the shelves and their contents.

He glanced at the apparently innocent bindings marching along the shelves behind him, but did not touch a one. He had spent the whole of the previous day battling, then banishing, his own licentious imagination. Drawings of men and women in impossible poses would not help keep his thoughts under control at all.

With his back to the shelves he set the bag on the library table and remembered the time he had come into the room to find Jessup and another gentleman with two women. His brother lived life on a scale that would kill him before he turned thirty.

That night cards and markers had been pushed off the table in favor of other pursuits. One of the women straddled his brother, her skirts raised and his pants obviously loosened. The other two watched with unconcealed excitement. David had left the room before any of them noticed him. Then David had left the house to stay at the inn, this being quite obviously a private party in which introducing a fifth would not be at all welcome.

Damn times six, everything in this house reminded him of sex, if not orgies, in some of which he'd participated. Of all the ungodly places to be trapped with a precocious virgin, Sandleton had to be the worst. In a brothel he could find relief elsewhere. In a convent he could spend hours on his knees in the chapel. Both were sure ways to come to terms with a weakness. Neither one was his first choice.

His headache reappeared, if it had ever truly evaporated, and David stared at the drawing of a steam engine, trying to bring it into proper focus. Damn it, this had better not be another symptom. He had no time for illness. He had too much to do.

First on the list was to read Sebold's letter. David hunted for his magnifying glass. The man showed his birth in his crabbed scrawl and bad spelling. He put the glass over the letter and began to read.

"Lord David, your reesons for delaying our apointment, serves to convince me to find a new co-owner for the Manchester

project. I have formed a partnership with a banker who has helped me in the past. It has beceome clear to me that you are not interested in this project as seriously as is necessary." The letter went on but David did not have to read another word.

This quarantine could drive him mad if illness did not kill him. Less than sixty miles separated Sandleton from Manchester. Styal lay even closer.

If it weren't for the damned quarantine he could ride there in less than a day and confront Sebold, try to convince him that the delay did not mean anything more than inconvenience.

David searched through the bag, relieved to see that Lyn had included the copy of the mill plans. He could find an engineer to amend these, substituting the newest steam engine. But that would mean nothing if he was not able to solve the biggest bar to success: funding.

With Sebold and his support gone it meant that all the money must come from the Meryon estate.

The enforced isolation of the quarantine at least presented the ideal opportunity to prepare proof that would convince Lyn and the trustees that a mill run by a steam engine was the way of the future.

Pulling a sheaf of papers from the satchel, David spread them out on the table that served as a desk.

"I beg your pardon, my lord."

David had seen the surgeon hovering at the open door and ignored him as he did his best to work his brain around this change of plans.

"Come in, Novins, come in," David said with as

much cordiality as he could muster. The health of his servants could be counted as even more important than the success of his plans. Not more bad news, he hoped.

"Thank you, sir." Novins perched on the edge of the chair on the other side of the table. "I examined both of the patients and talked to Mrs. Cantwell and Basil. In some way things are improving. I will speak to Miss Castellano later but first I will ask you if you have any signs of illness."

"A headache," David admitted.

"Nothing else?"

David shook his head.

"Head pain can come from many things, my lord. Worry for others. Too much close work." He nodded toward the papers spread out on the table. "What is that, my lord?" Novins asked with an air of sincere interest.

"A design for a cotton mill based on the Long Bank Mill in Styal near Manchester. I am considering building one."

"I know it, the Long Bank Mill," Mr. Novins said to their mutual surprise. "It's less than a day's travel from here."

"Yes." David nodded, pleased as could be that the man had not immediately implied that "going into trade" was beneath the son of a duke.

"Is this a joint venture?"

"Yes, and this quarantine is not advancing my efforts in any way. I thought to use these five days to learn all I can about the mill design." As if he did not have it memorized already.

"And there is the most likely reason for your headache. Walk at least twice a day, at the coolest hour, and see if that eases the discomfort."

"Then you do not think we are faced with some horrific contagion?"

"As to that, I am not a physician, trained in diagnosis, but a headache without any other accompanying complaints is not the way the illness started in the others."

So at least he did not have some dreaded and so far nameless disease. Yet.

"The prospect of this damn illness is like the sword of Damocles hanging over my head." David's headache worsened as he spoke, and it would not take a man of medicine to tell him that was from worry.

"Distract yourself with your plans, my lord. But do walk. I insist."

David nodded.

"Let me tell you what I found upstairs and then I will speak to Miss Castellano. Mrs. Cantwell told me she last saw her in her bedchamber, reading."

Chapter Fifteen

SITTING ON HER BED, dressed only in her shift, Mia stared at the drawing. Could a woman really bend herself into that position? Would any woman, other than a courtesan, even want to have sex that way?

After studying it carefully for a full minute Mia pulled a pillow toward her and used it as the other half of the picture, the male half, and bent her body into as close an approximation of the position illustrated as she could. It was a challenge even for her agile body. The pillow pressed into her most sensitive spot, which, she had to admit, was feeling some arousal after spending the last hour looking at the drawings. With a gasp she pressed against the pillow for a moment and then tossed it to the floor.

She blushed, even though completely alone—but that position did have something to recommend it.

I will consider that a learning experience. Jumping from the bed, she took a cold rag, pressed it against herself, and waited for the throbbing to abate. She knew self-pleasure was a sin in any religion, but she had just learned that it was a very tempting one, one that might be worth whatever penance was suggested. Unless one died from the pleasure and then it would be straight to hell. Did the Episcopal Church believe in confession? And, if they did not, then how did one atone for the occasional lapse?

She would ask Michael Garrett when she saw him next—though the idea of confessing this behavior to him would be more embarrassing than confiding in an anonymous priest.

Mia supposed a courtesan gave up all hope of salvation, unless in her old age she could use her wealth for good works and contrite acts.

What an amazing book, she thought as she carefully smoothed the pages and closed it. Sliding it into the drawer next to her bed, she decided to explore the library further. Given what this house was used for there were bound to be other books like it.

The second book she had chosen at random was not nearly as scandalous, a collection of poems in a language she did not know. She wished she did. The illustrations were quite sensual, though not nearly as salacious as the drawings in the book she had hidden.

A scratch at the door made her jump, then scramble under the covers. "Yes," she said, trying for a sleepy, half-dreaming tone.

"Miss Castellano? I am sorry to disturb you, but I

would like to speak with you in the main salon downstairs at your soonest convenience."

Mr. Novins. He would not come in uninvited. She relaxed. "Yes, of course." Then a horrible thought occurred to her. She jumped up from the bed, ran to the door, and opened it a crack. "Is everyone all right? Has Lord David taken ill?"

"No, miss, everyone is as I expected."

"Thank goodness." She relaxed her deathlike grip on her robe. "I will dress and be downstairs as quickly as I can."

"Thank you." He nodded and turned away before she closed the door. Mrs. Cantwell had explained his decision to come to the house. How noble of him to risk illness himself in order to care for them.

Now, if it had been Lord David at the door, he would have pushed his way into the room and berated her for still being abed. And, as a punishment for his rudeness, she would have made him wait an hour. Mr. Novins deserved her full cooperation, and surely he would have a few minutes to talk with her about Miss Horner. If she could find no novels to read, she could certainly enjoy a real-life story, particularly one she might be able to move along toward a satisfactory conclusion.

Mia raced through her toilette. She managed to lace her stays and slip into her gown, tie it, and find shoes, dismissing stockings. She left her hair down, settling for brushing it free of knots and tying it at the back of her neck. Janina would scold her endlessly for her casual air. Mia could hear her.

"You must always look your best. You never know when the man of your heart will appear."

"Mr. Novins will never be the love of my life, Janina," Mia announced as if Janina sat next to her. Then Mia held the brush close to her heart and closed her watery eyes. *Please, please be well, Nina, and come back to me soon.*

As she hurried down the steps Mia decided that she would write Janina today and tell her all that she learned about Mr. Novins and Miss Horner.

Mia hurried into the salon and then stopped short. She had not been in here before. This room had more light than the hall. It benefited from a west-facing window, and the light gave the space a golden glow that accentuated the yellows and golds that colored the walls and uphol-stered furniture. A huge arrangement of white and yellow summer blooms spiked with bright blue hydrangea brought the room to life.

If there had been a pianoforte she would have called this room perfection.

Mr. Novins stood at the window, his hands behind his back, as still as a statue. The view from the window had much to recommend it. The trees mixed green against a startling blue sky, but Mia knew the prospect was not what Mr. Novins saw.

She waited so long that Mia thought she would have to clear her throat to draw his attention, but just then the surgeon turned to face her.

"Good morning, miss," he said, as if just noticing her.

"Good morning," she echoed with a small curtsy. "This room is lovely and those flowers spectacular." Their earlier conversation came to her. "Did Miss Horner make this arrangement?"

"Yes, she did. But they are not half as lovely as she is," Mr. Novins said with a proud nod.

Oh, Mia thought, *his heart is so very involved.*

He cleared his throat and Mia pretended not to notice his embarrassment at so revealing a sentiment.

"I brought a package for you, Miss Castellano. It arrived last night from Pennford. I left it for you in the kitchen."

"A package! Is there a letter as well?" Of course Elena would have written. "Never mind, I will go see for myself." She spun around and had almost reached the door when Mr. Novins stopped her.

"Lord David told me today that he has a headache."

His words froze her in place.

"No." She spoke it firmly, her back still to Mr. Novins. "Lord David cannot be sick. No." She turned to face the surgeon. "I will not allow it."

"I hear desperation in your voice, Miss Castellano."

He went on talking but Mia had no idea what he said. Fear edged with guilt stole her breath and she sat on the settee, her legs weak, her head light.

This was her worst fear. If Lord David took ill, he who seemed as healthy and strong as an elephant, then what were the chances the rest of them would be spared? She rocked back and forth, fighting tears and anger.

"Miss Castellano, do not dissolve into hysterics." Through her light-headed fog it seemed that Mr. Novins sounded hysterical himself. "It will make me regret telling you." She felt him sit beside her and wave something under her nose.

Ugh. A vinaigrette. Mia gasped at the awful smell and coughed herself back to normal. "I hate that smell."

"Yes, but it does work." Mr. Novins slid it back into his pocket. "Are you steady enough to listen now?"

"Yes."

"Miss, Lord David is not sick, nor do I think he will be."

Huge relief overtook her fear.

"He is upset about the others and worried about you."

"Worried about me? No, he is not." Not because he cared about her or would be devastated if she took ill. "But I will concede that he is worried that my death would upset Elena, my guardian."

"Your death?" Mr. Novins took her hand. "Are you feeling unwell?"

"No. Not at all." The man missed the point completely. "Or Lord David might be worried that he is going to be late for his appointment in Manchester. But he is not worried about Mia Castellano, I assure you of that. Not any more than I worry about him."

"I see." Mr. Novins said the two words as though he were imbued with some sight other than visual.

"If all you wanted to know is if I am feeling well, the answer is yes. No pain, no aches, no bruises from the carriage ride." Mia was desperate to see what Elena had sent her. Instead she sacrificed that immediate pleasure to pursue Mr. Novins's best interest and felt all the more angelic for it.

"Since we have dispensed with my well-being, do tell me how the people in the village are handling this upset." *Especially Miss Horner. Especially Miss Horner.* Mia tried to send the ideas through the air and into his brain.

"Miss Horner tells me that everyone is concerned and fearful for Mrs. Cantwell."

"For Mrs. Cantwell?"

"Mrs. Cantwell is better known than you and Lord David. Even Miss Horner's mother went to church today to pray, and it is very difficult for Mrs. Horner to move about. She must use two canes."

"I am sorry to hear that." Mia winced at how perfunctory that sounded. She wanted to know about Miss Horner, not her mother. "Did Miss Horner come to church as well?"

"Yes, I spoke to her afterward. Very briefly." *I miss her.*

He did not have to speak those words. Mia could tell by the expression on his face that his loneliness went soul-deep.

"Why will Miss Horner not consider marriage? You would be willing to take care of her mother and siblings, would you not?" And if he said no then his love was as shallow as a mud puddle and as pure.

"Of course. Her family would be mine."

"Then, please tell me, what is the obstacle?"

"I have not asked her."

"Oh. Why in the world not?"

Mr. Novins blushed and looked at his hands.

The solution seemed simple, but men were such

prideful creatures. What she needed to do was meet Miss
Horner and find out if she returned Mr. Novins's affection
and then reassure him that his suit would be welcome.
But that could not happen for a sennight.

"Mr. Novins," she began, looking him straight in the
eyes. "Here is what you must do."

"Novins, need I remind you of all the reading that
awaits you?"

Mia jumped to her feet with a cry. Mr. Novins did the
same minus the little screech.

"You frightened me, Lord David," Mia scolded.

"Yes, I can see that."

He smiled like a self-satisfied prig. Or a bully. An oaf
and a bully. And a prig.

"Yes, my lord," Mr. Novins agreed. "I will see you later
today, my lord." Mr. Novins bowed to him, then turned to
her, taking her hand and bowing over it with a charming
grace. "We can continue our discussion then, Miss Castellano."

"I look forward to it." She flashed a look at Lord
David and hoped he could read her mind. *Take that, you
bully,* Mia thought even as she admitted to herself that calling him names made her feel like a child.

Mia followed Mr. Novins from the salon and closed
the front door after another brief farewell. Lord David had
followed her into the hallway but she ignored him. She
did not care about him at all, even if he did have a
headache. He seemed no more ill-tempered than usual.

She would find her package and most certainly a letter. Where had Mr. Novins said he left them?

She hurried down the hall and into the kitchen, mostly to avoid Lord David, and was rewarded with her mail. Mia knew exactly what the odd-shaped package was, but still pulled the ties off the cloth covering and exposed the leather case. Inside was the guitar that she had sent to Pennford months ago. She picked it up and hugged it to her. Even before she played a note, the smell of it, the feel of the strings, the way it fit so perfectly in her arms—it was just the thing she needed.

"A guitar."

Lord David did not surprise her this time. She knew he would follow her.

"I should have been able to figure that out from the shape of the package. But then I did not know you played the guitar, too."

"Yes, it is my favorite thing in all the world."

"I thought the pianoforte was your favorite thing in all the world."

"They both are." Why did the man bring out the snippy girl in her? She was a woman, completely grown, with a woman's wants and needs. She could not believe that she had pretended the pillow was him when she had been experimenting with the pose in the book. Not only sinful but stupid.

"If there is anything you need to discuss with me I will be in the study." He left the room without waiting for a reply, and Mia told herself she did not feel at all ungracious.

"Wait, Lord David."

He stopped at the door but did not come back into
the room.

"Is there no letter for me? From Elena."

"Oh," he said, and reached into his pocket. "There
was this note tucked in with Meryon's letter. He penned it
but it is dictated by the duchess."

"Would you have even thought to give it to me if I had
not asked?"

"Eventually."

She turned her back to him and read:

David and Mia,

*Elena asked me to write to you on her behalf. Mia,
she hopes that your maid returns to you shortly.*

*I told her that the pianoforte at Sandleton has been
sent out for repairs, so she asked me to send Mia's favorite
guitar and some new music by Fons so that she can have
some distraction from worry.*

*Alan Wilson jumped at the chance to ride by the full
moon to deliver this mail and the package to you so you
could have them as soon as possible.*

*Elena reminds you that this incident is no more than
an unfortunate accident for which neither of you is responsible.*

Mia read the note through again. It was not precisely
impersonal, but there was nothing particularly loving
about it. Why would Elena not write herself unless she
was beyond angry with her? Or perhaps she was too sick

from her pregnancy. Here was something else to worry about.

This incident is no more than an unfortunate accident for which neither of you is responsible. Couched in terms to spare David her anger, Mia knew it really meant that everyone was relieved that for once Mia Castellano was not the reason for this disaster.

With the guitar back in the case, Mia counted the months since she had played it. The pianoforte was so much more popular in London. Now she could play what she pleased. The guitar was so much more intimate an instrument, held so close to the heart.

Carrying the case by the handle, she decided to take it away from the house to tune it and practice so no one could hear her mistakes.

There were three doors leading from the kitchen and she chose the one on the right first, not sure which one led outside.

The one she chose opened onto a short narrow room lined on both sides with any and all items an angler might want, need, or wish for. Boots, rain wear, creels, nets, and the even more essential equipment: fishing rods and, on the wall, a padded felt square with at least fifty flies.

Mia took it all in with pure delight. You could angle with a fly here! This was proof that the river was filled with trout. Her papa would have loved this place.

Mia found that the door at the end of the room led to a path down toward the river. No fish worth its weight would be caught this time of day, so she headed to the river to play her guitar for them.

*   *   *

DAVID TOOK HIS second walk of the day after supper, a meal he had eaten alone since Mrs. Cantwell said Mia had sent word she would have something cold later.

The light remained strong but the sun sat low enough in the sky that the night air held sway. As he moved toward the river he could swear he heard music. He stopped, took two more careful steps, and recognized the sound.

A guitar. Someone played a guitar. And that someone could only be Mia Castellano.

David circled around the knoll where he found her sitting on a bench. As his eyes adjusted to the growing dark, what a picture she made. Mostly in shadows and not quite real. Since he could not see her clearly, he listened, gradually caught in the spell of her quiet guitar.

He moved to a secluded spot, lit a cigarillo, and found a dry patch of ground. David lay down flat, closing his eyes and listening to the musicale with no doubt in his mind that Mia would stop playing if she suspected she had an audience.

He did not recognize the composer and did not have to. The melancholy sounds coursed through him, leaving him feeling as alone and lonely as she must be. The music was just one more way that Mia Castellano had found to convey her feelings, but the way she plucked the strings of the guitar brought him more insight than her conversation.

If her words revealed her as a flirt who was only interested in adventure, the music she shared sang of loss and longing, announced it as surely as sobs and tears, an affect he had yet to see her employ.

Where did the sadness come from? he wondered. The loss of her father, most likely. Leaving Italy. The end of her engagement. Fear of illness.

He drew on his cigarillo and wondered if music was the only place she allowed her heartache to show. No wonder she had been so pleased to see her guitar. No wonder Elena had sent it as quickly as she could.

Mia stopped playing abruptly and began something far more cheerful, defiant even, using her hands on the body of the guitar for a stronger bass sound. The music required a speed on the strings that he could not even visualize. David smiled and closed his eyes, and shared her good spirits as he had shared her pain.

He persisted in thinking of her as indulged and spoiled when those were not the right words at all. She struggled to take care of herself, to be independent. In a man it would be admirable. In a woman it was seen as defiant and selfish.

The next piece was romantic, charged with a sensibility between lust and love. She played it with force at first and then more quietly and quieter still, ending with a note so soft it blended with the night song of the river and the breeze.

David stayed where he was, drawing on his cigarillo. Who was she thinking of as she played? He would be a lucky man when she decided to tell him, to share all her music conveyed.

He heard her put the guitar away and move on up the path. Just as she passed the spot where he lay, she whispered.

"Good night, Lord David."

Chapter Sixteen

DAVID DREW THE NUMBER THREE on the date in his pocket calendar, the third day of their quarantine. No one else had sickened; the groom was recovering, but John Coachman was worse and David himself woke with a headache for the second day in a row.

He grabbed some bread and fruit, went out the garden door, and headed for the river. The sun beat down as he crossed the lawn, making the trees along the river a welcome destination.

He found heat bothersome even without a headache so he hurried, too tired to outright run, hoping that the air would prove cooler in the shade.

Reaching the trees and blessed shade in five minutes, David surprised a deer nibbling on some green shoots along the trail. The doe scampered off, and he watched her disappear into the woods before voices from the riverbank drew his attention.

He heard the tone, out of breath and angry, but the words were unintelligible. Surely the villagers knew this was Sandleton land and off limits. He listened more carefully as he approached, and decided two people were bickering and the woman would not stop talking, though her voice rose and fell in strength.

David wanted a fight badly, so he bounded down the trail as he called out, "You there! You are not allowed on this property!"

When Mia Castellano jumped, the fish she had been playing took the advantage. The line flew back over her shoulder even as she tried to set it again with a practiced jerk of her wrist.

The wayward hook whipped toward him and pierced the pad of flesh below David's thumb as he raised his hand to protect his face.

Mia turned to see who called to her, and David watched her expression pass from amused to distressed to annoyed in a matter of a second.

David had never seen anyone, on stage or off, who could express so much with a tilt of the head, a quirk of the lips, or the look in her eye.

"Until you came, I was enjoying the peace and quiet!"

"Damn times five," David swore as he pulled the hook from his hand. The pad of flesh at the base of his thumb bled freely and hurt like hell. He pulled his handkerchief out and wound it around as a bandage. As he tied a knot and looked up he noticed how little she wore.

Too little.

Even as he had the thought, she stepped behind a tree that did not completely shield her, and turned her back to him.

"You can curse all you want, but the fault rests with you entirely. You gave Bruce the advantage and he escaped."

"Bruce?"

"Yes, the fish. I named him. My father insisted that the most worthy fish deserved a name. It is my goal to actually land him before we leave here."

She looked over her shoulder. He wanted an artist to capture that moment. Mia Castellano in her stays and diaphanous chemise, standing in the summer-lit woods like some dark-haired fairy playing at being human. Never mind an artist. He did not need a painting to recall this moment.

"Skirts are an encumbrance when angling with a fly. It requires freedom of movement." She pulled her dress from a branch and held it against her stays for a moment. "And petticoats are even worse than a dress. So I wear as little as possible."

"So I can attest," he said, his brain buzzing with the vision of her.

"This is Sandleton property," she continued, "and I hardly expected company, given that and our quarantine."

When it occurred to him that her embarrassment was why she jabbered on, David turned to walk down to the river despite the delightful view of her back, hips, and legs.

"I love fishing," she called out in a muffled voice.

David imagined her raising her arms, pulling her dress over her head, down the trim length of her body. "And I've found something to do, some way to help besides winding the clocks."

Would she need help with the fastening of her dress? He hoped not.

"Please do not turn around yet. I have this on wrong and must take it off again."

He heard the sound of low-voiced impatience, then the sound of material, most likely the dress, being shaken with force.

"You know, Lord David, if I catch Bruce we will have enough for a feast."

It flashed through his mind as he studied the water that she considered him another kind of fish. Whether she intended it or not, unless he took care he would be as well and truly caught as any trout named Bruce.

David concentrated on the clear clean water, its depth little more than three feet in this spot. He recalled there was a spot a little farther down with stones carefully placed so that crossing was easy. He looked across the river at the steep hillside, covered with brush and weeds. It wasn't the only reason no one used the crossing.

Here heaps of rounded rocks lay just below the surface, making for eddies and ripples that could hide the fish from view. After a minute his sight adjusted and he counted eight fish swimming by, all of them too small to name.

The sound of the stream and the feel of the breeze

made the heat of the day a pleasure. He bent down to trail a hand in the water, pleased with the fine distraction.

A scream destroyed his reverie.

"*Madre di Dio!*" The panic in her voice was unfeigned. "Help me. Oh no, please, no!"

David turned back to find Mia running toward him, holding her dress in one hand, brushing at her stays with the other. "There is a spot on my breast. I think it is a smallpox."

"Damn times ten, you scared me." So much that he barely noticed her dishabille. "I thought a bee had flown down your shift."

"I would rather have five bee stings than the smallpox. Bee stings disappear." She held her dress up in a pretense of modesty. "Look, please look, and tell me it is not the beginning of the smallpox. I cannot see well from this angle."

"Miss Castellano, it is not smallpox." He put his hands behind his back and stepped away.

"You cannot know until you look!"

"You have no symptoms. It is a bug bite."

"No!" she shouted, as if nature would obey her command. "You don't know for sure until you look."

Fear made her shake and he took her hand. "Come back to the house. Mrs. Cantwell will look. It will be no worse for waiting a few moments."

"But I will go mad by then." She gripped his hand so tightly that he could feel the blood stop flowing. "I would rather die from the smallpox than survive. You know as well as I do that my looks are all that I have. If I am marked for life no man would ever be interested in me."

Did she actually believe that? What complete and utter nonsense. He searched her face and saw no hint of deviousness. In fact, she looked as panicked as he had ever seen her. "All right. I'll look."

She lowered her dress and put her back against a tree. He came close and leaned over her. He could feel her soft breath on his head, smell the morning dew on her neck, but could barely see the mark that had so upset her. If this was her idea of flirting he would banish her to her room for the rest of their quarantine.

"You are wrong, you know." He turned his head to try to see the damn bug bite. "Men would line up to dance with you even if you had two noses." He spoke the truth, if only to distract her.

He would lie about the mark, though. The bite lay in a spot easier felt than seen, at the curve where the soft roundness was shadowed by her cleavage. Touching her in such an intimate spot asked entirely too much of both of them. Mrs. Cantwell could confirm his diagnosis later. "It's a bite from an insect, I am sure of it."

Without saying a word Mia turned from him and slipped the dress over her head. Despite the fact that he could have helped her, she reached around and tied the ribbon at her neck with an ease most women could not match.

She faced him again, her cheeks flushed. "Why would a man dance with me even if I had two noses?"

"Men are attracted to you, like hummingbirds to a

flower. You embrace every moment of life and think to make it dance to your tune. It is very appealing at a ball or in the park. But as Lord William learned, it is not nearly as appealing in the day-to-day stuff of life, when every hour must be styled to suit you. When *no* is the only word one hears."

She closed her eyes and shook her head. "I should have known better than to ask. With you even a compliment can be made into an insult."

If she thought him unfeeling, so much the better. He would not undo almost two days of separation by making her smile. Better that she label him with every unsavory word she could think of than to know how much one guitar concert had altered his understanding of her.

"I will leave you now," David announced. Without waiting for her answer he turned back.

"No."

He relaxed, relieved that his life was back in balance.

"I want to know how you can tell the difference between a bug bite and a smallpox."

David kept his place several yards away from her as he answered. "The surgeon told me that smallpox first appears as a rash. Your mark is distinctively a bite with a dot at the center. Completely different." He'd almost convinced himself. "And the rash almost always comes after the fever and starts in the mouth, then moves to the face."

"The rash is always the last symptom to show? You could not tell me that before?"

"Miss Castellano, you were not inclined to listen to

anything I said. Do *not* pose me as a man looking to take advantage." He calmed himself with a deep breath. "You begged me not to wait."

"I suppose so." She made a face, as though she had agreed just to appear civil when he knew she could not think of a way to use *no* in the sentence.

"Do not start sulking because I gave in to your hysteria."

"I am not sulking." She walked along the riverbank to a pool of water formed by a man-made stack of rock. "You cannot know what it is like to live with the fear of disfigurement and death."

"You are not the only one who worries about such things. I woke up with a headache yesterday morning, and it took all of Novins's skill to convince me I was not sick."

She had just pulled the creel from the water; she dropped it in again and stood quickly, without her usual grace. "You have not had the vaccination?"

"I was in Mexico when the rest of the family had the inoculation. The disease is common in Mexico. I never took ill and supposed that I was immune. Now I'm not sure. I will have the vaccination as soon as I can arrange for it."

"Now I must worry about you, too."

To his surprise, she didn't let loose a tirade over his lack of foresight. He wondered who else had a place on her list of worries.

She would worry about Elena, at least until her child came into the world. Janina. Not many. At least not many that he knew of. He should feel honored.

David watched her haul the creel out of the water again.

"I hope you like trout, my lord. There is plenty for dinner tonight. Even without Bruce."

How nice, he thought with some surprise, that she did not harp on the point of their mutual fear. He held out his hand and she gave him the creel. It weighed more than he expected. She must have read his expression. "I threw back the smallest," she said with some pride.

"How many did you catch?" he asked, astonished at her skill.

"About ten. I didn't count."

He laughed, which surprised her. "I don't believe that, any more than you would believe I do not mind losing a boxing match."

"Fifteen," she whispered into his ear. She straightened quickly and went on in a rush, "But Bruce escaped for the second time." She went ahead of him as they found the path from the river up to the house.

David moved automatically, wondering how one whispered number could undo hours of self-discipline. He watched the way the morning breeze picked at the strands of hair that had slipped from the knot she had fashioned at the back of her neck. Mia Castellano managed amazingly well without a maid, even to the point of lacing her own stays.

As he watched her climb the short, steep path to the lawn, David realized that she had an amazing suppleness. The way she had climbed up to the top of the carriage. Her ability to slip away from him.

Gabriel, the man of science, would call it double-jointed. David called it incredibly distracting, especially since it made him wonder what other ways she could bend and twist her body.

Add that to what he'd learned from observation. Despite her reputation as a chatterbox, David realized how little he knew about her. He'd learned more about her when he listened to her play the guitar than he had in conversation.

How interesting that someone so sociable kept her own counsel as thoroughly as he did. He never would have guessed that Mia Castellano could fish, for example, much less that she would like it.

"How did you learn angling?" he had to ask.

She stopped abruptly and he almost ran into her. He searched the grass for a rabbit hole or something else that might have given her pause.

"You asked me a question, Lord David."

She seemed genuinely surprised. Or pleased. Her smile always left him feeling confused. "Yes. I want to know where you learned to fish."

"You see? That is what you usually do. Command. You never ask."

He closed his eyes and wished for a rabbit hole that he could step into, sprain his ankle if not break his leg, and completely forestall the approaching lecture.

"This is important, my lord. I told myself that the first time you asked me a question, the first time you truly wanted to know something about me, instead of relying on what you have heard or what you assume, I would forgive all your past bad manners." She beamed at him as though he had given her the greatest gift and she returned the gesture.

If he had thought Mia only interested in buying elegant clothes, right down to an embroidered chemise, of buying hats she forgot to wear, or gloves she always left behind, he was wrong. She liked to fish, of all things, and seemed to find as much happiness alone by the river as she did in a crowded ballroom.

There was more to her than he had ever imagined. Shame on him for never being interested enough to ask her a question.

Before David could think of what to say, before he could think more than *Mia Castellano is a riddle it would take a lifetime to solve,* she started back across the lawn. He followed her. *Damn times two,* he did want to know how and why she learned to fish.

"I learned angling with a fly from my father."

"I thought he died when you were still a child."

"He died when I was twelve. I began angling with a fly when I was eight, closer to nine."

"But you're so at home in the city, I would have thought you joking if I had not seen it with my own eyes." *Dressed in a white-on-white embroidered shift and stays with roses picked out in pink.* Apparently that was another memory he would always have.

"Yes, but my father loved to fish and he took me with him when he went to the country. I do not handle boredom well, so he taught me how to cast a line. And he insisted that if I caught a fish I needed to know what to do with it."

"This must have been before you became an expert at the many variations of the word *no*." He was sorry the minute he looked at her. Her wounded eyes and the lack of a smile told him he'd offended her without even trying, and he felt the smaller for it.

"My father listened to my opinions and welcomed my insights," she went on, with more stiffness in her voice. "He knew how to ask questions and he listened to the answers. That is a talent few men possess."

If he had a woman's sensibilities he could have taken that as an affront. "Your father sounds like an interesting man."

"He was wonderful." She walked briskly, putting some distance between them. David suspected her eyes were wet. A minute later she slowed, so he made the effort to catch up to her.

"When I saw the river from my bedroom window I knew it would have fish in it. Yesterday I found a superbly outfitted room for anglers. But there weren't any boots small enough for my feet, and it is too warm to wear the covering that would have protected my dress."

As they drew closer to the house, she moved away from the most direct route and into the shade of the trees. Stopping, she turned to look back down toward the water, now mostly hidden by the trees that grew along the bank, though he could hear as it cascaded over the boulders farther upstream.

"This is the English version of Eden, my lord. When you told me about stopping here, I wondered why the duke held onto a place not quite a day's ride from Pennford." She raised her head, admiring the canopy the trees made. "Now I know." Resting her fishing rod against the tree, she sat on one of the oak benches, pulled off her shoes, stood up again, and walked into the grass. "I love this, the feel of grass on my bare feet. If we are waiting to sicken and die," she continued, "this is the perfect place, beautiful and serene, but there are a hundred things I want to do before that happens."

"I will make a list for you and put 'walk in the grass' at number one."

She turned her head, looked at him over her shoulder, and grinned. "Yes, I have lists for everything. Several of them have you at the top."

"I will not ask what the lists are, nor do I want to know, Miss Castellano." He could guess easily enough.

"Lord David, would you please call me by my given name? Miss Castellano is such a mouthful, and if we only have a few days to live, why waste any of the time we do have on five syllables when you can manage to have my attention with two?"

"There is a certain wisdom in being formal." David knew he sounded pompous, but alienating her was just what he should be doing, given the way his mind went to other things they could do if they "only had a few days to live."

"Nonsense. We might die." The drama in her voice

was more exasperation than fear. She flopped down onto the grass and spread her arms out, still looking more like a creature of nature than an untried girl, both begging for ravishment. "Wisdom is the least important virtue right now."

"Not if we survive, as I have no doubt we will." He went to her and held out his hand. "Now stop trying to tempt me. Let us go back to the house. Do you know Walton's *The Compleat Angler*?"

Though she accepted his hand she barely used it as she rose to her feet, winding up next to him. She put her arms around his neck, leaning back a little. Her mouth was not very close but her body was pressed against his.

"Yes, I have my father's copy." She looked him in the eye and dared him to keep talking.

"My father insists that his father hosted Walton here." He raised his hands to pull hers from around his neck. She took them and held tight as she leaned fully away from him and then closer again as in a dance. "The story is that he slept in the room that is your dressing room."

"Oh, that's wonderful. I will look for a copy on the bookshelves and read it aloud."

"Or use it as lyrics to 'God Save the King.'"

"Have you heard me?"

"Twice. Your words to the tune of 'Greensleeves' and 'Barbara Allen.' Why do you do that?"

"Another question, Lord David. That now makes three in one encounter. I do believe you deserve a reward." She pressed her lips to his without warning. That is if he did not consider her antics the last three minutes a warning.

The touch lasted the barest second. She would have let him go and resumed walking if he had not pulled her back into his arms. "Miss Castellano, if that was a kiss, you definitely need a tutor."

Her kiss on the corner of his mouth was chaste. His kiss was not. It would show her from the first that kissing was about more than reward. At the beginning it was like a testing of the waters before a deeper plunge into the surf. If that first touch felt right, and this did, he would plunge in, risking everything for the thrill of riding the wave of want and pleasure, taking her with him. His mouth wed hers, taking every bit of feeling she offered and gave, both at the same time.

This kiss opened them to a place where nothing existed but the other, what they were and what they could be. Complete. Complete in a way that words only hinted at, in a way touch proved inadequate. David Pennistan lost himself in that kiss, forgot everything and everyone else.

Her soft lips pulled him into this most intimate of worlds where everything was a jumble of clarity and confusion, heaven and hell, magic and mayhem, pleasure and anguish. His body longed for this union, so perfect, so much a completion that it was worth the risk of disaster. To forget the future, the past, all the fears and even all the hopes was the greatest gift he had ever been given. And just beyond that was the urging to give up control completely and take what the moment offered.

When he fell back into the world they'd left behind,

he was speechless. So was she, but her eyes sparkled and her lush lips showed an "O" of amazement that he understood completely.

If he had hoped to overwhelm her, he had made a grave error. He was the one overwhelmed. What was William Bendasbrook thinking to give this woman up?

Chapter Seventeen

STAY CALM, MIA ORDERED HERSELF. *Sit down on the bench, gracefully, so that he does not see your legs shaking. Smile, just a little. Or at least try to look as though you've been kissed like that before.*

Lord David cleared his throat. "Why do you wind the clocks at midnight?"

He'd asked her another question. He must be as nonplussed as she was. Now she *could* smile. "A fourth question, my lord? They are in danger of becoming commonplace, hardly worthy of a reward."

Mia stood up, pleased with her clever reply. Her legs were no longer unsteady, her heart had settled to a comfortable rhythm, proving to herself, at least, that she was in control of the situation.

Testing herself further, Mia tried walking. When her

feet obeyed her still-stupefied brain, she left the path and went back onto the lawn, a far less private spot.

Lord David followed her and then went back to pick up the fishing rod and bag she had left on the bench. He handed them to her, his expression guarded, which made her feel even better.

It was the best sort of kiss, she thought, filled with invitation and promise and very possibly more than Lord David intended to give. A thrill ran through her. "I wind the clocks at midnight because my bedchamber clock stopped ticking late the first night we were here, since Mrs. Cantwell had not had the time to wind it and I never thought of it. When I went to check the time on the great case clock in the front hall, I realized that none of the clocks were being wound."

Mia drew a breath and slowed the rush of words to a more conversational pace. "So I decided that winding the clocks was something I could do to help." She brushed at a bee that came too close and pushed a lock of hair behind her ear. "Mrs. Cantwell told me that I must wind the clocks at the same hour lest they become over-wound. Mr. Cantwell is a stickler for the correct time."

They went up the last rise and the back of the house came into view.

"So I do that small task close to midnight, just before I climb into my bed." *In case you want to know where to find me.*

The scent of roses greeted her as they moved through the small gardens. They were close to the terrace that ran the length of the rear of the house.

Full-blown roses were her favorite flower in the world. They were so generous with their scent and color. She did not know which she liked better, the spicy sweet aroma or the deep burgundy color. What would one be without the other? she wondered.

Despite the distraction of the roses, Mia knew the silence between them was strained. Lord David was not going to say anything unless she prompted him. Well, she excelled at making conversation in difficult circumstances.

"And you, Lord David, how have you been spending your hours?" This was more than difficult, Mia thought. Would she ever ask or hear another question without thinking of that kiss?

It was not so much that she wanted to still be kissing him. Well, yes, it was. Then, at least, the first kiss would be put in its proper place instead of lurking next to every thought she had.

"I have, most likely, lost half of my financial backing for the mill I hope to build. So I have been making a list of likely prospects and composing letters in hopes of forming another partnership with someone who is willing to provide half the funding. And I've been trying to make sense of the plans for the mill and the housing for the workers."

"Housing for the workers? That's unusual."

"Yes, it's an idea I suggested to the duke when he was so discouraged after the failure of his bill to provide care for orphans and widows. Then I found out that the Long Bank Mill already provides such housing. Mr. Sebold seemed to be the logical man to approach about a new mill."

"And Mr. Sebold is the one who bowed out?"

"Yes." His response was instant and final. He might as well have yelled that he was not telling her any more no matter how many kisses she offered him.

"Do you fish, my lord?"

"I do not."

"If you would like to learn to fish with a fly, I could teach you this evening." That was an invitation to trouble. She knew it as well as he did. What she did not know was how he would react to it.

"I have work to finish."

"But fishing is work." She glanced at him and wished she could make him smile. "You know, Lord David, work can be fun." She forestalled his comment with a raised hand. "You are going to say that I have never done a minute's work in my life. But you are forgetting hours practicing scales on the pianoforte. This is exactly the point. I loved music, so the fact it was work did not matter."

"Miss Castellano, I must compose a letter for more financial backing. The duke will not supply more than half from estate funds."

"You are too conscientious, and do not think that is a compliment." She was done trying to coax him. She was not a courtesan and could see where it would be a challenge to seduce someone so hardheaded.

"You can write the letter in the morning before Mr. Novins comes. Evening is the most perfect time of day to be outside. As the light fades and dusk and twilight follow."

"Twilight, then dusk," he said, as though she had made the mistake a dozen times before.

"Twilight comes first?" She stopped to face him. "I've always wondered."

"Twilight comes right after the sun sets or before it rises. In the evening dusk comes after twilight, before complete dark, and in the morning dusk is before twilight, then the sun fills the sky."

"Thank you." She blinked, surprised at his prompt response. "Come fish with me this evening just before twilight until dusk."

"We both know now that would not be wise."

"But don't you grow tired of doing what is wise?" She groaned out the last word and then smiled so he would know she was teasing.

Lord David did not return her smile, or answer her. He was the one who took the lead now, and Mia hurried to keep up.

"So you know about twilight and dusk from your man-of-science brother?"

"No."

"From your days in the navy?"

"Yes."

"You really were in the navy?"

"Yes."

"And you truly were shipwrecked?"

"Yes."

"You are not playing with me? You swear."

He smiled a little, and Mia thought that perhaps the

phrase "playing with me" had not been the wisest phrase to use.

"Miss Castellano, I really was in the navy, was truly shipwrecked, and, with God as my witness, I am going to build a cotton mill."

She winced as she realized that Lord David had told her nothing but the truth that night she had stalked out of the parlor. The night Janina took ill. She thought back to that conversation.

"I hope sometime you will tell me about your experience in Mexico."

"No." His eyes slanted over to her. "How do you like that word when I use it?"

Mia gave up; her disappointment was profound at the way he shut her out once again. Lord David was back to his favorite mode of conversation, one-word sentences.

"I do not know why I ever try to talk to you. You are hopeless!" she shouted. "Take the creel to the kitchen, Lord David. I am going for a walk."

"Do not leave the property." He hefted the creel but did not move toward the house.

"Oh, do be quiet. You are worse than a governess." She walked briskly. All right, she ran back down toward the river, wanting to put as much distance between them as possible.

Mia followed the trail to a spot where a rock marked a river crossing. Sitting on the rock, her dress gathered up to keep it from the wet, she traced the path stone by stone, across the river, wondering where it led.

Who knows where any path leads? she asked herself with a morose sniff. Now she felt like the philosophical Mr. Novins.

She cared more for Bruce the trout than for David Pennistan, so why did his behavior upset her? As profoundly intimate a kiss as possible one minute, and near-complete indifference the next.

Indifference. Made worse by the passionate connection of their kiss. The kiss meant nothing if it led nowhere, like a path that petered out before it reached any definable destination.

Had a kiss ever left her feeling indifferent? Mia could feel her heart sink as she realized that every single kiss before this one had been prosaic. Had left her unmoved. But this one . . .

Is that how courtesans felt about kisses? Unmoved? Perhaps, but kisses still would have meaning. For each one would mean money in the bank. The thought left her feeling vaguely ill.

Mia stood up, deciding she was in need of a small adventure to distract her. Carrying her slippers in her dress, which she gathered above her knees, she took a step onto the crossing.

Cold, it was delightfully cold. With more confidence than she had a right to, Mia found her way to the opposite shore. She dropped her dress and bent over to put on her shoes. She would climb to the crest of the hill and see what was over the rise.

"Mia! That is not Sandleton property. Come back here!"

She whirled. "But there's no one here to contaminate. If I see someone I will run back." She waved and turned to begin her climb.

"Come back! Now!"

"No." His imperious voice could be so irritating. "No," she called out again in a singsong voice.

"Listen to me. It's not safe." Lord David had crossed most of the way, still wearing his shoes. He slipped once and swore as he pulled himself out of the water.

Not safe? That gave her pause. It looked as bucolic as all the other hillsides they had driven by; the hills went up and down with trees and shrubbery in an endless parade.

Mia kept on, hiking more slowly. Within a few yards of the top, and the view, Lord David caught up with her. He grabbed her hand and pulled her back toward the river.

"It's Jasper Dilber. He owns this side of the stream and guards it with a gun and his dogs, his very fierce dogs. Come back."

"All right. All right." His grip was so tight that her fingers were turning numb. "But David, what are the chances that he will be anywhere near here?"

"The odds are very good, once he knows that Sandleton is occupied. You must have seen him this morning when you were angling."

"The old man? He walked the other side of the bank once or twice but I was busy with Bruce so I did no more than glance at him."

At that very moment she could have sworn she heard a dog barking. And there was no mistaking the sound of gunshot that echoed through this little valley. The bullet thudded into the earth about ten feet away from where they stood.

"Damn times fifty."

Lord David did not need to swear for Mia to understand trouble was rushing toward them. When she looked in the direction from which the shot had come, she saw the same old man, now pausing to reload. His dogs had no such encumbrance and raced toward them. They were black and not too big, but what they lacked in size they made up for with their snarling, barking frenzy. As if they could hardly wait to rip her throat out.

She grabbed a handful of rocks just as Lord David tore off his coat and wrapped it around his arm.

"Call 'em off, Dilber," Lord David bellowed. "I'll use my knife."

Dilber looked up with a sharp jerk and Lord David showed a knife.

Lord David carries a knife. On his own property.

The thoughts flitted through her mind with a dozen more practical ones. If she threw rocks, would that discourage the dogs or make them worse? Could they be worse than they were already? Could dogs be infected with smallpox? Would they go for her neck or her hands? If she ran to the river, would they follow? Could she and David cross faster than the dogs? Would she rather die of smallpox or a dog mauling?

"Stay behind me and lead us to the water," Lord David whispered. His direction cleared her mind, and Mia began to do as he asked. Half pulling him, she did her best to avoid anything that would trip him, watching the ground and trusting him to be her best defense.

The dogs were no more than five yards away when Dilber halted them with a sharp whistle. The command did not mean retreat but at least she and David had a better chance of reaching the water boundary before the brutes reached them.

"My guest crossed the river by mistake. She will not do it again."

They had reached the bank and while Dilber watched, David turned to her. "Cross and I will follow once you are safe."

How far did she have to go to be safe? Mia did not want to distract him by asking. So she made her way back to Pennistan property far more quickly than she had crossed before, not noticing the cold water at all this time. Only when she stepped onto the shore did Mia realize that she had forgotten to remove her shoes.

Before David could follow, Dilber whistled again, a different pattern this time, and the dogs charged forward.

Mia screamed as the dogs leaped at David and caught the arm he'd wrapped in his coat. She threw one rock as she moved across the water once again. She threw as many as she could find. Only one hit Lord David; the rest distracted the dogs so that he could back across the stream before the dogs attacked him again.

When Mia ran out of ammunition, she stopped to collect more and the dogs raced down to the water's edge. Dilber whistled again, and before they knew if the dogs would follow them across the river, the animals obeyed their master's summons and abandoned pursuit. The frenzied barking continued.

When Lord David stepped on dry ground, Mia grabbed his arm.

"Are you hurt?"

"Out of sight, first." He panted out the words as he grabbed her hand. They charged up the path to the lawn. Finally, with one last gunshot from Dilber and a whistle to the dogs, who fell silent, the adventure ended.

They both dropped to their knees on the grass.

"Are you hurt? Did they bite you?"

"No. They ruined a good piece of clothing but they did not draw blood."

She turned to him and searched his face. "You took no harm?"

"None, Mia."

He could have been angry with her. He could have been sarcastic. At the very least he could have been rude, but the sweetness with which he spoke, the reassurance of those two words melted something inside her.

He had risked his life to rescue her.

Mia fell back on the grass, her legs tucked under her. The lawn was dry and the sun was so welcoming that she thought this the perfect spot to recuperate.

"Are you going to faint? I will carry you to the house."

"No, no," she said. Reaching up, she took his hand and pulled him down on the grass beside her. "Stay here a bit and let the sun dry us. I did not fall in the water like you did, but somehow my dress is all wet. If we are at least dry, then Mrs. Cantwell is less likely to ask what happened."

They lay side by side for a few minutes. She could hear bees and birds and Lord David's breathing as it slowed to normal. She began to laugh; she could not help it.

"Are you having hysterics?" His tone made it sound more frightening than dogs or smallpox.

"No. I am not having hysterics." Another question. One more and she *would* stop counting.

"You are truly laughing."

Mia nodded, even though he was not looking at her. "The absurdity of it. Can you see the story in the gossip column? 'Lord David Pennistan finally loses a fight. To a dog.'"

"'Mia Castellano finds that dogs in England do not understand the word *no*.'" David made his own contribution.

"'Dilber, despite his sixty-plus years, easily defeats Pennistan without throwing a punch.'"

"'Pennistan lives in fear that Miss Castellano will eventually find herself in a predicament from which he cannot save her.'" Now he was laughing, too.

She had never heard him laugh before. She marveled at the richness of it, as though to compensate for how rarely he used it. He stopped too soon.

When she opened her eyes she saw him raised on his elbow, watching her.

"I'm sorry, Mia. I accept the blame completely. I should have warned you about Dilber. He is no more than a vindictive old fool but still, with a gun and those dogs, he is dangerous."

"Does he think you covet his property?"

"No, he covets whatever is ours."

His eyes made her forget what they were talking about. As much as she wanted to hear him laugh again, she loved his eyes when he was being serious, the way he spoke so much more eloquently with them than with words.

"Why is it that you handle emergencies with such a cool head?"

"That was an adventure, Lord David, not an emergency. You would call me a hysterical woman or some kind of green girl if I cowered when faced with an adventure."

"Since when does it matter what I call you?"

He did not wait for an answer but pressed his mouth, his body to her. Any remaining chill disappeared. For a hard, reticent, insensitive man, his soft dear kisses conveyed volumes.

She lost the ability to think as she began yet another adventure with him, a further step into a world she had never imagined before and now could hardly wait to become a part of. Their kisses grew more fevered, the feel of his lips on her neck, beneath her ear and trailing down until she could feel her breasts peak. Suddenly he made the cruelest move of all: Just when she thought the world had turned into a place for only the two of them, he rolled away from her.

Chapter Eighteen

DAMN HIM TO HELL times ninety, who did he think he was with? Some dairymaid who would enjoy a casual tumble? A courtesan who thought an outdoor coupling would be different? He was with a virgin, a girl under his family's protection.

David sat up and began to pull bits of grass from his suit. He felt her doing the same to his back and wanted to yell at her to leave him alone. Not to touch him. To run as far and fast as she could.

"No," Mia said as if she could read his mind.

"I did not say a word."

"You did not have to, Lord David. Your body is as tense as a string pulled taut. You do not want me to touch you. You want me to leave and never come back. That is what I said no to."

"You don't sound insulted."

"Because I'm not. I think urging me to leave when you are so obviously, um, interested in something else is a very noble, or perhaps even a romantic declaration."

"Oh, God, spare me the predictability of women."

"I suspect that women are predictable because they are right."

"I am not being noble, Miss Castellano."

She laughed and took a pile of the grass she had just picked off him and rained it on his head. "Call me Mia, at least when we are in private, and admit that two kisses, two kisses like the ones we've shared, take us beyond 'miss' and 'my lord.'"

"We will not be in private again."

"We are in quarantine, David. We are in private no matter where we are."

He stood up, did not offer her a hand. He knew what that would lead to. "I am going to collect the creel."

"From where we kissed before?"

"Where I left it when I suspected what trouble you would find. I am going back to the house and changing my clothes, unless you are too cold and wish to go first."

"Thank you, but I am quite dry now and too warm. How did that happen? I wonder." She raised two fingers to her mouth as if she had to think very, very hard. She felt absurdly happy even as he turned and headed toward the house.

Then she remembered exactly why they were trapped there, alone.

*   *   *

"I AM CERTAIN that is a bug bite, my dear."

"Oh, thank you, Mrs. Cantwell." Now Mia knew exactly how Catherine Morland felt in *Northanger Abbey* when she insisted that the dresser be moved only to find it did not cover a secret door to a hidden passage. Relief and embarrassment.

"It's beyond strange to have life be so normal, or at least appear normal, and then all of a sudden I remember why I'm here and not at Pennford." *Or London. Or Bath.*

Mia could have fastened her dress but turned around so that Mrs. Cantwell could help her. Gathering her hair, she held it over her head so that it was not in the way.

"How is the coachman?"

"He is not improving as quickly as Mr. Novins would like, miss, and the surgeon will not speculate on what is causing his illness."

"How troublesome, or maybe he does not wish to be wrong."

"Or he has no idea." The housekeeper patted Mia's shoulder. "There you are, my dear. Would you like help with your hair?"

"No, I am only going to tie it back."

"Then I will see to the fish." She paused at the door. "May I suggest, miss, that I cook the trout for dinner, perhaps stuffed with onion? And that you and Lord David have dinner at midday rather than in the evening? I will use the chicken bones for stock and make a soup for supper. It is hardly the sort of meal you are used to but I trust it will serve in an emergency."

"That would be excellent, Mrs. Cantwell. Shall I come help you by cutting, or is it chopping, the onions?"

"Cutting or chopping will both serve the purpose and you will count as an angel if you are willing."

She was being a help. She did not loll in her room all day reading her book and demanding someone bring her tea. And except for the sore arms from fishing she felt perfectly healthy. What a relief that was.

In the kitchen they found the bread and the basket with the meat pies.

"It will be a while before dinner is ready. After I clean the fish, I must make the beds and check on the sickroom before I start. If you are hungry, miss, have a meat pie now."

"I should wait." Mia's protest was halfhearted but she firmed her resolve, ignored her hunger, and took the three onions that Mrs. Cantwell gave her. With an apron to protect her dress, Mia took up the knife. "I can make the beds when I am finished with the onions, Mrs. Cantwell."

"No, miss. When he came in Lord David made it clear that I am the only one to go into his room."

"He did? How insulting." Anger surged through her.

Mia raised the knife and began cutting, or chopping, the onions, and despite the very sharp knife within a minute tears were flowing.

"The things I've seen, miss, they would shock you. Women are forever trying to find a way to hide in a gentleman's bedroom. Gentlemen are much more direct."

"I would never hide in a man's bedroom. It would be

too demeaning." She wanted men to come to her, would settle for nothing less.

"Of course not, miss. You have enough pride not to stoop to such behavior. You and Lord David are alike that way."

Alike? That could not be, Mia thought but was too polite to say out loud. Though it could explain why the kiss had been so amazing.

Mia wiped the tears and grabbed the last onion. "Tell me more. Please," she added with a smile that invited secrets.

"One lady hid in the armoire. Another had herself made up into the bed. There was a time when two ladies were both hiding in different places in the same bedroom. Neither one of them came out until morning."

Did that mean that the gentleman found both of them and sent neither one away? Mia wanted to ask but did not want to betray her lack of sophistication.

She would look through the bookshelves more carefully this evening. Maybe she could find a book of drawings that would explain what three people could do together.

Mrs. Cantwell handed her some lemon soap to remove the smell of onion from her hands, and just as Mia was drying her fingers her stomach growled.

"Eat a meat pie, miss. You can pretend you are not hungry but your stomach insists otherwise."

"All right. The only thing I've eaten today is one of Janina's sweets. Indeed," she said in surprise, "I was up at first light so it's the middle of the day for me."

Choosing the smallest of the four meat pies, she broke off a tiny portion and ate it. "Oh, it's delicious. Made with minced pork, onions, and some seasoning I do not quite recognize. Coriander, I think."

"Indeed? I thought that they would be from Mrs. Henderson's recipe. She is a dab hand at meat pies. Her crust is as flaky as possible but she does not favor spices beyond salt and pepper."

"Do you know who made the bread? I should like to send them our thanks."

"I could guess it comes from Miss Horner. She always puts raisins and cinnamon in her Sunday bread."

"Miss Horner? Then I will definitely write a note." Writing to her would establish some contact and then, perhaps, Mia thought, she could suggest a meeting when they were free of the quarantine. Of course it was Mr. Novins who had to act but she would like to meet the lady who had won him so thoroughly.

"No special thanks are necessary. Helping in hard times is what people in Sandleton do."

Mia took another bite and used a cloth nearby as a serviette. Hardly good manners, but the situation did allow for some leeway. No one needed to wash more plates and cutlery than absolutely necessary.

"Stop eating that!" Lord David commanded as he came into the kitchen. "We don't know who made it."

Mia's answer was to pop the last bite into her mouth and swallow without chewing it. "Do you think the villagers are out to poison us?" Her tone added, "You, sir, have a problem with paranoia."

"You've only had one, I trust."

"Yes, and I am still hungry, but I will leave the rest for you just in case they are poisoned and have another of the sweets that Janina gave me." She picked out the biggest, did not offer him any, and put the box, carefully rewrapped, back on the pantry shelf.

Without another word, Mia went to the door with every intention of staying in her room until dinner. She needed a small rest anyway after rising so early. The door almost toppled her as Basil pushed it open from the other side.

He charged into the room and hurried on without a word of apology.

"Mrs. Cantwell. Lord David." He looked from one to the other. "Please come. John Coachman is not breathing. I think he's dead!"

Basil had not commanded Mia's attendance, but no one could keep her away. She followed the other three up the stairs to the sickroom. The second groom was wide-eyed and had moved as far away from the coachman as he could, pressing himself into a corner with a blanket wrapped around him.

There was no doubt John Coachman had gone to God. Mia knew that look at least as well as anyone in the room. The peace, the complete repose of the face, all the lines gone as though he had lost twenty years and was young again. It had been the same with her father and even Elena's husband, though his death had been more sudden.

Mia stayed by the door, feeling slightly ill, and wondered

what had caused the coachman's death and how long it would be before they all were sick.

"Listen to me, Basil," Lord David said, giving the groom a steadying look. "Go to the gate and tell the man there to fetch Mr. Novins. The surgeon has been expecting this."

Basil nodded at Lord David and hurried away.

"What did you say?" Mia left the door and went to stand in front of Lord David. "This is beyond tolerable, you mean-spirited dictator. You thought John Coachman would die and you did not tell any of us?" Mia looked from Lord David to an unsurprised Mrs. Cantwell. "Oh, I see. I was the only one you would not tell. Because you thought I would not handle it well. Let me tell you, keeping the truth from me is what I do not handle well." She wanted to slap him but had some presence of mind, though not quite enough. As she spoke she pushed him once, twice, and would have done it a third time if he had not grabbed her wrists to stop her.

Lord David closed his eyes but she saw the anger and distress before he hid it from her. "Miss Castellano." He spoke very, very quietly, in great contrast to her raised voice. "You are in the presence of a man who died in my service. You will treat him with the respect he deserves and stop shouting."

He was right. Oh, God, he was right. The poor man was dead and she was acting like a fishwife.

Mrs. Cantwell put her arm around Mia and whispered, "It was Mr. Novins who suggested keeping it a secret. Even Basil did not know."

Once again Mia Castellano was on a par with the servants, the lesser servants. They moved nearer the door. Mia found her self-control and prayed for John Coachman's soul, for his family, for any sins that would keep him from heaven, even as her hands began to shake with fear.

After a few minutes, Mia left the room. Her stomach was beginning to ache in earnest. She should never have gobbled that meat pie so quickly. In her room she curled up on the bed, still dressed, and allowed herself tears.

How many days had it been since she swore she would never cry again? Well, someone's death was a valid exception, was it not?

When she heard Mr. Novins arrive, she rose, washed her face, and went to the front parlor so she could have a word with him when he was ready to leave.

She was a grown woman and was determined to be treated like one. If she was going to die she wanted to know the details, every detail, from the man in charge. And that was not Lord David, who had a way of making her feel as big as a peach pit, and as important.

Her stomach rumbled, not from hunger this time, and she rubbed it with her hand, wishing that Janina was here to take care of her.

If Janina was still alive.

Mia sat down and began to sob in earnest. Not quiet tears that trailed down her cheeks but gasping sobs that sounded as though they were being ripped from her.

Oh, Janina, poor Nina, please be well soon. With a monumental effort she controlled her gulping sobs, and with two shuddering breaths she was almost calm again.

Mia picked up her guitar, but only plucked a few of the strings, notes that would be a song if she made the effort. But she did not have the strength at the moment.

"Miss Castellano?" Mr. Novins came into the room when she stopped playing. "Lord David said it would be all right if I came to speak with you."

"Thank you, Mr. Novins." She wanted to tell him that Lord David was neither her husband nor her lover and had no right to dictate who should talk to her, but she was so tired she could barely make her lips move.

"I wanted to reassure you. I believe that the coachman's death was from a head injury and not from the illness that led to the quarantine. The other groom is most fully recovered from his distress, and once I receive word about the well-being of your maid I will be able to release you all from quarantine. That should happen any day now."

It was a veritable speech for Mr. Novins and Mia nodded, raising a hand to her face to rub at her eyes and clear her vision. "Thank you, Mr. Novins. I appreciate the information."

"Miss Castellano, now may not be the ideal moment . . ." Mr. Novins began, quite in earnest. Of course, Mia thought, now when she was so fatigued and her stomach hurt, he wanted to talk about Miss Horner, or at the very least express amazement at her good humor through the ordeal.

Mia did not want to hear one more person express surprise at her ability to be thoughtful, especially in the face of her most recent failure. Maybe later. Right now all she wanted was her bed.

"Mr. Novins, please excuse me. I was up early and am very tired. I am going to my room for some prayer and some rest."

Mia left the room and made it up the stairs and into her bedchamber before she accepted that she was about to be most unwell. She grabbed the chamber pot, and before she could take another step was thoroughly and completely sick.

In that way of sickness the few minutes afterward was free of nausea. She changed out of her dress, stays, and chemise, ruining the laces of the stays with her impatience, and put on a clean chemise. Mia knew there was no hiding her nausea in a house this small, even with no staff.

Oh, hell, she thought, quite deliberately using the word, *I should have stayed dressed long enough to tell Mrs. Cantwell so she could tell Lord David,* to whom Mia was still never going to speak.

Mia went back into the dressing room and wrapped herself in a dressing gown the moment before the insidious pain began to build. She pulled open the door, intending to call for Mrs. Cantwell, but dizziness overwhelmed her and she careened into the passage and Lord David instead.

He took her by the shoulders—why was he always doing that?—and as she began to gag she tried to turn away from him.

"No," he said. "Do it right here on the floor. It will be easier to clean up than if you trail it across the rug."

She wanted to shout, "Do you think you can give permission for everything?" but she knew what would happen when she opened her mouth, so she bent over and let what was left of her stomach's contents land on the hardwood floor, not feeling one whit of regret when some fell on his highly polished boots.

This time the retching left her weak and the dizziness added to her confusion. Lord David used a handkerchief to wipe his boots and left the bit of linen on the floor. He swooped her up in his arms and took her back into her room, putting her on the bed.

Mia was well enough in the moment to have the vague thought that this was the second time he had carried her in his arms and it was even less romantic than the first time, which she would have thought impossible.

She propped herself up in bed, feeling better in a sitting position. Lord David left the room without explanation and came back a moment later with a clean chamber pot, which he left on the table next to the bed.

He took the used pot with him and left the room still without saying a word. Mia closed her eyes and settled herself against the upraised pillow as the nausea began to build again. God help poor Janina if this was how she had felt.

Mia endured the torture of repeated bouts of nausea alone, and was grateful for it. It was too humiliating an experience to share with anyone.

She offered her suffering up for any sins the coachman

may have committed. It was a very Catholic way of think-ing, but at the moment it was the only good she could see coming from this wretchedness. She was in such misery she would not even wish it on Lord David.

Periodically Mrs. Cantwell would come in and wipe her forehead with a damp cloth and bring a clean chamber pot. Where was Mr. Novins? Was she so far beyond hope that he was not even going to examine her?

Sleep, the only escape, was impossible, and she could feel her body growing weaker and weaker. Finally she fell into a state that was somewhere else. Not asleep, not awake; a preview of hell. Death did not seem so bad if it would mean an end to the constant cycle of nausea and vomiting.

Lord David came in once, at least she thought he did. Or could it have been a dream? No matter, it was a wel-come break from the nightmare.

He was so gentle, carefully pushing each strand of hair from her face, smoothing the sheet, all while at eye level, as though he had knelt beside the bed.

"Listen to me." His voice sounded different, too, as though he had a hard time speaking. Still, the command she knew so well echoed even in his whisper. "You are not going to die." He took her hand and squeezed it, silent for a long, long time. "This will pass and you will recover."

Gentle or not, he was still telling her what to do—as if he could choose life or death. But this one time she would try to do exactly what he wanted.

Chapter Nineteen

MIA HEARD SOMEONE open the door. It was the most wonderful sound in the world. The blessed click of the door handle was, for her, a celebration of life. For the first time in an eternity of hours she was aware of something outside of herself.

Mr. Novins came into the room. With Lord David behind him. The surgeon came over to the side of the bed nearest the window.

Neither spoke at first. Lord David walked over to the mantel and wound her clock, and then came to stand on the other side of the bed.

"You do not have smallpox," Lord David announced.

"You are not God." She was too weak to say anything else. With all the strength she had, she turned her head away from him and looked at Mr. Novins.

"Yes, I do realize that despite being able to command

most of this small world at Sandleton, I cannot decide what illness you have."

She wondered why he was humoring her unless she was about to die. "Where have you been?"

"Here, at least five times. The question is, where have you been?"

She shook her head. Talking took too much energy.

"Yes, you are better, but exhaustion can still take a toll."

Mr. Novins looked at Lord David, who gave a curt nod. What secret did they have?

"Mia," David began, "Mr. Novins has a posset that he and the apothecary devised for Miss Horner's mother."

Mr. Novins picked up the story. "She grows so weak sometimes that Mary is afraid she will slip away."

Mia drew a breath. She could understand that. Even breathing seemed like work.

"The posset will help you regain strength, but it may well dredge up unpleasant memories. It's as if the body is trying to dispel anything that weakens it. Would you try it and see if it will help you?"

They both waited, as though afraid of her answer. Well, she was not a fool. Of course she wanted to be better as soon as possible. She could withstand a few more bad dreams. She gave Mr. Novins the slightest nod and closed her eyes.

"Stay awake a moment more, Mia." She felt David sit on the edge of the bed and gather her close. "Open your mouth and let Novins dose you."

She did as he wished and felt the cold tasteless syrup

slide down her throat. Mia felt it trickle all the way down
to her stomach and thread its way to her extremities in a
most peculiar way.

"Don't leave me," she whispered, forcing her eyes
open to look at Lord David, unable to see his expression
through her watering eyes.

Mr. Novins cleared his throat. She had already forgotten he was there. "Miss Castellano, I will explain what
happened when you are feeling better."

Mia felt Lord David nod to the surgeon and heard the
door click shut.

"Tell me what I can do to make you more comfortable."

"Just hold me."

He could have argued. He could have refused. He
could have patted her hand and assumed she was deliri-
ous. Instead David Pennistan let go of her only long
enough to tug off his boots, pull off his coat, loosen his
cravat, and then set himself on the bed, on top of the covers, lifting Mia into his arms again.

Lying against his chest was the most comfortable
place in the world. If death was going to take her, this
would be the perfect place from which to leave this world.

"You will tell me if you are going to be sick again? I
think it's over. Mr. Novins said four hours."

"Forever," she whispered.

"Yes, I know it feels like an eternity since it started.
You must talk to Gabriel about how time is distorted by
pain."

His voice, the way it sounded so everyday and normal, was as comforting as his arms.

"Contagious?" she asked.

"No." He was quiet a minute and as if sensing that she loathed his one-word sentences added, "Rest now and let me explain later."

Let me. Had he asked her permission? How very unique. She must be on her deathbed. But if she was, then there would be no "later."

"Heaven." It was all she could manage, but thought that he should know the joy of conversing with someone who used one-word sentences.

"Shh." He smoothed her hair, which she was sure was tangled and damp from her fever. "Rest now, Mia."

"Talk." She was almost asleep but was afraid that she would not wake up if she closed her eyes.

"All right. I'll talk about anything you want if you will rest and try to sleep."

"Mexico."

She was asleep. He could tell by the even breathing and the lack of tension in her body. David lifted his other leg onto the bed since it appeared he was going to be with her a while. He might as well be comfortable. Mrs. Cantwell was napping and, frankly, he was sure he did not care, and did not think Mia would, if the housekeeper came to the room and found them together. There was no doubt in his mind that Mrs. Cantwell had seen far more shocking sights in this house.

Mia Castellano was not going to die. He tried to believe it, and for the first time in hours he felt his fear ease, the tension leach from his neck and shoulders.

Not from smallpox, at any rate, or any other disease. Novins had been sure from the beginning that this was food poisoning. Despite his suspicions earlier, when faced with the evidence, David could hardly credit that someone had tried to harm them, kill them, to make sure that whatever contagion was among them was not spread. Fear made monsters of some people and weaklings of others.

He'd all but cried, hadn't he, when he had come to the room with Novins to find her so weakened that her head lolled back when Novins shifted her away from the soiled sheets. She'd looked more dead than alive. The fear that gripped his heart had stunned him.

Her breathing changed, coming now in an odd gasping sound, but she slept on. He hoped that this would be the worst of Novins's predicted "unsettling memories," and that when she awakened she would be on the mend.

It was hard to believe that he missed the way she moved, jumped up from a chair, hurried from one side of the room to another. Mia Castellano did nothing slowly and yet managed to be as graceful as any lady he knew. He told himself he would have another chance to watch her fish, that she was going to be healthy again. He pictured the elegance with which she cast the line and played the fish that tested it.

He would love to watch her do any number of things, he thought, and wondered if she would make love with the same energy with which she did everything else. He imagined that bed would be one place where *no* was not her favorite word.

Her breathing grew more restless and she began to mumble words that were unintelligible at first.

"I'm sorry," she mumbled, and he tried to think of what she felt the need to apologize for.

"It's all right, Mia." He felt her tears on his shirt.

"Papa! Papa! Please."

That was when he realized it was a dream. He continued to hold her, at times quite firmly, as she struggled against the nightmare memory, giving him no more clue to its content than her father's name.

At times her "Papa" was accompanied by short rapid breaths as if she were doing some kind of physical work. He tried to shift her a little so that she could breathe more easily but she grabbed his shirt and pulled herself up farther into his lap. "Help me, help me."

He had never heard her beg before this and wished he could help her. Novins had not told him how difficult this would be for him to listen to, powerless to help or even give comfort.

She flung out her hand and banged the headboard, accidentally or on purpose, he had no idea. "Help, please help me." Then she lowered her voice to a whisper. "Papa. Papa."

David was not sure if she was shaking or if he was, but her breaths finally evened out and he thought she had fallen into a more restful sleep. He rubbed her shoulder, hoping she would sense his presence.

She stopped talking, but he could feel the tension in

her as she dreamed in silence. He was no stranger to nightmares, nor was Gabriel's wife, Lynette. She insisted that it was better not to awaken dreamers. Often they remembered nothing if allowed to continue sleeping. Waking them brought the memory to their awareness when it was the last thing any of them wanted.

David wondered if Gabriel found the experience of watching Lynette dream as maddening as he did, when the only help you could offer was waiting it out.

Then without warning, Mia threw herself at him, kissing his chest through his shirt, pressing herself against him as if she was an experienced woman with needs she could not control.

"Please, make love to me." She moved her hand lower.

"That is enough, Mia. Wake up." David moved his body so she could not feel his arousal.

"I hate you, William. Hate you. *Dio mio,* must you be a gentleman all the time?"

She stopped suddenly, as though someone had slapped her, and began to cry, not real tears and the more frightening for it. Mia collapsed to the bed and thrashed around for a few moments. When she settled, he picked her up and held her against his chest. He had no idea why he did it. Yes, he did. He wanted her to feel, even if she could not understand, that she was not alone.

Chapter Twenty

WHEN MIA WOKE a little while later, she gave David a smile that reassured him. He hoped it meant she did not recall her nightmares and, more important, that she was feeling better.

"Talk to me," she commanded in a sleep-slurred voice. "Tell me about Mexico, Lord David."

"First look at me," he said.

She braced herself on her elbow and stretched as she turned to look up at him. Her breasts pressed against his ribs. He reminded himself that she was recovering, but not before he wondered if the bite mark that had so frightened her was still visible.

"I'm looking, Lord David."

"You are definitely improving." She was fully awake, unlike the first time she had opened her eyes. "I hear it in your voice." Though her eyes were still not as bright as they should be. "Let's try a different position."

This time her lips did tilt up. He ignored his own double entendre and stood up, letting her settle back on the pillow.

"My arm is cramped. I need to move about." He went to the door.

"Don't leave."

David had his back to her but could hear the alarm in her voice. "I am only going to find you some soothing tea. Listen to me; I will not leave you."

She did not answer him and when he looked back at her, her face was turned away, as though she were staring out the window. Only the curtains were drawn and he could hear her sniffles.

"If you are feeling unwell again—" he began, but she interrupted.

"No, but I can't stop crying and I do not know why."

"All right," he said, meaning the opposite. He came around to the other side of the bed, between the bed and the window, and stooped down to look into her face.

"Stay," she said softly. "Tell me about Mexico."

His relief was out of all proportion. Her peremptory command should have annoyed him; instead, it convinced him that Mia Castellano was on her way to recovery. He laughed, his relief so great that he could not contain it.

"What is so funny?" Her voice brimmed with suspicion.

"I think I must be laughing for the same reason you are crying. Relief."

She nodded and both of them did their best to control the excess of sensibility. Finally David cleared his throat.

"I am going to send Mrs. Cantwell to you. She will help you change and bring clean linen so you do not take a chill. Then I will bring you some chamomile tea. Olivia insists that, after her chicken soup, it is the best cure-all there is."

"Mrs. Cantwell is busy. I can take care of myself." She tried to prove it by throwing back the covers and standing up. Instead she proved she was as weak as a newborn. David caught her and held her against him.

"You have to test everything for yourself. You never trust anyone to know better. That will only find trouble, Mia."

"I'm sorry." She snuggled a little closer. "Well, not that sorry." He all but tossed her back on the bed.

"Stop that. You have been a valiant soldier." He suspected that under normal circumstances she would never have told anyone she was ill. "Do not ruin it by behaving like a spoiled courtesan." David moved away from the bed and her hurt expression. "I am going to send Mrs. Cantwell to you. She has no other patients and we all want you well as soon as possible."

He meant that in the kindest way, but she turned her head away from him and he was sure she was crying again. It was the illness, he told himself. And his poor choice of words. If he apologized he was sure he would only make things worse.

"THERE YOU ARE. Clean clothes and fresh linen make all the difference, don't they, dearie?"

Mia nodded. She did feel better. Cleaning her teeth and rinsing her mouth may have been all she really needed, because now she was completely exhausted all over again. "What time is it? How long have I been ill?"

"It's been almost twelve hours, my dear."

"Twelve hours! Is that all? I feel as though I have been in this bed forever."

"It is close to midnight of the day you first took sick."

Mia shook her head. Mrs. Cantwell would have no reason to lie. She yawned and settled back onto the pillows.

"No, miss. No sleep yet. You must have some tea, a little something to start your body working again. It's right here. Lord David brought it while you were changing. Wasn't that kind of him? This house is topsy-turvy when a gentleman is doing a servant's work. One or two spoonfuls and you can sleep as long as you want."

Mrs. Cantwell supported Mia's head with her arm as if she were a baby and spooned some of the weak tea into her mouth. Mia swallowed and felt the warmth all the way down her throat. Another two spoonfuls were all she could manage.

"Sleep now. When you wake up I will give you some chicken broth and toast."

The thought made her want to gag, but she nodded and turned her head into the pillow. Her stomach muscles ached from the way they had been abused, but that was the only discomfort she felt. If she had been through hell before, she now had a glimpse of heaven. Not paradise, but comfort and quiet and this one moment of peace.

She was very aware that Lord David had not come back and talked to her as he promised. There was nothing surprising about that, she assured herself. Mia had learned that men often said one thing and did another.

She fell asleep, convinced that if she could recover from this illness alone, she could face anything and win.

"I TOLD YOU that I wanted to talk with her before she went to sleep again." David could not believe the housekeeper had not called him.

"I'm sorry, my lord." Mrs. Cantwell's voice held no regret. "Now that life is almost back to normal, now that we know we are not subject to some contagion, I think it would be highly inappropriate for you to be in Miss Castellano's bedroom for any reason."

"Mrs. Cantwell, I appreciate your sensibilities, especially when I consider what goes on in this house, but as long as there are only three of us here, then no one will know unless we tell them. Miss Castellano is still recovering and I know how important it is to her that she not be alone when she is in distress."

"As you wish, my lord, but she is asleep now."

"And when she wakes up the first thing she will think is that I did not come back as I said I would." At her continued expression of disapproval he added, "I will leave the door open."

Mrs. Cantwell shrugged.

"I promised her, and I keep my promises." *Damn times four,* this woman was not his mother, his tutor, or his first lieutenant. He could do as he wanted. David left the kitchen without trying to justify his actions any further.

Mia's room was dark, the moon too old to have risen yet; besides, the curtains were drawn. He left the door open as he said he would and pulled the chair some distance away from the bed. He could see she was sleeping more naturally now. What a relief.

The clock in the front hall chimed four before she woke up. He had lit a second candle so that when she turned her head she would be able to see him sitting nearby. She stared at him but did not say anything.

"Good day to you, Mia."

"What time is it?"

"Close to sunrise."

She showed no emotion or anything more than vague interest.

"Why are you here?"

He leaned forward, his elbows on his knees. "So you would not be alone when you woke up. I promised."

She gave a slight nod. He allowed the silence. It was a long one.

"I feel so much better."

"You are going to live a hundred years to torment as many men as you can find."

"Has anyone else died?"

There was that unexpected generosity again. "No, we are all safe and, except for the groom, everyone is well."

"Even Janina?"

"Yes. Basil came back from the inn to tell us that Romero is there and will accompany your maid here so that we can all go to Pennford together."

She closed her eyes and pressed her hands together. "Thank God. Oh, thank you, thank you, God."

He stood up. She did not stop him.

"Mrs. Cantwell seemed to think that it was not proper for me to stay with you. I will leave if you agree."

"Nonsense." She sounded bored. "Though I imagine you are tired."

He knew he should be tired. But at this moment elation banished fatigue. Mia was on the mend; his world was brighter, and it had nothing to do with the first light of day. David almost blurted out the truth. That his world would be incredibly dreary without her.

Thank the good Lord he had enough sense to keep his mouth shut and not give her that weapon.

"Mia." David pulled the chair closer, sat, and touched the hand that lay outside the covers. It felt cool, any fever well and truly gone. "Mrs. Cantwell left some chicken broth for you, and some toast that may still be edible."

"Perhaps she can bring me the toast but I do not want anything else yet."

"Mrs. Cantwell is abed, but I will bring it to you."

When she did not answer he tried a different tack. "You have to eat."

"No."

He could grow to love that word. He leaned even closer, took her hand, and kissed it. Her surprise was embarrassingly genuine. "I am going to bring the toast and you will eat it."

She laughed.

Perfect. It was a pathetic breathy sound but he was happy to be able to predict her so well.

"I will spit it out before I swallow it."

"I can almost believe you would. As a matter of fact I can see it." He came even closer, lifted her in his arms. She tried to wiggle out of his hold. "You see, you are too weak to escape. So I will hold you against me and push a small bit down your throat. You will start to gag, but the thought of being sick again will be so repugnant that you will swallow and I will win."

"That is not a fair contest," she said, with a coquettish smile. "I almost died. You are supposed to be nice to me."

"I am being nice. If I was my usual callous self I would insist that we leave for Pennford today and not wait until you are strong enough."

"Oh." She was silent a moment. "Well, then bring the toast. What are you waiting for?" she added, as if she were not the one who had resisted the idea of food.

He ran down to the kitchen, afraid she would change her mind if he did not hurry. The toast was still edible, and he brought some more of the chamomile tea.

She had worked herself into a sitting position and had

a pillow on her lap to hold the tray. She took a sip of tea and nibbled the toast, and even nodded when he asked if she would like a little peach jam on it. She managed half of the toast and jelly and the whole cup of tea, then laid her head back. "I am tired already," she admitted with reluctance.

"Go to sleep. It is the best way to heal, to give your insides a chance to right themselves again."

"We are free? There is no smallpox? No other disease?"

He took the tray and put it on the chair behind him. "It was food poisoning."

She blinked her surprise.

"From the sweets Romero sent with Janina."

"No!"

He could see her real distress.

"Accidental, purely accidental. There were some sweetmeats in the mix that were rancid. The honey masked the taste. At least that is the best explanation Mr. Novins has."

"Romero's mother will be so upset."

"I understand she is, and that's the reason she was more than willing to let her son come to escort Janina."

Mia nodded, as though that seemed like a fair penance. "Where is Mr. Novins? Why has he not been to see me?"

"He was called to the next village to deliver a babe and has yet to return."

"Of course. How selfish of me. Mr. Novins will have quite a number of calls to make now that his own self-imposed quarantine is over."

"That is not something you have to fret about. You have to eat and regain your strength so that we can be at Pennford when Elena's baby comes."

That gave her pause, but only for a moment. "I will eat, but each time I do, you will have to tell me something of Mexico."

"I will tell you about Mexico only if you tell me about your father and your life in Italy."

"All right," she agreed readily. "Start now and I will eat more of the toast."

Her instant response made him realize that there would be happy as well as sad tales. Unlike those of his years in Mexico.

His head began to pound and David wondered if he was about to take his turn in a sickbed.

"The toast first." He returned the tray to her lap and refilled her teacup.

"You talk while I eat."

"This is like bargaining with a merchant."

"Isn't it fun?" She took a bite of the toast and waited.

"No more than a bit of geography this time, as you are already half asleep."

"I'm waiting," she said around her bite of toast.

"Not Mexico. I was shipwrecked on Isla Mexicado."

She swallowed and shook her head. "I never heard of it." She wrinkled her brow, looking suspicious. She did not believe him.

"Not many people have. But it did exist. It is gone now."

"This sounds like a fairy tale you are devising for the sickroom."

"I know, but if you will let me tell the story you will see that it is the darkest sort of fairy tale."

Her smile winked out and her eyes grew wider.

"Now that I know you are an angler I will no longer be surprised at the scope of your knowledge. Are you an expert in globes and maps?"

"Not an expert, but I was very good at it in the school-room. I always wanted to visit the Galapagos. It has such a musical name. Tell me where to find Isla Mexicado."

"Somewhere to the east of Mexico. That's all I know. I have never found it on a map or globe and I think I may have been the first European to ever set foot there."

"Oh my." She was quiet a moment. "You are promising me that you are telling the truth?"

"Yes, Mia. I am."

"Did they treat you as a god?"

"Most definitely not." He stood.

She finished her toast and grabbed at his sleeve, her words coming out in a rush. "I was born in Naples. My mother died when I was three and my father and his sister took care of me until she married. I was nine, and so Papa and I managed alone. He played the harpsichord but his real genius was in building them." She paused, lifting the teacup to her lips. "Now tell me how you escaped."

"I didn't." Why was he doing this? It was like inviting her into his nightmare when she had enough of her own. "Sleep now and you can tell me more about Italy later."

"But I want to know. I need to know what they did to you."

His head was pounding, his admittedly limited patience pushed beyond bearing, so he told her the truth.

"Once they had nursed me to health they sold me into slavery."

Chapter Twenty-one

MIA DID HER BEST not to choke on the tea. "David! Slavery! *Dio mio,* for how long?"

"A little more than three years."

He remained standing, obviously eager to escape, but he was not such a coward. She would have the whole story. She stretched her hand out as she spoke, but he stepped away from the gesture. She dropped her hand and, with an effort, calmed her voice. "Did no one try to find you? How could that be?"

"The rest of the crew was drowned. The officers, too. According to the Admiralty I was among the dead."

"But you were not. You were the only one to survive. Surely that was a gift from God." *His family. What they must have suffered to think him dead.*

Now he did sink into the chair near her bed, leaned back, and closed his eyes.

"If surviving that storm was God's idea of a gift, then the thought of what hell must be like terrifies me."

She wished she had some brandy. This story was difficult for him and tea hardly seemed the right restorative. "How is it that you lived and no one else did?"

He opened his eyes and looked at her with both anger and anguish. "You do manage to ask the most pertinent questions."

Waiting was hard, but Mia was afraid that if she urged him on he would leave. The silence lasted a little longer, and then he raised his hand and rubbed his forehead. "The only reason I survived was that I disobeyed the captain's order and did not go below when the storm hit."

"You disobeyed an order."

"Yes." He put his elbows on his knees and his head in his hands and went on. "I was not a very successful midshipman." He looked up at her hum of understanding. "Yes, I do prefer to be in charge, and if the shipwreck had not ended my naval career then I would have been sent home a failure after that first voyage."

"Well, I see that one could hardly call the shipwreck a blessing, but you did survive. Both the sinking and your captivity."

"Damn times ten, Mia. If you repeat a word of this to anyone I swear I will cut your tongue out."

She pressed her lips together, actually believing him for a moment. "I will never tell anyone, David. I swear in the Virgin's name." Then she gave him the most generous gift she could. "You do not have to tell me any more tonight. Not if it's too difficult."

"It's the last thing you need. You have been sick and are weak." He seemed to consider what she offered but did not move from the chair.

"It is exactly what I need to make me appreciate how minor an inconvenience this illness is. And perfectly timed, as I was just beginning to feel sorry for myself." That was a lie, but he nodded.

"There is not much to tell. It was a bestial existence, all physical work and punishment which I managed to avoid because I was young and strong."

Mia let him tell the story in all its hideous vagueness.

"When I had been there so long I had almost forgotten my other life, a man came to the island, recognized me for a European, and bought me." He stopped and thought a moment.

Mia was sure he was editing the story for his female audience. She had no idea how she was so sure of that, but she waited, then finally asked, "Was he English?"

"No, he was Spanish, from Mexico. He took me to Mexico City and I spent the next few years earning my way to England."

"And paying the man back," she added.

"Yes."

"Why did you not write your father for help?"

"Damn it to hell, Mia. I was a total and complete failure. I was not about to beg him to send money so I could come home. I knew they thought me dead, so what would it hurt to wait another year or two so I could come back with something besides a borrowed suit of clothes?" Now he did stand up, angry and humiliated. "But I paid a price for that, too. When I did come home to Pennford I found that my mother had died the year before. So I failed even her. The one I missed most of all."

Mia stared at the canopy and would not let him see her tears.

"Now try to sleep," he said brusquely. "And if you have more nightmares do not blame me."

He left, and Mia let him go without a word. When the door closed, ever so quietly, she blessed herself, a papist habit that was an odd comfort, even after all these years, and prayed for the boy and the man who had lost so much.

I WAS A TOTAL and complete failure. The words had haunted Mia for days, but there was no chance that she would hear an explanation any time soon. Not only was the house filled with servants again, but Lord David had scrupulously avoided her company. He had not come back to her room, and even now that she was up and dressed for the first time she had seen no sign of him all day.

She sat on the terrace at the back of the house. The warm air and sun felt wonderful and the late breakfast of coddled eggs and bread had been perfect.

If it were not for the nagging questions about Lord David's past, Mia would not have a complaint in the world. During the two days she had been abed, everything had changed.

Janina had arrived the very next morning. She spoke for Romero as well as herself when she fell onto Mia's bed, crying with remorse. "Was it not awful, signorina? Romero's mother says she will eat one as a penance, which is nonsense. She is old and could die, so I have sent him to destroy every one remaining. I am so sorry that the coachman died, but it was not really because of the sweets." Janina had convinced herself that it was the hot day that had caused him to pass out and fall, not the poisoned sweet. No one needed that on their conscience.

Mia patted her head soothingly and let the tears flow until Nina was quiet beside her. It felt so good to have her nearby. When Nina was composed again, Mia went on.

"I have convinced myself it was a kind of adventure. One that has made me much more sympathetic to your travel sickness."

"By the grace of God, Mia, I think you could be on your way to the guillotine and call it another kind of adventure."

"Well, yes, I would, leading to the greatest adventure of all."

"Only you would describe death that way," Nina said, crossing herself as she spoke.

How could sisters view life so differently? Mia wondered, and changed the subject. "I will regain my strength more quickly than you have, Nina. You were sick from the carriage as well. Do you need to rest now?"

"No, I feel in excellent health." She yawned. "I am only tired from three days of travel."

"Three days?" The trip was less than fifty miles.

"Romero is so clever. He drove me here in a dog cart that he rented and the fresh air kept me from being ill.

Sometimes when I was feeling not quite well, I would walk a little. It was an excellent trip. If I can ride outside and we go slowly enough, I do not think I will ever have a trouble traveling again."

Three days to go less than fifty miles. Mia thought she would go mad if she had to travel that slowly, but it was a problem she would bring up later.

The sweet sounds of summer enthralled her. Mia closed her eyes, breathing in the smell of newly cut grass, the scent of summer flowers, and fell into a doze where she was as much a part of nature as the shrubs and trees.

She half dreamed of David sharing the day with her and wondered if he ever made the time to enjoy the world he lived in instead of planning for the world he wanted.

Mia heard the door open and opened her eyes to find Janina watching her. "I feel wonderful." Mia hurried to speak before Janina could ask if she was feeling ill again. "It is wonderful out here. I was just thinking that Lord David should take some time to enjoy such perfect weather. Where is he?"

"In the study and asked to be left alone unless you take ill again. He says we will leave for Pennford as soon as you are well, but not for at least another two days to be sure you are strong enough."

With that news the hope that she and Lord David would have any time alone together faded to nothing. And so it had been for the last twenty-four hours. Now that she was dressed and on her feet again, she would have to return the books she had borrowed. That would give her an excuse to see him, if only for a moment.

Nonsense. She did not need an excuse. Regardless of how he treated her, she was not a servant. He had held her through her nightmares and told her his, or at least the bare bones of it. After that they should not have to stand on ceremony.

She stood, drew a bracing breath of the warm summer air, went into the house, and moved briskly across the hall to the study. After a perfunctory tap at the door, she waltzed into the room without waiting for permission to enter. Exactly as he had done to her a dozen times before. The room smelled of books and leather, though the room was only half filled with shelves. A billiard table took up more space than the library table.

The weak light of the north-facing room was augmented by candles and the huge chandelier over the billiard table.

Mia said nothing, watching the way his fingers traced something he was studying. After nearly a minute of silence, Lord David looked up from the paper and stood as quickly. "You are among us again."

"Yes." She curtsied and he bowed to her. Rather a nice beginning. "What are you examining so intently?"

He stayed behind the table and she came farther into the room.

"I am trying to familiarize myself with Newcomen's steam engine. I have to decide between his and Watt's. Both are proven, and their prices are comparable. I have to present my choice and reasoning to Meryon." He shrugged off business. "I can't imagine you came to learn about the mill."

"I am very interested in it, my lord." She sat in the chair across from him. "Would you care to practice your presentation? I am a very good audience."

He gave her a smile Mia pretended was not patronizing and launched into a description of what his cotton mill would do. There did appear to be such a machine as a "slubber." It was used to draw out the loose fibers from the carding machine. The slubber twisted the fibers together to make them strong enough for the next step in the process.

She stopped him once or twice and asked basic questions, and finally he finished with "the cotton is then ready for weaving."

"All that, and you still have so much more to do before it is calico or some such fabric."

"Yes, and that process is as complicated. And now that Sebold has withdrawn from the partnership I have decided to reconsider where to build the mill. It will take much more study but I am inclined to favor Birmingham." He spoke the last as much to himself as to her.

"Well, I can see why you spend so much time working."

David nodded, his eyes already drifting back to the papers in front of him.

Not before I have my reward, Mia thought. "I need some exercise and you need some time away from this desk. I think your shoulders are beginning to grow rounded and you are definitely starting to squint."

He straightened and then stopped himself from raising a hand to rub his eyes.

"Shall I ring for tea or would you prefer to go for a stroll?"

He didn't say anything, but did begin to stand.

"I wanted to thank you for confiding in me about your time away from home." She was rather proud of her discreet description of his shipwreck and slavery, but the sense of good humor Mia had felt in him disappeared.

"It is not something I will ever talk about again."

Not only had his good humor disappeared, anger was only a breath away.

"But why the change of heart, David? I thought we were becoming friends."

"Your maid has arrived and the house is filled with servants again. Our quarantine is over. Life returns to normal."

"And you will never talk to me again? I am now no more than a silly woman who is not worth any of your time?"

"Mia, do not paint me heartless. It's just that I am no longer at your beck and call."

That hurt, but at least he was using her given name. He had not forgotten *everything*.

"We both said things that it would be unwise to think on too long," he went on, twisting the knife deeper. "You were, and are, in good hands now, with people who can give you better care than I can. What we shared here is in the past."

"You make it sound as though we had a torrid affair and now it must end." *How stupid,* she thought, swallowing over the lump in her throat. Nothing made her more angry than stupid men.

"We may not have been intimate, but society will find that hard to believe if we continue to spend time together, to share stories better forgotten, and if we are seen as friends rather than barely cordial relatives." He sat down again.

He shuffled a few of his papers and then looked at her. The measuring expression he wore told her the real reason he was trying to discourage her. *He was afraid that he had told her too much. Afraid of allowing her to know him any better.*

"You said once that you would never marry me," he said. "And I have no desire to marry you, or any woman. So you had best leave me alone for the next two days lest we be forced into that situation by appearances."

"All right, if you insist." Mia came closer to him, determined to show him that it was not so easy to cut short what had grown between them. She half sat on the edge of the table so that she had only to lean down and turn her head to touch his face with her lips. "Thank you for taking care of me, for holding me, for staying with me all night." She brushed her lips against his cheek. He hadn't shaved today and the feel of his whiskers made her lips tingle.

She delighted in his warmth, in the feel of the muscles in her arm when she touched it. The smell of tobacco, leather, and ink was as distinctly a part of him as his blond hair and blue eyes. She closed her eyes and realized that she could find David Pennistan in a group by his scent alone.

Mia buried her face in his neck and could feel the pulse racing. "I want you to hold me again. Now that I am healthy you do not have to be so careful."

David pushed her away from him. If she had not been leaning against the table she would have fallen to the floor.

"Damnation, woman! Have you ever considered being a courtesan? You have everything one needs. You are beautiful, graceful, talented, and as selfish as the best of them. And most important of all, you know exactly how to bend a man to the breaking point."

He yanked her to him and began to kiss her with such a ferocious passion that her knees weakened and she sat on the table to keep from falling.

Pushing her legs apart, he moved his body between them, without ending the assault on her senses.

She barely had a moment to think: *Did she want this?*

Yes, she did. Her body knew it was what she wanted more than anything else.

More than a sensible engagement.

More than a cautious courtship.

She wanted to be swept off her feet and into a world where nothing mattered but the way it felt to have this man lose control and share all the passion he had with her.

But a small, barely coherent spot in her brain knew it would be a mistake. Even as he pulled her hips closer to his arousal, even as he teased her breast through the thin dress she wore, even as she pulled him closer, Mia knew this was the wrong way to start. It would end before it began and he would hate her for it. They had bypassed any number of steps along the way, important steps.

"Stop," she breathed against his neck. He didn't hear her or didn't listen.

"No!" she said, more forcefully. "Stop right now." Her body arched to him, making her words a lie, and she thought that she could no more stop than he could.

"No, David. Not like this."

Some part of him heard her and he stopped kissing her. He still held her close, both of them breathing hard as they tried to gather some self-control.

He stepped back, his face filled with anger, his body still aroused.

"If you slap me, Mia, I swear before God that I will slap you back. This is what you have been asking for since we first set out on this trip. Do not dare deny it."

She swallowed hard against a protest.

"Now leave this room and do not come near me again in private."

Mia nodded and stumbled toward the door. She paused and turned back to him. "I'm sorry, David."

He made a sound like a disgusted laugh, and sat down to continue working.

WHEN THE DOOR CLOSED with a click, David threw his pen down and swore when ink spattered over the plans for the cotton mill. As he blotted the spots, he cursed the pen, the paper, the tabletop, yesterday's rain, today's sun, and the hopeless mess that tomorrow was sure to be.

He had just shown, conclusively, that if he had anything to do with it, Mia Castellano would not leave Sandleton an innocent. So far from being her protector, David Pennistan was now Mia's greatest threat.

Yes, yes, yes, her endless flirting made it half her fault. But if he and Mia found their way to bed, he was the one who would be held accountable.

Everyone expected trouble from Mia and everyone was so sure that he could handle it. Even that madman William Bendasbrook had been able to resist her. What did it mean that he had less control than a man years younger than he and with a reputation for wildness?

David would never forget Mia's nightmare words, asking William why he "must be a gentleman all the time." Damn him times ten, no one would ever accuse David Pennistan of being too much a gentleman, as he had just proved.

And she had so thoroughly rejected.

He would lock the door to this room, block it with a chair if there was no key, and stay there until the bags were loaded and the horses were chomping at the bit.

If Mia was not ready, he would leave her behind and ride on to Pennford. She could ride in that infernal dog cart her maid's man had found. Or Lyn could send Michael Garrett if he thought that a Pennistan should accompany his wife's ward.

Within arm's reach there was a bottle of brandy and plenty to read that had nothing to do with cotton mills and steam engines. He could entertain himself, in more ways than one, and then drink himself into oblivion.

Chapter Twenty-two

MIA WALKED BACK to the terrace in a daze, her brain working only well enough for her to reason that the breeze and the warm air would explain her tousled hair and reddened cheeks.

She sat in silence, unaware of the sun or the trees or the rhythmic sound of the scythes as the workers cutting grass moved to the shady side of the house.

Mired in guilt and frustration, Mia wondered when, if, she could ever stop making such a ruin of her life. Why had she made him stop? Because it was not the time and place of her choosing? He had not scared her. She loved that his desire for her overcame his scruples. *Be honest,* she chided herself, *it's* your *sensibilities that frightened you*. To feel so intensely, to want beyond reason. She put her head back on the soft cushion and fell asleep before she could start crying.

Mia woke as Janina carefully spread a shawl over her lap. Mia bit her lip to keep from snapping at her. "Nina, I am not chilled. The temperature is perfect and I am done resting. I think I will take a walk down the drive."

"Alone? Miss, you cannot go alone. And I am still not as strong as I was before. What if you weaken and faint?"

Mia suspected it would be at least six months before Janina felt herself fully recovered. "There are men everywhere today. You're the one who told me Cantwell sent them out to scythe the grass and polish the brass at the gate. If I need help I will have one of them come for you." She stood, and felt perfectly fine. "I have to think about what is next for me. I think best alone."

"Yes, signorina." Her maid's resigned tone was as close as she would come to disagreeing with her mistress.

The trees shaded the drive very nicely and Mia walked slowly, even stopped once to sit on one of the benches that were set amidst a seemingly random planting of flowers.

It was despicable to play with David's manliness that way, to arouse him and leave him angry. And unsatisfied. But she had been punished. David was no longer a friend. That was penance enough.

On standing, Mia did feel a slight weakness in her knees and decided that a walk all the way to the gate was too ambitious a prospect. She had just turned back to the house when she heard the crunch of carriage wheels on the drive and stepped to the side to allow whoever it was to pass.

It was a coach and four, not at all what she expected. The carriage was almost past her when it stopped, the door opened, and a man leaped out, not waiting for the steps to be lowered.

"Miss Castellano?"

Lord Kyle? Yes, it was the duke's good friend Lord Kyle. And he was not alone. She returned his bow with a curtsy and nodded. "Yes, Mia Castellano. Good day to you, my lord."

What was he doing here? She knew just how to find out. "I wonder if I could ride with you and your party to the house."

"But of course." He was all kindness as he pulled down the steps. "We will be a little crowded but it is only for a moment."

There were two ladies and another gentleman in the carriage, and after a slight hesitation, Lord Kyle introduced them. He spoke so quickly that Mia was left in some confusion. Not that anyone noticed. They were having a merry time of it. There was one empty champagne bottle on the floor of the conveyance and the other man was drinking from a bottle, while the two ladies waved their empty glasses.

How fascinating, Mia thought. She knew Lord Kyle was not married, and the ladies were much too forward to be true ladies. But what were they doing here?

"We thought our house party would be only four in number," Lord Kyle said. It sounded as though he was as curious about her presence as she was about his. "Won't we be cozy." His guests all laughed good-naturedly. "Who are you here with?"

"Lord David Pennistan," she answered, before she realized how they would interpret that.

"David Pennistan is here?"

The delight in the woman's voice, the one nearest Lord Kyle, gave Mia pause, though Lord Kyle did not seem fazed in the slightest. He was looking at her speculatively.

"Kyle, we have not seen him since that boxing match last fall."

Kyle nodded, distracted by something Mia could not guess at.

"I do so enjoy talking to him. His view of the world is so very unique."

This woman talked to Lord David? Mia wanted to ask her what the magic words were but did not want to admit that she was not on nearly as good terms with him as this woman.

"As long as it's only talking, Ettie," Kyle reminded her with a cautionary glance.

"Only talking." She patted Kyle's arm. "But you know I find that as provocative as any other sort of foreplay. The three of us—" she began, and then stopped at Kyle's warning glare.

"What a fine catch," the other woman said.

"And so soon," the other man said.

Mia pretended not to understand. "Do you fish, my lord?"

"Yes. Do you?" His expression was teasing and she realized that he, too, had drunk a fair amount of champagne. She wondered how many bottles had been tossed from the carriage on their way from . . . wherever they came from today.

"I do fish, Lord Kyle. I angle with a fly mostly, and have had some very successful mornings here. The weather may be warm but the river is deep enough for the fish to find cold spots and rise to the hatch."

Complete silence followed her words, and she looked from one to the other as she tried to determine what she had said that was so off-putting.

"Miss Castellano, what are you and Lord David doing here?" Lord Kyle asked in a more sober tone. One of the women giggled, and Ettie put her hand through Kyle's arm and whispered something to him.

"I know what you will be doing here, Ettie, since I will be doing it with you, but I suspect we may be in the way."

"Why?" the other gentleman asked in an offended tone. "You told us this has been on the calendar since last winter."

"You are quite right, sir, I'm sure," Mia said. "Our prolonged stay here was unexpected." She was about to explain the quarantine when his companion broke in.

"Castellano. Are you the girl who ended her engagement to the viscount?"

"Yes," Mia said through a clenched jaw.

"Ooooh, tell us what happened. We all want to know. Lord William left town so abruptly." The woman, who smelled of a citrusy perfume that was pleasant, if a little strong, leaned close and whispered, "Too bad, dearie, he might be short but he isn't short everywhere. He's as adventurous in bed as he is out-of-doors."

Mia swallowed her embarrassment, pretending she was not one step away from outright humiliation, and hoped that the others had not heard what the woman said.

"Lord David is vastly entertaining in his own way," Ettie added.

"How do you know him?" Mia asked, curious and horrified.

"One cannot know Lord Kyle without knowing all the Pennistans."

"Lord David is so rugged," the other woman, Blanche, said, as if she did not wish to be outdone by Ettie. "That roughness is very appealing after all the smooth hands and short-cropped hair."

"He is not the kind who marries, miss," Ettie insisted, ignoring the other woman's commentary and looking Mia straight in the eye.

"Neither am I."

That announcement drew all attention to her. Lord Kyle looked at her quizzically and the other man's eyes opened wide. His companion slapped him on the wrist and pulled him toward her ample bosom.

Before Mia could explain herself any further, the carriage halted at the short rise of steps at the front door. They waited for the groom to open the door and announce their arrival.

The group stumbled down the steps with Mia following more carefully. Lord Kyle offered her his hand with a genuine smile, and she smiled back as she accepted his help.

Janina waited for her at the steps, wringing her hands with worry. "Did you faint or feel ill?"

Before Lord Kyle or his guests could comment, Mia pulled her maid aside. "I am fine. I rode back in the carriage to find out who these people are."

"Yes, what are they doing here? I would not think this house so popular that the minute a quarantine ends, guests arrive."

Even as Janina spoke, Mrs. Cantwell came out, totally flustered and in obvious distress.

"I beg your pardon, Lord Kyle. Did you not receive my message?"

"No, Mrs. Cantwell, but I have been away from home for several weeks. We come from Brighton and the Prince Regent."

"The house is always ready for you, my lord, but Lord David is here and it will be crowded."

"Why is she saying nothing about the smallpox?" Janina whispered to Mia. The woman who wasn't Ettie looked at them with some suspicion, if not dismay, and Mia thought fast and spoke just loud enough for her to hear. "The doors have locks, Nina. We will be perfectly safe."

With an offended "Humph" the woman turned to her party and ignored them, just as Mia hoped she would. While Mrs. Cantwell welcomed the unexpected guests, Mia pulled Janina toward the back of the house.

"Who are those people?" Janina repeated.

"It is a house party of courtesans and their patrons." Mia was so excited she felt like someone had just given her a gift she never expected. She would have the opportunity to see what the life was like.

"Oh no!"

"Oh yes, a wonderful little adventure before I go on to God knows what at Pennford."

"But what about Lord David?"

"What does he have to do with anything?" Let him just try to tell her that she could not dine with the party. "Now stop asking questions. Please."

"Very well," Nina said with a sigh. "I understand that means you want to be alone. I will go find some tea and biscuits for you, as I am sure dinner will be later than we are used to."

Janina went on toward the kitchen garden while Mia tried to figure out why Lord Kyle, who was all charm and good looks, did not interest her nearly as much as Lord David. Why, when David was in the room, did she barely notice anyone else?

Foolish thought, she decided. Before tonight there had been no one else worth noticing. Dinner this evening would be different, very different indeed. If David didn't want to be friends with her, she would be friends with someone else.

Mia hurried upstairs trying to recall which dress flattered her the most, but stopped short at the door to her room. Ettie was talking to her maid, acting as if she owned the place.

"That daybed in the dressing room is perfect for me if Kyle wishes to sleep alone. You will have to sleep upstairs with the other servants but I will make it up to you." The maid nodded, with a sniff of annoyance.

"Lord David Pennistan is here," Ettie went on. "A very intriguing man. I should love a few moments with him. I just have to find a way to make him look at me and not that too-young, too-beautiful Italian woman."

"Well, Ettie, you are on your way, as you have taken over my room. That must be the first step." Mia stepped into the room.

"I beg your pardon, Miss Castellano." Ettie nodded with just a hint of apology.

"You are begging my pardon for calling me young, beautiful, and Italian? Please do not take it back." Mia laughed, truly pleased at Ettie's description of her.

Ettie smiled.

"I had thought you were here with Lord Kyle," Mia said. "But if you are interested in Lord David, please do not let me stand in your way. We are almost relatives and have no other attachment."

The courtesan looked intrigued, but shook her head. "I only wish to converse with him. I am to be with Lord Kyle this weekend."

Not at all sure of the etiquette of the demimonde, or even if there was any, Mia nodded as though she understood perfectly. "Well, I must go find out where my maid was told to move my things."

She was on her way back down the passage when she saw Janina coming out of the set of doors that led to the family suite.

"Janina, what are you doing there!"

"Shh, signorina, Mrs. Cantwell wants to speak with you. Your room is now that one across from Lord David's. I will find her. I do believe she is in the kitchen. I left your tea. You can drink it while you wait."

Mia shrugged and wandered down the corridor to the room she had not been in since the night she had wound the clocks for the first time.

This room was far larger than her original bedchamber, its accent on green and cream colors as pleasing as the blue and pink had been. There was a lovely arrangement of late-blooming hydrangeas; their lush arrangement spoke of Miss Horner's hand.

Before she could investigate the dressing room, she heard Janina chattering, most likely to Mrs. Cantwell, and went back into the passage to meet them.

"I am sorry, Miss Castellano, but I could think of no other solution. I cannot move Lord David and I do not want a young lady," she emphasized the word, "anywhere near those women." Mrs. Cantwell was obviously distressed at the situation. When Mia gave no more than a cautious nod, the housekeeper hurried on.

"The rooms are not next to each other. The hallway separates them. They each have their own dressing room and they have locks. I think your reputation is perfectly safe."

In the end Mia agreed that it made sense and told the housekeeper as much, reassuring her that all would be well. Mrs. Cantwell curtsied and left as quickly as she had come. Mia imagined that she had a huge list of things to do now that every bedroom was occupied.

"It is your only choice, I suppose," Janina said, "but this is becoming very difficult, and I am afraid your reputation will be ruined and you will have to marry Lord David. He is a gentleman only by birth and has no wealth. I cannot imagine anything worse." Janina spoke as they walked down the passage. Mia noticed that the door to Lord David's room was slightly ajar.

They both jumped at the sharp snap of the door shutting securely and Mia grimaced at the snippet of conversation he might have heard, but Nina did not seem to notice.

"Sit down, Mia, and have some tea and one of these little tarts or some cheese. You need to eat more or your dresses will not fit."

Mia did as Janina ordered while Nina finished arranging Mia's things in the attached dressing room and announced the cot in the dressing room would be "very comfortable for sleeping."

"You are to go to bed early tonight," Mia commanded as she offered her maid a tart. "I will wake you up to help me undress. This is an order and for your own good, Nina. I want you to be strong for the drive to Pennford."

"Of course." Nina nodded. "I will do as you say. I would have even without your prompting. I want to stay well on the journey so that the duke and Elena do not think I have failed you."

"Never, Nina." Mia sipped her tea and then sat back. "Sit down a moment."

Nina sat in the chair on the other side of the small tea table. "I am afraid for you."

"I want you to know that I will never marry Lord David. I would see my reputation in tatters and worse rather than accept him."

"But if your reputation is ruined then you will wind up like my mother." Nina began to wring her hands.

"That will never happen, Nina. I have money. I will never be destitute like she was."

"But you still might die alone and lonely." Nina's eyes filled with tears, even though she had been only two when her mother had died and always insisted that she did not remember her.

"Dearest, Papa would never have allowed your mother to die that way if he had known."

"Yes, yes," Nina said through her tears. "I do understand that. But still, it happened."

"And our papa took you in and would have given you anything you wanted."

"I have exactly what I want. I am with you and will not ever have to leave you. You treat me like the sister I am and respect the secret because it is what I want."

"If you say so, but I think it is because becoming a servant was the only option you were given by my aunt and that ghastly governess before we were old enough to understand what it would mean."

"But I am happy. I do not want to be a lady who is always being measured by what she wears and who she visits. Mia, you know I have not even a little adventure in me."

They hugged, and Mia knew she had best change the subject or Nina would be morose for hours.

"You must not worry about my reputation."

"Then you will not go down to dinner tonight?" Nina brightened visibly.

"Of course I am going to dinner."

Nina's smile disappeared.

"Nina, this is a very private party and Lord Kyle is too good a friend of the duke's to gossip about me when the duke's wife is my guardian."

"But the others . . ." Nina began.

"Will do exactly what Lord David and Lord Kyle tell them." She sat down. "Now come fix my hair and then help me choose a dress, one of the new ones. It will not be as risqué but at least it is the latest style. Admit it. The neckline that will make Elena frown is actually too conservative among these women."

Janina relaxed, all trace of tears for her mother gone, and, as always, she allowed Mia to have her way. She was the more cautious of the two of them, there was no doubt about that, but Mia was far more stubborn.

Chapter Twenty-three

MIA'S TOILETTE TOOK TWO HOURS. By the time she made her way to the study where the others were already gathered she was afraid that Lord David would try to stop her. That would be beyond humiliating.

Lord David did not even notice when she came into the library.

He was engrossed in a hotly contested game of billiards. When Cantwell announced dinner was ready, the men ignored him as well. Were they foxed already? Mia espied three or four bottles and empty glasses and had her answer.

In the end Lord Kyle and David were the only two in competition. Franklin—Mia did not know if that was his first name or his last—was so far into his cups that as the last shots were taken, Mia was afraid he would ruin the felt. Finally, he gave up, broke the cue over his knee, and insisted that he pour champagne for the ladies.

Soon he and Blanche were by the drinks table bickering over something that had to do with the number of rings each was wearing. Too many, Mia thought.

That left Mia and Ettie to entertain themselves at the other end of the room. They spent the required few moments admiring each other's gowns. Blanche's was a disastrous choice for someone so well-rounded, but then Mia was sure that the gentlemen's examination of her gown went no farther than her oversized bosom.

Ettie was dressed to perfection. She had used the time efficiently and well. Her hair was swept up in a confection that left her lovely neck bare, and a gorgeous egg-sized amethyst emphasized the deep décolletage of her gown.

Mia felt much too young beside her and wondered how a courtesan cultivated an air of superiority rather than the complete lack of sophistication that Blanche showed.

"You look lovely, and much more of a threat than you did this afternoon," Ettie said, looking Mia up and down and shaking her head.

Mia did not know if the woman was serious or pretending. Well, this was one place where she did not have to worry about fitting in, so she decided to be honest and see what that won her.

"I should like to sit next to Lord Kyle this evening."

"So I can have some time to converse with David?" Ettie asked. "Or to make him jealous while you flirt with Kyle?"

Before Mia could take offense, Ettie waved her hand.

"I will wager a guinea that I can make Lord David laugh before you can make Lord Kyle cry."

Mia laughed and accepted the offer even though either scenario would be impossible.

"Neither of us will win," Ettie said, echoing her thoughts, "but it will be fun to try."

Mia nodded, and with a word to Mrs. Cantwell, she changed the seating at the dining table. She knew that even if Lord David noticed, he would not say a word.

When they reached the table, the only reaction from David was the searching look he gave her and then Kyle, as if he was not sure which of them had made the change.

She was now seated at the end of the table, with Kyle to her right and Franklin to her left, while Ettie was to David's left and next to Lord Kyle. Not that much of a change except that Mia was no longer anywhere near Lord David. Let him think that Lord Kyle had developed an interest in her and arranged for the change. Perfect. Let the adventure begin, Mia thought at the exact moment that Cantwell led the footmen into the room.

Their party of six was presented a dinner that showed exactly how talented the cook was. A skill wasted on the visitors, as most of them were more interested in the wine than the food.

David did not touch his wineglass, which made him more sober, or was it somber, and his attention to Ettie was perfunctory at best.

"No wine, Miss Castellano? You will miss half the fun." Lord Kyle held the bottle at the ready.

"No, thank you, my lord. Not tonight." Her stomach

would be tested by so many courses. The last thing she wanted was to add wine.

Kyle set the bottle down with a wry smile. "Tell me, Miss Castellano, exactly what you are fishing for tonight?"

"Fishing? I don't think that is quite the word, my lord." She hoped she did not sound coy, but rather amused. "Fishing implies I am casting about for anything that fits a general description. One fish is as good as another," she added in case he did not understand. "This evening my interests are very particular." She said the last two words slowly while looking directly into his eyes, a sort of blue-green, she noted, and not nearly as commanding as David's blue eyes were.

Kyle sat back, a dumbfounded expression lurking beneath his now somewhat forced smile. "Am I wrong to feel as though I have won the lottery when I have not even bought a ticket?"

"How flattering." Mia laughed, not too loud, as she did not wish to draw attention to their conversation.

"I am the one who is flattered." He sampled the fish and looked down at his plate. "This is so fresh." Then he looked back at her. "You really have been fishing, in the river," he clarified, "haven't you?"

"Yes, and that should prove to you that every lady has a secret or two."

"I imagine that you have more than two." He leaned closer and offered her a taste of the fish that she had refused when the footman proffered the platter. She accepted the morsel and let her mouth slip slowly off the fork. It was so obvious a gesture that she could not keep from smiling.

Mia risked a glance at David, who glared at them, as though he was irritated that she and Kyle were the only ones having a good time. At that moment Ettie said something to him. He turned to Ettie and away from her quite deliberately, and suddenly Mia realized a man could play the game of flirtation as well as a woman could.

"Miss Castellano."

"Yes." Mia turned her attention to Lord Kyle, who was not serious precisely, but no longer smiling. He had his elbows on the table with his hands folded and resting under his chin.

"If you are using me to make Lord David jealous, I cannot believe I have to tell you that is not a wise idea."

"Oh please, Kyle, Lord David is like a brother to me. We have been together here for a week and have barely seen each other." It took all her control not to blush furiously at the memory of the kisses they had shared or the complete happiness she had felt when in his arms.

Mia leaned closer to Lord Kyle. "He has been all day in the library studying the mill plans as though he would be tested on the subject. I have been fishing and then, if you must know," she looked away, a little embarrassed, "I was ill. I am sorry to bring that up at dinner, but you would ask such a silly question." And then, just in case he was not convinced, she added, "You do know that his brother is married to my guardian."

"Oh, yes, I know that as well as I know my own

name." He watched her intently, as if trying to make sense of her perfectly sensible conversation. "You're almost twenty-one, are you not?"

"Yes, in fourteen months, right before Michaelmas."

"And when you have your independence, what do you plan to do?"

He sounded just the tiniest bit patronizing. So she straightened. "I plan to live independently and establish my own salon for musicians." She announced it in a voice just loud enough for all of them to hear, if they were listening.

Blanche and Franklin could not have cared less. He was busy licking some of the delicately seasoned fish from where it had fallen on her décolletage.

Ettie was laughing in an effort to draw at least a chuckle from Lord David. David, however, had heard what she said. He stopped chewing whatever he was eating, and his expression dared her to continue.

"For men and women who appreciate music. Not only those who play." She spoke directly to David. He must remember her solo guitar recital for him the second night of their quarantine.

"At twenty-one you plan to have your own home." Kyle patted her hand. "How intriguing."

"Do not make me sound a fool, Lord Kyle. I know what most people will think. And I no longer care."

"Music is that important to you?"

"Yes, it is." Her anger evaporated at his understanding. "I want to be able to spend time with what I value instead of what the ton dictates. I will make all my callers welcome."

"Oh, Mia, it seems to me that you are walking a fine line between the life of a respectable woman and that of a courtesan. Or do I misunderstand you completely and are you thinking of establishing a music school?"

"My lord Kyle, I plan to do whatever I want. I have never in my life been able to choose more than what color to wear, and there were times when even that choice has been limited if I wished to be welcomed into society. When I turn twenty-one I will embrace the freedom to choose with joy. I will pay whatever price I must for that freedom."

Chapter Twenty-four

"LORD DAVID, do not tell me there is no chance of anything but the most conventional conversation with you."

David heard what Ettie said and nodded, as he watched Mia wrap Kyle around her finger.

"There is a charm about her, is there not?"

David closed his eyes. Charm? Is that what it was? The way she constantly drew his eye even when he was seated next to a courtesan who was that rare combination of intelligence and sympathy? He shook his head and Ettie went on.

"Yes, Miss Castellano is charming. She flirts with such naïveté, and I imagine she is as passionate as she is lovely."

"Willful, spoiled, and she thinks of no one but herself." Even as he said that last he knew it was not true.

"You are wrong, Lord David."

"You've only known her for a few hours, Ettie."

"And that is quite enough, with someone who is as open as she is. They are a rare few." Ettie glanced toward Mia and Kyle before she spoke again. "Girls like that were the bane of my existence when I taught at the young ladies' seminary, but they do know how to enjoy life."

David took a bite of his fish, wondering if it was the one Mia had named. Then he almost choked when he heard Mia announce her plans to become an independent woman.

Damn it to hell times ten! She might as well have announced that she would become a courtesan. It was certainly how everyone here would interpret it. And he had been the one to put the stupid idea in her head that very morning. "If Kyle takes advantage of her I will beat his lordly face into a bloody mess."

"David, look at me."

He did as Ettie asked in an effort to control his anger.

"She is in no danger from Kyle. He is a rake, I will give you that, but he is your brother's dearest friend. He would do nothing to Mia. Nothing but try to show her the truth."

"Truth?"

The woman sighed as though she were trying to teach an idiot how to tie a foursquare knot. "Mia announced in the carriage that she has no plans to marry. And now she says she will live independently. Not to mention the fact that she is here alone with you. What were we to think?"

"That we were quarantined here by the threat of illness, as we said."

"Ah, yes, the quarantine. Vouched for by the staff, right down to the grooms."

He'd always thought Ettie Loughton a good judge of character, and sensible. If even she thought that the quarantine sounded suspicious, what was he to do? End Mia's flirtation with Kyle for one thing. The sooner the better. Before David could jump up, Ettie tapped his hand.

"She's doing rather well, if her blushes are to be used as a measure. Kyle appears vastly entertained. She would make a refreshing change in the demimonde. Though I doubt her guardian would approve of the venture."

He was only half listening, caught between fascinated and infuriated at the way Kyle and Mia had their heads so close together. "It would be an adventure, not just a venture." He could feel a smile and pursed his lips to erase it.

"What?" Ettie asked.

"Mia considers everything an adventure. Everything from runaway horses to kneading bread."

"Oh, you lucky man." Ettie fortified herself with a long drink of wine.

"Lucky?" Ettie was near lunacy if she thought acting as Mia Castellano's escort counted as a stroke of luck.

"David Pennistan, you supreme man among men— and I do mean that as a compliment—Mia is willful and spoiled and argumentative when she is afraid. Women like her, the ones who are so flirtatious, use it as a protection."

"I am no threat to her." If anything it was the other way around. Her very presence tested all his control.

"Oh, for God's sake, David, stop lying to yourself. You want her. Admit it. And if you do not act on it I will not hesitate to call you a coward."

"I would not tolerate that word from a man."

"Yes, I know, and I use it with care. What is the worst thing that could happen? That you would be compelled to marry her?"

"It would be a nightmare to marry her."

"David, she acts as she does because she is afraid of falling in love with you." The woman raised her serviette but he heard her mumble, "you stupid man."

"Ettie, stop drinking the champagne. She flirts with every man she sees, including coachmen and surgeons."

"Coachmen can be very entertaining, David. They have not learned the finer elements of lovemaking, but they make up for it with their enthusiasm."

"I am not one of the circle that wants to hear of your conquests." He was as annoyed as any man would be in such a discussion, while he tried to dispel visions of Mia in a close embrace with Novins or one of the footmen. It appalled him.

"I can't say I blame Mia for being afraid," Ettie went on. "Not to be cruel, David, but I cannot imagine the words 'I love you' ever coming from you. Not because you are unfeeling but because you are even more afraid of it than she is."

He heard what she said, and it was the last bit of wisdom he wanted from this too-keen observer. Then he saw

Mia sit back with an expression of dismay on her face, and Kyle smiling like a spider beyond pleased with what had fallen into his web.

That bastard. David threw his serviette on the floor and stood. It was time to sweep Mia out of the room, if only to protect her from her worst enemy. Herself.

Chapter Twenty-five

"Miss Castellano and I are going fishing," Lord David announced, and Mia realized that he had left his place at the head of the table and was striding toward where she sat.

She stared up at him in astonishment that quickly gave way to delight.

"We wish you all a good evening." He gave Mia a look that demanded her cooperation. She gave David a quick smile and turned to her dinner companion.

"Thank you for an enlightening conversation, Lord Kyle, but let me assure you that despite your very paternal attitude you have not convinced me to abandon my plan."

Kyle stood, took her hand, and helped her to her feet. Then he kissed her fingers. "I will look forward to seeing you, then, perhaps at a house party shortly after your birthday."

He smiled at her and she laughed with the pure pleasure of victory. "Good night all!" she called out as David pulled her along behind him.

They left the room to a chorus of ribald comments until Kyle silenced the group with a crude word of his own.

In the kitchen they found a mirror dinner. Janina and Romero were at the table with the other house servants. Cantwell sat at the head of the table, his wife at the opposite end. Ettie's and Blanche's maids and the gentlemen's valets were seated with excruciating attention to what was proper, far more attention to precedence than they had observed in the dining room. There was no conversation, only the sound of forks clinking against china.

"We are going fishing," Mia announced. "It is just the right time for the evening hatch."

Mr. Cantwell nodded as if granting permission, at which point Mia realized that she should not have said anything to them. She, and certainly Lord David, did not have to explain themselves to the servants.

The yells and laughter from the other room made it clear what they had left behind.

Romero moved from his seat and closed the door that separated the house from the kitchen, and a sense of gentility settled over them again.

David led Mia out to the fishing porch and closed the connecting door firmly behind him. She knew he was angry. Or maybe he was only frustrated that he did not know what she and Kyle had been talking about. Or maybe it was not anger or frustration at all but the same thing she felt.

When he backed her against the door and kissed her, Mia had her answer. His ruthless kiss felt wonderful. Just what she wanted: to lose herself in feeling, to not have to think of something clever to say, some reason for behavior that seemed, to her, perfectly ladylike. She could just let her body speak for her.

She pushed her fingers through his hair and clasped her hands behind his neck. When she could stand the temptation no longer she opened her lips, and the deepening kiss made her weak with longing. Mia thought she could spend the rest of her life kissing this man and never tire of the way his mouth felt, never want less than everything he had to give.

David ended the kiss with his forehead pressed to hers. He whispered, "If anyone is going to take you to bed, it will be me." He kissed the corner of her mouth, her cheek, her neck, and she felt his hand cup her breast.

"Then why," she whispered, "are we going fishing?" It was perhaps not the cleverest thing to say but she was in a daze and very happy there.

A few hours ago she had said no. But now the word was beyond her. She wanted him. She wanted to know his body as well as she knew his mouth. She wanted to feel him as close to her as a man and woman could be, in a way that made words unimportant, in a way that spoke of love without ever saying it.

David stepped back, one step, then two. Mia would

not move from the door until her legs were more capable of supporting her.

"We are going fishing because if I had to watch Kyle fawning over you for another minute—" He stopped, turned around and adjusted his clothes, ran a hand through his hair and started over, still with his back to her. "If I leave you alone you will find more trouble than I can handle without hurting someone." He looked over his shoulder, his face grim. "Show me what I will need to fish."

His distress was so sincere that Mia went through the steps of gathering what she needed, even though it would be too dark to have a hope of catching anything. David made a show of following her directions and finally tossed it all to the floor.

"I will watch you. Or go for a swim in the coldest water I can find."

"That will scare the fish away."

His expression alone would scare the fish away. Without another word, Mia put the fishing rods back in their braces and opened the door that led outside. "If we hurry we can see what insects the fish are rising to. Then tomorrow I can show you how to choose a fly and the best way to cast."

"Mia, I have no desire to learn to angle with a fly."

"Then come and smoke one of your stupid cigarillos." Could he not tell that she just wanted to spend some time with him, alone?

She began to not-quite-run down to the river. The stays and her narrow skirt made an actual run impossible.

He followed her at what was, given his longer stride, merely a stroll. When they were far enough away from the house that Mia felt they were committed to a walk, she slowed.

"You are not the only one who observed at dinner, David. Ettie talked to you endlessly and Blanche could not keep her eyes off you."

"Blanche? Franklin kept calling her Candy," David said, and after a beat added, "She does look good enough to eat."

Mia turned her head slowly to see his expression. When their eyes met they both began to laugh, and continued until Mia had tears in her eyes and David had to stop walking to catch his breath.

"Oh, that was so much fun!"

David was not sure if Mia meant the laughter or the dinner.

"I know you have seen it all before, my lord, but the way Blanche let the fish fall on her bosom. It was so obvious. And yet Franklin was all too willing to help her remove it."

"Did you see that? I hoped that the least Kyle would do was distract you from their goings-on." David resumed walking at a slower pace. Mia followed.

"Yes, and I heard her ask the footman to have some of the whipped cream delivered to her room." Mia almost asked why she would want that later, and then realized that with a little whipped cream in the right place, dear Blanche would be good enough to eat. "And the footman did no more than nod," Mia finished, rather proud of her sophistication.

"He's seen worse here, I'm sure."

For just a second Mia wondered how the duke found servants willing to tolerate his guests, then deliberately did not think about how often the Pennistan brothers had made up a party. "I always thought Lord Kyle was such a gentleman, and he proved it tonight. He might have been a little bold or perhaps risqué but he never went too far."

When David's brow furrowed she hurried on.

"He did not insult me in any way, David, but he was quite willing to play the game."

"Kyle is less roué than he pretends."

"But why?" Mia faced David and danced backward toward the river. "He has so much to recommend him."

"He does it to upset his father, who persists in treating him like a schoolboy. So Kyle acts like one. He will inherit an earldom with virtually no idea how to handle it."

"The complete opposite of Meryon. How odd they are such good friends."

"Not at all. Have you not observed how often opposites attract?"

"Are you talking about us?" She stumbled a little but did not fall.

David laughed.

Exactly how much had he drunk? Nothing, she thought, but he never laughed this much.

"You are not all that I think about, Mia."

"Then who did you mean?"

He thought for a moment, proving that she was who

he had been thinking of. "You and Bendasbrook prove it. You are too much alike. Elena and Meryon are a good example of opposites. She loves the crowds at a party and Meryon would as soon find a quiet room. And he cannot sing at all."

"Nonsense. Elena might not seek privacy, but she will talk to the same person for an hour. They both are exactly the same. Except for the music." She turned to face him, her hands on her hips. "Admit it, you were talking about us."

Perhaps he had been. But he would never say it aloud.

"David," she said, taking his hand and swinging it between them. "When was the last time you had fun?"

"Fun is for children."

"Well, there is one way in which we are opposites, because I have fun every time I play an instrument. I have fun when I angle. I have fun when I shop for new clothes. I have fun when we laugh together. So, when do you have fun?"

He shook his head but she could see he was thinking about it. He had fun when he was in a boxing ring. He had had a grand time intimidating Mr. Cole, and he had enjoyed provoking that man who had insulted her. And he and she both definitely had fun when they kissed.

"David, admit it. If we can laugh together, surely we could have fun together?" It was as close as she would allow herself to come to asking him for more attention.

As she waited for possibly the most important answer of her life, Mia heard Janina calling to her. When she turned Nina was running across the grass.

"Signorina, what are you thinking? You cannot wear that dress to catch fish! You must change first."

Mia let out a sharp breath. There were times when Nina was too scrupulous.

"Nina, we are not fishing. We are only going for a walk."

"Think of all the times during the war when we had to make do with old styles, even patching our favorite gowns! Come into the house this instant and change."

"We are *not* going fishing." *Go away, Nina,* Mia thought in as loud a voice as her imagination could summon. *We are talking about something important. Do not destroy the mood.*

"That is quite enough." David stepped in front of Mia and spoke directly to Janina.

Why could he not mind his own business?

"Miss Castellano is the one in charge here. She can do as she wishes."

"Do not criticize Nina. She is not at fault. She is sweet and fragile and your ill will is appalling." Mia grabbed Janina's hand. "He is not angry with you." Janina nodded doubtfully and Mia turned back to David. "If you are angry, yell at me." *It does not upset me.* He took her suggestion to heart.

"You seem to delight in associating with all the wrong kind of people, Mia. Those women tonight were courtesans and you actually seemed to enjoy yourself."

"What you need is a boxing ring to go a round or two with Lord Kyle. Please do not lose your temper."

"I am not losing my temper." He parsed the words out, proving the opposite.

Oh dear, Mia thought. Then she saw Romero coming across the lawn, striding in a purposeful way. *Oh hell,* she thought, using the word quite deliberately.

He confronted David with his fists raised. "You are insulting the woman I am going to marry." He stood slightly shorter than Lord David but that did not stop him from stepping closer. "Prepare to defend yourself, you arrogant aristocrat."

Dio mio, they were going to replay the French Revolution here on the lawn at Sandleton. Thank God there were no knives around. Then Mia remembered the one that David had on him during the confrontation with Dilber. She ran around the two, who were preparing to fight by taking off their coats. Nina was wailing quietly, almost to herself.

"Nina, we must stop them." Mia grabbed Nina's arm and began to pull her toward the combatants, who were now loosening their cravats.

"Yes, yes, or Romero will kill him." Nina grabbed Mia's other hand and stopped their advance.

"No, he won't," Mia said with some exasperation, pulling her hands out of Nina's. "David will kill Romero."

They might have argued about it themselves but there was no time.

While Mia took a moment to consider the best approach, Nina wrapped her hands around Romero's waist. "You will stop this nonsense now."

Romero growled and dropped his hands to try to pry Nina's off him.

Mia did her one better and jumped up onto David's back, wrapping her legs around his middle. She heard something rip and hoped it was David's coat and not her dress.

David grabbed her hands but did not try to push her off; rather he held her as though afraid she would fall.

"David," she whispered into his ear and refused to be distracted when he shivered. "Listen. Janina is my sister."

"Drop off my back, Mia. Do it now."

"David, why must I say everything twice? Nina is more than a maid. Did you hear me?"

"Yes." He paused as if patience would come to him if he waited a moment. "This is no position in which to have a discussion."

"I don't know. I do have your complete attention."

"Off me, Mia, or I promise you are the one I will punish."

"I'd like to see you try," she murmured as she slid off his back.

Nina and Romero waited, arm in arm, though Mia thought it was more to keep Romero under control than a gesture of solidarity.

David straightened his clothes and ran a hand through his hair. "Did you say that Janina is your sister?"

"Oh, Mia." Janina's two words were laced with disappointment.

"Explain your relationship with Janina."

"Lord David!" Janina almost shouted. Her raised

voice made even David pause. Having gained his attention, she gathered her composure around her like armor. "If we are going to talk about my relationship to the Castellanos, I must swear you to secrecy." Janina spoke in a firm voice.

"I promise discretion, miss, but I will not promise silence until I know the story."

A tense silence settled between them, but finally Nina gave a little nod.

"Shall I begin?" Mia asked Nina.

Nina nodded again, this time with more certainty.

Mia turned to David. "My father had a years-long affair of the heart with the seamstress who came to our home. It began shortly after my mother died and lasted until the signora's own death from an inflammation of the lungs." Mia heard Nina sniff and saw Romero take her into his arms, resting her against his shoulder.

"I was six, and one day my father brought the prettiest little girl to the schoolroom and announced that she would be my companion." Mia smiled at Nina. "I was delighted. It was like having a live doll with which to play. She was three and so tiny and her eyes were so big and she cried so easily. I loved cosseting her and making her feel better with treats."

Mia watched David look from one to the other of them and shake his head. "How could I miss the resemblance?"

"No one sees it. She has her mother's temperament, which is the exact opposite of mine. She detests adventures." A thought occurred to Mia. "You said before that opposites attract. Janina and I are proof that is true. There are times that I think she is the only reason I am not the most thoughtless, selfish woman in the world."

"You are kindness itself, Mia," Nina said fervently.

"Thank you, but all that I learned about kindness I learned from you." She blew her sister a kiss. "Well, Lord David, my aunt—my mother's sister, who was raising us—did not like that Papa had brought Nina to me. When she left us on her marriage, the governess that came to the house felt the same."

Mia remembered Signorina Devoto's sense of propriety as suffocating. "She did not think Nina an appropriate companion for a wellborn child and did her best to do what my aunt did—that is, to convince both Nina and me that Nina had no place in our house other than as a servant.

"In the end she so convinced us that a maid is all that Janina wanted to be. I think differently now, but Nina does not want anything else. I will accept that as long as she will allow me to treat her like the sister she is."

She waited for David's response. If he laughed or told her she was stupid, or implied any failing in Janina, she would be the one to take the first swing at him.

David did not react to her story for the longest time, but stared at the ground, or maybe his boots. The three of them waited in silence.

Finally, finally, David looked at her, bowed, and then turned and gave an even more gracious bow to Janina. "First, I apologize for my rudeness before. It was inexcusable.

And thank you, for entrusting me with this story. I promise I will never speak of it unless you ask me to."

"Thank *you*, my lord." Janina curtsied to him and gave Mia a hug that stole her breath. Mia could feel her sister's tears on her neck and wished she had a handkerchief.

David pressed one into her hand, and she gave him a smile out of all proportion to the gesture and whispered, "I will give you handkerchiefs at Christmas."

He really could be the most thoughtful man. As she handed Nina the bit of linen she realized how carefully he hid his kindness. Why?

She noticed that the anger was gone from his face, softened now with understanding and even compassion. What would he and Romero fight over now that everyone was curtsying and bowing?

"Romero, when you arrive at Pennford I invite you to join me in the boxing ring. It would be a pleasure to go several rounds with someone as well built for boxing as you are."

"It will be a pleasure, my lord." Romero bowed as though David had promised him an unequaled treat. With that he took Nina's arm and they walked slowly back toward the house.

"David, please, let's sit on the bench where we can hear the river. I think we both need some time away from the house."

Chapter Twenty-six

WHAT THEY NEEDED, David thought, was time away from each other. But with the barest of good nights to *her sister* and Romero, David set out across the lawn toward the benches under the trees where they had first kissed. Not a wise spot to visit again, but wisdom did not seem to be in his makeup these days.

The air had cooled considerably but it was still comfortable enough to stay a while. Mia sat, playing with her skirts, humming a little.

He leaned against the sundial and looked back toward the house. It was brightly lit and he could even see the shadow of people in the library. Why were they not in the salon and out of their sight? David turned and found Mia with her eyes closed, her head thrown back as if she were absorbing every bit of the night magic that surrounded them.

Her dress was cut low, not scandalously so, but low enough that he did not need much of an imagination to see her as she would look naked.

"David, I am serious about becoming an independent woman."

What nonsense. He kept the comment to himself and waited, knowing how poorly she tolerated quiet.

"I will come into my own money when I am twenty-one, which is only a year or so away. First I will find a house, and then I will invite all those who are interested in music and hold a musicale. We will see who comes. That will tell me, more than anything else, where I fit in society now."

There was bitterness in her voice as she said that last. He had never heard her sound so hostile to the world in general.

"Why are you not optimistic?"

"Look at Lady Belfort. I thought her a friend, and she shunned me as though I had committed a crime by breaking my engagement."

"She is only one person." He sat on the bench next to her and handed her his coat. "Olivia likes you."

"She has to," Mia said, accepting the coat but only using it to cover her lap. "We are practically family."

Her cynicism should have been unbecoming, but underneath he heard her upset.

"Before I left London, after I ended the engagement, there were whole days when no one called on me at Penn Square."

She took a moment to actually put his coat on, her

arms in the sleeves, rather than just draping it over her shoulders. She raised her arms and buried her face in the fabric, drawing a deep breath, and then sighed. "It smells like tobacco."

The way she said it made tobacco sound like an aphrodisiac.

"Then I was invited to Bath, and I thought it was because Mrs. Giddings and her daughters liked me. But then I found out it was because their grandfather wanted to have a pretty girl around to look at." She laughed. "I tell you, David, I could have had a proposal from him if I had wanted. But I did not want to marry him. Or anyone else."

"Why did you not say something to Elena? Write and tell her how unhappy you were?"

"I was not about to share my heartache when she is so happy. Especially when there was nothing she could do about it."

He paused, impressed with this selflessness, and not wanting to be. "Then you are creating your own misery and cannot complain."

"I am explaining my decision to you. I am *not* complaining."

She stared at her fingers and he looked at them, too. It was almost dark and he could see nothing but their outline. He had never noticed how long they were. The better to play instruments, he thought, and let his imagination go no further.

When she raised her head, he read her expression as a dare. "Well, you do the same thing. You never tell anyone about Mexico because there is nothing anyone can do about it. So perhaps we are more alike than we think."

He laughed, short and harsh. "William is still very popular—" he began, but she did not let him finish.

"Exactly. And I am not. So now I am persona non grata. Until my birthday I will do whatever the duke and duchess tell me. Or say no if it is impossible, like a suggestion that I marry someone or that I take a vow of chastity."

He bit back a laugh. It was more likely that they would beg her to stop causing the locals such heartache.

"While I am waiting to come of age, I will contact an agent and arrange to rent a house." She paused, drew a deep breath, and announced, "In Bath."

"Bath? Why in the world would you pick Bath?"

"Because I like Bath. Why did you pick Birmingham? You know, your plans are as insane as mine but do I spend all my time trying to talk you out of them? No. I hope they work. I hope you find the financing you need or are able to talk the duke and his trustees into funding it totally from the estate."

"Thank you, but my plans do not compromise my place in society."

"Oh yes, they do. Very soon you will reek of trade and no one in the ton will want to associate with you."

"We have had this argument before and I do not care what society thinks."

"Neither do I. Haven't I said that often enough as well?" She stood and faced him, pulling his coat off and straightening her sleeves. "I have this all thought out. Bath is a city that will always attract visitors. Visitors of rank and wealth and those who have neither, but who do love music. They will be invited to my salon. In time I hope it will be the one place to which every visitor longs to be invited."

"It sounds like a fairy tale." David looked at the sky and the glittering stars, and wondered if there were other men on other stars who had easier lives. In truth, the plan was well thought out, but he couldn't see her doing it. Did not want her to do it. But that was no argument.

"Oh, please do not be such an old man. It will be an adventure, and you will always be welcome at my home."

"Thank you," he said with a bow, longing to be welcomed in a far more intimate setting.

"David," she said, stepping close enough so he could hear her whisper, "you know we could have such fun together."

"Let's walk." He stood up and set off, sure she would follow him. She did, and walked beside him in silence at first.

They made their way across the lawn toward the edge of the property that ran along the road. His eyes had grown used to the dark but still they walked slowly, not arm in arm, but next to each other.

"Why do you not use your wealth to become part of society someplace other than London if it no longer appeals to you?"

She smiled at him, and he felt ten times happier. He knew that smile came because he had asked a question. Really, she was amazingly easy to please.

"Because success in society for a single woman depends on other women. And I do not know many well enough to be sure I can count on them. If I go to Bath and make myself known in musical circles, the pianoforte and the guitar will be as good as an introduction from Lady Jersey."

"You see this like you see everything else. As an adventure, without realizing how risky it will be."

"I don't need to think of the difficulties. I have you to tell me."

Mia blew him a kiss and danced ahead of him. Half a day with two courtesans and she was well on her way to joining their ranks. How long would it take before her salon in Bath offered more than music?

They were coming up on the stables and they could hear the horses shuffling in their stalls. One of the grooms was outside.

David watched as the young man stood and brushed off his clothes.

"Miss Castellano." He bowed and called out to Lord David. "Good evening, my lord. Can I help you?"

"Good evening to you, Alan Wilson." Mia's genuine welcome made the boy smile, though it was not his usual brilliant grin. "How are you?"

"Well enough, thank you, miss. John Coachman was always very good to me. It hurts to hear of his passing."

"He was such a good driver," Mia said, filled with sympathy for his grief. "I am sure he taught you a great deal."

"Yes, miss," Wilson said with a smile. "He was as

good a teacher as he was a driver. Did you know his given name was Elmer Elmerton? I would have preferred to be called John Coachman myself."

"Perhaps you will be someday."

The boy bobbed his head, as though admitting out loud that it was his fondest wish would make him sound prideful.

"Thank you for making the trip at night. That must have been quite an adventure. But tell me, why are you still here?"

"His Grace said that I should wait to come back with you in case the other groom is not well enough."

"But who is taking care of Magda?"

"The dog will manage well enough at Pennford, though she does prefer the city."

David watched as the boy relaxed and his answers grew more enthusiastic. He did not think it was just because Alan Wilson loved talking about the dog.

"And she will try to escape every day so she can play with the field dogs. I expect that she will have a time of it while I am away."

"Well, I am sure that Magda will miss you almost as much as you miss her."

When the boy gave a curt nod, she laughed. "Good night, Wilson. I think we will be leaving tomorrow so you will see your Magda again soon."

"Yes, miss." He bowed and sat back down.

"He loves that dog as much as he loves any person." Mia took David's arm as they walked on.

"Not surprising. His father walked out on the family.

His mother beat him. Two of his siblings have died. He is very much alone in the world."

"Like me," Mia added.

"Yes, but without the money," David added with a sarcastic edge to his voice. The girl did see the world through only one lens.

"Are you trying to annoy me? I am too happy for that to work. Besides, one can feel abandoned with or without money."

"Yes, but money makes one so much more comfortable in their misery." He winced a little, thinking he may have pushed her too far.

"Yes, I am lucky, aren't I? But so is Alan Wilson to have come from such difficult circumstances and to now be doing work he loves. He has found his own kind of wealth. David, happiness and wealth are two completely different things."

"Yes, yes, I see your point." He admitted it with annoyance, sure she would preen over her minor victory. But she didn't.

"You know, I've always thought Alan Wilson was so much more than he seems. Perhaps he is the heir to property in Scotland and was kidnapped at birth. Or he has family in Bermuda that thinks he was lost at sea."

"Wilson is a groom and happy to be one." He was not jealous of the boy. Mia cared about everyone she met. Even him.

She shrugged. "Maybe I should find a pet to keep me company like Wilson has Magda, perhaps a poodle. I've always thought them cute, and they do not shed their hair on everything. Janina would hate a pet that sheds."

So she was not done comparing herself to the loveless groom. Did she really think herself so alone? Mia went on about different breeds of dogs as he thought back through their time together.

And cringed. He was so busy trying to suppress his attraction to her that he had made her feel less than welcome and succeeded in convincing her that she was just another task he must complete before he could do something much more important.

"A poodle, I think." She finally ended her discussion.

"I will give you one at Christmas."

"A poodle? Next you will be offering me a necklace." With that suggestion between them they were silent the rest of the way to the house.

The front hall was amazingly quiet. For his part he hoped that their fellow guests were abed—alone or together, he did not care; nor did he want to see them again tonight. Or tomorrow, either.

She followed him up the stairs. At the double doors that led to the owner's suite, he stepped back and waited for her to brush past him. He loved to watch the way she moved, as if the next adventure lay around the corner or beyond the door. And always she would do as she did now, turn to see if he would join her.

Would letting her into his life be such a big mistake?

God help him, he would at least wait until she was twenty-one. He would. It could be that when they were apart the attraction would fade to nothing. Waiting was the sensible thing to do.

"Mia."

She turned to him as though she had no idea what he wanted. He closed the double doors, took her hand. He knew that look. Her lips pressed together lest she laugh out loud with excitement, her eyes amazed and full of anticipation. She could hardly wait.

"One more kiss. We go on to Pennford tomorrow. Let's call the kiss a farewell to this adventure."

Her laughter disappeared. Her eyes flashed with anger.

"It's all we can share," he insisted. "You know it as well as I do."

She said nothing but stood very still, so he pulled her closer, lifted her chin with his finger, laid his lips on her mouth, and waited for a response.

He could feel her shaking as if she were upset or afraid, and he stopped. She raised a hand and would have slapped him if he had not grabbed her fingers before they landed on his cheek.

"I hate you, hate you, hate you," she whispered, though there was no missing her anger. "You think you can play with me, with my feelings, with my fears, with my plans." She drew a deep breath but before he could say a word she went on. "No. No. No. You cannot kiss me *one last time*." She said those three words like they were a joke. "Why won't you make love to me?"

"Because I would be taking advantage of your youth

and curiosity. It would hurt Elena and by extension the duke, and I would sooner die than hurt any of you."

"Oh, you would rather die. Then where is your knife?" She felt around his waist. "I know you carry one."

"I don't carry a knife with me when I'm in evening clothes." Thank God.

"Then I will go to the kitchen and find one."

"You sound like a child, Mia. Act the adult you are."

"I assure you this is not the anger of a child. Just because you find it easy to dismiss my upset because I am a child does not mean I am one. Soon, very soon, I will start making my own decisions."

She whirled around as if she would carry out her threat.

Let her leave. It's the right thing.

David grabbed her around the waist, lifted her, and carried her into his room, for once not caring what was right.

"Listen to me. You will stop this tantrum and go to your room."

As if further proving his point she kicked his shins with her heels and, in the end, he tossed her on the bed.

"The only thing you care about is your cotton mill!"

The cotton mill. The cotton mill. He thought the words like a chant, hoping it would distract him from the only thing he *did* care about. Holding her, feeling her all around him. Sharing an adventure with her that would be worth the risk. He could lose everything.

Mia rolled off the bed on the other side and looked

across the rumpled expanse. Her anger disappeared and she smiled at him as though she knew what he was thinking. She reached up and pulled a few pins from her hair so that it fell down her back. She dropped the pins in a cup on the table by his bed.

In that moment she was not a girl, but a woman.

Her beautiful hair fell halfway to her waist. Its dark color showed black and brown and auburn. He felt drained by the constant battle.

He could lose everything, he reminded himself, but what of value did he actually have? At this moment nothing mattered more than she did.

She came around the end of the bed, right up to him, as close as she could come without touching him. He thought she was going to try to seduce him, but she stood a moment, watching him, her smile as sad as a smile could be.

"Is there anyone, anywhere who will ever care about me as much as I care about them?"

"Sweetheart, I don't think that's possible."

"I know," she said, misunderstanding him, her eyes filling.

"But only because you do everything with such intensity." He could see it so clearly.

"Please make love to me. I am begging you." Mia blinked back the tears, but the longing remained.

He had not been drinking, so he could not blame his decision on spirits. He did not forget for a moment that he was supposed to protect her. He had not lost sight of what this would mean to him and to her, possibly to the rest of their lives.

What changed his mind was the look on her face and her words. *Please make love to me.* As if he would be doing her the greatest favor in the world. As if her life would not be complete without this night together. As if he was the answer to all her prayers.

Ettie's words still echoed in his head. *"Stop lying to yourself."* So he did. And in that moment of freedom there was no doubt in his mind that wanting Mia more than anything was a truth he had ignored for much too long.

She stood still, waiting. It never occurred to him to step back, much less push her away. He was done lying to himself. He wanted her.

He gentled her with little kisses at her temple, and felt her pulse, faster than usual. Was it the residue of anger or passion waiting? He kissed her neck, and the pulse there beat stronger and quicker. She drew a long breath but it sounded more like a sigh than a thrill.

David touched her cheek and then the corner of her mouth and felt her lips turn up in a smile. That was much better. His relief was so profound that he picked her up and whirled her around.

She gasped, then laughed. When he stopped and she slid down, he kissed her mouth and found everything he had ever hoped for in her response.

Her throat worked as he kissed her there and she laughed. "Oh, that feels so wonderful. Do not stop." He was happy to comply even when she would keep talking. "I love the feel of your tongue, the way your lips feel so soft and full." He ended her comments with his mouth on hers. She did not need words to convey her delight, but wrapped her arms around his neck and fell with him onto the bed, both of them still fully dressed.

"Do we need to take our clothes off? I do not want to stop for anything."

"Yes, part of the fun is the anticipation."

"*Dio mio,* David, we have had enough of that!"

She had a point.

"And my dress is already ruined from when I jumped on you."

He rolled her over so that she was on her stomach, and with a hand on the first button pulled at the material so that it ripped along the buttons all the way to her waist. She laughed in surprise as he held her down and began to kiss his way down her back.

"Oh there, again, right on that spot, or there. Oh, this feels so good that I will not let you stop."

He slapped her lightly on the buttocks and then pressed a kiss to the spot, though it was still covered by her shift and a petticoat that was tied at the waist.

He massaged the spot he had spanked and kissed, then rolled her over so that he could watch her face as he caressed her from neck to waist and below. She lay very still until he touched her breast with his fingers.

"Oh," she said, "I thought it would hurt." She sighed again, a sound he was beginning to love. "If you stop I will beat you with a pillow." She raised her hips and he knew she was as thoroughly aroused as he was.

Moving his hand ahead of his lips, he trailed caresses and kisses over her breast to her stomach, and then felt for the entry with his fingers to be sure she was ready.

She writhed against him and with her eyes closed begged with sounds that were not words but which needed no translation. When he stopped she cried out, a quiet scream, but he dearly hoped that Janina was sound asleep, across the corridor and two doors down.

"Why are you stopping? That cannot be all there is."

"Take your clothes off or you will be going back to your room naked." He was pulling off his boots and breeches. She struggled to kneel behind him.

"I could wear one of your shirts." Her hand was at his neck and then he felt her rip his shirt down the back. "Oh dear, I guess I can't use this one."

Mia began to do what he had done to her. Only she used her hands as well to knead the muscles at his neck. How did she know that was his favorite sort of foreplay?

With his clothes in a pile on the floor, he turned to her and with a deft movement pushed her onto her back. Her breasts were full, her stomach flat and even her navel a perfect little circle. "Do you wish you had some whipped cream?" she teased, then promised, "Another time."

"I told you once that I am not gentle with women."

"I am *soo* afraid," she said, laughing at him.

"I will try not to hurt you."

"Oh, David," she said, "it's very hard not to love you." With that she pulled him to her, arching her body to entice him. He should have waited, he should have made sure she understood what he was doing, but the feel of her hand on his erection left no other choice but to slide into her. He felt the moment of resistance that marked her virginity, but she did not seem to notice as he filled her body as completely as she filled his mind.

"It's so perfect," she said in short gasps as she began to move in time with him. It took less than a minute, he hoped more than five seconds, before he spilled his seed into her, before she arched against him to take it all, before he did not care about anything but the feeling of triumph and completion that spun in his head and ensnared his heart.

Lying entwined he heard her sigh again.

"Listen to me. Let me satisfy you, too." He kissed her sweetly and then began to move inside her again. He was not as aroused as he had been, who would expect that, but it was all the better as his manhood eased against her most sensitive spot and her sigh turned to a gasp.

"Oh, please, if you stop I will be so unhappy. I will—" Finally she stopped talking. Her body tensed and he could feel the pulse of her pleasure. David gathered her to him, holding her tight against his own body, his own arousal renewed by the throb of her own. With Mia this close the world was his, no bigger than this bed and the woman with whom he was one. He wanted no more than this. And no less.

When they separated but were still in each other's arms, he kissed the top of her head.

"You must have lied about being a virgin."

Mia smothered his chest with kisses and then sat upright, dragging the sheet with her, turning to face him. "I consider that the most wonderful compliment in the world."

"As I meant it to be." He pulled the sheet away from her breasts, but looked into her eyes.

Mia leaned closer so that the tips of her breasts touched his chest. He was almost sure she did that on purpose, and was even more certain she knew the consequences.

Chapter Twenty-seven

MIA LEANED CLOSER and pressed her breasts fully onto his naked chest. She wanted to make love again. And again. And again. How long before he would want her? She moved on top of him, acting on instinct, fitting her body to his. "Oh, I can feel you grow hard." It was amazing to have that effect on a man. She felt powerful and protective at the same time. Most of all she was hungry for him to give her, to share, the glory of that overwhelming feeling that became her only thought.

She raised herself on her knees, but before she could touch him, he grabbed her hips and pulled her to him so that he penetrated her in an instant. A gasp was all she could utter as she began to rise and fall as if riding a horse.

Was this right? She didn't care. It felt right and she kept moving until she could feel the explosion of satisfaction envelop them both. She heard herself cry out, "This is too much, too much," even though it wasn't and never would be.

David seemed to know that, too, though he did not react with words but by holding her hips against him, so that they were still but for the immense pulsing sensation that bound them together. Then she lay on top of him, wanting to feel their whole bodies touch. They stayed still as statues for a long time, until Mia began to doze. She slid down beside him again.

Sex could not be this wonderful with every man, or every time. If it was, then courtesans would be the happiest people in the world.

She cuddled beside him and wondered why husbands and wives slept apart. Mia felt him kiss her on the head again. That was one place where his kisses were not at all arousing.

He should be kissing her with passion, declaring his undying love. This was like being kissed by a cousin or some distant relative, an old one at that.

"Mia, you have to sleep in your own room. You cannot be here in the morning when the maid comes to light the fire."

"Must you always be practical? I do not care who knows we are lovers." She buried her face in his neck and kissed the tender skin there.

"But I do." He turned so he could look down at her. She loved the feeling of being overwhelmed by his size, his strength, his manliness. She loved it so much that she almost missed his next sentence. "Mia, this must be our secret."

He sat up, and though she hoped she made a pretty picture lying on the bed with her hair curling and her body his for the taking, David did not sweep her into his arms and declare devotion, but turned away.

"For how long?" she asked, finally giving up the hope of more kissing. "Until I am twenty-one, or for as long as you can hide it from the duke and Elena?"

David moved from the bed and stood, magnificently naked, broad-shouldered, with a body that would tempt a nun. He grabbed her chemise from the floor and tossed it to her.

"Mia, do not start an argument. Put on your chemise and go to your room."

"No." She sat up and wiggled to the far edge of the bed, putting some distance between them. Two angry people close to each other had to be as unwise as two aroused people. "You must explain to me how you can make such love to me one minute and the next be as practical and as cold as you are to a stranger."

"Because I have some common sense. We are not going to parade this relationship from here to Pennford unless you wish to announce our engagement!"

"*Dio mio,* no!" She scrambled out of bed and pulled her chemise on. She found her ruined dress, her petticoat. As she looked for her other garments and slippers she glanced at David. "I will do what you say. I will tell no one. I can even make up a story for Janina."

David nodded. "It will give both of us time to decide what we are going to do. Mia, you know what we must do if you are pregnant?"

She'd never thought of that.

"Yes, I can see by your expression that it never occurred to you when you were pulling pins from your hair and otherwise making yourself irresistible."

She would not be pregnant. If she was, she would have to go off to Scotland and pretend to be a widow and what would she do with the darling baby after he was born? She could not give up a child, David's child.

"It would mean marriage."

"No!" Mia tried to control the feeling of panic at the thought. "I could never marry someone who does so because they must." She felt ill at the thought that she would have no say. *Dio mio,* was this to be her whole life, never having a chance to make her own choices? Or did one choice dictate others not as desirable?

"We will talk about it later. Go now."

Mia wanted to argue about it. To annoy him so much, to make him so angry that all his bad feelings were used up and the love he must hide somewhere came out.

Because she knew he had feelings for her; she could feel them. He could not touch her as he had, hold her, make love to her, without them. She knew him that well. David Pennistan had compromised himself tonight, and he'd done it because of how he felt about her. And there was only one way to make him see that.

"No, David, we will not talk about it later. This is the end. When you find you can speak of love, when your first worry is not your precious cotton mill, then, if you are very lucky, you can find me and beg me to take you back."

Without waiting for an answer, Mia tiptoed across the

passage and into her room. The candle that Nina had left flickered its last light, the colors of the elegant room as muted as her spirits. At least the door to the dressing room was closed.

Dropping her clothes in a pile on the floor, Mia slid under the covers and closed her eyes, hoping that David was as wide awake as she was.

Marriage wasn't the only option if she was with child. She could go to America as a widow, and after it was born stay and raise the child there. She had the money, but it was unlikely that David would allow that.

She could give the child to David to raise, but to never see her own child, never be a part of his life, well, that could not be borne.

There must be other possibilities, something besides marriage to a man who did not love her. She fell asleep telling herself that the chance of pregnancy the first or second time a person shared love must be very rare.

WHEN DAVID WENT TO BREAKFAST the next morning he found himself alone. Cantwell told him that Franklin and Kyle were at the river, angling, and the ladies were taking breakfast in their rooms.

"Miss Castellano," Cantwell began, and David noted that he did not group her with the other women, "is dressing for a visit to the village. She said that before you leave for Pennford there is one call she must make."

"Tell her we leave before noon."

Cantwell nodded and left the room.

In the study he set about putting away the plans and papers that he now knew as well as he knew the road home. He should be thinking about what to tell the duke and how to convince his brother to support the venture wholly.

But all he could think about was how and when to announce his engagement to Mia. There was no doubt in his mind that they must marry. The sex had sealed their fate, even if the two of them never breathed a word of it to anyone. Even if neither of them wanted it. Not because he had ruined her, at least not entirely, but because he knew that his longing was too great to overcome.

If his lust for Mia wore out in time, then they would be no different from the rest of society's married couples, though they would be an oddity in the Pennistan family. First Gabriel, then Olivia, and, most recently, the duke himself had married their lovers and seemed the better for it.

Yes, there were periods when Olivia spent more time in the kitchen than seemed necessary, or the duke spoke in short, curt sentences. Both actions meant arguments with their spouses. But bright smiles from Olivia and a much more relaxed air from Lyn far outweighed the discontent.

If his marriage was not a success then he would accept it as the cost of one night of the most perfect lovemaking he had ever known.

Once Mia Castellano was Lady David Pennistan, he could refocus on what was most important. Financing for the cotton mill. Employment, money, a step toward the future that the Meryon dukedom badly needed. And success that had eluded him for so long.

He finished with his leather traveling bag and then turned to the bookshelves to find the ideal engagement present for his adventurous bride-to-be. Along with something that glittered, so Mia would not even notice that love was not part of his declaration.

He was capable of love. He had learned that in Mexicado, and learned the cost of it so well that he would never make the mistake of loving again.

Chapter Twenty-eight

"MISS CASTELLANO, IT IS a pleasure to meet you." Miss Horner curtsied gracefully, despite the boy hanging on her leg.

"Mary, I want to play ball and Robert won't come out-doors with me. He's reading." The boy's disgust with the written word was obvious.

"It's that kind of day, is it not," Mia said, trying to ease Miss Horner's embarrassment at her brother's inter-ruption. "The sky is so blue, with a few clouds to make sky-watching interesting."

"What is sky-watching?" the boy asked, still clutching his sister's leg.

"You lie on your back and watch the clouds until you find one that looks like something you know, like a rabbit or barn."

"It sounds like a *girl's* game," the boy said scornfully.

"How old are you?" Mia asked.

"Almost six."

"He turned five a week ago."

"Five is a fine age, Master Horner. Old enough to sky-watch all by yourself."

"Thank you, miss." He bowed to Mia and ran off toward the back of the house.

"What good manners."

"It's baking day. He knows there are treats in the kitchen, so he will detour that way before he tries sky-watching. Do you know more games? I could always use new ideas."

"Oh, I have an endless supply. I was easily bored as a child and my papa was very good at finding things for me to do."

"Then you will be well prepared when you have your own family."

Mia nodded, but she had to work to keep smiling. What would she do if she was pregnant already? What sort of games did David play as a boy? Would he want to teach them to a son, or would he leave all that to the babe's mother and nurse?

"I was about to step outside and see what flowers might be ready for cutting," Miss Horner continued, blithely unaware of the direction of Mia's thoughts. Thank heaven. "Would you like a walk in the garden with me?"

"That would be lovely."

A door slammed and a girl, older than the boy but still

young, came pelting down the stairs. She stopped short when she saw her sister with a visitor.

"Elizabeth, Mama is resting in the parlor. Please move about more quietly."

Well, Mia thought, that was one good reason not to have this conversation in the parlor, of which there appeared to be only one.

"Mama is asleep?" The girl covered her mouth with one hand and whispered, "Oh, Mary, I am so sorry. I promise to be as quiet as a mouse." Elizabeth eyed the newcomer with curiosity but merely nodded to both of them as she went toward the back of the house on tiptoes.

As Mia and Miss Horner headed out to her garden, her hostess filled the silence with talk of weather.

Mia wondered at Miss Horner's placid demeanor. More than that, she exuded an air of serenity that was as relaxing as sitting in the shade. It was more than show, for she had not said one harsh word to her brother and sister. Mia suspected that "selfish" was not a word in Miss Horner's vocabulary.

"Don't you agree, Miss Castellano? The hours of summer sun are not nearly as tiring as the short winter days."

"Yes," Mia said as Mary opened the garden gate. "I always want to sleep in the winter, but in the—" Mia stopped talking abruptly, her mind filled with the beauty in front of her.

The garden was a wonder, an explosion of color tempered by green, enlivened still more by light, and shade from one tree on the far edge of the walled space.

Reds, yellows, purples, blues, all competed for attention. The luxurious white blooms gave the eye some rest. There were large flowers like the hydrangea and others smaller, so small they bloomed in clusters so they would not be missed. Even the moss between the stepping-stones was lush.

"My apologies for knowing so little about flowers, Miss Horner, except that I love them. Your garden is exceptional."

"But that is the joy of flowers, is it not?" her hostess said reassuringly. "One does not need to know anything about them to enjoy them."

Mary Horner led her to a bench in the shade of the tree where a jug and some glasses were set under a linen cloth. Mia was slow joining her, stopping to smell and admire, and envy the bees who visited one bud after another, obviously drunk with delight.

When Miss Horner offered her a glass of lemonade, Mia laughed. "You are fey and you knew I was coming."

"I always have the maid bring some here after breakfast so I can stay out as long as possible. And the boys help weed and I reward them with a glass."

The lemonade had more lemons than sugar. And where did Miss Horner find lemons? The tang was the perfect counterpoint to the garden's overwhelming sweet smell.

Now that they were seated with their drinks, Mia could not quite think of how to start this conversation.

"Mr. Novins says that you are the liveliest woman he

has ever met," Miss Horner began, "and we are all so relieved that the food poisoning did not cause any lasting harm."

"Thank you," Mia said as graciously as she could. Then she added, "Mr. Novins talks about me?"

"Constantly," Miss Horner added in a dry voice.

"Oh, I am so sorry." Mia echoed Elizabeth's phrase, with equal sincerity. "I know how wearing that can be. Let me assure you that Lord David considers my liveliness a besetting sin." *Except in bed,* Mia added very quietly, to herself.

"Oh, Lord David may say that is so, he may even think he believes it, but I find that gentlemen will protest about what they truly like the most."

"Do you think so?" And what experience did Miss Horner have of men, Mia wondered, stuck here in this little village with no man in the house?

"Yes, most assuredly. I went to Bath for a few months, and I had plenty of time to observe; I daresay gentlemen are the same the world over."

Mia nodded encouragingly. No doubt Mary Horner had gone to Bath because her family did not have the money or the connections for a London Season. Though Mary did not say that, precisely, it was obvious from her surroundings.

What did it say about the world that they could converse in her garden today but if Miss Horner were to come to Bath next year, they would most likely not be in the same circles?

"And then there is Mr. Novins."

The mention of the surgeon's name drew Mia's attention from her musings.

"He will complain—in a very circumspect way, mind you—that I care too much for people, do too much."

"And you do not agree with him."

"Not at all. My responsibilities to my mother and my brothers and sisters are more important to me than my own comfort. Surely you feel the same way about those you love?"

"I do not have any family." Except Janina, and she hoped she would do anything to keep her sister happy. But she was not completely sure.

"That must be very hard."

"And I think that the sacrifices you make are hard."

"Not at all. Love makes all things possible."

"Do you think so?"

"Yes," Miss Horner said with a laugh. "I did not say it was easy or simple, but love is the storehouse of strength." She sipped her lemonade.

"Does Mr. Novins understand this?"

Miss Horner shook her head with the first scowl of annoyance Mia had seen. "I cannot convince him that becoming his wife, the mother of his children, his companion in all things, would be not a sacrifice but exactly what I want."

Ah, Mia thought, "his companion in all things" was such a sweet term for lover.

"Helping him minister to others would make my life complete." She stood up, moved to the closest bed of flowers, and pinched some dead blooms off an otherwise thriving plant.

"Men can be so . . ." Mia paused, and then said exactly what she was thinking. "Men can be so stupid. There is no other word for it."

Miss Horner pulled scissors from her apron and continued to clip off the dead flowers and cut others to use, but she was smiling at Mia's blunt statement. "Yes, I suppose so, at least they are when it comes to matters of the heart."

Mia pinched off some of the dead flowers, too, looked to Miss Horner for approval, and when she nodded kept on. "Why is it so impossible to convince them that women often know what is best?"

"Because, Miss Castellano, they have been raised to believe that we are mere ornaments."

"Then why aren't they the ones that have babies?"

Miss Horner looked shocked and then started laughing. Mia smiled at the sound. She could make people laugh, if only by stating a truth they were too genteel to say themselves.

They continued with their work in a companionable silence. How intriguing that both Mr. Novins and Miss Horner had the same problem. They were generous to a fault. Well, that was one problem neither she nor Lord David had to worry about.

Then a solution occurred to her, once again proving *no* the most useful word in any language.

"Mary," Mia said with such intensity that Miss Horner stopped her work and gave Mia her full attention. "Did you know that Mrs. Cantwell asked if you could come to Sandleton and help with the sick and Mr. Novins said no?"

"He did?"

"Well, I believe his exact words were 'absolutely not.'"

"But I would have helped."

"Of course, and he knew that if you did your mother and your family would have been neglected, or put at risk if we were ill with a contagion. So he said no for you."

"I'm not sure if I like that or not."

"Perhaps what you two are meant to do is say no for each other. How often is Mr. Novins called away when you think it unnecessary?"

"All the time. The Irvings call for him at least once a week for such silly things as splinters."

"If you were married, you could say no for him when you thought it an imposition and not a medical necessity."

"I don't think I could do that."

"But you could say no when it came to other things that were neither medical nor emergencies, could you not?"

"Yes, yes, I could do that."

"Then marry him and practice saying no for each other for the rest of your lives, and you will be very happy together."

By the time Mia walked back to Sandleton she was very pleased with herself. Mr. Novins was a fool if he did not marry this woman as fast as he could. She was a gem.

Was it true, as Miss Horner insisted, that love made all things possible? Not easy, but possible.

Maybe if David loved her enough, just maybe, marriage was a possibility. But could she love him enough to take second place to his cotton mill, his family, even his boxing? If at night, in bed, was the only time he loved her, would that be all she would need? If he never could say the words I love you?

No.

She knew from her father, her friends, and her own failed engagement that love from the heart and the mind was essential to a happy union. Even then it could be a challenge, and certainly would be for David Pennistan and Mia Castellano.

For she was just as guilty as David at hiding from the words that would set them on a path to a lifetime together. Did she love David Pennistan?

Well, it was not a decision she would have to make today. Or ever.

Unless she was with child.

Chapter Twenty-nine

AS MIA MADE the last turn on the curved drive back to the house, she saw the Meryon coach and four standing at the front door. Exactly what time was it? And more to the point, who was going to act as coachman for this part of the trip?

Hurrying up the front steps, she went into the house, dropping her pelisse and bonnet on the table nearest the door. The hall was empty, but the pile of baggage confirmed that packing was well under way.

Mia looked into the study and found it empty as well. There was no sign of Lord David or his papers. Had he dared to leave early, as he'd suggested he might?

Angry at the very thought, she hurried up the stairs, into the family wing, and into his room with the barest of knocks. It was empty. Who had packed all his things so quickly?

With a harsh breath, and half afraid that he had, indeed, left without her, Mia picked up a book and threw it at the wall. The clunk it made was not particularly satisfying; for the first time Mia understood why men liked boxing so much.

She hurried back into the hall and into her room to see if Janina knew of his whereabouts.

"Be sure to carry that right side up as the hats are fragile."

The command in her voice reminded Mia that Janina was best avoided on travel days. She had very particular thoughts on how everything should be packed and could be quite the dictator.

Mia ran back downstairs, her feelings of panic increasing out of all proportion. He would not, could not go to Pennford without her. He would not dare talk to Elena or the duke about her before she arrived.

Outside, she broke into a run toward the stables to see if his horse was gone. Before she reached the building, Franklin came round from the side of the house.

"Whoa! Miss Castellano." He grabbed her arm. "Stop a moment. You are just the morsel I hoped to find today."

"Good morning, sir." She gave him a quick curtsy and would have moved on if she could have pulled her arm from his grip.

"Slow down, my girl. I would have a word with you."

"No! I have to go to the stables. I'm in a hurry."

"No one there that can give you what I can."

Mia stopped struggling. If David had left already, racing to find out would not bring him back. "What do you want, Franklin?" Her tone of voice was hardly gracious, but Franklin did not seem to mind.

"You were much the topic of conversation this morning, with all of us trying to define what your idea of being an 'independent woman' means."

"Lord Kyle was talking about me? With everyone?"

"To me, Candy, and Ettie. How flattering that you consider that everyone. Last night you seemed most interested in Lord Kyle, and he thought Ettie might have a word with you."

Last night's dinner seemed a hundred years ago.

"My thought was, Mia," he used her given name quite casually and stepped even closer, "that if you wanted a little practice in dealing with gentlemen, I would be very happy to tutor you." With that, he moved beside her, put his arm around her so that she could feel him touching the side of her breast, and urged her onto the lawn. "I found a little love nest on this side of the house. It is the perfect spot for us to become better acquainted."

That was the last thing she wanted. His touch disgusted her, made her feel physically ill. Of course that could have come from running too fast while wearing stays, but she didn't think so. She wanted to scratch his eyes out for no other reason than the way he was holding her.

"No!" She jerked her arm but he did not loosen his grip. "Franklin, I am not interested in becoming better acquainted with you."

He laughed and offered her the flask he had just drunk from. "Here, this brandy will help."

"No. Unhand me now!" She was contemplating whether to kick him in the knee or higher if he did not release her.

"Here is your first lesson: This is the point at which you should end your protests, feel faint, and allow me to lead you to someplace more private."

"No. I will show you how faint I feel." And with one of those deft movements that she had learned as a child when eluding a spanking, Mia escaped his hold and ran directly into Lord David.

Oh, how wonderful. He had not left.

She grabbed David's lapels and held on.

"NICELY DONE, MIA," he said, letting his lips rest on the top of her head.

"You were watching?" She leaned back to look at him.

"Yes." David should not have been surprised by the flash of steel in her eyes. He was almost sure it was leftover rage with Franklin's behavior and not with him.

"Yes," he said again. "I was about to pummel him when you escaped."

"I thought you had left," she said, hands on hips, and now he knew her displeasure was aimed at him.

"And leave you with these randy fools? Never."

"I say, Lord David."

Franklin's blustering attempt to draw his attention reminded David of one bit of unfinished business. "Would you like me to teach him a lesson?"

"Yes, my lord, I would."

He turned around, strode over to Franklin, steadied him by grabbing the lapel of his coat, then punched him square in the face. It felt so good he was sorely tempted to do it again.

Blood gushed from Franklin's nose. He staggered backward and screamed like a girl. "You broke it!"

"Maybe, maybe not." David did not care one way or the other. "But if you do not leave Miss Castellano alone now and forever, I promise you I will break your jaw, your arm, and your leg."

"You didn't have to do that." Franklin's tone was man-to-man now. "Just tell me you had a claim."

Franklin had ruined one handkerchief. David watched as he pulled his shirt from his pantaloons and used the ends to try to staunch the blood and save his coat from ruin.

"Claim?" Mia said, her voice a sure clue to her outrage. "You think a woman is something you can claim?" She would have kicked Franklin if David had not taken her hand and pulled her away.

"Mia, listen to me," David said as he urged her toward the carriage.

She stopped and faced him.

"This is what you will face all the time if you insist on establishing yourself without a chaperone."

She said nothing but began to turn away. "Don't you see that eventually you will lose yourself in the demi-monde? You have to listen to me."

"No, I do not."

Her tone provoked him beyond civility.

"I do insist." He let go of her shoulders. The urge to shake her was too real. He raised his hand, gesturing toward Franklin, who was almost at the front door. "Is that the sort of life you want? Consorting with men who make your skin crawl?"

"My salon will not be like that," she said with an insistence that made him want to shout. He did his best not to.

"Mia, once you make this choice, once you leave Meryon's protection, society will reject you. You think what you feel now is hurtful. It is nothing compared to what could happen. There will be no turning back."

"I will be discreet. My salon—"

"Damn times five freaks. Your salon is a fairy tale," David said, cutting her off. "It's what every courtesan wishes their world was. In truth, someone pays and then they fuck you. There is nothing elegant or discreet or charming about it."

David could feel anger explode out of her. Mia pulled out of his grasp, and when she raised her hand to slap him he allowed it.

"You disgust me as much as Franklin does!"

David watched as Mia ran toward the house. She might be disgusted with him, but not half as disgusted as he was with himself.

He turned toward the stables. Leaving in a timely way was the least of his problems.

David hoped his blunt words had shocked some

sense into her, shown her the reality of her absurd dream. She was stung, and angry, either because of Franklin's abuse or his own words, or both. In any case, he did know that he had ruined any hope of her accepting his proposal.

So he'd best come up with another plan.

Chapter Thirty

IT WAS SOME TIME after noon before they departed, and not only because Mia had taken as long as she possibly could to make her farewells to the Cantwells and the rest of the servants. Their departure was slowed even further by the last-minute arrival of a breathless Mr. Novins, who was anxious for a personal good-bye.

Mia gave the last of her traveling items to Janina. "I promise I will not be long," she assured her and went to greet Mr. Novins.

He bowed to her. She curtsied.

"I want to thank you for visiting Miss Horner. I saw her today and she asked if I would extend her farewells with my own."

"You spent some time with her?" No suit could have prospered in the few hours since she and Mary Horner had met.

"We talked," he said.

She waited, hoping that silence would prompt details.

"I know it will sound odd, miss, but she actually said no to me when I asked her to do me a favor. She said no, and when I showed my surprise and perhaps a little disappointment, Miss Horner laughed and said that I should thank you.

"I left in some confusion but as I thought about it, I do believe the word *no* from Miss Horner is one of the wonders of the world."

"I hope so, for both your sakes, sir." He nodded, and if he thought that an odd wish he gave no sign of it. "Mr. Novins, I want to thank you for the care you gave us, and I promise you that the duke and duchess shall hear of it and send their own thanks."

"I appreciate that, Miss Castellano. I hope that the angling will bring you back to Sandleton."

Mia said all the right things one more time, while she marveled at the fact that a suit *could* prosper in so little time. She would write to Miss Horner and encourage her to respond. Until news of an engagement came to her, Mia would not consider her conversation with Mary Horner a complete success.

Mr. Novins escorted her back to the coach where he waved farewell to the others, including Lord David, whose horse was pawing the ground, as ready as his master to be off.

Romero, of all people, was acting as coachman. "He is a man of many skills," Janina bragged as they set out.

Alan Wilson rode alongside Romero in the coachman's box and the two grooms rode in the rear behind the trunks lashed on top.

Even though they were leaving late, Lord David announced that they would stop every five miles or so.

"Why are we to stop so often?" Mia called to him, but Lord David had already urged Cruces into a canter. He was out of sight before they had left the edge of town. Mia watched him until she could not see him anymore as she untied her bonnet and tossed it on the seat. It was too small and made her temples ache.

"Where is Lord David going?" Janina asked as they passed through the cloud of dust that Cruces had stirred up.

"I do not care."

"What happened?" Janina asked, her eyes narrowed.

"He is awful and crude."

Janina raised a hand to her mouth. "Is this about last night? Oh, my God, did he force you to have sex with him?"

"What? Force me? No, never." Then Mia realized what Janina's comment meant. "You know we were together?"

Nina gave a tiny nod that was as much apology as confirmation.

"How did you find out?"

"Mia, your dress was ruined. When I saw it this morning, I thought it was because of a passion that could not be denied, but now I see I could have been gravely mistaken."

"No." Mia sighed. "You were right the first time. It was the most wonderful evening of my life."

Janina nodded encouragement.

"It is much too private to discuss, but please believe me when I say that the seduction was totally mutual."

"So now you are going to marry him." Janina clapped her hands.

"No. Never." Mia closed her eyes and waited until she could talk without shouting. "He does not love me. He would be forever saying 'Listen to me,' and telling me things I do not want to hear." She swallowed her heartache. "If love makes all things possible, trying to live without love in a marriage would be horrible."

"But he must like something about you to propose."

"He has not proposed, Nina. He only asked what I would do if I found I was with child."

"Oh, dear, that is not even a little romantical."

"Not even a little." Mia pulled off her gloves and dug through her bag for her own handkerchief. "And there is something even worse."

"What could be worse?"

"He told me that my idea to live independently was a fairy tale. That if I live without a chaperone in no time I would become part of the demimonde."

Mia slipped to the floor, put her head in Nina's lap, and began to cry. Nina smoothed her hair and then made matters worse. "I have always thought the same thing."

"What!" Mia stopped crying, bolted upright, and pushed herself onto the seat next to her sister.

"I have never understood why you could not invite some poor but wellborn woman to live with you, to convince everyone that you are and always will be a lady. You could even live at Penn House in London. It is more like a palace than a home, and you could have your own apartments and never even have to see the duke when he comes for Parliament."

"Nina, have you forgotten my ruined engagement? I have no idea how Elena will react to that. She may send me to my room for a month. She may refuse to speak to me. William is her dearest relative. And I hurt him badly."

"But think how much this choice of living alone will hurt Elena."

Would it? Mia wondered. She would not know until she reached Pennford and discovered how Elena felt.

"I will think about my plans, Nina. Not because of what David said but because you've asked me to."

Janina took her hands and kissed her cheek. And all was right in their world. Mia settled back and closed her eyes.

"Mia?" Janina asked in a timid voice. "Has it been five miles yet? Do you think we will be stopping soon?"

Oh, so that was why David had insisted on the frequent stops. His kindness was as guarded as everything else about him.

Those first five miles were the last that Janina could handle inside the coach. With her hands pressed to her stomach and her face too pale, it was decided Janina would squeeze into the coachman's box with Romero and Alan Wilson so they could move a little faster than a snail.

Mia tucked herself into the corner of the carriage so she could see out both windows, one over her shoulder and the other across from her. The sun was moving west and the air was still dry. There was enough shade that the inside of the coach did not feel like an oven. If she could doze off she could escape her worries. It would be a relief.

Instead she would pray. That she would be allowed for once in her life to make her own choice.

That Nina and Romero would find the happiness each deserved. That Mary Horner and Mr. Novins each grasped the value of the word *no,* except in bed. That Elena would understand that Mia's ending her engagement to William was the right thing for both of them, and even that William would find someone worthy of all he had to give.

That David Pennistan would discover such a powerful love— She stopped that prayer before it fully formed. To pray for love was too much like asking for a miracle, and how dreadful to ask for one and then discover it was not the answer to all her problems. So the last thing she prayed for was that she was not with child. It was a prayer for both her and David and, she hoped, not too much to ask.

Sleep, blessed sleep, spared her any more self-pitying thoughts.

She woke up when the coach slowed to a stop, but kept her eyes closed. The carriage rocked as Janina climbed back inside, and once they were under way again Mia opened her eyes.

David sat across from her; Mia blinked the sleep from her eyes to be sure that she was not dreaming. No, he was still there, looking at her with an intensity that would have been flattering if he had looked at all happy.

"Is Nina all right?" she asked as she struggled up, and

winced when she realized she had been sleeping on her now-crushed bonnet.

"Janina is fine. She remains in the box with Romero, who assures me he knows how to take very good care of her."

Mia tried not to smile. "And Cruces?"

"Alan Wilson is riding ahead to alert Pennford that we will be there before dark." His expression relaxed a little, though he still did not seem inclined to smile. "I do believe he is jealous of me."

"He is?" Mia looked out the window but could see no sign of the young groom.

"Yes, he is very protective of you." David took a breath. "Who do you think called for me when he saw Franklin stop you by the stable?"

"Do not ever remind me of that disgusting man again." It was possible that with an effort she could forget Franklin's insults. David's diatribe was another horror entirely.

"As you wish." He nodded as though he agreed with himself about something even more important.

"So you are in here with me because you have no other choice."

"I am in here because I want to tell you what will happen when we arrive at Pennford."

"You can see the future and know what is going to happen?" Did he even know that he talked as though he were responsible for the whole world?

"Oh, yes, I can predict with unerring certainty."

"I am not at all interested in your *opinion*." Mia looked out the window. There wasn't much else she could do to ignore him in such a small space.

"When we arrive at Pennford we will go our separate ways. You will spend your time with Elena and Olivia and I will spend my time with my brother and Olivia's husband."

"In the boxing ring?"

"Undoubtedly."

With that one word he made it sound all her fault.

"We will not see each other except at dinner."

She shrugged and watched a leafy branch rub against the side of the carriage.

"Within a few weeks, or less, we will know if you are with child. If you are, then we will marry as quickly as possible. Between the duke and Michael Garrett, who is a priest, that can be arranged. If there is no reason for us to marry then we do not have to see each other ever again. You can make any arrangements you wish with the duchess and I can build my cotton mill."

Pain tightened her chest. He could barely wait to be rid of her. "There must be some other option if I am going to have a baby."

"Yes, there is, but we will marry. You may not feel the need but I have a responsibility to my family name, and I will do what is right."

Responsibility. That was the reason he would marry her. Of course it was. He would marry her so his brother would not be unhappy. Anger began the slow burn that meant trouble. "If we go our separate ways we will never make love again."

"That's right." There was the reasonable tone again. It was beginning to annoy her.

She leaned forward. "That means that making love two times was enough?"

"Apparently."

And that single word was exactly the answer she was looking for.

"Oh, my lord David Pennistan, you are so wrong." She moved a little so that she was more directly across from him. "Two times is barely a beginning. Have you ever made love in a moving coach with people all around you?" She moved over to his side of the coach as she spoke.

"Mia, stop."

"We would have to be very quiet," she whispered, and nipped his earlobe before settling back on the bench. "You know I am very dexterous. I could sit on your lap, splay my legs on either side of you in a way that would seem impossible. Do you want me to show you?"

"Mia, I do not—"

"Shhh." She pressed her fingers to his mouth. If he thought he was immune to this, she was about to prove him a liar. His erection pressed against his trousers, making his interest clear. "I want you as much as you want me, David Pennistan. I want to feel your fullness in me and move with you in time to the way the carriage sways back and forth. I want you to swallow my cry of pleasure as your seed fills me."

He turned to her, both angry and aroused, his hands

grasping her waist, which was exactly what she had been waiting for. She patted his cheek as she slipped away out of his arms.

"I would say that I have just proved that two times was not enough." Mia moved back to her side of the carriage and resettled her skirts decorously around her. "But that is all you will ever have from me, my lord."

She raised the fan that she'd brought along and waved it. He was not the only one disappointed and overwrought. "I agree with your suggestion. After tomorrow we will go our separate ways."

She resumed her spot in the corner of the carriage, looking out the window, so lost in thought that she saw nothing outside the window but a blur of green.

Chapter Thirty-one

DAVID WATCHED MIA through narrowed eyes. There were words to describe a woman who would do that to a man. Tease was the least of them.

If she had done that to prove how weak he was, then she had made her point quite adequately. He could take her again and again, and he knew as well as she did that they would lose count before they ever had enough of each other.

Lying in bed last night, as sleepless as he hoped she was, he had tried to imagine what their marriage would be like. Exciting for a while. But then he would have to turn his attention to the cotton mill, funding it, supervising the construction. She would feel neglected, and only Mia knew what she would do if she felt abandoned.

If she were carrying his child they would marry. He had no doubt of that, and they would make the best of it.

But he would never call it a love match. She was too young and he was too hardened. But whatever it was, he hoped it would see them through a lifetime. Otherwise they would end up mired in hatred and not above inflicting more pain on each other than either of them had ever experienced before. He'd had a glimpse of that shared pain today when he lost his temper and she had slapped him, and just now, a totally different kind of suffering. It was as close to hell as he ever wanted to be.

MIA DID NOT OPEN her eyes from her faux nap until she was sure they were passing through the town of Pennsford. More than one of the townsfolk waved in greeting. Mia waved back, even though they could not possibly recognize her as she had never been there before. David ignored the greetings.

The carriage moved on, the horses climbing steadily and slowly to Pennford. Well, it was a castle and would be set on the highest point. How she wished she was up in the driver's box so she could see what was coming. Instead she folded her hands together to hide her nerves and inspected the grounds while she waited for the castle to come into view.

The grounds were as lush and green as all the other parts of England, but she noticed that this lawn was perfectly cut, the trees were well pruned, and the shrubbery showed not one dead or dried branch. There were few flowers in bloom and she wanted to ask David if there was a garden somewhere, but held her tongue as the castle itself came into view.

It was huge, designed to impress, and it did. Parts of it looked very old. Hopefully the dungeons were no longer in use.

She had seen castles aplenty in Europe, but she had always been a welcome guest. Her uncertainty as to her welcome at Pennford added to the intimidating air that enveloped her as they drew closer.

The carriage drove through open gates and passed a charming gatehouse with apparently no guard in residence. She felt one of the grooms jump down and heard the sound of him pulling the gates closed behind them. Once on Pennford grounds, David banged on the roof and Romero slowed the carriage to a stop.

Janina let Romero lift her down from the coachman's box. Without a word, David left the coach and began walking toward the castle while Janina took his place across from Mia.

"Oh, Mia." Janina's voice was filled with anxiety. "The castle is daunting, is it not? I did not think any place could be bigger than Penn House in London!"

There was yet another drive to negotiate but the castle dominated the landscape. The building still had the giant doors that reminded Mia of armor-clad men on destriers. This part of the castle was not old enough to have need of such doors. Some duke before Lynford Pennistan assumed the title had commissioned them to intimidate whoever came to call. It worked, Mia thought.

Nina reached over and pinched Mia's cheek gently.

"Are you nervous? I will come with you. Have you thought about what you are going to say?"

She had not. She had been so caught up in her contest with David that her broken engagement seemed ancient history now. They stopped in front of the grand door and Mia felt her heart in her throat.

"Janina, please supervise the unpacking. I will see Elena myself and then come to you."

Janina accepted the task without complaint. David waited at the carriage door and offered Janina his help stepping onto the drive.

When her maid had gone to the rear where the trunks were secured, he gave Mia his hand and helped her down from the coach. She took his arm. It was like taking hold of a piece of wood. Was that because she was working so hard to control herself, or because he was?

He took her to a smaller, almost invisible door to the right of the ceremonial doors. Before he lifted his hand to knock, the door swung open, and a very distinguished gentleman bowed. "Welcome home, my lord." Then he saw her. "Welcome to Pennford, miss."

"Mia, this is Winthrop. He keeps this pile of rocks from crumbling down around us. Winthrop, this is Miss Castellano, the duchess's ward."

Winthrop bowed formally to her. "The duchess is resting. She does not come downstairs these days, but asked that I show you up as soon as you arrive."

"I will take her up, Winthrop."

"Very good, my lord." Winthrop made to step back, and Mia turned to hand her hat and cloak to the footman.

"And the duke, Winthrop. Where is he?" David asked.

"He is in his study. Shall I send a message that you have arrived?"

"Yes, and that I will meet with him at his convenience."

David gave his things to the footman and offered Mia his arm. She took it, and closed her eyes for just a moment. As long as she did not think about his opinion of her, David's touch, strong and confident, was wonderfully reassuring. At the same moment it occurred to her that if Elena sent her away, she might never see him again. The thought should please her; instead, her eyes filled with tears.

They moved toward the stairs. Mia cleared her throat and whispered, "I want to clean up before we go to see Elena."

"Are you crying?" He sounded shocked.

"No, I am not."

"Very well," David said, and she knew he did not believe her. "Winthrop said the duchess wanted to see you as soon as you arrive."

"He did not mean that literally, David."

"You cannot put this off, Mia. The sooner you see the duchess and explain your broken engagement, the better you will feel."

He annoyed her the most when he was right. Putting on as brave a face as she could, Mia walked toward what awaited her at Pennford, desperate for the next year to pass. How could her life have changed so completely in less than a week?

She had been terrified of smallpox. She should have been as terrified of the games she had played with her heart. No one need ever know about her so-brief affair with David. It was in everyone's best interest to keep that secret. But she would know, and the knowledge caused a heartache from which she desperately wanted to escape.

So now she had to look back to her life, before David, and decide how to use her failed engagement as a way to convince Elena that an independent life would suit her best.

She and David climbed and walked and wound their way through a number of corridors, in silence. There were footmen stationed in various alcoves and at turning points, and though each one bowed to David, he barely nodded to them.

"I could have easily asked for directions and avoided this endless parade."

"Listen to me."

She could see the muscle in his jaw work and knew he was, if not nervous, very uncomfortable. Or was it worried?

"I said that I would see you safely to Pennford and I will not let you from my sight until you are with the duchess."

"Are you afraid I would run away rather than face her?"

"I no longer have any interest in what you will do, but I will see my responsibility to its complete end."

Before Mia could tell him exactly how it made her feel

to be called "a responsibility" yet again, they rounded a corner and stopped before a footman standing at a door.

The servant bowed from the neck and tapped lightly on the wood. A maid Mia did not recognize opened the door immediately and stepped back to let them in.

"Your Grace," the footman announced, "Lord David and his guest have arrived."

David came into the room but stopped before he was halfway to where the duchess was resting.

"I will visit with you later, Your Grace," he said, releasing Mia's arm without so much as a reassuring pat.

"Thank you for bringing her safely to me, David." Elena nodded and David stepped out the door.

Elena struggled up from the chaise she had been lying on. She was huge, and Mia could not believe that the babe did not simply burst out of her with every move she made. Despite her size, Elena still managed to look very fragile.

"Mia, *cara.* I am so relieved to see you. So happy that you are with me."

Mia nodded. Truly? Still unsure, Mia took Elena's extended hands and kissed both of them with tears. "I am so sorry, Elena, so very sorry to have hurt you."

"Hurt me?" Elena pulled her into an embrace against her side. "Oh, Mia, it is you I worry about. Only you. If anyone hurt me, it is William. He makes the words 'grown man' and 'fool' synonymous. If he could not figure out how to keep you happy then he deserved to lose you."

Confusion overrode Mia's anxiety. "But then why did you not write to me? I was sure you were furious with me."

"Did you not receive the note I asked the duke to

write? My hands are swollen and I cannot hold a pen easily." Elena held out her fingers. They looked awful, the skin stretched and her fingers stiff. Mia tried not to show the shock she felt.

"Sit down, please, Elena." Mia guided her once-elegant guardian to her chaise where she and the maid helped the duchess seat herself comfortably.

"Should I change? Lord David insisted that we come to you right away. I'm hardly at my best."

"You look lovely, if a trifle road-weary." Elena patted the chair next to her chaise. "But humor me and sit a moment. I do have a few questions for you. I find the stories that have reached me both confusing and inadequate, and my imagination has been working much too hard with so little to do but wait."

Mia nodded and settled in the chair closest to the chaise. Was what Elena had heard better or worse than the truth?

"Bring us some tea, Destin."

The maid nodded and left the room. Elena waited until the door clicked shut.

"Now that we are alone, I will tell you what I have heard and you tell me the truth. It will help both of us decide what is to be done."

Mia nodded. She already knew what needed to be done. Mia folded her hands and prayed that Elena would agree.

"Word reached me in a letter from Letty Harbison, written with great apology, that William and his friends found you with the Duke of Hale, in a very compromising position."

"No!" The Duke of Hale was a widower and even older than Meryon.

"Indeed, Letty did not think that sounded likely. But hers is not the only letter I received. I trust Letty more than the others. She is a good friend and will tell me the facts as she has heard them rather than fill her letter with pointless speculation. The Duke of Hale, Mia? That cannot be true."

It took an unholy amount of time and embarrassing detail to explain the truth, up to and including the fact that it was not a crowd of William's friends but only Lord David who had been with him when William had come upon her and Lord Arthur.

"Oh, dear. That must have made traveling with Lord David this last week uncomfortable for you."

Mia nodded, her honesty evaporating. She was not going to explain the last week to Elena. It had nothing to do with her failed engagement. "I deserved the discomfort and more."

"I blame myself as much as anyone."

"No!" Mia raised her head so fast that Elena jerked back in surprise.

"Yes," Elena insisted. "I wonder what would have happened if William were not my nephew and I had not given him the run of the house in Bloomsbury."

It was true that Mia and William had met and become fast friends over those months, but what happened later was not Elena's fault.

"He really did help me with my English," Mia insisted, though she and William had spent more of their hours together finding ways to outwit her governess, who had been the most inadequate chaperone on this side of the Channel.

"I should never have permitted him to spend that much time with you before your come-out. It allowed an attachment to form before you had a chance to meet anyone else."

"But he was my best friend then."

"Precisely. But a best friend is not someone you marry." Elena looked away for a moment. "Mia, why did you not talk to William about your worries? Why did you have to find such a public way to draw his attention?"

"I didn't know until this past week if I was in love with him or not, much less if he was in love with me. Kissing Lord Arthur was a test."

"You are saying that it was not the unfortunate kiss but this last week that convinced you that you were not in love with William?"

"When I realized it is not so important, Elena." *Dio mio,* she wanted to avoid the last week and here she was the one who had brought it up.

Elena's soft expression changed to something maternal and not quite as kind. "Mia, tell me what happened between you and David."

"Nothing." Mia knew it was the most unconvincing word she had ever uttered.

"You were in quarantine. Do not tell me that you have

fallen in love with one of the grooms." Her tone indicated that she would not believe that for a minute.

"Of course not. But Lord David does not like me at all. And I think he is a bore who only thinks of his cotton mill."

"I hope that's the truth."

Mia noted that Elena did not press her further. Whatever the reason, Mia thanked God for it.

"Mia, what David wants from the duke and what Meryon is willing to give is very much in discussion right now. David dares not do anything that will compromise the faith Meryon has in him." She smoothed the light rug over her gargantuan stomach and patted it as though settling the baby inside.

"My husband is conservative when it comes to the interests of the estate. He knows how important this mill is to his brother and he is pulled two ways. On one side he wants to take the financial risk to give David a chance to prove himself. On the other side he firmly believes that preserving the estate's capital is his mandate."

"But if David is successful . . ." Mia pressed her lips together and began again. "*When* David is successful the mill will mean even more wealth for the estate."

"So you have talked to David about this."

"A little." But obviously not nearly enough.

"Then you know how important this project is to him."

"Yes," Mia said, but she must have sounded doubtful because Elena went on.

"Securing the financing and completing the project

means more to David than anything since he left to begin his naval career."

"Oh" was all Mia could think of to say. Why had David never explained any of this to her? With that weighing on his mind Mia was amazed that she had been able to distract him at all.

"The last thing David needs is to weaken his position with his brother, so please tell me that your behavior together was above reproach."

"If you saw us when we arrived, you would have no doubt that we are barely on speaking terms." That, at least, was the complete truth.

"It would be best if it stays that way. It will be in your and David's best interests."

Mia saw Elena wince and, despite the fact they had yet to discuss the future, Mia realized that Elena's new and more urgent responsibilities came first.

"You rest now, Elena. I will come back later and play for you."

Elena nodded and Mia stood. When it seemed that Elena was comfortable again, Mia bent over and kissed her cheek. *"Ringrazio, la mia duchessa."*

"Ti amo, cara."

Chapter Thirty-two

"NOT NOW, DAVID." The duke spoke as he rifled through a ledger, then handed it to his secretary. "I'm having dinner with the duchess. I will see you in the morning." He signed two items and passed those on to Wentworth. The field manager added the papers to the others he held. "It will keep, will it not?" the duke asked when David did not answer.

"Yes, Your Grace." David felt his jaw throb. His brother could not spare five minutes to tell him if he had heard from the trustees. He needed no further sign that this project was not of any more interest to Lyn than how many sheep could be raised on the farm in Kent.

David's terse answer did, finally, draw the duke's attention. "Is there something else? Did everything go as expected in Sandleton? I've taken care of a pension for the coachman's family." He made a vague gesture with his hand, as much as asking if he had forgotten anything and, if not, why was David wasting his time.

"All went exactly as I thought it would."

The duke nodded, once again absorbed in the paper he was scanning before signing, not actually hearing the ambiguous answer. But Meryon's secretary shifted his gaze from the duke's papers to David.

David avoided his eyes.

"Yes, so I thought. Tomorrow at nine." The duke was out the door before any one of them could command his attention for something they thought more important than the dinner with his duchess.

"If you'll beg my pardon, my lord." Roland bowed with all the deference of a secretary used to the occasional harsh word. "The duke is very preoccupied these days. Even Lady Olivia has trouble holding his attention."

"Thank you, Roland," David said, and turned to leave. He had to get out of the house.

Puffing on a cigarillo, David made his way down the road to the vicar's house, considering that very unsatisfying meeting with his brother.

Olivia was Meryon's favorite, so the fact that he found her an annoying distraction was significant. They all, to a man and woman, understood that the duke was worried. His first wife had died in childbirth, and now his beloved second wife was about to deliver.

David knew he could not postpone his project until a more opportune time presented itself. He would fail. He would lose the site he had already negotiated to buy, as well as the architect he had hired on promise of payment.

On the other hand, he would fail if Meryon declined to fund the project.

Damn times five fat men, he would rather think about Mia than consider that dark possibility.

He'd had no word on how she'd fared in her meeting with Elena and he would probably not see her at breakfast. In any case he was leaving for Birmingham as soon as he had the duke's decision. He would not delay any longer. It was becoming the most overused word in his vocabulary. And there was nothing more destructive to the new industries than delay. He would not tolerate it again.

"Have I ever told you the story of how I met the old vicar on this very path one night when he was out looking for 'lost sheep'?" Michael Garrett fell into step alongside him.

David started and then swore to himself. Even when she was not beside him Mia Castellano was a distraction.

"Good to have you home, David." Garrett slapped him on the back. "And how long has it been since someone came upon you unaware?"

"I'm going to be at your house in five minutes."

"Still a master at not answering questions, I see."

"Garrett, despite your priestly vocation, you still annoy the hell out of me." David pinched out his smoke and stuffed it in his pocket.

"It's not the priest that annoys you. Whoever would have guessed that those years as a spy during the war would be such good practice for seeing straight through to the secrets in a man's soul?"

"You're wasted in Pennsford. A man with your skills could reform the Regent."

"No, thank you. I am very happy with my little church, my very loving Olivia, and our son." He waited only a second before going on. "So how was your meeting with the duke?"

"He put if off until tomorrow."

They spent the next few minutes discussing the best way to present the need for funding to the duke. Garrett was a master at convincing men to do what he thought best. "Let's discuss it over port after dinner."

"You should make the speech for me," David said, ignoring the suggestion.

"No, you are the one who cares passionately about this, but I will be there to offer my support."

"Thank you. You on my side may be all it will take. I know how Lyn listens to you and values your opinion."

"After dinner you can practice with me and I will point out the shortcomings."

Garrett laughed, and David gave him a sarcastic "How generous of you."

The vicar waved off the faux compliment. "So now tell me why you refused to bring Miss Castellano to dinner with you."

"Mia does not like you or Olivia."

"Nonsense. Everyone likes Olivia. And Mia would love to flirt with someone as safe as I am. Happily married and a priest."

"She is angry with me."

"Closer to the truth, I think."

"Oh, damn times twelve tyrants, Garrett, leave it alone. Mia and I have just spent a week together under very uncomfortable circumstances and have no desire to be in each other's company."

"Which means she bores you. Which I do not think is possible. Or is it that you need time apart to think clearly?"

"It's even more simple than that. She hates me."

"Because?" Garrett prompted.

"Because I refuse to treat life as an adventure. Because I do not know how to have fun. She thinks only of her own world and not what others need." Not completely true, but adequate to the purpose, which was to convince Garrett that Mia was of no interest to him.

His words did silence Garrett, though the fact that he was walking very slowly, David knew, meant he had more to say.

"David, tell me what happened at Sandleton."

"Damn it to hell and back, Garrett." David stopped and willed his heart to slow. "Even one of Olivia's dinners is not worth going through this inquisition."

"Then I will take an even less pleasant tack. Miss Castellano is right. You do not know how to have fun. You have not allowed yourself to even consider happiness, not once in the years I have known you. Olivia thinks it is because of what happened in Mexico, even though she has no idea what that was."

David wanted to punch the superciliousness out of the man there and then, but Michael put his hands behind his back and kept talking.

"I do know what happened in Mexico and agree with my wife that that is the reason. You live with it every day and you will not allow yourself forgiveness."

"People died; innocent men, women, and even children were tortured and murdered because of me."

"No, David, not because of you," Garrett corrected, his voice adamant. "They died because the diabolical mind of an overseer found a way to punish you for being smarter, stronger, and more clever than he was."

"Why did I ever tell you about Mexicado? Will you never let it go?"

"Not until you do," Garrett said, his voice echoing the shared pain. "Every time you broke a rule some other slave, men and women who were your friends, was put to death. You were too valuable to lose. It's the overseer who has earned a place in hell."

David stopped walking. "I could have killed myself. I could have ended it." He could feel the water in his eyes and looked away, then started walking again, hoping Garrett would not notice.

"No, you are a Pennistan and they survive. Killing yourself would be like losing in the ring on purpose. That's not in you, David. Not in you at all."

David shrugged. That was the truth.

"If you are afraid to love again because you fear loss, then it is too late."

"You have no Romany blood, Garrett. So stop speaking like a gypsy and tell me what you mean."

"You are surrounded by people you love. If that bastard overseer were here now, whom would he choose to kill? And if you are afraid that God plays the same sort of game, then you are a worse heretic than Luther."

They had reached the path to his front door and Garrett stopped him.

"I am going to preach for less than a minute and then change the subject."

David shook his head. "You've said it before."

"Yes, but have *you* been listening?" Garrett pulled open the gate but stood in the middle of the opening. "God wants us to be happy and fulfilled. Anything that brings us joy is good."

David looked down at the ground and thought of laughing with Mia.

"Do you hear me, David?"

Garrett's voice vibrated with such feeling that David thought he'd best agree to avoid a fistfight.

"Yes, I do. It's a refreshingly brief recount of your favorite sermon."

Garrett seemed to relax a little. "And it brings us back to Mia."

"Who does hate me."

"Ah, hate is such a wonderful sensibility. So much better than if you bored her, or frightened her, or even if she cordially disliked you. It's even more significant that you do not hate her."

Now the priest was gone and the man, the friend, was baiting him.

"She'll be twenty-one in a little more than a year and, she has informed me, will be making her own decisions."

"Oh God, don't tell me you tried to make decisions for her."

"Yes, yes, I did. And I assure you it was as disastrous as her ideas were bad."

Garrett clapped him on the back. "Nothing new about that, David. Women want to make their own decisions. The sooner you learn that, the better."

"What are you two doing out there? Have you lost your way? Come here right now, David. I need a hug, and Garrett, your son is asking for his papa."

Olivia stood at the door, wearing an apron. If her command was not pointed enough, the enticing smell of dinner was an allure neither man could ignore.

Chapter Thirty-three

"YOU SEEM MUCH HAPPIER, Mia." Janina fixed a flower in Mia's hair and then stood back to admire her handiwork. "I am so glad that it went well with Elena and you two are on happy terms again."

"Yes, and I found a pianoforte which is in excellent tune."

"Good," Nina said perfunctorily. "So now you are hoping Lord David will propose and make everything perfect?"

"No! What would be perfect about that? I do not want to marry without love, and he will never say the words."

"Who won't? That short man, the viscount? What does he know?"

Mia clenched her teeth and did not correct Nina's

misunderstanding. She'd said too much already. "Are you sure this dress isn't too much for a family dinner?"

"You look beautiful in it. The varied color in the ruffles is very flattering. Pink always makes your face glow."

Mia stopped for a bit of perfume, a dark spicy scent that reminded her of a late-night rendezvous. She picked up her book in case she had to wait and, with the help of a footman, found her way to the room where the family gathered before dinner.

The room was empty with no fire, but Mia poured herself some sherry and sat to wait for the others. It would most likely be a small group. Perhaps Olivia and Michael would join the duke, David, and her. That would be perfect. After dinner they could all go to Elena's room for coffee.

She took a sip of the sherry and stood when she heard someone come to the door. The majordomo, Winthrop, came into the room, looking pained and unpleasant. Did the man ever smile?

"Miss Castellano, did no one tell you that there is no formal family dinner this evening?"

Mia put her sherry glass down very, very carefully. "Is that so, Winthrop?"

"Lord David has gone to the Garretts'," Winthrop said, apparently reading a question in her civil reply. "And His Grace will have a private dinner with Her Grace. The housekeeper arranged for a tray to be sent to your room."

"Very good." Mia nodded, pretending not to be completely mortified. Winthrop waited a moment, then bowed and left the room.

Draining the sherry in one sustaining gulp, Mia stared at the picture over the fireplace.

She had so wanted to see David tonight. To see if she could learn more about the cotton mill from him or from the conversation. If she understood enough, she would have taken part and showed that she did care about what was important to him.

Mia looked at the glass she held, squeezed it tight, then threw it hard into the fireplace. It shattered, and she sank into the nearest chair.

Maybe it was childish of her to throw things when she knew how busy and upset the household was by the duchess's approaching confinement. It wasn't even very satisfying and it certainly did not accomplish anything. What she would do is find the music room and play all the Beethoven she could recall. His music was most satisfying when she was unhappy.

Summoning what dignity she could muster, Mia left the room. She refused to further discover how little she belonged in this house by asking the footman on duty for directions. She had been to the music room once and could surely find her way on her own. Mia began to walk purposefully down the corridor.

DAVID CAME BACK UP to the castle even less aware of his surroundings than he had been on the way down. The wine and food had been followed by a port that a friend of Garrett's had sent from Europe. Olivia had gone up to say good night to their son, a convenient excuse to disappear for the rest of the evening. That left David free to discuss his hopes of the Meryon estate financing for his cotton mill.

Between the two of them, they had finished off the bottle before Garrett was satisfied that David's presentation was as sound as it could be.

Garrett had not brought up David and Mia's relationship again. The man's ability to drop a subject was the only thing that made him tolerable. That and his willingness to meet David in the boxing ring. Tomorrow, he had agreed, and was looking forward to watching David's match with Romero.

The boxing matches would be no more than a temporary distraction. Garrett might not have mentioned Mia again, but David was still all too aware that his future with Mia Castellano was not settled.

Garrett's insistence that David had as much right to happiness as anyone had not left his head all evening.

He was so sure he had done with even thinking about happiness. In Mexicado, the cost of caring had taught him to hide his sensibilities carefully, to forsake any hope of happiness for the greater good. He was not going to risk his heart or people's lives. But he had risked love again when he came home to the circle of his family.

As much as Lyn could annoy him as duke, there was a love for his brother that was at the core of his being. The same was true for Gabriel, who lived so far away that they only saw him once or twice a year. Distance did not lessen the affection. Even Jess, lost to them these last four years, had a place in his heart. And Olivia was loveable by her very being.

He pulled the half-smoked cigarillo from his pocket and lit it again.

If he admitted that he loved, then Garrett would argue a fulfilling life and happiness should follow. The cotton mill would bring him fulfillment. He had no doubt of that. But he had no idea what would make him happy.

It seemed such a selfish way to judge an action. David decided he would be happy if the mill project was a little easier to bring into being.

If happiness and ease went hand in hand, then his life would be easier if Mia was not increasing, infinitely easier if they did not have to marry.

If he never saw her again. Oh yes, life would be much easier, but not nearly as entertaining. Or "fun," as Mia would call it. If she were with him now she would be dancing along beside him, for she never did anything as simple as walk. She would be teasing him, more like tempting him, because they were alone in the dark. Even this prosaic walk back to the castle would be more fun than it was. And once they were back she would insist he come turn the pages while she played the pianoforte, when he should spend a few more minutes reading the papers brought up from London to see what changes were afoot.

So if he allowed Mia to distract him with fun, then he would ignore his true responsibilities.

Did God mean for him to be happy at the expense of those responsibilities? Now, there was a question he would wager Garrett did not have a pat answer for.

David went in the side door where the night porter

greeted him with a message. "Miss Castellano's maid is waiting to speak to you."

Damn times five merry milkmaids. What could be wrong? David was not often in the guest wing and had to ask one of the footmen which suite was Mia's. He tapped at the door.

Janina opened it in a flash and began to cry.

"My God, what is it, Janina?"

"You have been so kind to me, my lord. Please, please do not fail me now."

"Of course, of course." He grabbed her hands. "Tell me what's wrong."

"Mia is gone! I cannot find her. She did not eat her dinner. It was here on a tray and cold as death. I had them take it away but it sat here forever, I am sure." Janina pulled her hands from his and waved them in the direction of the table, empty now. "Mia went down to dinner, looking so beautiful with flowers in her hair, and she never came back."

"She went to dinner? No one told you that there was no formal dinner?"

"No one told me, so no one told her. But someone must have. They did bring her a tray, but she has not been back."

"How do you know?"

"She always leaves things on the chair or the bed or the floor. Of all people, you must notice the things she leaves behind when she has been in a room."

He wasn't entirely sure what Janina meant by that, but it was true that he had found her shoes in his room, and her hairpins in a cup after their first night together. "Have you told anyone?"

"No, my lord. I have only been here myself for a few minutes. I sent the footman to ask for you to come to me thinking that you and Mia might be together."

He shook his head. "I'm sure she is not missing. This is a big place. She is just having an adventure. That is what Mia would say even if she were truly lost."

"I hate adventures," Janina said, and for the first time David could hear Mia in this sister's voice. "Please, my lord, I will wait here. You go look for her. If she is lost she will be very embarrassed if many are looking for her, and she will not want to upset the duke and duchess. If she has run away it is best if no one knows. And if she was kidnapped and is being held for ransom . . ." Janina's voice trailed off and tears took the place of words.

"She has not been kidnapped." Olivia had been kidnapped once; to have that happen again was patently impossible. He would not even allow the idea into his head.

"All right," Janina said, as though he had a shortcut to God and knew it for a fact.

"I will go look in the most likely places and be back in an hour. Or less."

"Yes, you go look for her and I will do what I do best."

She was going to cry for an hour? Or maybe she meant pray. David left the room without asking.

He started with the Oriental Room; it was the logical place since it was where the footman would have directed her before dinner. He found nothing out of place, but the servants would have cleaned already and gathered any-thing left behind.

He saw a book on the table and went over to it. Books were one thing the servants knew not to move. It was the Jane Austen novel Mia had been reading, *Northanger Abbey*.

David left the room with the book in hand, turned right, and began to walk slowly, as though he could feel his way by a sense of her presence.

When he'd gone down one hall, he realized what he sensed. Music. She had found the pianoforte and he needed no more than to listen to her play to know her mood.

Following the music, he did not have to be much closer to know that she was lonely. He did not recognize the composer any more than she would recognize his ar-chitect's name, but if he were to draw a picture of the music he heard, it would be of a woman, lost, lonely, sad, and as beautiful as the notes she played.

He stood just outside the music room in the dimly lit passage and waited to see if she would continue playing when she finished the first piece. She did, and this melody was some hymn whose title he could not recall. He could hear her singing but could not distinguish the words, for as the song progressed she played with greater force until he wondered if the instrument could stand the insult.

Pushing open the door, he went into the room, which had only one brace of candles lit. Mia looked up and stopped singing. Looking down at the keys, she finished the hymn with a sonorous crash of chords.

The echo evolved into complete silence. He walked over to the bench and sat on the edge of it, beside her. It was not made for two and their shoulders touched.

"I'm sorry, I was playing too loud." She moved a little so they were no longer touching, but he could still smell her perfume. The one that reminded him of incense and spicy flowers and the way her hair looked against her skin.

He started to speak and found he had to clear his throat before words would come out. "No one sleeps on this side of the house. We use it as a shortcut to the bedchambers on the east side, but it is late enough that I do believe everyone is abed."

Mia nodded and played a few random notes, her long, supple fingers a contrast to the flat rigid ivory of the keys.

"Janina thought you lost and asked me to find you."

Mia stopped fingering the keys. "*Dio mio,* she could have asked one of the footmen."

"She did seem genuinely upset, though now that I think about it, what did she think had happened to you?" Was the girl playing matchmaker?

"She worries about every little adventure I have. Exploring the castle without a guide would make her nervous." Mia began to gather the music. "How was dinner at the Garretts'?"

"Very nice." He moved a little closer to her again, amused at her effort *not* to touch him. "I'm sorry that I didn't invite you to come, too." Taking her with him would not have been so awful. No wonder she thought she never fit in. Add to that arriving at dinner to find no one there. What a miserable first evening at Pennford.

"Well, I am with you now." She stood up. "David." She waited until she had his complete attention. "I wanted very much to see you this evening to tell you how sorry I am if anything we did at Sandleton will endanger the cotton mill project."

"It shouldn't, as long as we tell no one." He tried for a practical answer, when the mention of Sandleton filled his head with anything but sensible thoughts.

"Elena tried to explain to me how important it is to you. I wish I had understood that. I wish *you* had explained it to me."

"It wasn't enough that I spend every available hour studying and writing letters?"

"I thought it was no more than an excuse to avoid me."

"Mia—" he began, then stopped himself. He could hardly take her to task for thinking that when there was some truth to it.

"Admit it, David, you *may have* been working, but you were also doing your best to avoid me. Just as you did tonight." She seemed just then to notice how dark it was. "What time is it?"

"Sometime after midnight, I think."

"Oh dear, that's too late for us to be alone like this."

"Where is your longing for adventure?"

"I found out today that my adventure at Sandleton could well threaten a project very important to you." She spoke as if that was not clear to him. "I will not be blamed for that. Just because I long to be an independent woman does not mean that I will think only about what I want and what I need."

David moved to stand and the book fell to the floor.

"What was that?"

"You left your book in the Oriental Room."

Mia sank to her knees in front of him to retrieve it, brushing against his legs. Even that innocent touch sent sparks through him. He tried to ignore them, to ignore the possibilities of this situation, to ignore just how alone they were.

"Mia, don't. I'll get it." Her perfume was as exotic as his dreams of her. He tried to push her away. His fingers brushed her cheek, slowed, lingered.

"David," she whispered, "you must know I still always want you." She knelt back on her knees, abandoning her attempts to retrieve her book. Her glance told him that she understood the situation, understood how she looked kneeling in front of him.

Mia dropped her gaze, but only to rest it there, on the front of his breeches. He could see her smile a little, in that mischievous way that meant what she would call fun and he would call trouble. She looked up into his eyes, and back down, quick as a wink.

She pursed her lips and blew.

It was no more than a breath, but his whole body shook in response. "I wish you could have wanted me enough to defy the world and make me yours no matter what the cost."

David reached down and put his hand on her hair,

wishing he could say the words she wanted to hear, accept the invitation she offered. His body begged him to take a half step forward. To bring them into greater contact and to let what would happen just happen.

"David. Mia."

Mia gasped. David's arousal faded instantly at the sound of his brother's voice.

"I am not going to ask what you are doing in here, postured as you are."

Mia jumped up. "I am looking for a book that I dropped. It is under the bench. Truly, Your Grace. The pianoforte is in the way and you cannot see."

"Do not insult me with made-up stories."

"It's the truth, Lyn." David stood up and moved behind Mia, his hands on her shoulders.

"That does not explain what the two of you are doing in here alone at this hour. Aren't there enough bedrooms? Or are they too conventional for the two of you?"

There was a long, deadly silence that was as good as words at conveying Lyn's disgust. Finally he spoke. "Come to my study tomorrow morning at ten. Both of you."

David reached down and covered Mia's mouth with his hand. That was how sure he was that she was about to shout no.

"Yes, Your Grace," he said. "We will both be there."

He spoke to his brother's back. Meryon had not waited for an answer.

"*Dio mio*, David, what will we do?" Mia faced him,

two fingers on her lips as she seemed to consider their options, as if there were any.

"Be in his study at ten and tell the truth."

"But what is the truth?"

"That nothing happened here tonight."

"Yes, yes, all right. Do not tell him the complete truth."

"And what is the complete truth, Mia?" *That I want you and am afraid that to claim you would be the ultimate selfish act.*

"That neither of us wishes to marry the other, of course."

"Of course."

Chapter Thirty-four

MIA FOLLOWED THE FOOTMAN to the duke's study. The sun was absent that morning; clouds and rain matched her mood. She felt as though she were walking to her execution. How ironic that she and David were about to be punished for sex they did not have.

There were two other footmen on duty outside the door. She stopped the one who made to open the door for her and tried to hear what was being said, hoping she was the last one to arrive.

She heard no sounds. No voices, no furniture creaking, no shuffling of feet. It was much later than ten. She must be the last. She hoped the duke understood that she would no longer allow him to intimidate her. She would not allow him to punish David for her actions.

After a nod, the footman opened the door and announced her, and she went in. She found the duke and

David and, oh dear, Michael Garrett already in place but waiting in complete silence.

Only men could argue without moving their lips, she thought. She could feel the tension in the room and knew her presence would only add to it.

David did seem relieved when she came in. The duke's expression, gravity with a tinge of anger, did not change, and Michael smiled at her in such a gentle way that she wanted to sit next to him and hold his hand while the duke cast them into hell.

All three men were looking at her and she realized that the duke had asked if she would prefer to sit.

"Oh, no thank you, Your Grace. I think it more proper for me to stand." Then wished she had not said it quite that way. Who was she to tell a duke what was more proper, especially in his own study?

"Very well." Meryon looked at her and then at David before he began to speak. "You will not insult me with that tale about looking for a book that fell to the floor. If it was too dark to see it, then you could not have been reading it. Even if it was only pictures."

Mia's mind flew disastrously back to the picture books she'd looked at when they were at Sandleton. She pushed the images from her mind.

He was going to go on and on, which would make her more aggravated than distressed. The duke stood behind his desk, which was on a small platform that raised it so he would always be taller than anyone standing before him. Mia wondered if there might once have been some sort of throne in this spot, or maybe the duke who built this house had been so short that he wanted to appear taller.

"No, Your Grace."

As much as she would have liked to think about anything else, David's words brought her back to the moment

"And you, Mia, do you have any explanation for your behavior last night?"

"No, Your Grace." Well, she did actually, but he was not willing to believe the truth. Her hands began to shake and she clasped them tight in front of her.

"I have an explanation," the duke said, which appeared to surprise David as much as it surprised her. "Several possibilities, in fact."

The duke closed his eyes and Mia could see that for all his cold behavior he carried his own version of the Pennistan temper, under very precarious control at the moment.

"I will not list them, as they are an insult to both of you, but rest assured I have thought of little else since I found you last night."

David nodded and Mia tried, but she was sure it looked more like a shiver.

"In fact, with regard to you, David, last night it became clear to me that you have no control over your baser instincts. You seduced or allowed yourself to be seduced by, it really does not matter which, a young woman under your protection."

The duke looked at Garrett and the man nodded. Did he agree or did he simply understand how it could happen?

"My wife is facing the birth of our child, facing life or death, and still you could not control yourselves. Mia, Elena loves you like a daughter, and this is how you repay her, acting like a courtesan in her home."

Mia shut her eyes. The duke looked so bereft at the thought of her toying with his wife's sensibilities that guilt overwhelmed her.

"David, you are the older and I asked you to protect my wife's ward, not compromise her." The last came out in a raised voice and Mia began to feel faint.

It was not David's fault. Mia wanted to tell the duke that. She prayed to the Virgin that she would say the right words and that the duke's affection for his brother would not be ruined. But when she opened her mouth to speak, the duke gave her a look that was so like a dare, she pressed her lips together instead.

"Very wise, Mia," the duke said. Then he drew another deep breath and Mia waited for the sentence. "I do not care what kind or how much sex you have had, but do not try to convince me you have not been together. You both will tell Elena that you are going to be married. The banns will be announced beginning this Sunday, and the wedding will take place as soon as that phase is complete and we are certain that there is no impediment to the marriage."

Married? The duke was going to force them into marriage. "No," Mia announced, in the same slightly raised voice that the duke had used. "I am the one responsible. It is all my fault. It was all my idea. You can ask my maid. I thought it would be an adventure."

She stopped until she was sure she had their attention. "David may be older, perhaps even wiser, but he is after all only a man. Seducing him is the most selfish thing I have ever done."

"Mia, that's ridiculous," David began. "Do not make it sound like I was—"

"Stop, David," she said with enough force to silence him. Mia looked at Mr. Garrett and then the duke. "You see, we will even argue over this, which is why I will not marry him. We agree on nothing. Well, almost nothing."

With that she turned toward the door. The three of them could fight this out in the boxing ring. She would stay in her room for the next year and never see any of them again.

"Mia, if you persist in hurting Elena this way—" The duke stopped, then started again. "If you walk out that door and persist in actions that hurt the people who love you the most, I will not welcome you at Pennford again."

The duke's ultimatum only firmed her resolve. She turned back to Meryon and saw an expression on David's face that made her heart ache. "Welcome me, Your Grace? Elena loves me, and William, well, at least William understands me. But your family has never *welcomed* me. At best I have been considered a responsibility, an obligation. But do not fear, Your Grace; the moment I am able, I will absolve you of that burden."

With her eyes she tried to tell David how sorry she was, how much he meant to her, how he held her heart in so many ways but that she would be a fool to give him such a treasure when he had no idea how to care for it.

Without another word, Mia left the room. The footmen stood straight and impassive on either side of the door. They had probably heard everything.

"YOU IDIOT," DAVID SWORE at his brother. "I told you that demanding an engagement would not work with Mia. I told you that dictating to her never works. And it did not. Damn time ten dense dukes."

His brother ignored the insult. "Miss Castellano's categorical refusal leaves me with only one alternative." He folded his arms across his chest. "I entrusted you with her care because I wanted Elena to rest assured that Mia was safe."

The duke shook his head. David knew Lyn was disappointed in his own judgment as well.

"You have proved yourself unreliable in the most important of ways, David."

Ah yes, the Pennistans carried guilt in large measures and shared it freely.

"Until you can convince Mia that marriage is the only honorable action, there will be no money, no support of any kind for your proposed cotton mill. Not until you prove yourself worthy of the trust. I will not burden my wife with a disgraced relation."

"Do not call her disgraced, Lyn," David shouted, and then, with an effort, lowered his voice. "She is as bright and happy as any woman I have ever met. Most of the time I've treated her as an inconvenience, and did you know that last night she went to dinner and no one else was there? Winthrop had to tell her that there was no family dinner. No wonder she thinks no Pennistan has ever appreciated her. Because, I'm afraid, it's the truth." He wished Lyn would come down to the boxing ring. He could teach him a few home truths there. "As for your refusal to fund the cotton mill—"

"David."

He had forgotten Garrett was in the room.

"David, His Grace did not say he would not fund the mill. Only that you must prove yourself all over again."

"Prove myself? By convincing Mia to marry me when she so clearly does not want to? No, I will not do that. I will not force her into anything that would make her so unhappy, any more than you can force me."

The duke flexed his fist and David wanted more than anything for Lyn to take a punch at him.

"What's more, I will never accept even a guinea from you, Your Grace, much less capital for a cotton mill."

"Calm down, both of you." Garrett came and stood in front of David as if physically deflecting the insults. "Your Grace, as your spiritual adviser, I suggest that you show some compassion. David and Mia obviously have a strong bond that they have not yet resolved."

Garrett looked from one to the other. David did not so much as blink. His brother relaxed his fist, but his expression was still angry.

"Your Grace, your efforts to force them into a commitment that neither is ready for is ill-advised and wrong.

You were young once, too." He nodded toward the door, obviously referring to Mia. "And David had his youth stolen from him. Is it any surprise he would be so attracted to someone who wants to share hers with him?"

They both turned to look at him. David dismissed them with a shrug, even though Garrett's words had given even him insight. "I have nothing more to say. I will be in the boxing ring with Romero. The two of you can discuss me and insult me, but leave Mia alone. Despite what you may think, she is the innocent in this."

David left the room without waiting for permission from either of them.

To his surprise, Garrett came after him almost immediately. "He is upset, David. He is worried to his soul about Elena's lying-in. Do not make it more difficult for him."

"This is one time that I know exactly how Mia feels. She loathes rules and orders from on high. Did you know that she plans to live independently once she comes of age? To move to Bath and host a salon that specializes in music?"

"Oh my." Garrett laughed. "And I thought that Olivia was the most naive woman in the world." They walked on in silence until the door to the old castle was in sight. "The duke once used that line on me, the one about being the seduced or the seducer, or something close enough to it that I relived it when he used it today."

David could not have cared less.

"It must make him feel very old when he hears the

same words come out of his mouth over and over." Garrett laughed again at the thought.

"Maybe he should keep his mouth shut. He is my brother, not my father. The dukedom has made him old before his time. I'd be afraid to meet him in the ring now. He'd probably fight like he's sixty instead of forty."

"Once Elena is safely delivered of her child his good humor will return," Garrett insisted. "In the meantime, David, try for patience."

David shook his head. "Not if he continues to insult Mia."

They pushed their way through the doors that led to the oldest part of the castle and the boxing ring set up in the old forecourt. Garrett pulled the door closed behind them and followed David to the ring. "I do feel sorry for Romero."

Chapter Thirty-five

"BUT WHY IS THE DUKE so mean to you?" Janina collapsed onto the chair. "The duke is a man, and all men like you."

"He saw how much trouble I made for Elena last year, before you came. He thinks me rude, selfish, every bad word you can think of."

"That's not fair. There are many good things about you, too."

"I hope so, Janina, but the duke does not know me any other way. Lord David treated me the same at first. I suppose it is only fair, after I made Elena's life so difficult." *And William's. And now David's.*

"What will you do?" Janina's question was filled with despair.

Mia faced her sister, afraid that she would lose her, too. "I am going to leave as soon as Elena has given birth and recovered. I will see if I can go back to Sandleton and wait there until my majority. If Elena will not trust me that far, then I will ask to live in the gatehouse until I can claim my money and leave."

She dreaded the next year. It would feel like a punishment, but it was a punishment she deserved if she had ruined David's chance at success.

"When the time is right, I think I will still go to Bath. Definitely not to London. And I will find a lady to act as chaperone." She would find a way to assert her independence, even if it meant a compromise.

"Romero and I will go with you." Janina covered Mia's clasped hands with her own.

"Thank you, Nina. But perhaps you should talk to Romero first."

"We have talked. He knows that you are my only family and I will not abandon you. Not ever."

It meant everything to Mia to have that commitment from Janina, even when her sister had no idea what she would do with her life.

"But before I do anything else I have to find out what the duke decided about the mill. If the duke will not support him I have to find a way to change his mind. I have to come up with a plan."

She was spared the task when one of the younger maids came into the room, breathless from running or from excitement. "The duchess is in labor! The babe is coming!"

*   *   *

EVERYONE IN THE CASTLE settled in to wait. The first three hours were uneventful. The servants completed the essential tasks of the day, but then one of the housemaids dropped a vase and a footman knocked over a suit of armor. Into the fourth hour, two maids argued each other into tears and one of the kitchen maids burned her hand.

At the end of the fifth hour, with half a workday left, Winthrop allowed the servants who lived at home to leave and sent the rest to the servants' hall to help the housekeeper with mending and polishing silver in shifts. Not a one complained.

Hanging like a pall that dampened any excitement was the memory of the last birth in this family. The first duchess had not survived the night.

As the house grew quieter, Mia realized that the child's birth touched all their lives, not just the duke and his wife. That everyone under this roof and in the town of Pennsford was praying for the safe delivery of the next Pennistan.

She and Janina waited in her sitting room, trying to convince each other that Elena would have no trouble at all giving birth. Women did it every day without a threat to their lives. But as Mr. Novins had said, women understood too well that life and death were only a breath apart.

Each time Nina said something encouraging, Mia would remember the Regent's daughter, who had died in childbirth, and Mia's own mother, who had never fully recovered from her birth.

With dinner still hours away, Mia announced that she

was going to the nursery to see how Alicia and Rexton were preparing for a new brother or sister.

The nursery was a bright and airy suite of rooms that even on a rainy day seemed welcoming. The main room was filled with serviceable furniture and a large open space, the floor covered with an old thick rug that was obviously a perfect spot to roll and tumble and otherwise play. Had David spent his childhood playing here? Mia tried to picture him as a boy and wondered if he had always been serious or if his time in Mexico had made him so.

There was an alcove with a cozy fire and a table and chairs where the duke's son and heir, Rexton, was working with his tutor. Disappointment showed when he realized that his caller was not his father.

"Papa comes every day, but he is with the duchess and might be late." The boy was pretending not to worry right along with everyone else.

Mia wondered if Rexton remembered that his mother had died just after her lying-in. She wasn't sure how old he was, surely more than ten, so he would recall in his own right the day his mother died. For the first time in her life Mia found herself relieved that she had not been old enough to know or even really miss her own mother.

The tutor seemed to welcome her addition to the circle, and so she sat down next to the boy who would someday be the Duke of Meryon.

"I know I am a poor substitute for your papa, but do tell me what you are studying today."

"The meaning of names," the young earl answered promptly.

"And what is the most interesting thing you've learned today?"

"That the name Miles means soldier," Rexton answered. "I always liked that name above all others."

"I wanted to change my name to Damiana or Julietta." She still thought Mia a rather unimpressive name. "What does Rexton mean, my lord?"

"It's my mother's maiden name," Rexton explained to her. "It's a Pennistan tradition for the firstborn."

Well, Mia thought, *that explains the odd choice of Lynford for the duke's first name.* "But, my lord, what will happen if you marry someone from Germany whose last name is, for example, Baumgardner? Or someone from Italy with a name like Castellano? What do you think of those for a given name?"

Rexton thought for a minute. The tutor showed his value by waiting for a comment and not offering his own before the boy could consider it.

"I do not wish to be rude," Rexton said.

Much too adult a sentiment for a young boy. Did they not live to be rude?

"Baumgardner Pennistan would certainly be a mouthful," Mia said, prompting the boy with her own frank assessment. "And Castellano Pennistan makes even me want to laugh out loud."

The tutor tried to control the way his lips twitched. "What I suspect would happen, my lord and Miss Castellano, is that your heir, my lord, would be given the traditional name but be called by some more conventional name among the family."

Rexton seemed relieved at that solution, and they played the "weird name game" for another few minutes until the boy was snorting with laughter. The tutor nodded his approval, but remained above the silliness that in Mia's opinion was just what the boy needed.

After twenty minutes of nonsense, Mia decided she had been the entertainment long enough. With a curtsy she went into the day nursery to find that little Alicia was taking a nap. How nice that at least one member of the family was not at all worried about what was happening in the duchess's suite.

Mia refused to look at any of the clocks she passed. Time had lost its usual meaning. Every minute was more like an hour. She was sure that time was now measured by Elena's breaths.

With a little help she found the Long Gallery. The steady rain outside made it the only place to walk and pray and walk some more.

All the chandeliers and sconces had been lit and the room was warmed by four fireplaces, making it almost comfortable despite its size.

Mia took her time, examining the portraits. How many of these men had been afraid their wives would die, and how many wished they would? How many thought life a great adventure, and how many wished it would end so the misery would go away?

Mia stood in front of the painting of Rowena Rexton Pennistan, the first wife of the current duke. The elegant pose didn't convey much of the woman's strengths or weaknesses, nor could Mia imagine how this woman looked when she went to God. Much too soon.

She bent her head and began to cry. Tears welled in her eyes and ran down her cheeks in a river of sorrow and loss that was a mix of both groundless fears and what was all too true.

Mia allowed the tears, hoping God would see them as proof of her love for Elena and not her selfish fear that she would lose someone else she loved. She prayed and promised that she would do anything if Elena survived.

"The first duchess was a very sweet woman. The artist missed that completely."

Mia recognized Michael Garrett's voice, her eyes too filled with water to actually see him. She nodded. "Should you not be with your wife?"

"She is with Elena and the midwife."

"The duke must need you."

"No, he is in the chapel and prefers to be alone with his fears." She could hear him coming closer to her as he spoke. "I'm exactly where I'm supposed to be."

Mia nodded and kept on crying, still not looking at him. He stayed next to her, rubbed her back, and waited. When it hurt to swallow, Mia made herself stop crying but did not move away. "I am so selfish. I am crying because I do not know what I will do if Elena dies."

"We all feel that way. You are the only one to admit it aloud."

"Maybe." She shrugged a little. "The duke must be so afraid. It is the worst thing in the world to lose someone you love. Grief is one thing I understand. If Elena dies I know it will break his heart. And there is nothing he can do to save her." The tears escaped again and she concentrated on slowing them.

"We are all praying."

At her shock of guilt for not praying at this very moment, he patted her arm.

"In times like this, Mia, our very thoughts are prayers."

She relaxed a little.

"Tell me about David."

"*Dio mio,* how could I forget! What did the duke tell him?"

"I don't think the decision will be final for a while yet."

"Do you think if I spoke to the duke it would help?"

Garrett took her hand and kissed it. "You are not the heart of the problem."

"How can that be? I'm the one who seduced David."

"Tell me about him."

She swallowed hard and took a moment to think. "I wish he loved me."

"Mia, dear, that tells me about you. What I asked is for you to tell me about David."

"He is a hard man to have a conversation with. If he would talk in more than one-word sentences then I would know him better."

"Yes, I suspect that terseness is the first thing one notices about him."

"Well, Mr. Garrett—" Mia stopped and folded her arms as she considered how honest to be with him. "I think what women first notice is how handsome he is and not at all aware of it, and his quiet then makes him very mysterious. He is hard for a woman to resist."

"Hmmm," Garrett, said which apparently meant she was to go on.

"He is immensely capable in all situations. He can rescue a coach from a disaster and calm people who are afraid of plague by knowing exactly what to do. He will comfort you when you are ill. Is that not every kind of situation?"

Garrett nodded.

"He is kind, even though he would never ever admit it or perhaps does not even realize it. And when he gives you all his attention there is no other thought but you."

"When you have all his attention?"

"Yes," she said firmly, "and I will not elaborate on that."

"No need to, my dear. No need to at all." Garrett's devilish laugh was not at all priestly.

"He is not perfect. The ridiculous boxing and those ghastly cigarillos he smokes . . . and really, does he have no valet? And he must argue with every single thing that I say and tell me that fun is only for children."

"Not perfect at all," Garrett agreed. "But it seems you do know him even without conversation."

"I suppose one would say he is a man of action."

"And do you love this man of action?"

"I could." *I do,* she thought, but she would not give even Mr. Garrett that piece of information. "But he does not love me. And that makes it impossible."

After glancing at a few unappealing portraits from Elizabeth's time, Mia guessed at the reason for this conversation. "You want me to stop living in sin and marry him."

"Impossible." Garrett laughed. "We all live in sin every day. I want you both to be happy."

"I do not see how it could work." Her eyes filled with tears again. "I want my own way too much and he is too harsh. Once the fun of sex wears away—though I cannot imagine that happening, but it must—it would be like when he was in Mexicado, but this time there would be no chance of escape."

Mr. Garrett stopped short and looked at her in amazement. "Has he told you about Mexicado?"

"Only a little." She would say no more, not wanting to speak of a secret, if that's what it was.

"With God all things are possible," Garrett declared with a laugh of pure delight.

She'd heard that before somewhere. From Miss Horner.

"Dear God, woman, don't you know that even a little of the story is more than he has ever told anyone but me?"

"Really?"

"Yes," Garrett said with emphasis. "It is a nightmare he does his best to forget."

"He has not told me everything about his time there."

"And he may not ever, but please know that if he has spoken of it, you are not some casual flirtation."

"Perhaps not casual." She thought of Janina's mother

and her long *affaire de coeur* with their father. All Mr. Garrett wanted was to have her agree to marry David so the Pennistan family would be at peace again.

"You do not believe he could love you." He shook his head. "Of course you don't. You are a woman and must hear the words. You do not understand how a man says 'I love you.'"

"And I suppose you are intimately familiar with it."

"I'm a man, aren't I?"

"Oh, yes," Mia said. "You certainly are. Beneath your priestly title, I think you are very much a man." She hoped she didn't sound flirtatious.

"Exactly. So I speak with authority on the subject." They were at the door that led to the duke's apartments, and continued their circuit, now passing marble busts of long-dead Pennistans. "After you left the duke's study this morning, David told Meryon that he would never accept a guinea from him as long as you were made to feel unwelcome." He nodded. "That was quite a declaration from a man who came to beg for a small fortune to build his mill."

"How could he even consider such a sacrifice? There are so many people depending on him. He must not give up."

They were in front of a picture of four young men. Lynford, David, Jessup, and Gabriel, the four Pennistan brothers in their youth. It must have been before Olivia was born.

Lynford Pennistan looked no more than sixteen.

Which would make David twelve. Even before his maturity, David looked too serious. This must have been just before he left for the navy. Had they had the portrait painted in case he never returned?

"Take a few minutes and think of all the ways David has said 'I love you.'"

Garrett wandered off as Mia sank onto a bench and stared at the young David.

He had given up his mill for her? Well, he would change his mind about that. It was too important.

But he had come to her last night when Nina had asked, even though he had no doubt she was safe. With that insight, the memories came so fast that they were a jumble in her heart with the refrain "all things are possible."

He had been there when she awakened from her illness and held her through her awful dreams. He had punched Franklin so she would not bruise her knuckles. He had carried extra handkerchiefs in case she should need one.

He took time to explain the workings of his cotton mill when he must have had more important things to do.

Then there was the time he had stuffed a branch of roses into the carriage so that she would have "something live" to talk to. Could his love be traced back that far?

And, *Dio mio,* most of all when they made love. The truth came out when they were in each other's arms and it always would. In those moments she had never felt more desired, more treasured, more important than anything else.

A door down the hall flew open and a woman, Olivia Garrett, came running down the hall. She ran into her husband's outstretched arms and kissed him on the cheek. "Michael, Michael, go find the duke. It's a boy, a very healthy boy! And Elena made it look easy!"

Chapter Thirty-six

"A SIX-HOUR LABOR!" Mia knew very little about childbirth, as was appropriate for an unmarried woman, but even she knew that such a short labor was not common.

"Let's find Lyn!" Olivia insisted. And when Mia would have bowed out of the group, Olivia grabbed her hand and pulled her along. "You are part of the family in all the ways that count! Lyn will be delighted to have you join him."

Clearly Garrett did not share everything with his wife.

They found Meryon in the receiving room of his suite, looking both dazed and elated. According to this very proud father the boy was already showing his temper, crying—"bellowing" was the word the duke used—to be fed.

The duke was a different man. Almost jolly in his happiness. It gave Mia hope that Meryon would reconsider his refusal to help David.

After a few minutes of back-slapping and congratulations, Meryon announced, "Elena insists that we have a party this evening in her sitting room. That way everyone can meet the newest Pennistan and we can all toast Elena's good health."

That was the signal for all of them to depart. The castle was as alive now as it had been quiet before. Maids hurried down hallways, bobbing curtsies and smiling. The footmen stood alert and volunteered information even when no one asked. Mia debated trying to find David, but then decided it would be better for him if they were not seen together, because, in fact, nothing had really changed between them.

Janina had already laid out four different dresses for the evening. Mia chose the most modest. The color, a pale green with lavish lace ruffles, elevated it from ordinary. She'd thought it too young but now decided it perfect for the occasion at hand. Leaving her hair down, she used two combs fixed with incredibly lifelike artificial flowers, and hoped there would be no mistaking her as the only unmarried woman in the party.

Which was, of course, not the same as innocent, but for tonight she was sure that the duke's opinion of her affair with David would not even occur to him.

Mia arrived later than the rest the family proper, slipping into the room as champagne was being poured.

The duchess's bedchamber was filled with people, including the duke's two other children. Rexton was old enough to take part in the conversation, but he was standing near the window with David. They were both watching something outside. Alicia was still young enough to hide behind her nurse's skirt and suck on her knuckle.

Besides the children, it seemed that "family" included any number of upper servants, too, and Mia was sure the younger women were nurses for the various needs of the newest family member.

She accepted a glass of champagne and moved to a spot where she could observe but not intrude. No one called to her to come over and see the child, so she would wait for a quieter moment.

"God save the King!" the duke began. "To Elena!" Everyone cheered and drank again.

As the toasts continued, to the newborn and to the Pennistan name, Mia looked at David and realized he was still standing by the window, but now alone, looking as much an outsider as she was.

He must have felt her gaze because he looked her way. She raised her glass and smiled. "To life." She murmured the words and he responded in kind. They both drank their own quiet toast, separated by a dozen people but as close as they had ever been.

"TO LIFE!" DAVID THOUGHT. Here he stood, thinking about the failure of his dearest plan, and Mia reminded him that life is a celebration.

I love that about her, he admitted to himself. I love her sense of adventure, her vanity, her interest in people, her choices, both silly and wise. I love the way she gives herself so completely to her music, to fishing, to the people she cares about, to me.

The crowd began to thin and he noticed that the servants had left and the children, including the new babe, had been taken to the nursery.

The duke sat at the foot of Elena's chaise with that look that David always thought of as a fool's smile, the besotted expression of one hopelessly in love.

Mia, Olivia, and Michael were smiling fondly at the tableau, and David realized that he was, too.

"I am never going through that again," the duke declared as though he had done all the work.

"Oh, yes, you are," Elena exclaimed. "The consequences do not bear thinking about."

"What consequences? I think that three children are quite enough."

"You dolt," Olivia said.

David noticed that Olivia's insult shocked Mia.

"Lyn," Olivia went on, "you do know how these things happen. Are you saying you prefer celibacy?"

"I think it's time to put the champagne away, my dear." Elena took the glass from her husband's hand and set it on the table. Lyn tickled his wife's toes and then kissed her hand.

David wondered if he had ever before noticed how much more relaxed Lyn was when he was with his wife, as though he shed his ducal shell and the person David had known as a boy came out again.

He watched Olivia and Garrett. He could hear Olivia

insisting that despite the long day she wanted to prepare something special for breakfast. Her husband took her hand, kissed it, and said no. They seemed to bicker about it for a moment, and then Olivia nodded grudging agreement.

Is that what the best marriages were? Two people who kept each other in balance, like playing on a seesaw, and seeing how long it could stay level before swooping one way or the other?

Not very long, but if the game was with the right person, he imagined the seesaw could be a lot of fun.

He considered his short but intense time with Mia in terms of the seesaw. Up and down, with very little balance except for their time in bed. And when the horses had taken the carriage on that wild ride. When she had played the guitar that night, aware that he was listening nearby. The time Dilber's dogs had threatened them. When they had stood before the duke. Had it only been that morning?

He watched Mia and Elena with their heads together, exchanging a proper hug, and then Elena's farewell. "I will see you tomorrow and you can tell me your plans."

I'm going to be part of those plans, David decided. He had thought it once of Bendasbrook: He would be a fool to let this woman go.

But he had to come up with a way to let her think she was making the choice to marry him, instead of doing exactly what he wanted.

With no clear idea how he would make that happen

and the briefest of farewells to Lyn and Elena, David left the couple who, at this point, only had eyes for each other.

Mia had already disappeared from sight. He had an idea where she would be, but the music room was dark. When he sent a footman to her suite, the man came back to report that the rooms were empty.

All right, so he did not know where she was. Damn times ten naked nymphs, the woman never made anything easy. As he rounded the corner to his room, he realized he had not yet checked the most likely spot.

"What took you so long?" Mia asked as he came through the door from his bedroom into his study. She stood near the door to the corridor, as though not fully committed to staying. How unusual.

David went to his desk but remained standing. *What took him so long?* David didn't answer her. The question could be considered on so many different levels.

He asked a question of his own. "What are you doing here?"

"Was that not the most touching moment between Elena and the duke?" She walked to a shelf and touched a piece of pottery, a rock, and a statue of some ancient Mayan god he had never been able to identify.

"Which moment was that?"

"When the duke tickled Elena's toes," she answered as she turned to face him again. "It was such a sweet, intimate gesture. Not at all what I expected from the ogre he is when he thinks like a duke."

He'd be happy to tickle Mia's toes anytime she wanted. With great effort he managed not to say that aloud. "I was thinking something similar. That when they are together he is the boy I grew up with before the dukedom so weighed him down." He straightened, pointlessly, a stack of papers on his desk. "Interesting that we both saw the same thing." The seesaw was in balance for just a moment.

Mia walked to the center of the room and made a slow turn, taking in all the bits and pieces he had collected. "How can you work in here with all these strange statues watching you? They must be from Mexicado."

"From Mexico." The seesaw swung him high so that she was on the ground and in control. This was not a conversation he wanted to have.

"There is nothing from Mexicado?"

"Memories" was all he said.

"Oh, yes, and they cannot be given away or hidden, can they?"

The seesaw swung back, in balance again.

Chapter Thirty-seven

MIA UNDERSTOOD THE REASON for the one-word sentences. David did not want to talk about this. So she would.

"I think we all have some of those. When my father was dying I was desperate for medical care for him but all the medicos had gone to the front." She drew a bracing breath. This was not at all easy. "Papa and I were alone in a dark, cold, empty house. The servants had gone to watch the fighting or to see to their own families. Janina had gone for help and had not come back. I was afraid she was hurt, or worse."

Mia closed her eyes and waited until the tears that threatened subsided. When she continued, tears filled her eyes anyway. "I knew Papa was going to die, sooner than he had to, and all I could do was tell him how much I loved him and beg him to stay with me. Help came, finally, only he had been dead for hours. That is a memory I would gladly give away."

He nodded, his face filled with sympathy.

You see, she thought, *we are not that different.* But she kept the thought to herself for fear he would laugh at her.

"This room is filled with memories, David. Would it not be easier to forget if you began to make new ones?" *With me.* Again, she kept that to herself.

"These," he waved at the statues and jars, "are the good memories. As you say, the bad ones are with us in a place that is impossible to expunge."

"Tell me one." *Let me share the burden.* Mia stood very still, afraid that if she made any gesture of affection or understanding she would scare him away.

David looked away from her and stared at a wall plaque, a figure that looked like a rising sun full of power and glory, possibly a god from some ancient times. She saw him pat his pocket as if smoking would help, but either he did not have a cigarillo with him or he remembered how much she hated them.

He went to his desk and sat down, shuffling some papers until he uncovered a small shaped piece of stone which he held tight in his hand, still saying nothing with eyes or words.

Mia gave up. *Hell,* she thought, quite deliberately. *This man does not even want my love.* His words cut into the tirade forming in her head but not yet spoken.

"I had as hard a time obeying authority as a slave as I did as a midshipman. Whenever I broke a rule I was punished, but I was a very valuable commodity, a strong, healthy male. When punishing me physically did no good, the overseer took one of the other slaves and made them suffer in my place."

"How awful. I'm so sorry. It would be like punishing one of the footmen every time I said no."

"Worse than that, much worse." He looked away from her, and she was glad she could not see the agony in his eyes. "He would always pick someone that I cared about."

Loved, she thought.

"Not just men, but women, and the children of people I knew. It would be like someone killing Janina because of something you did."

She felt vaguely ill at the thought and wondered how many times this had happened.

"Is that a bad enough memory to satisfy you?"

Mia was taken aback by his angry tone and could only nod.

"Telling you does not make me feel any better."

"Then we will never speak of it again."

He had no answer for that.

"But you see, David, I feel better for hearing it. It brings me closer to you in a way that has nothing to do with making love."

"What are you doing here, Mia?"

She did not want to tell him. She did not want to be the first one to say "*I love you.*"

"I wanted to speak with you in private and I knew eventually you would come here. What took you so long?"

"I was looking for you."

"Really!"

Before he could answer her, there was a tap on the door.

"Enter," David called out, and the Duke of Meryon joined their small group. He seemed surprised though not completely shocked to see Mia there.

"We were just talking, Your Grace," Mia said in a rush of words as she curtsied deeply to him.

"Yes, I can see that. I appreciate your discretion."

As was almost always the case, Mia could not tell if the duke was being kind or still regarded her with contempt. "If you wish to talk to Lord David, I will leave."

"Please stay, Mia." David glanced at the duke. "I have no secrets from you."

Mia's heart skipped a beat. If he truly meant that . . . If . . .

She sat in the chair nearest the door and listened while the duke explained that he had given David's situation further consideration.

Someone had changed his mind. Mr. Garrett? Elena? Mia did not care who, but pressed her lips together to keep from laughing out loud. Her mind spun off into an adventure worthy of Jane Austen until David's terse voice called her back from the happy ending.

"Then I am exactly where I was before, Your Grace. If you are only willing to provide half the funding then I must spend months, if not years, finding other financial support. It is as good as you saying no."

She wanted to shout at David to accept it with thanks and make the most of what the duke offered. The man could be so stubborn. There were ways and ways of finding the money he needed.

"David, I cannot risk that much of the estate's assets for any project. It's about being cautious. Your passion for the mill blinds you to the chance that it might fail."

"It will not fail!" Mia could contain herself no longer.

"Thank you, Mia," David said, "Your confidence is—"

"David," she interrupted him, since he was sure to say something annoying. She could tell by his tone of voice. "I will invest in your project. I will provide the other half of your financing."

The two men stared at her.

"I am sorry, but it will take a while. I will not have control of my money until next year, but surely you can move ahead with the project with that promise in mind." She nodded as if they would both agree without hesitation.

"I will not take your money," David. "You need financial security."

"But I will have it if I invest in your cotton mill."

She looked at the duke.

He did smile, but then shook his head no. "A very sweet gesture, Mia, but acting on sentiment is a sure way to financial disaster."

"It is very clear to me that you two have the same blood and were raised by the same hidebound antiquarian tutor." *And father.* She was going to throw rotten fruit at the old duke's bust if this did not work.

She walked up to David so that he had to look at her

and not the duke. "If you will not use my money, then marry me and it will be your money to invest."

"You're proposing to me?" David looked and sounded dumbfounded.

"If that's what it will take to convince you that I am serious about this investment."

"Mia, I love your generosity and appreciate your faith in me, but to marry would mean a life considerably different from the one you have now."

"It will be an adventure, *and* we can make love whenever we want."

Her outrageous comment had the effect she had hoped for.

The duke broke in. "I will go and let the two of you resolve your differences."

He could not leave fast enough. The room was quiet for a very long moment while Mia waited to see what David would say. Silence was often as good as action.

"Listen to me," David said, taking her by the arm.

Of course the right action could never be underestimated, either, so before he could say any more, Mia kissed him.

David could not doubt the intensity of her feeling. Tumultuous, overwhelming, so intense that her body was shaking with need. They clung to each other with their mouths, their hands, their bodies admitting with each caress that they were so much better together than they were when split apart.

She leaned back in his arms and tried to catch her breath.

"I love you," David said.

They were almost the most wonderful words Mia had ever heard, even if she didn't understand his added "Damn the seesaw."

"David, my dear and only lover, that sounds like an ultimatum rather than a declaration." She kept her arms around his neck and kissed his chin.

A smile touched his lips. "I love you, Mia."

"Much more loverlike and nearly perfect. And I love you." She punctuated each word with a quick kiss and ended with a kiss that left him in no doubt.

He grinned, almost let loose a soft laugh. "Aha, so the seesaw is in balance."

"What seesaw?"

He explained his theory to her.

"Why, it's wonderful. It will be the way to measure our lives for years to come."

She moved against him, seeking a different kind of balance. He started to untie the ribbons at her back. "Wait," she said, and when he stilled his hands she asked, "David Pennistan, will you marry me?"

He laughed and kissed her. "Only if you will marry me."

"Yes, of course. As soon as you wish."

"If you want an adventure, we can elope to Gretna Green."

How sweetly generous that was, but this was all the adventure she needed for a good long while. "To elope would only convince your whole family that conventions mean nothing to us."

David laughed again, for as she spoke she led him into his bedroom, then walked over and locked his door.

"And while that may be true, we do not want our behavior to estrange you from your far more proper brother and my guardian, who would understand but take his side as is only right. Can we marry here?"

"Yes."

She waited for more but he shook his head.

"Mia, my dear, you are living in a dream if you think I am going to abandon one-word sentences. They are so efficient."

She narrowed her eyes and considered his statement. "Just as long as you're prepared to hear the word *no* on a regular basis."

"Not in bed," he said as they helped each other undress.

"Never," she agreed, and proceeded to demonstrate that where showing her love for him was concerned, the word *no* was not in her vocabulary.

Epilogue

THE NEXT MONTH passed in a haze of happiness. They argued regularly, and his taciturn answers and her *no*s were as much a part of their engagement as they had been a fixture of their unconventional courtship.

The night before their wedding was typical as they discussed whether she should stay behind while he found them a house in Birmingham. Absolutely not.

"You can be so practical. And unyielding." *But it also means that I can rely on you to always be there.*

"Your liveliness is too much of a distraction."

How sweet that he would not say it annoyed him.

"But you make me laugh. Mia, you truly make me laugh."

"But making someone laugh is so frivolous, not that I'm fishing for compliments," she added.

"It fills me with joy and I no longer see that as frivolous, any more than you are."

She curled up alongside his body and kissed his chest.

"There is one more thing that drives me mad," he said.

"Really?" She could guess what it was.

"You do talk too much."

He loomed over her and she giggled. Neither one of them said another word that night.

MIA'S DECISION TO BE MARRIED at the church in Pennsford by Mr. Garrett surprised everyone.

What surprised them even more was when David and Mia announced that they would take a wedding trip to Manchester to see firsthand the Long Bank Mill, and spend a week or two at Sandleton before moving on to settle in Birmingham.

There were any number of risqué jokes bandied about at their wedding breakfast. It seemed everyone knew about the collection of erotic books in Sandleton's library. The duke asked them to send one of their favorites to him. Elena looked as if she were about to take his wineglass away again.

Mia leaned close to David and whispered, "And this is the man who considered celibacy for the rest of his life."

David burst out laughing. She watched the laugh lines deepen around his eyes and mouth and vowed to make them permanent. Then she noticed that all conversation had stopped and everyone was looking at the two of them, varying degrees of surprise on their faces.

"I'm sorry," Mia said, "though I have no idea what I am apologizing for."

They all relaxed, smiling again. Olivia leaned across the table. "It is just so wonderful to hear David happy. We have not heard him laugh for more years than I want to count."

"But he laughs all the time with me. And sometimes at me."

The duke raised his glass. "To David and Mia. Marriage will surely be their greatest adventure."

Author's Note

Quarry Bank Mill in Styal near Manchester is the inspiration for Long Bank Mill. Quarry Bank Mill is still in existence and is operated by the largest waterwheel in the world. It was built and originally owned by Samuel Greg, and by 1832 it was the largest cotton-spinning business in the U.K.

David Pennistan very much wanted to be part of that growth, but he founded his own cotton mill, steam powered, in Birmingham instead. David's (and Mia's) success will be an element in my next book for Bantam.

In post-Waterloo England the country began to move toward the Industrial Revolution. Manufacturing was growing more important, with an increasing emphasis on city employment. Barges were still used to transport goods, but within twenty years trains would become essential to efficient movement of both raw and finished materials.

Another major change of the period was in the world of fashion. Around 1818 dresses became more fussy, edged with ribbons and ruffles around the skirt and neckline. The shoulders showed more of what we today call shoulder pads. Gone was the elegant simplicity associated with the early Regency, as waists lengthened and fashion headed toward the elaborate designs of the Victorian era.

Mia loved change in fashion, as most young women

do. The more elaborate gowns suited her exotic beauty, and since she was older and could wear stronger colors, all was right in her world of fashion.

In case you were wondering, Mia did in fact become the proud owner of a poodle, whom she named Slubber, a word that still makes her laugh every time she says it. No wonder Slubber thinks his mistress is the happiest woman in the world. It's true, though I suspect that David has more to do with that than Slubber does.

Lisa Reppert deserves special mention for her comment when I told her that Mia of *Stranger's Kiss* was the heroine of *Courtesan's Kiss*. "I can't believe that vanity smurf Mia is going to be a heroine. I can't wait to see how you do it." I'm sure Lisa, at least, will let me know if I succeeded.

Also, please be assured that William Bendasbrook will find true love. I knew from the beginning that he and Mia would be better friends than lovers. I'm sorry if you were disappointed by their breakup.

My thanks, as always, go to my critique group, the Lifesavers, also known as Lavinia Kent, Marsha Nuccio, and Elaine Fox. They must share first place with editorial genius Shauna Summers and her talented assistant, Jessica Sebor. Their input always makes my books better.

Can't wait for more riveting romance
from Mary Blayney?
Don't miss her upcoming novel . . .

One More
Kiss

Coming soon from Bantam Books

Turn the page to take a peek inside. . . .

*We are so used to disguising ourselves from others
that we end up disguising ourselves from ourselves.*
— François de La Rochefoucauld

LYDIA CHERNOV DID NOT put on her cloak or gather her things until the hackney drew to a halt in front of the shop. Chernov Drapers might be on the best street of shops in Birmingham, but at dusk and beyond one could not be too careful.

Pulling the wool cloak over her gown, Lydia did her best to control the hum of excitement that made her heart beat a little bit faster, but she could feel herself smiling and knew that tonight could change everything.

She calmed herself by mentally running through the list of items: umbrella, satchel with periodicals, trim kit and reticule; then she stepped out into the evening, miserable as it was.

The fog hung just above the rooftops, turning to

rain as it came closer to earth. Not a heavy rain, but enough to make protection necessary. Holding the umbrella and her bags, Lydia made short work of locking the door. She hurried to the conveyance stepping carefully, holding her skirts a little higher than proper, all to avoid the widening puddles.

Calling the direction to Mr. Leopold, she climbed into the cab. She settled back and considered the periodicals she had chosen. Lord David promised fabric that would be a delight to both eye and touch. His wife would be the perfect model for the new cottons. And Chernov Drapers would be the only shop to carry the yard goods. The trick would be to choose the designs that would show the fabrics to best advantage.

The hackney moved more quickly than usual and Lydia had to hold on so as not to lose her seat. With the streets wet and slick, speed seemed unwise.

Controlling a stab of alarm but not her annoyance, she was about to knock on the roof with her umbrella when the conveyance skidded to a halt. Before she could lean out and scold Mr. Leopold, the street-side door swung open.

Cold wet air was not the only intrusion. A man jumped aboard. At the same moment the hackney began moving again and Lydia felt affront and an even stronger dose of alarm. Thank God she was not the type to be paralyzed by fear.

"What do you think you are doing?" She tried for indignation and held tight to her umbrella, quite prepared to use it as a weapon. "Mr. Leopold!" she called. "Do you have your pistol?" She had no idea if he carried one or not but hoped the question would give the intruder second thoughts.

The man, a very large man, laughed and settled in with his feet propped against one door and his back against the other so that she could not reach either handle. "Leopold is counting his bribe money and heading for the whorehouse." The man made himself more comfortable but still blocked the doors.

"Mr. Chernov wants to see you." He spoke with an all-too-familiar accent.

"My husband?" That was not possible.

"If you wish to call him your husband." He spoke the word as if it were a nickname and not a state blessed by God and the church.

"Mr. Chernov is not in England and I have no travel papers with me." Which would hardly matter if he intended to force her to go abroad.

The man shrugged. "No papers will be needed where we are going."

Her mind worked as fast as the machine at the new cotton mill. Lydia was sure that Mr. Chernov was dead. He would have found her much sooner than this if he still breathed. The shop, after all, bore his name. But even dead, a line of those who wanted something from him would wind around the block. This man thought to use her to find him.

Lydia had made a vow that she would not become embroiled in his problems. Not ever again. "This is a kidnapping. I will not go with you willingly."

"Call it what you will, you are coming with me." The man took out a large knife and pretended he needed to clean his fingernails.

The knife erased her fear, replacing it with a cold truth. Her mind moved at double speed. She would rather die. Yes, and leave Paul an orphan, than obey this man. If she went along with his demands she might never see the boy again anyway.

The carriage was still in the city, nowhere near the river but surely headed that way. Once they were out of Birmingham it would be more difficult to find help.

Lifting her umbrella, holding it by the tip, she used the curled handle to hit him where it would hurt the most. The man bent double, cursing in Russian, and Lydia grabbed the moment to open the door and leap from the hackney, dragging her invaluable bags with her.

Stumbling on the wet cobblestones, she twisted her ankle and cursed a little herself. Ignoring the pain and without the slightest idea of where she was, she headed for the noise coming from the one lighted building glimmering through the fog.

Within a few yards of safety a man stepped out of the shadows. She ran full into him. Raising the satchel holding the periodicals with strength born of desperation, Lydia beaned him before his words registered.

"Do you need help, miss?" was followed by a sound between an *oof* and *ow*.

"What in the world did you hit me with?" He stepped back and looked about for his hat but showed no sign of abandoning her. Finding his hat, he brushed it off, seemingly unaware of the scoundrel from the hackney hurtling down the street, his knife raised, all the more menacing for silent dispatch.

With his hand firmly on his head, the man from the shadows stepped in front of her, easing her anxiety enough that she could breathe again.

In an instant her rescuer released a sword that was sheathed in his walking stick. What was a gentleman doing on the streets at this hour?

"Begone, you villainous thug. Leave this woman alone."

Lydia almost laughed, as inappropriate as it was. The words could have come straight out of a Minerva Press novel.

"She's my wife and trying to run off with her lover."

"I am not his wife!" Lydia hoped she was stating the obvious.

"Of course not. No woman with your taste and manner would ever be seen with a pig like this."

The pig lurched forward, and without a moment of hesitation her rescuer stuck him in the arm with his sword.

Bleeding like his namesake, the pig stumbled back, tossing his knife into his other hand but making no move to attack. "You'll pay for this!" The venom in his voice made payment sound life threatening.

"Ah, but first you have to find out who I am." Her rescuer wiped the blade with a bit of linen and held it at the ready again.

"Not you, you dandy-headed fop. The bitch, Mrs. Chernov, will pay. I'll see to that."

The rescuer glanced at her, apparently taken aback for the first time since the encounter began. For her part, Lydia had no idea what was afoot, other than the mention of her husband's name, and that was as puzzling as knowing nothing.

The gentleman nodded as if she had spoken her confusion aloud. He took several steps closer to the thug, holding his sword in front of him.

"If you so much as come near her again, I will butcher you and leave you for the dogs. I have my ways and my contacts in Birmingham—I can find the likes of you, Novokov, without a moment's trouble."

Novokov's startled expression showed his shock at being named.

"Begone!" the man shouted again, causing both Lydia and Novokov to jump.

"I'll find you. I'll find you both!"

"Empty threat, Novokov. Mrs. Chernov is now under my protection. You know better than to challenge me."

Did he? Who was this man? At the moment he sounded almost as threatening as Novokov.

"Damn you both to hell!" Novokov called out as he stumbled backward and away from them.

Her rescuer wiped his sword again and sheathed it in one easy move. He turned to her and bowed. "I beg your pardon for his offensive language."

"How did you know who he was?" It was the first of at least five questions to which she wanted answers.

"The man is tall with a girth to match and an accent he didn't learn at school in England. Not many like that in Birmingham. It was an educated guess."

"And who are you?"

"A man when you needed one. Names are hardly necessary."

"Then you have the advantage of me."

He smiled and his face went from dangerous to delightful. "You don't believe that any more than I do. Ladies always have the advantage."

Was he flirting with her? She hefted her sample bag and used the voice that cowed her help. "You, sir, are a rogue."

"And you are not the first to say that." The smile tempered to an amused disappointment.

"Oh dear." Lydia hated it when she stated the obvious. It was an awful habit. "I would so much rather be original."

"You are definitely an original, Mrs. Chernov. I have no doubt of that. From your name, to your vicious weapon disguised as a bag, to your presence in this neighborhood at this hour, you are very much an original."

Before she could decide how to answer, he continued. "Tell me where you are bound and I will see you there safely."

What a conundrum, Lydia thought. She hardly wanted to walk on alone but neither did she want to tell him where she was going. It was supposed to be a secret.

"I can guess. To see a customer, a lady, someone you call on in the evening because you would also like to see her husband."

Lydia almost dropped her satchel. How could he know that?

"We are within a short walk of Posey Hill, which I assume is your direction, but I do think that a carriage would be far more comfortable."

As if by magic, a covered conveyance rolled to a halt behind him.

"Who *are* you?" Lydia asked again.

"If you must have a name, call me Jessup."

"Thank you, Mr. Jessup, but I think I will send a message to my customer and tell her that I will not be able to keep the appointment. I am more than a little distracted at the moment."

"You disappoint me, Mrs. Chernov. I would think that someone with your obvious independence would not be deterred by the idle threat of a man like Novokov."

It was not Novokov who was making her nervous. Mr. Jessup showed signs of being a bully himself. With a much more charming approach, but a bully nonetheless. She had enough experience of the type to know how to deal with them.

She made her eyes fill with water and looked up at him. "I need to return home. I will send a boy to cancel my appointment. Please, can you help me?"

"Of course, madam. I would be a pig myself if I did not." Mr. Jessup opened the carriage, offering his hand to help her inside as he called the direction to the driver.

She was wearing gloves. He was not. He squeezed her hand a little and the heat of his fingers traveled to warm parts of her that had been stone cold for much too long.

She missed the carriage step and almost fell. Mr. Jessup caught her by the waist and steadied her and made to lift her into the conveyance.

She shook her head and moved out of his grasp. She did not want Mr. Jessup any closer.

"Good-bye, sir."

"Good night only, Mrs. Chernov."

She shook her head and knocked on the roof for the hackney to move on. No one knew better than she did that station and place in life meant nothing when it came to one body responding to another. A man in her life or, God help her, in her bed was a complication she would never entertain again. This was good-bye.